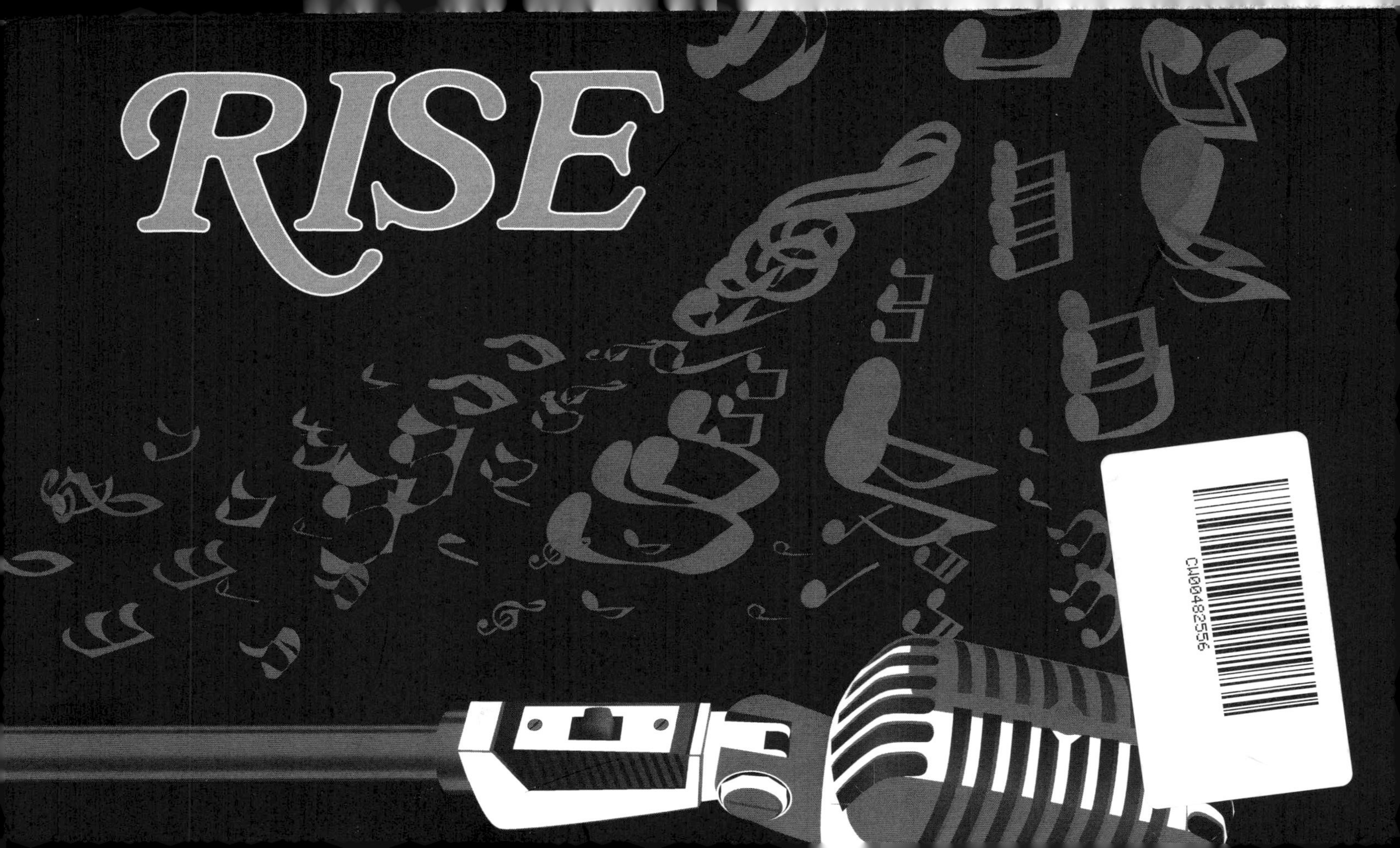

RISE

Edited: Nikki Busch Editing
Cover Design: Lori Jackson Design
Formatting and proofing: Elaine York, Allusion Publishing
www.allusionpublishing.com
Cover Photo: Michelle Lancaster
Cover Model: Mitchell Wick
Tattoo Artist: Mathew Franklin

RISE

USA TODAY BESTSELLING AUTHOR

CASSANDRA ROBBINS

PLAYLIST

Your Guardian Angel – The Red Jumpsuit Apparatus
Silver and Cold – AFI
Mountain Man – Crash Kings
Champagne – Cavo
Cocaine – Eric Clapton
The Night We Met – Lord Huron
I Found – Amber Run
Forever – Labrinth
Love is a Bitch – Two Feet
Do It for Me – Rosenfeld
Snow White – Dennis Lloyd
You Really Got Me – The Kinks
A Little Wicked – Valerie Broussard
Voodoo – Bryce Fox
Devil Inside – London Grammar
Don't Let Me Down – Stereophonics
She Talks to Angels – The Black Crowes
Glycerine – Bush
House of Pain – The White Buffalo
Where Did You Sleep Last Night – Sleigh Bells
November Rain – Guns N' Roses
Within Your Reach – The Replacements
In Your Eyes – Peter Gabriel

For my loves,

Mark, Jack, and Sophia

PROLOGUE

She stands in the rain, droplets of water running down her face to her feet. The moonlight makes it seem even more ominous than anything the daylight could spread.

Her pain seeps out of her, almost as if her tears are the reason she's wet, rather than the rain that has soaked the parking lot.

The pulse of rage pounds my temples along with my adoring crowd behind me. The stadium energy is alive. It vibrates through me as I watch her.

"Why?" she yells at me. Her long, wet hair sticks to her face.

The guitar solo behind me wails as they chant my name. I wonder if they know how much I need to hear them?

This is the moment I die and become reborn.

Her grief will heal; mine will fester and ooze. It's poison, growing stronger daily until my heart will not beat for her anymore.

She is, was, my anchor. My fucking lifeline to the real me.

I watch her beautiful face in the moonlight, her pale skin never looking more striking at this moment, until she backs away from me, taking my soul with her.

Agonizing pain seizes my chest as I let her go.

I don't reach for her.

I don't stop her, though the pain's so excruciating it's as though I've swallowed a knife. The slow descent slices my insides.

The bike waits for her like a living creature. An angry, living beast, its exhaust fills the area. It rumbles and vibrates on the pavement, reminding me that no matter how high I rise, I'll always be the man who hemorrhages grief.

She hesitates, her hand on his shoulder.

Time stops.

One. Two. Three.

I hear my heart pound and know it's hers calling to me.

"I hate you, Rhys Granger," she screams. Her thin body trembles as she swings one long leg over the seat and climbs on, clinging to the biker in front of her.

I can't see him. Don't need to. I know his rage, and I'd feel the same if the roles were reversed.

His dark bike shines, almost glows in the moonlight. The sky blasts an eerie white zigzag across the black night. The pelting, almost stinging rain burns my sensitized skin. I open my mouth to try to take back all that has happened, to make her stay.

But I stop myself.

I owe her more than that.

The guitar solo is almost over and the lights from the stadium lasers fill the wet night with color.

My followers never leave. They're what I need to focus on. Even with Mother Nature sharing her grief for me, my people love me. They know I bleed for them, and in return they give me their undying devotion.

The bike, like a dark demon, speeds away, the red taillight illuminating the two figures who seem to evaporate into the wet night.

For a second, I move as if I can actually catch up with the lead horse. I rip off my soaked shirt as if to shed my skin, or at least her scent, but stop as I acknowledge the truth: this is it.

She's mine and she's gone.

I'm not good.

All the people I love end up getting hurt.

The rumble of the crowd stops me, calls to me. Like a junkie with his addiction, I slow. We never had a chance.

Timing. The one thing you never escape. Our past formed our future.

Tossing the wet shirt to the ground, I reach for my heart, then look up into the rain-filled night and let it wash away my guilt.

Betrayal stings like a bitch, and no amount of Mother Nature's cleansing tears can rid me of who and what I've become.

I've lost my muse, the one love of my life.

The crowd chants my name. I embrace it, let it fill me, build me up, the adrenaline of their screaming love allowing me to accept who I am.

Rock God.

As if the universe agrees, it lets out a loud, explosive crash of thunder.

She's gone and taken my heart with her but *this...* I still have this.

I start to walk, but the water weighs me down. Hands touch me, and someone passes me a bottle as I make my way up the stairs.

It's chaos.

Mayhem.

The crowd roars as if my very presence has brought them to life.

I lift my fist to the sky and close my eyes.

I am home.

I am the Rock God.

CHAPTER 1

GIA

Present – Twenty-five years old
Paris, France

"**A**re you going to fall asleep at the table, or can I order us something to eat?" Sebastian kicks my crossed leg, causing my eyes to snap open and my leg to drop with a thud.

"Stop it," I hiss, straightening up. "I'm jet-lagged already." I breathe in and look around, mostly for a waitress. I need coffee. Wealth and entitlement bounce from one table to the next as I roll my neck and try to focus.

"Get your shit together. The day just started." He smirks and leans back in the comfortable chair as his eyes scan my face.

I cock my head and stare right back, but let's be honest—he has an unfair advantage. The jerk slept the entire plane ride from Los Angeles to Paris. I think he woke up once for some water and a warm cloth for his eyes, then went back to sleep. While I stayed awake, torturing myself for eleven hours, worrying that at any second this might be my last. I have a flying phobia. It started years ago. Maybe I've always had it. I can't pinpoint when it started to be out of control. I guess it kind of crept up on me slowly, one flight after another until *Bam*.

I've tried everything: yoga, counseling, hypnotherapy. You name it; I've tried it. But no matter how Zen I am, as soon as I board the plane and smell that recycled air, all meditation is gone.

It's irrational, but the plane could go down. The thought of having to go through those last seconds...

Sebastian, on the other hand, orders a screwdriver, pops some Valium, and is out in minutes. Meanwhile, I sit in silence, fighting myself not to jump up and scream for the pilot to make an emergency landing.

Which is why I'm exhausted. I need coffee, or a ten-minute nap, not Sebastian's *stare*.

"Damn it." I don't look away but grab my purse from the floor. Obviously, my appearance is lacking.

"I don't know why you never listen to me. I begged you to take a Valium or Ativan." His voice keeps bugging me.

"Because I hate relying on them. I'm stronger than that," I snip right back at him. He continues giving me *the stare*. I take a deep breath because I want so badly for it to be true. Unfortunately, this time he might be right. I'm exhausted, physically and mentally, and we do have a full day ahead. I give him a giant eye roll as I pull out my makeup bag.

"And I hate that stare," I say dramatically, opening my compact to assess myself. He throws back his head and laughs as I blink at my reflection in the small mirror.

I've got the smoky-eye thing going on, but I'm rolling with it. It's fashion week, after all, and with the eleven hours of panic I've been through, I'm shocked I look this good. My lips are still stained red from the matte lipstick, and my hair has held up well.

I bring the mirror away from me so I can see more of myself. What the heck? I look pretty damn good. Sebastian has no reason to give me his infamous stare.

"You're strong, Gia. But even Wonder Woman needs a little help sometimes." His beautiful brown eyes are serious.

I run my hand through my hair. "Fine. You've made your point." I glance over at the cute, dark-haired waitress who's approaching and mumble, "I'll take ten Valium on the way home and swallow them down with a bottle of vodka. Happy?"

"I'm dead serious, Gia. This is getting absur—"

"*Bonjour, est-ce que tu veux que bois quelque chose?*" The French waitress thankfully saves me from the lecture my best friend is about to give. I hate when Sebastian gets on his soapbox or worse, displays his "brotherly" concern.

I have a brother and trust me, *he's* enough.

"*Bonjour, beaute.*" He instantly shifts so that he can give her his full attention, flashing her his beautiful smile and causing the poor girl to blush.

Perfect. I'm never going to get coffee now. Women go crazy for Sebastian when he decides to show interest. The man oozes self-confidence. That, and he's fucking hot.

"You want your usual?" He speaks without breaking his stare with the waitress.

"Yes, please." I feel like kicking him with my new heels. He's being ridiculous.

Sebastian orders in flawless French. He's from Montreal, so he speaks the language.

I snap my compact shut, tossing it back into my bag and forcing them both to look at me.

"Coffee, s'il-vous-plait." My accent is horrendous, which is why I always let Sebastian order, but I have zero patience this morning. If he wants to flirt, he can do it after I get a cup of coffee. I recross my legs and sit up straighter.

"We just got off a plane and I'm in desperate need..." I trail off as Sebastian leans forward and takes my hand, smiling at me as if I'm not quite right.

The waitress looks at me blankly as if she doesn't speak a word of English, which is a lie. *Everyone* speaks enough to understand coffee. I'm sure she's wondering what's the deal between Sebastian and me.

If I wasn't so tired, I'd try to smile at her so she could be reassured that I have no interest in Sebastian sexually. We're strictly friends.

Best friends.

Well, best friends who used to have sex. I met him my freshman year at UC Berkeley. I was nursing a broken heart, and he was drop-dead gorgeous and willing to fuck without asking questions. Thankfully we're two peas in a pod. Within months, we both knew that we're definitely better as friends than lovers.

I'm not the type of girl who's ever going to be in a serious relationship, and Sebastian is a playboy. He's also my partner, my rock, my voice of reason. I'd do anything for him, which is why I'm in Paris. *He's broke again.*

Sebastian likes to live way above his means. His theory is that if you live like you're the best, you will, in fact, become the best.

As absurd as that thinking is, it works for him most of the time. I'm the opposite. It makes me nervous if I have to dip into my savings account. Sebastian doesn't even have a savings account, another reason why we're better as friends.

Crossing my legs, I glance down at my new heels. They're soft black Italian leather and crisscross up my ankles. I admit it—I have a weakness for shoes, and even though I pride myself on not being impressed by wealth, I was excited to see the shiny black box waiting for me on my bed when I checked in. The shoes were a welcome gift from Alberto, the designer we're shooting. Timing is *everything.*

Alberto exploded this year in the fashion world. I met him backstage at the Emmys. Some of the actresses were wearing his dresses and I was there to shoot the cast of *Schitt's Creek.*

We hit it off, drank way too much champagne, and ended up at the Abbey doing shots. He passed out that night at my cute

Venice bungalow and we've stayed close. He's young, talented, and has a fresh take—not the same crap we've seen over and over.

When he called me two weeks ago and begged me to come to Paris to shoot his upcoming collection, I turned him down.

Fashion Week is a lot: the crowds, parties, celebrities, egos. I've done it twice and vowed never to do it again.

Unfortunately, he had already gotten ahold of Sebastian who was over the moon about being able to make rent and spend a week in Paris first class.

So... here I sit, dead tired, no coffee, and all-around feeling off. I keep thinking it's exhaustion, but it's more like an anxiety or nagging feeling. As if I forgot to lock my door or left my flat iron on.

Yawning, I try to ignore the laughter from my best friend and the waitress. Coffee and breakfast seem forgotten. Might as well check my phone for messages.

Quickly I scan all the missed calls to make sure none are from my mom or brother. Zero from them. Unfortunately, I have ten, no, twelve from my ex and soon-to-be-former agent.

Perfect. I glance up at the gorgeous hotel. Its stunning, giant floral displays are tastefully arranged all over the hotel filling the space with a soft but fresh smell. Whites, creams, and golds grace the lobby and restaurant we're sitting in. I lean my head back to admire the ornate turquoise beams that house the glass ceilings.

My phone vibrates *again.* I don't need to look down to know it's my ex. I can sense his craziness across the ocean.

I try hard not to regret things, but Jeff is one big fat mistake. This is absolutely the last time I get into a relationship with my agent.

Why? Why do I do these things?

Maybe I was feeling pressured to find someone or I was sick of sex without some sort of connection. Whatever it was, in a moment of weakness I said yes to Jeff. He's older, powerful, and rich, not to mention one of the best agents on both coasts. All signs pointed to him being stable and secure.

God, was I wrong. I've never been with a more paranoid, borderline narcissistic man. Not to mention the sex was beyond bad. Cringeworthy, really.

I close my eyes and try not to let my mind remember his body. Great, now I see him naked.

Jesus.

Clearly I have shit judgment when it comes to men. It has to be hereditary, maybe even a Fontaine curse. After all, I do come from a long line of bad decision-makers.

My mom. Worst taste in men.

My Grandmother Fontaine. Miserable for thirty years, and now that my grandfather is dead, she's speeding around Pasadena in a red Corvette. And don't get me started on my dad and his numerous failed marriages.

I reach for my glass of ice water and almost laugh. There's only one Fontaine who is happy and in love.

My brother.

It's unfathomable.

Axel never even wanted to fall in love. He hated it. Made fun of it, yet somehow he's happy.

With kids. I'm an aunt to twin girls. Surreal if I take the time to think about it. Axel is actually living my childhood fantasy. The house, kids, maybe throw in a dog. He even has a white picket fence around his yard.

It's kind of a drag. He doesn't even care when I tease him, just laughs and agrees, then grabs Antoinette and kisses her as if there is no one else in the world. Which makes me feel like shit. I'll never have what they have. Then that causes me guilt because I do love my brother and I'm happy for him.

Back and forth I ping-pong. It's why I've kept myself busy working and avoiding Antoinette's calls. She's knee-deep in planning their wedding, and she wants me around for it. But she has a whole crowd of women who love her, most in happy relationships. I'm like the third wheel.

My phone vibrates again, bringing me back to the now and the waitress's over-the-top laughter. Can she be any more obvious? Sebastian isn't going to be into her as soon as we pay the check. That's mean but true.

"Rock God," a girl screams as she runs past our table.

Time stops.

For one terrible moment I break out in a cold sweat. I take a breath as dread slithers up my spine causing goose bumps on my arms.

I'm hearing things. My brain is just tired. No way did I hear her correctly.

"Gia?"

I almost scream, or puke. Either one is close to happening. Sebastian frowns at me, but who cares. My eyes dart around to look at the crowd lined up at the entrance.

"What did they just say?"

Breathe. I need to breathe. He wouldn't be here. I'm hearing things, that's all. I blow out some air and wave my phone.

"What are you talking about?" Sebastian snaps. "Answer your phone or turn it off." Then he turns back to the waitress again.

"We have to go." I slam my hands down loud on the table, causing the silverware to clank together and water to spill onto the white tablecloth. Both Sebastian and the waitress stop.

"What's wrong with you? It's a celebrity, for fuck's sake." He scowls and turns sideways to look over at what seems to be the coming attraction.

"*Mon Dieu*, this has to be someone big." The waitress rubs her hands up and down her pants and I want to scream numerous things at her... like *I knew you spoke English*, and *Why didn't you get me coffee?* And most importantly, *Is there an emergency exit?*

"Gia?" Sebastian's voice makes me jump. Christ, I'm completely unraveling.

"What?" I sound hysterical, but fuck it, I am, so why pretend. I need to save us... me, whatever... Holy shit, I'm full-on panicking. *Breathe, Gia. And think.*

I'm not doing either.

"Rock God! It's him. Rock Godddd, I love youuu," a woman wails as she clings to her friend.

"Sebastian. Now." I grab my bag and vault out of the chair, causing both waters to spill over. It's like a bad dream that I want to wake up from but can't. I feel rather than notice the ice water that's soaked my white pants and drips onto my new heels.

"Goddammit," I say, wanting to burst into tears, but screw that. I have to get myself together and think.

Okay. One. It's him.

Two. I need to either toss my phone into my purse or throw it against the wall because it's vibrating again.

Three. I'm acting ridiculous. Rhys Granger is a nobody. A part of my past—that's all. Eventually, this was bound to happen. In fact, I'm surprised it took this long.

"O-kay. I guess we're going." Sebastian finally stands and I'm tempted to throw myself into his arms.

Electric energy pulses around the large space. I clear my throat and dump my phone into my purse, swinging it over my shoulder.

"Maybe we should wait for the crowd to move." He nods toward the door.

"No. We need to go *now*. I don't have time to get into this—"

"Oh, it's Granger, from The Stuffed Muffins." His eyes focus above my head.

"Shit." Biting my lip, I stare at a button on his shirt.

"Interesting... he's coming over here."

"What?" I want to cry but that can wait. *Don't look back,* I chant in my head.

"Yep... and he's got Paulette with him."

The waitress squeals. "I love them! Granger is magnificent..." Thankfully she switches to French. She was bugging me before. Now I really dislike her.

I close my eyes to brace myself. He's as bad as they come. A viper waiting to strike, and once bitten, his poison will take you down.

The hotel is a swarm of noises: hushed, excited whispers, gasps of adoring sighs, feet pounding, and a pulsing electricity of chaos that only *he* can bring.

Then silence.

And I know he's behind me. I can feel him. His body heat seeps into me.

"Gia." That voice, it goes straight to my core and slithers up to my stomach. It's deep, melodic, almost gravelly. I haven't heard it in years. Sounds flood back in as I take a breath and turn.

And there he stands.

Intoxicating. Riveting. A legend. And my greatest mistake.

A crowd forms around him as usual. He's like the Pied Piper, but instead of the rats following him, it's people. He draws strength from them, lets their adoration make him grow stronger. I have no idea how he knew it was me, or maybe I do—I've had this sense of foreboding for the last twelve hours.

He's wearing black Ray-Bans. He must be high or inebriated. I remember a time when he'd make fun of famous people wearing sunglasses inside.

"Rhys." I nod, my voice slightly raspy, which aggravates me.

I don't need to see his bourbon eyes to know he's dissecting me. He's an addiction that's always been unhealthy for me.

His full lips turn into his signature smirk—actually, more like a slight snarl—and my heart thuds.

Lucifer. With dark hair, looking like he hasn't brushed it in days. My fingers tingle as I fight myself not to reach out and try to tame the untamable.

"Who's this, Granger?" Paulette. Her loud southern drawl breaks all his dark magic. I puff out air and smile. How did I not see her? She's over six-feet tall and clinging to him.

Her eyes travel up and down my body, stopping to stare daggers at my face. I stare right back. She's everything I hate. Not because she's a famous supermodel, but because I see myself in her desperate eyes.

She wants him so bad she's willing to humiliate herself for one more moment, one last scrap of his attention.

It's what he does best, and no matter how much self-esteem you start with, by the time Rhys is done with you, you end up exactly like her.

"You fucking dick, you promised." Paulette lunges for me.

And I'm done.

I step back and straight into a warm, hard chest. Strong, familiar hands wrap around me. I'm dizzy, completely off balance, as if the breath has been knocked out of me.

"Let go of me," I sneer and watch in horror as Paulette clumsily reaches for the table, misses, and grabs ahold of the tablecloth instead. The sound of her hitting the floor, along with the breaking glass, makes him move us backward.

One tan, tattooed hand has wrapped around my stomach, while the other snakes up to my neck, bringing my head slightly back.

I smell him.

Fresh, clean, with a slight hint of smoke. I used to be obsessed with his scent. Loved it. For some reason it calmed me.

Today is different. This day, I hate it because it's gonna haunt me. It's all happening too fast, like a whirl of colors and loud cursing with Paulette sitting in a pile of water, silverware, and glass.

"Brat." His voice is like a caress, and my whole body feels alive, tingling, as if liquid heat has been injected into my veins.

I try to move, only to be jerked tighter; he has to be high. My heart is pounding so hard I know he feels it.

People are screaming. Phones are filming and yet none of it matters.

"Fuck you, Rhys," I snarl, the pain I've kept locked up escaping. I shift so I can look up at him.

He's tan and his face sports days of dark stubble. A shiver of unease and excitement runs through me. He's trying to intimidate me. His rage radiates off him, seeping into me. Like an infusion, it gives me strength.

I'm not the same girl who worshipped him my whole life. He can play the brooding rock star. But he's in the wrong.

This is bad, so very bad.

He never should have touched me. We're like a match ready to set fire to dry brush, incinerating and destroying all in our path.

My face is inches from his mouth; his breath kisses my lips. I'm so close I can see through his dark sunglasses.

Our eyes lock and do battle.

Pain.

It's a new pain, fresh and powerful. I'm actually grateful he's holding me. Because this agony wants to steal my soul and never give it back.

We're ugly and damaged.

Damaged people should never be together. But then that's the allure: it's forbidden, addictive.

"Who is she?" Paulette says, her face a puffy mess.

Sebastian reaches down to help her, frowning at Rhys.

The restaurant is a buzz of activity. Security is clearing people out; busboys are cleaning up the glass.

He holds me tight, and I can feel his hard cock on my ass. I hiss at his gall. Then he lets me go. I reach back for a chair to steady myself.

"*She's* nothing," he says tightly, then turns and steps over to Sebastian. "Who the fuck are you?"

Sebastian looks shocked. "I'm the one helping your girlfriend. The fuck's wrong with you? Gia, get over here." And I almost groan out loud. Because unless Rhys has changed...

He hasn't, and in seconds, Sebastian is on the floor.

"Rhys, stop it, you maniac. You're going to get arrested." I grab his arm, looking around at all the phones filming us.

He looks up at me, then down at Sebastian as he stands, sneering.

"Has his cock been inside you?" His eyes narrow, and I hate that my stomach dips.

"Stay away from me." I drop to my knees to help Sebastian.

"What is wrong with you?" I hiss up at him. A jolt of energy zings through me as it dawns on me that I can see his eyes. His sunglasses must have come off when he attacked Sebastian. For a split second, I swear I see pain. But it's gone so fast, I might have imagined it.

"Here. Breakfast is on me." Rhys snorts. Reaching into his pocket to toss a wad of money at us, he takes Paulette's hand and drags her toward the exit.

"Jesus, Sebastian." I grab a napkin from the table to dab his bloody lip. "Are you okay?"

He pushes my hand away. "I'm suing that motherfucker. What the hell just happened?" He glares at me, kicking the pile of hundred-dollar bills away in disgust.

"He's a friend of Axel's." As if that should explain why he acted like a lunatic. "I'm so sorry."

He looks over at the crowd following Rhys. "I'm calling a lawyer. Take pictures, Gia." He motions for the police who were talking to the manager.

Suddenly I'm forgotten as he switches to rapid French. I assume he's telling them that Rhys Granger attacked him for no apparent reason.

I sit down in the chair and wait for Sebastian to finish, trying not to think about Rhys, his smell, and the past. Rhys Granger was a fantasy. He's clearly not stable. The drugs and booze have caught up to him. Another cliché fallen rock star, only he's far from fallen. If anything, he's at the top of his career.

Rock God... that's what they call him.

But to me, he'll always be the one who makes all the girls cry.

PART 1

CHAPTER 2

RHYS

Past – Seventeen years old
Burbank, California

"**D**ude, hurry the fuck up." I glance over at Nuke. He stands, twirling his drumsticks completely interrupting me and Stephanie.

"Give me five more minutes." I'm a dick, but Nuke's an asshole. Can't he see I'm dealing with shit? It's pretty obvious that she's hysterical. I can't even understand her.

"Steph, it's gonna be okay," I say half-heartedly because there's no silver lining here.

We're fucked.

Stephanie lives down the street. I wouldn't call her my girlfriend since I don't believe in labels. But she's someone I fuck and apparently got pregnant.

"How? How is it ever going to be okay?" She pulls back to look up at me. Her eyes are bloodshot and puffy, and her hair looks as if she forgot to brush it. She's always so perfect; it's kind of jarring seeing her like this. I sigh. My head pounds. I glance to where Nuke was standing. Thankfully he's gone.

"Just... everything will be fine tomorrow." God, I really am a dick, but what else can I say?

"Stop it!" She jerks away, which is fine. I'm not one for physical affection unless I'm getting off.

"God, what am I going to do?" She stares, almost dazed, at my mom's latest boyfriend's truck.

I stay silent. We've been through this. Neither one of us is parent material. I'm seventeen, don't want a kid, and neither does she. So, her incessant talking about what we're gonna do has to be her anxiety about getting it done.

"It's gonna be over tomorrow, and we can pretend it never happened," I say again, reaching into my pocket to light a cigarette. Her eyes grow huge as she waves a hand in front of her face.

"Oh my God, you can't smoke in front of me. I'm pregnant."

"Jesus, Steph, what is wrong with you? We're not keeping it, so stop." I'm losing patience. This has been a fucking nightmare, and the way she's looking at me makes sweat trickle down my back.

"We're still on board with tomorrow, right?" I'm not being mean, but I'm definitely not being nice. We both agreed on this. "Right?"

She jumps at my harsh tone, then covers her face and silently weeps. Christ, I'm completely out of my league. I hate women crying.

"Look." I glance around my backyard, which is mostly concrete. Good thing since we can't afford a gardener. "You said you were on the pill. I'm gonna be really honest, Stephanie. I can't be a dad—"

"This is not my fault." She drops her hands and screams, causing the next-door neighbor's dog to bark.

"Shh. Jesus, Stephanie, be quiet. I gave you all my money, and your mom is taking you. It's done."

Why am I trying to reason with her? This is her fault. I mean, yeah, I should have listened to everyone and wrapped it up, but she promised she was on the pill.

"I need you to go with me." She hiccups and looks up at me.

Tomorrow is school—not that I can't forge a note—but her mom is taking her. I already feel like shit. And she wants me to sit there and be like what... a boyfriend?

I stare down and take a long, hard look at her. I don't know if I ever really have. She's not hot, but she's cute with short brown hair. I've known her for years, and yet I couldn't tell you what her favorite color is.

This is a horror show. I just want it fucking over and done. I take a deep inhale and toss the cigarette onto the concrete as I try to think. As soon as she said she was late, I knew, and it's messed with my head. It also doesn't help that my friends seem to think it's not a big deal.

She tries to wrap her cold hands around my neck, almost startling me. She tilts her head back.

What the fuck? One second she's screaming, the next she wants me to kiss her? This is over, has been for a while.

"Steph, look at me." Her eyes pop open.

"If you absolutely need me tomorrow, I'll go, but I'd rather not." The one thing I owe her is honesty.

She slides her hands down to hang at her sides and looks up at the sky. "No, my mom is taking me, and this is the right thing for both of us. I don't want to be a mom any more than you want to be a dad."

Before I can say anything, she turns and walks toward her house. I close my eyes, trying to get ahold of these emotions that I should feel, but the truth is I'm relieved.

All my dreams would have been just that, dreams, because I would have had to get a job and help out. I mean, I never had a dad, and look at me.

A flash of dark hair and dirty bare feet make me look up. "Christ." I rub my hands up and down my face.

"What the freak? What's happening to Stephanie?" Gia Fontaine sits perched on top of one of the trees in our backyard.

"What are you doing? And I told you to stop saying that," I say, looking around. You never know with Gia. I call her *the Brat* because she really is. She's Axel's baby sister.

She's seven, almost eight, and is like my shadow. If I had a pet puppy I don't think it would be more loyal.

Lately, she's started spying on me, taking pictures with the camera she got for Christmas. It's a nice camera, older version, a Nikon and she loves it.

"Freak is not a bad word." She waves the camera that's around her neck at me. "And what does it look like I'm doing?" Both her knees are skinned, and the bottoms of her feet are black from running around with no shoes.

Sighing, I hear Nuke playing the drums. "Gia, get down. You can't spy on people." I hold out my arms for her to jump. She leaps like a frog, and not for the first time do I wish I were her.

She's fearless.

I know it makes Axel crazy, but I think when she grows up it will be an asset. Her zest for life is usually infectious. Today, she's testing my patience.

"You made her cry, Rhys. Why do all the girls cry around you?" I stop for a second as if she's gut punched me. Leave it to the Brat to tell the truth.

"I guess I'm just not good." I shake my head. "Look, Gia, this is grown-up shi... stuff. You wouldn't understand. Steph will be fine. Let's just go to your house," I grumble, not bothering to see if she's following. I know she is.

"Why is she saying she's gonna have a baby?" She runs so that she's at my side, then brings the camera to her face and snaps a picture of me. Jesus Christ, I didn't think this day could get much worse, but two minutes with Gia has done it.

I stop. She almost trips on the sidewalk, which is broken and elevated from the roots of a tree. I take a deep breath. This fucking seven-year-old brat is making me feel worse than Stephanie.

"You misunderstood her. She's sad about—"

"I heard her. She's sad about the baby. I know all about it. I asked my mom last night."

"What?" My temples pound. "Wait." I crouch down so I'm on her level. "Did you tell your mom about Steph and me?" Because if she did, I know Mrs. Fontaine will call my mom, and that is something I can't handle right now. My mom has all of a sudden found religion. Her last hospital stay she met a man, and together they think that through prayer they can cure all ailments.

I can't wait to graduate and get the fuck out of here. Hit the road and play my music. But right now, I need to know what damage the Brat has done.

"Gia? Did you say anything about the baby?" It comes out harsh, but surprisingly she looks right back, not even affected by my tone.

Her green cat eyes narrow as she puts a dirty hand on her hip. "No, Rhys, I'm not a rat, and since I'm gonna marry you anyway... I'm the only one who's gonna have your babies." She tosses her hair over her shoulder as if she's mimicking some of our groupies.

"Christ," I mumble. This is screwed up. Gia's a kid. She shouldn't be hanging around with seventeen-year-olds. I need to talk to Axel. Doesn't she have friends her own age who play with dolls or shit? Thank fuck she hasn't said anything. Wait, did she just say she's gonna marry me and have babies?

"Gia," I say, my voice tight.

She turns and snaps another picture of me as she walks backward. She's a fucking mess. Her dark hair hangs down past her butt in wild curls that are in need of a good brushing. I have no idea what she does with her shoes because she seems to be barefoot all the time. And her shorts and shirt are stained with what looks like chocolate milk and dirt. I saw her this morning and she didn't look like this. Axel and I usually take her to school since Mrs. Fontaine leaves early to teach. Traffic is crap in Los Angeles, especially in the mornings.

"What?" She spins and starts to skip across the street.

"Stop spinning." Again, sharper than it needs to be, but this is fucked up. "You're seven and I'm seventeen. We're *never* getting married."

Her big eyes blink at me and she giggles. "Not *now,* but when I grow up." She twirls again and I shake my head. Fucking Gia. She's a brat. Been a thorn in my side from the day she was born.

Axel and I were nine when Gia came along. All I remember was chaos in that house, but it was still better than mine.

My mom has bipolar disorder. So, she's either really high, believing that she can conquer the world.

Or low.

So low she's in bed and I'm searching the bathroom for razor blades. When my grandfather was alive, it was easier, maybe because I was younger. I don't know or care anymore. She's a train wreck. I love her and would like to believe she's done the best she can. Although, given her issues, it would be nice if she'd stay on her medication.

And my dad... I barely remember him. Only that he was an ass to my mom. As a child I hated him for that. Today, I'd like to take a baseball bat to his head. This is why Steph must take care of this. I'm not father material, but I'm also not the kind of person who would fuck her over either.

That's what my old man did. Just left and never came back. If my grandfather hadn't taken us in, we'd have been homeless.

At least I would have been.

My mom would have gone off on one of her manic spells and left me. One time she decided to go to Vegas. You know, to become a millionaire. She was gone a week, and me and my grandfather had to bring her back and put her in the hospital.

This is why I loved Axel's house.

At Axel's house, I was allowed to play my music. They had food, and even though his parents worked all the time, it still felt like a family.

Until the Brat.

From the first time I saw Gia, she was loud and constantly moving. She also cried if Axel and I played our guitars too loud, which is how we ended up in the garage.

That was actually the best thing to happen. I've spent more time in that garage than my own room. Sometimes I pass out in there. We have an old mattress in the corner loaded up with blankets.

It was supposed to be a no-Gia zone. But somehow that went out the window. I think Axel's parents' divorce probably instigated it, but as soon as Gia found the garage, it seemed to be her favorite place too.

I can't help but grin. She was our first fan. She'd dance and sing and go wild with all our stuff: our equipment, posters, amps, Nuke's drum set. You name it, it's in the garage and it's fucking awesome.

We even have a minibar. A neighbor was giving away a cabinet and some old barstools. He offered them to us since he digs our music.

I frown as I smell marijuana. It's so pungent I can smell it thirty feet away.

Jason and David are sharing a pipe with Axel as Nuke twirls his sticks in between pounding on his drums.

"'Bout fucking time." Axel inhales, his eyes narrowing on me as he holds, then releases. "Everything okay, man?" He motions with his head to the couch in the corner. "How much longer do we have to deal with this?"

I look over at our sad excuse of a couch that's being held together mostly by silver duct tape. Stephanie's sitting there, still crying and looking like a wreck, surrounded by some of her girlfriends.

"Christ. I thought she was going home." I rub the back of my neck and motion for him to hand me the pipe.

"Sucks, brother, but at least she's gonna take care of it," Jason says all this while staring at one of the girls who's comforting Steph. He's good friends with Axel. His dad is the president of a biker club called the Disciples. I can't remember how we started hanging out with them, but they're cool as fuck.

"Snatch. All of them nothing but liars." I arch a brow at David, Jason's cousin, as he slurs slightly and brings a bottle of Jack Daniel's to his lips. I'm actually better friends with him than Jason. David writes poetry, so we have a lot in common.

"Granger," Skylar purrs as she sashays by us. She leans over to open the minifridge, her dress so short we all stare at her ass. David shakes his head and tosses himself onto the mattress.

"Fucking snatch. Although, you might like that one, dude. She's pierced in special places." He snickers, pointing the bottle at Skylar. He brings the bottle of Jack to his mouth but spills a good portion down his chin and onto the mattress.

"Christ, David." I grab the bottle from him.

He grins. "Go get her, Granger. But wrap up your dick." He shakes a finger at me then passes out, the smell of spicy bourbon coming from the mattress.

We probably need to think about getting a plastic cover for it. It has to be crawling with all sorts of dried fluids, most of them bodily.

"We gonna rehearse or just talk about Granger and his dick?" Nuke pounds the drums and sits back staring at us. Stephanie starts to cry louder, and I feel like punching Nuke. He's been kind of a dick throughout all of this. I know he's had a rough life, but who hasn't? His lack of patience is making me want to leave, because without me, the Dicks don't really exist. I'm the lead singer. Axel and I create all the songs. He needs to give me some space to at least try to get Steph and her girlfriends out of here.

"Heyyy, that's not nice, Nuke," Gia yells.

I turn to Axel. "Gia should not be hanging out with these girls. She's starting to understand things."

Axel frowns and takes the pipe back. "What do you mean?"

"I mean, she knows that I knocked up Stephanie. She needs to be playing with kids her own age."

"She's seven," he growls and looks over at Gia who's sitting on the end of the couch talking to Jenny, one of the girls Jason likes to fuck. Her small hand twirls her dark mess of hair as if she's twenty instead of a child.

"Gia?" Axel scowls at her. In return, she rolls her eyes dramatically at him and turns back to Jenny.

"What the...?" Axel says and looks at me as if I can explain why the brat is *the Brat*. "Get over here."

She stares at him, then mimes that she's talking to the groupies.

"Christ." I shake my head, ready to grab her by the hair and drag her over here.

Jason cracks up. "Gia kills me. Fucking kid's got balls." He crosses his arms and smirks at both of us.

"Are you kidding me?" Axel roars, causing Gia to finally move and the girls to scream.

She stomps over as if she's missing out on a chance for a million dollars. "What?" she huffs and stands with her hands on her hips. "I'm comforting Stephanie." She stares up at us, her big green eyes defiant, and for a second I almost grab her and put her over my knee.

"I don't want you hanging out with them anymore," Axel states, then turns for his guitar.

I almost choke on the swig of bourbon I just took because that can't be it.

"Why?" she whines and stomps a foot. "Is this because they all said Rhys is a *dick* and that he will never be happy because he's not capable of feeling true—"

"Gia, watch your fucking mouth." Axel glares down at her.

Jason just stares at her as if she's some sort of genius. I look at her smug face and then at Axel who starts strumming his guitar.

"You kidding me? That's it? That's all you're saying to her?" I ignore Jason who's laughing.

Axel grabs the baby powder for his hands. "Dude, relax. She's seven. She doesn't understand what those gashes are talking about."

My hands clench because this is fucked up. "Axel. She needs friends her own age, not this shit." I motion to the crying mess of Stephanie and her posse.

Axel looks at me and Gia who is sticking her tongue out at me. "Knock it off, Gia. What happened to your blond-haired friend... Katie?"

"You mean Kelly. Her mom won't let her come over if Mommy isn't here. Apparently, she thinks you're scary." She rolls her eyes.

Axel frowns as if this is a shock to him. It dawns on me that there is a reason Axel is Axel. He's completely out of touch. Either that or he doesn't care. Which is fine for him, but he's allowing Gia to become exactly like him.

He does one loud strum, nodding his head as he smirks. "Well, fuck her then."

"Christ." I shake my head and glance down at Gia who stares at me victorious. "Go play in your room," I snarl.

"You're not the boss of me, and I'll never be like those girls, crying because you don't love them. When I grow up, I know you're gonna love me the best," she announces, spins around, and walks back to the girls.

"Fucking Brat." I take another deep swig of Jack.

"Granger, you did this, man." Axel glides his hand up and down the neck of his guitar. "Wrap. It. Up. That's what we all do. That's what *you* didn't do." He stares at me as I fight the urge to throw the bottle against one of the walls.

"And leave Gia out of this. My sister is fine." He starts to strum and tune his guitar.

I nod, the blood pumping in my temples. "Fuck this." Just one day it would be nice if I could play my music and not have drama. As long as I can remember, drama has followed me. My mom, and then the girls, and now this. I look around the garage and take a deep breath. Everything seems to be pressing down on my chest like a fucking heart attack that takes away your breath.

"Skylar?" I bark at the one David says has piercings. She looks up and smiles as she pushes off the wall.

I'm done trying to be good, or even trying to be understanding. I'm not perfect, but I don't deserve all this shit either. I take her hand, ignoring the shriek from Stephanie. Her loud cursing in my direction is lost on me.

Stephanie's right. I'm bad luck, but I don't care. I drag Skylar across the street, my head swimming with music. It starts soft, and by the time I have Skylar pushed up against the back door of my house, it's pounding and vibrating through my head.

I take her lips. This is what I am, and I'm done feeling guilty about it.

I might be the worst, but at least I own my shit. I should have a warning tattooed on me. Because they all deserve better.

I thrust my tongue into Skylar's willing mouth and groan at the large barbell that twirls and fucks my mouth.

I pull back and look at her flushed face. "What?" She cocks her head and smiles.

I lean down to murmur in her ear. "I'm gonna fuck you."

"Okay." She shudders, excitement radiating off her.

"Then after I've blown my load..." Her chest is rising and falling in somewhat of a pant. "You're gonna pierce my cock." She puffs out some air and looks down at my erection. Reaching to grab it, she rubs it hard.

"Absolutely."

CHAPTER 3

GIA

Past – Eighteen years old
UC Berkeley, California

"**A**re you sure you want to do this?" Julianna, my roommate and bestie, flops down on her bed and looks at me.

"What are you talking about? This is the opportunity of a lifetime." I pivot and reach up for a pile of jeans, then toss them into my suitcase.

"I can't believe you actually pulled this off." She lies down, resting her head on her hand as she watches me pack.

"Jul, I'm kind of insulted that you doubted me." I shoot her a glare as she laughs, falls onto her back, and stares up at the ceiling.

"Rhys Granger. The Stuffed Muffins. This is crazy." Her long blond hair covers most of the pillow, and for one small second, I'm grateful that I'm the only one going. Not that I think Rhys would be into her, but Julianna is beautiful. What's wrong with me? I never feel like this.

"Hello? Gia?" My eyes focus and I realize she's holding my cell phone, which is playing "Lost in You," the Stuffed Muffins' latest hit.

Dread flows through me as I snatch it out of her hand. "Don't answer it." Her horrified face should make me pull myself together, but I'm slightly off right now.

"Geez, Gia." Julianna shakes her head at me as I frantically decline the call. I look at her and back at my phone before sinking down to sit on the edge of my bed.

I need to think. This might be nothing—just my mom wanting to tell me to be careful and that she's excited for me.

"You okay? You're starting to worry me." Julianna's big blue eyes show concern. I must look as bad as I feel. And I feel like I want to puke.

"I thought you said your mom was fine with you going on tour with them over winter break." She cocks her head, and the kindness in her voice makes me want to cry because I've worked so hard, and if this phone call is what I think it is...

"I did." I jump up and pace in our tiny dorm room, which is so limited on space that my giant suitcase takes up a big portion of the floor.

"Shit." I make my brain think. Julianna was right. It's a miracle I've pulled this off. It all boils down to the fact that both my photography and English professors are giant Stuffed Muffins fans. So much so that I was pretty much given a guaranteed A. All I have to do is an exclusive interview that my professor, Mr. Berry, can submit to *Rolling Stone* for me and provide some recent pictures, and it'll probably put me on the map. Over the years, I've stayed in touch with Nuke, their drummer, and if his drunken phone calls complaining about how the band is not in sync are any indication, Rhys absolutely needs me. I mean, who else knows him like I do?

The time is now. I'm already late—this is the tail end of their tour.

Six weeks.

Six weeks to make Rhys realize what I have always known. That we're soulmates. It doesn't matter that I haven't seen him in years. Or that he has become one of the biggest stars in the world. What matters is us. He needs me. It's why I'm so determined to get out of here. They're playing tonight in Seattle. Nuke was a bit fuzzy on how long they were staying.

My phone starts singing again and I take a deep breath. Might as well deal with it because I'm absolutely going to do this.

Exhaling, I toss my hair off my left shoulder. "Hey, Mom, what's up? I'm super busy, so if it's not an emergency, I really need—"

"Gia, you need to stop and listen to me," my mom yells through the phone, halting my rant. Damn it, I had hoped I could talk right over her.

"You need to call your brother." And those are the last words I ever want to hear out of my mom's mouth.

"Why?" I almost explode at her. Why the hell did she tell *him?*

"He's not happy," she says flatly.

I huff. "Axel's never happy." Taking a deep breath, it's hard not to go off on my mom, but I hold back. I glance over at Julianna who sits at the end of her bed looking like a Disney princess, except for her gross and annoying habit of picking her nail polish off. I almost swat her hand, but I need to focus.

"Look, sweetheart, I know this is through the university, but Axel has some concerns."

I go to open my mouth but she continues. "Call him. You know he's only looking out for you. If he says yes, then by all means go, and do the best job in the world." She says the last part as if she's on a talk show. She's so phony and completely see-through. God, I can't believe I felt guilty because technically this has nothing to do with Berkeley. But now I don't. Of course, she's trying to make Axel happy. That's what everyone does. It's all about not upsetting Axel.

Pathetic.

All but me—screw that. He's my brother but I can see his flaws. I take another deep breath.

"Fine." I huff. "I'll call Mitchell, but just for the record, I'm eighteen, so I don't need permission from either of you."

The line goes silent. "Hello?"

"I'm here." Her voice is loud and clear. "Call your brother, young lady, if you want to continue using your credit card." And then the line really does go dead.

"Goddammit." I toss my phone on the pillow. "Goddammit." I jump up and pace.

"What?" Julianna tries to follow, her blond hair slapping me in the face as I turn quickly.

Sighing, I look up at the dull white ceiling. "I have to call freakin' Mitchell." I clench and unclench my hands.

"Who's Mitchell?" Julianna's voice goes up. She gets flustered easily.

"*Axel.* Mitchell is Axel," My eyes flash at her. "Never mind." I wave my hand, already rehearsing what I need to say.

Hey, big brother. I'm going to spend my whole winter break with the Stuffed Muffins. Why? Because I need to convince Rhys Granger that we are destined to be together. So, deal with it and don't stand in my way. Somehow that's not going to fly. In fact, he might lock me up. He and Rhys are not close anymore.

"Screw this. He can't control me," I mumble and push on his number. It's like a Band-Aid that you know is going to burn and sting when you take it off, so you rip it off fast. That's where I'm at. Might as well rip it off.

"Oh dear." Julianna wrings her hands as I straighten my shoulders back, frowning at her. I don't need any bad juju. I love her to death, but she worries way too much.

I'm about to sigh in relief because he's not picking up and I can leave a message when I hear, "What?"

"Hey, Mitchell, so—"

"No."

"Um, rude. You don't even—"

"Listen, Gia." He sounds grumpier than usual. "I have shit going on, so I'm gonna make this fast. Over my dead body would I ever allow my baby sister to be anywhere near Granger."

Holy shit, that's harsh, and kind of vicious. "Axel. I'm doing this through the university. It's comple—"

"Do you think I'm Mom? That's the stupidest thing I've ever heard. You're lying and the answer is *no*." He barks the last part, causing Julianna to cover her mouth as I hold the phone away from my ear.

"Fine, I won't go. But you're making a huge mistake. Completely clipping my wings. This is my career, you kn— Axel? Mitchell?"

I look down at my phone. "God, he's such an asshole. He hung up on me. Can you believe it?"

Julianna sinks to her bed, her eyes full of tears, and I have to fight myself not to yell *What the hell are you crying for? My whole life plan has been ruined.*

Or has it?

"Julianna?" I drop down next to her, my mind spinning. This could work. Julianna's dad is rich, not wealthy, but *rich*. And Julianna is freakin' perfect. She's so responsible, she has access to money—aka she can give me a loan.

"I'm so, so sorry, Gia. I know you truly wanted to do this but... you know what they say. If it's meant to be then—"

"Screw that," I interrupt her kind but unnecessary pep talk.

"We make our own destinies. And I need your help." Taking her cold hands in mine, I give them a supportive shake. I'm dealing with a complete rule follower here. Julianna never did anything adventurous until the day we became roommates. Thank goodness I came into her life.

"You do? Oh God, what?" Her eyes grow huge.

"Stop it. It's not a big deal at all really." I smile at her, and she stares back befuddled.

"Okay. Listen, if my mom and Axel are going to be like this, then I can't use my credit card because..." I trail off. Of course, she looks confused.

I smile. "Julianna, I need you to give me a loan and cover for me if my mom calls." I squeeze her hands again as her eyes get bigger, if that's possible.

"Don't panic." I let go of her hands. They're clammy. "She's not going to call."

"Oh, thank God," she whispers.

"*But* in case she does, just pick up and tell her I'm working." I do jazz hands and smile encouragingly, trying my hardest not to lose patience.

"Oh dear." She blinks at me and again, my conscience nags at me. I jump up and move to close my suitcase, needing to get away from her responsible energy.

"Please, Julianna. You need to believe in me. If you don't, then I don't think I can handle it."

"You know I believe in you," she snips.

"Fantastic, I need a loan."

"But *they* said no, Gia." Her voice is calm, and I don't need to look at her to know she's picking at her nail polish again. I can hear the annoying scratching.

"I mean, you can't disappear for weeks and think they won't know."

I hold up my finger and sit on top of my overpacked suitcase. "Watch me. Throw me my phone." I motion with my hands while blowing a piece of hair off my face. She leans over and hands it to me. I give her a saucy wink and push on my mom's number.

"Watch and learn." Surprisingly it goes to voicemail, which I take as the universe telling me this is one-hundred percent right.

"Hey, Mom, so after thinking about it and talking to Mitchell, I'm not going to go." I sigh dramatically because there is a fine line between obvious and spot-on perfect.

"I'm super disappointed." Another deep sigh. "Butttt... Julianna has offered me an alternative." I shake my head and glare at her since the mention of her name has made her moan in despair.

"Her dad is a big commercial real estate guy. And he's hiring her over the break to help out. Anyway, he was getting ready to hire a professional photographer to take pictures of his properties and update his website. But Julianna convinced him to hire me instead." Gazing at my shoes, I avoid the look on Jules's miserable face. "I want you to know I'm devasted about not being able to get the scholarship. I'll check in when I can."

I push end and turn to Julianna. "See, easy peasy. Now how much can you loan me?"

"You're like a Jedi master at lying." Her face is flushed and I smile because again, thank goodness she has me. She hasn't been this excited since I made her go to TJ with me for a fake ID.

"You're seriously going to do this no matter what?" She licks her lips as I motion for her to sit on my bag so I can zip it up.

"Yep. I need enough for a plane ticket to Seattle and emergency money... a couple thousand should do it in case I need to buy some things." I'm pulling numbers out of my head.

"Whatever, I don't care about the money. Gia?" She grabs my hand.

"What? And you can get up." I almost laugh at her but that would be horrible. It's not her fault she's a truly good, innocent person.

She stands and takes a breath. "You promise that your mom will not call or... or *Axel?*" She whispers my brother's name and turns pink. Christ, I forgot she has a crush on him.

"You have zero to worry about. In fact, don't answer our phone, okay?" I turn and start to dump my moisturizer into my makeup bag.

"I'll have Rhys pay you back as soon as I get there." I flip my hair off my shoulder.

"Please, don't worry about the money. What I'm concerned about is... I mean..." She takes a deep breath and closes her eyes.

"You're positive *he's* going to want you, right? I mean, you've built this up in your head, been saving yourself for one of the most famous men in the world." She says all this lightning fast and for a moment, I falter. Her words make me sound crazy.

"I'm sorry. But as your friend I feel I need to at least say this." She straightens her shoulders back.

My eyes narrow on her as I stop to think. Jesus, what if he doesn't want me? I've spent so much time getting to this point that I haven't even let one bit of doubt enter my plan.

"Gia, you're sure he feels the same way? You haven't seen him since you were twelve."

I sigh and drop down to sit on the end of my suitcase. "Eleven, and it was a funeral. I can't get into it, but it was a bad time."

She lowers herself to sit next to me on the case. "Please, don't be mad at me. I just don't want to see you get hurt is all." She wraps her arms around her knees.

I nod. "I know, and to be honest, I have no idea if this is going to work out." I rub my temples. I'm starting to get a stress headache—either that or a huge reality slap.

"Look." I bop her shoulder. "Worst-case scenario, I get a bunch of exclusive photos of the band and sell my story to *Rolling Stone*. Then Cameron Crowe reads about me and turns it into a movie." I smile at her.

She shakes her head at me. "If anyone could make that happen, it would be you." She rubs her face as I hug her.

"I have to do this. I know you think I'm crazy, but he's the one."

"You are crazy, so crazy, but I believe in you. Now give me your account number."

CHAPTER 4

RHYS

Past – Twenty-seven years old
Seattle, Washington

"**G**ranger, get your ass over here." I look over to see who's screaming at me. I'm seeing double but grin anyway. I hold up my bottle of exclusive tequila and nod at the person. I have zero idea who it is.

"God, people are so obnoxious. Why do they think we would talk to them?" Tea calls out, making me turn my face away in distaste. This one's a disaster, even for Nuke. She's a model he met in New York a couple days ago who's somehow followed us to Seattle.

She flips the poor guy off, then wraps her arms around me, trying not to spill her martini.

"Wipe your nose, Tea." Peeling her claws out of my side, I let go of her waist. Her waifish body sinks into the velvet purple couch as her martini spills everywhere.

"The fuck, man?" Ammo yells up at me as Tea tries to lean on him, screaming that her shoes are ruined. I raise the bottle of tequila to my lips and smirk. Ammo and Tea belong together.

"Where's Nuke?" I grit out, not sure why I'm so aggravated with Ammo. Maybe because he seems happy and content and I'm the opposite.

He sits there, looking relaxed and snorting coke with Gordon, one of our new record execs.

Ignoring them, I look out at the massive crowd of bodies. This club has to be over capacity. I can barely see the dance floor. It's nothing but a swirl of colors and bright lights. The loud beat vibrates through my chest.

"He's at the airport," Tea shouts, still trying to climb onto Ammo to save her shoes.

"Jesus Christ," he mumbles as he dumps her on the other side of Gordon who smiles and makes room for her. Ammo takes the rolled-up hundred-dollar bill to snort more of Gordon's cocaine.

I stare down at the scene, completely detached. We're not even trying anymore. None of us gives two fucks.

In the old days, we would at least make an attempt to be subtle. Now we leave a pile of cocaine or whatever drug we're into on the table and dare anyone to say anything.

Rolling my neck, I relish in the slight dizziness. It reminds me I'm alive. I reach into my jeans pocket for my cigarettes and grin as I light up, thinking of Cynthia, our stylist, groaning at my wardrobe. Fashion is not my forte. But I'd rather take a bullet than wear the shit she convinces Cash and Nuke to go out in.

"Granger... Oh my God. Remember me? Granger!" a hysterical fan shrieks as one of the bouncers holds her back. I don't encourage her. Otherwise, it'll be a free-for-all. If you show attention to one, they all come.

It's shitty, but a sad fact. Most of the time I enjoy my fans, but not tonight. Tonight, all I want is to find someone who won't talk, but will blow me before I pass the fuck out.

I rarely fuck random women anymore. Not worth the huge shitstorm in the morning. Usually, I let them suck me off. If they sign an NDA, I'll consider dipping my dick into them.

I can't remember which one of us started having the women we fuck sign shit. Maybe it was after Ammo got slapped in the face by a jilted girlfriend who wrote a tell-all on him and the band. Half the shit was a lie; not that it mattered. It instantly became a bestseller anyway. Needless to say, it didn't go over well, and we all decided to protect ourselves after that.

Ammo takes negative shit and allows it to fuel him. I, on the other hand, was fucking pissed. I hate when my privacy's invaded. The book was not about me, but I was in a hell of a lot of it, and it portrayed me as an egomaniac who gets off on being a tortured artist.

I take another swig, letting the tequila slip down my throat without even tasting it. Fuck, maybe I am all the things she wrote. The day my fans labeled me the *Rock God*, I gave up being me and morphed into what they needed.

I have everything and yet nothing. Fame, money, women. You name it, I can have it. I'm at the top of my game, and lately all I want to do is get on a Harley and ride until no one knows my name.

Fame happened way too fast. One day I was playing in my buddy's garage, and the next we were in front of a hundred-thousand adoring fans.

I must have missed something along the way. There's a void in me. I try to embrace it, but it's like fucking herpes—it never leaves you. It's always ready to ooze its blisters into your psyche, until you wake up and decide that maybe you've sacrificed everything for nothing. Just a goddamn curse, a slow noose that tightens with each bit of success you achieve.

I should get the fuck out of here. We've played three concerts in four days. All of us are burned out, living on Mexican food, tequila, and cocaine.

I'm surprised I even know what state I'm in. I crouch down, ready to take the hundred- dollar bill from Ammo when a flash of dark hair and silver lamé catches my eye.

"What do you think, Granger?" Gordon leans over Tea, his bald head more pronounced with the moving lights dancing above him.

I hold up my hand to silence him as I straighten. My eyes search for the vision that made me stop and actually feel something.

"Granger?" He stands.

"Ask Rafe," I grunt, zeroing in on her. She's a goddamn vision with dark hair and legs to die for.

"Dude." Ammo shakes his head as he snorts and wipes his nose. "You need to listen to Gordon. This could be good for the Muffins."

"Tell it to Rafe," I repeat as I let my eyes devour her. She's in a silver dress that's nothing but a second skin with straps. Her fucking tits are full. Christ, I can see her rock-hard nipples from where I stand.

"Who's that with Nuke?" Ammo wipes his nose again and stares at my goddess.

"Oh my God, that's who he was picking up from the airport." Tea's annoying voice brings me back to the fact that the woman in question is indeed dancing and laughing with my drummer.

Which sucks for him. I'm absolutely gonna fuck her tonight.

"Brother." Ammo's hand stops me from moving. I stare at it, almost confused. Last thing I'm in the mood for is his shit.

"I'd let go, *brother*," I sneer in his face. This is not a threat. If he doesn't let go, I will not be responsible for my actions.

"Jesus, man." He lets go, dramatically holding up his hands. I'd like to punch him in his perfect face for that.

"You need to respect the code, Granger." Ammo shakes his head. "Nuke got to her first, picked her up from the airport, clearly she's special to hi—" I don't wait around to hear more. The way I feel, I don't care if she's his fucking wife.

"Shit." Ammo signals for our security.

I move toward Nuke. He looks like a fish out of water jumping circles around my goddess while she laughs and twirls. People start to rush us, screaming "Rock God" and "Ammo."

"Goddammit, Granger," Ace, my bodyguard, gripes as he makes a huge production of trying to keep people from touching us.

I despise having security. Pussy-ass shit, in my opinion. But apparently the record label and Rafe, our manager, disagree. I don't run or hide. Anyone wants to come at me, I'm right here. I smirk. Guess this is why we have security. I storm a path straight up to Nuke.

"Hey, man," he calls out and looks up at me, his face filled with excitement.

"Nuke." I nod then turn to the woman. She's stopped dancing. Her chest rises and falls, almost as if she's been waiting for me.

Her long dark hair is pulled up, revealing her stunning face, allowing me to admire her puffy lips, high cheekbones, and big eyes that slant up like a cat's.

"You remember—" I hold up my hand for Nuke to stop. The club has pretty much ceased to exist anymore. My eyes go up and down her thin form, stopping at her incredible tits. Jesus, my cock is so hard I have to shift it to the other side.

If she's with Nuke, she's not anymore. A slow smile graces her incredible lips as I ignore him and whatever he seems to want to tell me. Instead, I move closer, blocking him out as I reach for her tiny wrist, which is adorned with numerous bangles.

She's delicious, intoxicating. As she glides into my arms, I fight the urge not to lick one side of her face, if only to see how she'd taste. I breathe in her scent, savoring the smell.

It's *vanilla*.

Maybe caramel. Fuck, it's crème brûlée. I want to lose myself in her, savor her as if she's dessert. Dipping my head, I feel her shudder. *She's mine and she knows it.*

"Hello, beautiful," I say lowly into her lips.

Her eyes narrow on mine, then dip to my mouth. "Hello, Rhys." Her voice is like a slight breeze, a gentle feather caressing my lips.

Warning bells pound through my intoxicated trance and I lift my head to stare at her. The neon lasers and lights are chaotic, adding to my unease. No one calls me Rhys anymore.

It's a name from my past. I even correct people if they try to use it.

"Rhys?" Her voice is slightly raspy, sensual.

"No one calls me that."

"Well, I'm not anyone," she purrs.

"Fuck, Granger. You looking for a world of pain? What the hell are you doing?" I barely register Nuke yelling. It doesn't matter what he says or what he's warning me about.

I want her.

I grab her face with both hands, bringing her lips to mine. A premonition that this one is dangerous flashes through my head.

It doesn't matter though. I'm all in.

Roughly, I claim her lips, thrusting my tongue deep inside her mouth. She moans and wraps her hands around my neck. Her body fits perfectly. As if I hired a sculptor to mold her to me.

She tastes like sugar and berries and all I want to do is live inside her honey core for days.

Hunger.

I haven't felt starved like this in years—that need, drive to obtain something, to want something so desperately that you don't care if she ruins you.

Lifting my head, I say, "Let's go."

"Yes." She nods, her eyes slits and lips swollen. I have to fight myself not to wrap my hands in her long dark tresses and take her mouth again. She digs her nails into my forearms as we start to walk.

"Granger, this is a mistake. People are filming you." Ammo's and Nuke's voices blend together. I let Ace clear the path for us.

"Fuck, man, he'll kill you. Don't you know who she—"

I'm getting pissed. Don't they get it? *I don't care.* Who do they think they're talking to anyway?

Hunger.

I let the adrenaline flow through me. For the first time in years, I want something.

I want it, crave it more than anything.

CHAPTER 5

GIA

Past – Eighteen years old
Seattle, Washington

Holy fuck, the world is spinning and my lips still tingle from his kiss. My eyes devour the tattoos on his forearms as a wave of pure excitement flutters through my body.

He's dressed all in black. As I cling to his strong hand, a large black man in a suit shields us, making sure we aren't mobbed. This is out of control.

I knew the Stuffed Muffins were famous, but I had no idea how monumental *this* truly is. They love him—no, they worship him as if he's not human but a god who can give them eternal life. Women and men reach out to touch him as he storms past, maneuvering us out into the cool, wet night.

I take a breath, trying to get ahold of my emotions. This is happening fast. From the moment I boarded the plane and landed in Seattle, it's been crazy. I barely had time to panic I was so excited.

Nuke was actually on time picking me up. His genuine happiness that I'm here reassured me that this is right. All of Julianna's doubts and fears that kind of stayed with me on the plane evaporated as soon as he grabbed me and swung me around.

45

Nuke and I are close. He's the only one over the years who came and visited me and my mom.

He'd show up and crash in Axel's old room, stay for a week or so, and go back. I used to ask him why he never wanted to see Axel. He'd give me that faraway smile of his and kiss the top of my head. He's kind, and even though he tries to act tough, Nuke has a sadness in him. No matter how much fame he gets, or how many people tell him he's the best, he can't seem to shake it. Deep inside something's chasing him, and unless he deals with it, he's never gonna find peace.

It must involve his parents and the way he grew up. He rarely mentions them, and if he does, his words are not kind. But I've never been around a person who craves a family more than Nuke. Unfortunately, he has a major self-destructive streak and sabotages any relationship that might bring him happiness.

Aside from some of my brother's friends, I've never seen a guy have worse taste in women.

He's beyond hot, striking, really, with pitch-black hair shaved on the sides, so you can see his tattoos. Nuke is covered in tattoos and has been getting them for as long as I can remember. As a kid, I recall thinking he looked like a beautiful painting.

He's loyal and supportive. Again, I push aside that nagging guilt because I might have also told him there was a scholarship involved...

"I've got Granger." The bodyguard talks into his earpiece, bringing me back to the now.

I'm with Rhys.

And... he wants me.

His warm hand squeezes mine, causing a small shiver that has nothing to do with the cool, misty rain, and everything to do with the electrical charge that goes through me every time Rhys touches me.

"Come here, beautiful. You're cold." He graces me with his famous smirk and pulls me tight into his arms.

"Christ, can I have some privacy?" He shakes his head at the horde of paparazzi screaming and taking pictures of us.

"Granger, who's the woman? Sweetheart, look over here. What's your name?" They're firing questions at me so fast, even if I wanted to lift my head from Rhys's chest to answer, it would be impossible.

A large, black SUV pulls up and another man in a suit jumps out and opens the door, and it's like I'm in a movie or something. I slide in, glancing around at the mob forming, phones, flashing, people screaming.

Mayhem.

"Go," Rhys orders. His strong arm reaches out to protect me from flying forward with the jerk of the SUV. The driver holds his hand on the horn. I grab Rhys's arm and press myself against the soft, buttery seat to keep from falling forward.

"Where to, Mr. Granger?" The bodyguard turns his head.

My stomach flips. Puffing out some air, I try to stay calm. Thank God I drank that champagne and had a couple shots of some kind of exclusive liquor that tasted like candy.

"The hotel," he says, his voice gruff. I turn to look at him in all his glory. He's shadowed but I can still see his beautiful features. He looks different. More mature and... hard.

Confidence radiates off him as his presence commands everyone to bow and know their place. He used to be a pretty boy. Scratch that. Both he and my brother were. He's still pretty... but now he's almost dangerous. Goose bumps pebble my arms, which I rub to no avail.

This is not some college boy I can boss around. He sits in the darkness with only the headlights from the passing cars allowing me to see him staring at me.

Holy fuck, he looks like he wants to eat me, devour me whole. His signature smirk tells me he must know my panties are drenched for him.

It's so hot. He's hot. Jesus, his whole persona screams nasty, filthy, sexy...

No wonder women lose their minds around him. He's the most exciting man I've ever been around. And that's saying something if you knew my brother's friends.

I wish I had a cigarette, or something to help my nerves, because holy fuck, he's everything I've dreamed about.

Clearing my throat, I cross my legs, knowing he's watching. I search my mind for something dazzling to say.

He smiles as if he knows what he does to me, which kind of bugs me, but I can't seem to speak. Until I can stop my pulse from racing in sexual excitement, maybe it's better if I remain silent.

"How do you know Nuke?" His voice is seriously amazing. I've been listening to it since as long as I can remember, but tonight... tonight it seems more deep, intense, like caramel dipped in dark chocolate. *Wait,* did he just ask me how I know Nuke?

I turn slightly so I can see if he's serious, willing my brain to work since the champagne is making me somewhat dizzy.

What the?

My mind races. I sense the power of his impatience as he waits for an answer. Is he serious? Does he seriously not know it's me? The way his eyes hold mine in the darkened vehicle, I have my answer.

Shit.

I never dreamed he wouldn't recognize me. Okay, there are two ways of handling this. I tell him the truth, or...

I smile and say, "We go way back." He reaches for a strand of my hair and twirls it around his finger. His eyes scan my face, then dip to my breasts.

"Oh God," I whisper. My nipples harden and I lean back into the cushioned seat again, this time to get ahold of myself.

"You a liar, beautiful?" He reaches for my breast, his thumb roughly rubbing my nipple and I almost moan out loud.

"No. I'm an old friend." This time I do kind of moan.

As he continues to rub and pinch my nipple, his other hand wraps around my neck, bringing my face inches from his.

"I know all his friends, and trust me, I'd remember you," he says gruffly, and if I wasn't so freakin' ready to grab his hand and shove it in my panties, I'd laugh.

Thankfully, the SUV saves me from myself and slows in front of his hotel.

"Granger, do you want me to clear the lobby?" The hot bodyguard turns to look at us and my cheeks turn hot. Rhys brushes my lips with his, then lets me go as he opens the door and steps out.

I clear my throat and pull down my dress. God, the bodyguard doesn't look fazed at all. Clearly this is not the first time he's witnessed this.

"I'll take it from here, Ace. Thank you." He holds out his hand for me.

I slide out and decide that if I'm going to make this work, I can't be getting jealous. There are going to be a million women throwing themselves at him. Again, that voice in the back of my head makes me hesitate, if only for a second.

Am I doing this wrong? I feel like I've been telling a lot of white lies, starting with my mom. Is karma going to slap me in the face?

"Holy shit, it's Granger," a group of men in suits call out, making me push aside my thoughts and focus on my future. His hand lies firmly on the lower part of my back. Nodding, he moves us fast. I barely glimpse the gorgeous lobby when the elevator door closes on the few people brave enough to have followed him.

"This is crazy," I whisper.

His tall, hard body pushes me against the glass wall. "Welcome to rock 'n' roll, beautiful." In a moment, his lips are on mine and I cling to him, opening my mouth to let his tongue take mine. He tastes like smoke with a hint of citrus. My head is spinning, and every single cell is buzzing with need.

This goes beyond wanting him, or fantasy about the famous Rock God. I've never felt anything close to this before.

He grips my chin, forcing me to allow his tongue more access. His other hand roughly jerks my dress up, and my leg wraps around his thigh.

"Fuck," he says into my mouth as he rubs his erection on my wet panties.

The elevator dings, but Rhys reaches over to stop it, and like the dark magician I suspect he might be, he pushes aside my underwear and thrusts two fingers into my wet core.

"Jesus, tight." His eyes look into mine, and for a split second I think he might realize who I am. Instead, he captures my lips and slides his fingers in and out, finger fucking me hard and fast.

"Oh my God," I gasp as he roughly rubs my clit. Nothing about him is gentle. He's powerful and primal. I groan into his mouth as my tongue twists with his.

"Fuck, this is the tightest cunt," he says huskily, and my head falls back against the cool mirror.

I cling to his shoulders. Climbing as if I'm possessed, I rub my pussy on his hand.

"That's it, beautiful, fuck my hand. Fuck it hard." His nasty voice makes my core pulse.

"I'm going to come," I say hoarsely, not even recognizing myself when I lift my head and dig my nails into the back of his neck.

"Yeah, that's it, baby. Squeeze my fingers."

"Rhys..." Vaguely I'm aware that I'm chanting his name as I orgasm. Wave after wave of life-altering pleasure spirals through my body.

"Fuck. I want this tight cunt," he murmurs in my ear and I shiver. I'm gone, beyond caring about anything but him. His fingers slowly slide out of me, and I move to drop my leg.

"Tell me, beautiful, you think this tight pussy can handle my cock?" His fingers rub my swollen clit, hard and fast.

Jesus, he's full-on nasty, dirty, and fucking amazing. I can't answer, or maybe I do. I'm not making sense because I'm getting ready to come again.

"That's it, just like that. Give it to me, beautiful." His eyes penetrate me, and it takes my breath away.

I'm spinning, seeing stars as I cling to him and convulse, pulsing on those magical fingers. I'd almost be embarrassed that he's seeing me come apart, but I'm floating, holding on to him while the world comes back into focus.

"Mr. Granger, is everything all right?" a male voice comes from outside the elevator door.

"Oh God, Rhys," I whisper into his mouth. My eyes dart to his. Slowly, he smiles and again, I'm struck by how beautiful he is. He makes my heart hurt; he's been my everything for as long as I can remember. But the real man who stands here with me... this is a feeling I've never had. It's raw, brutal. Suddenly, I feel a bit desperate. I might not be okay if this doesn't work with him. He's that addicting. I might be ruined.

He cocks his head, his eyes caressing my face, then turns and presses on the intercom. "Yes, fine," he assures whoever and returns his attention to me. "Let's go."

Thankfully, he holds my hand tight, since my legs feel shaky as we walk to the end of the elegant gold and silver carpet. Of course, he has the penthouse. The key card lights up the entry slot, and he pulls me into a room that is four times the size of my Venice bungalow. The blinking lights of Puget Sound tease through the airy glass windows.

"This is gorgeous," I murmur, taking in the suite. The darkness and slightly wet windows make it almost romantic. I rub my hands up and down my dress, all of a sudden nervous.

"It's a room. Most of the time, I can't keep track of where I am." His breath tickles my ear, but his tone is different.

I turn to look at his face. Half is shadowed, but he's different. Everything about him seems to have changed. I'm at a slight disadvantage since the man standing behind me is dangerous in a detached, almost bored way.

The Rhys Granger I knew would have been thrilled to be in this type of hotel. Beyond grateful for anyone to even listen to the mad ramblings he had in his head and put into song.

"What are you looking for, beautiful? I can assure you I'm not half as interesting as you seem to think I am."

"Wow." I clear my throat, while trying to make my legs move. But the orgasms and champagne were making me almost sluggish.

He easily snakes a tattooed arm around my stomach and jerks me back into his chest. "Speak, and don't worry—nothing you can say will make me not want to fuck you." His breath tickles my ear and I gasp as he bites the tip and sucks on it.

I need to be outraged. I need to speak and tell him the truth. But all I can do is groan and think that I'm glad I forgot to wear earrings tonight while his tongue fucks my ear.

What the hell is wrong with me?

"Oh God," I hiss as his rough skin slides up my body to my breasts. He's so forceful, so confident... it makes me feel secure.

"This needs to come off," he grunts as he rubs his hard erection on my ass, and all thoughts of telling him anything are gone. It's only me, his magical hands unsnapping the clasp at my neck, and his hard dick.

My dress falls, stopping at my hips, and I arch back into him. The slightly cool air makes me shiver. My hard nipples ache for his touch yet he doesn't oblige. He turns me by my hips and steps back, his eyes raking over my body. The rain must be feeling the energy from us. It pelts the glass windows harder.

I lick my lips and straighten my shoulders. At this point, I need everything I've got to give me confidence, or at least match his arrogance.

He flashes me his signature grin and crosses his arms, allowing me access to admire his chest and biceps. They're large; everything about him seems large. I smile back at him and try not to sway. I feel like Alice in Wonderland, except I'm getting ready to go down the Rhys Granger rabbit hole.

Clearly, I'm drunk. But whatever. This is it. I'm in Rhys Granger's room.

And he's freakin' hot. No, *he's perfection.*

My eyes trail up and lock on his. He's almost too intense. It's intimate and scary. I open my mouth to speak but he thrusts his thumb inside.

"Suck," he snarls and jerks the rest of my dress off my hips so that I'm standing in nothing but my black G-string and heels. Clinging to his arm so as not to fall, I suck hard and let my tongue twirl around his thumb. It tastes like smoke and liquor.

"Fuck." He pulls my hair back, forcing me to lock eyes with his fierce ones. I'm connected to him, and it kind of throws me for a second. I like to think of myself as a free bird, someone who loves to experiment. Sure, I'm still a virgin in the traditional sense, but that's because I've been saving it for him.

Yet as he stares down at me, I realize that all my experimenting was child's play compared to him and how he makes my body respond. As if I'm his instrument, he brings me alive. And now I know that there are boys and then there are men. Apparently, the guys I've been messing around with were boys. Either that or Rhys Granger truly is a god.

He pulls his thumb out of my mouth with a pop and trails the wetness all the way down my chin and neck to rub one of my nipples. His eyes hold mine hostage as I try to breathe. Screw that, I'm trying hard not to pass out.

"You're fucking beautiful." His raspy voice makes my skin feel as though it's on fire, yet goose bumps emerge on my arms and thighs.

I reach for his shoulders. "You are."

He doesn't smile and merely cocks his head. It's dark, but the lights from outside let me see his glorious smirk as he jerks me up to his mouth.

And then he kills me.

Damages me for anyone else. His mouth takes mine in a kiss that can only be described as my awakening. I groan and let him guide me. Slow and deep, his tongue plays with mine. *What's happening to me?* This is not at all how I played this moment out in my mind. I never imagined he wouldn't recognize me. Or that he could make me feel like this. I never even knew I could feel like this.

"Take off your panties" he growls. I blink at him, then quickly slide them off and step out as he reaches down and lifts me up. My legs easily wrap around his waist as he starts to walk. Vaguely I notice a fireplace and white couches. The smell of flowers clings to the suite.

All at once, he tosses me onto the bed and my back lands on the white down comforter.

God, I shouldn't have drank this much. It's clouding my judgment. Somehow I thought I would tell him that I had been saving myself for him and it would be magical. Instead, he's getting me off in the elevator only moments ago and doesn't even know my name.

Is that bad?

Fuck it, I'm rolling with this. I've come this far. Plus, I came all over his fingers in a matter of seconds. Without a doubt, this is going to be the best night of my life.

I scramble to sit up, my heels giving me traction. They dig into the comforter, and I swear I hear a rip but don't care because Rhys Granger is taking off his shirt and that's all that matters.

Even with the lights off, I can see his numerous tattoos, but it's his freakin' lean eight-pack that's making me take small breaths so as not to hyperventilate. Although I might be making myself worse, considering the room is slightly spinning.

I lick my lips and watch him roughly jerk his zipper down and kick his jeans off. Of course, he's commando.

"Holy shit, are you... oh my God." I answer the question myself and sit up farther to see the silver piercing on his dick.

"Spread your legs, gorgeous," his voice rumbles. Though I try to focus on his face... his cock is huge... and thick... *and pierced.*

"Rhys, I need to tell yo—" I whisper something that doesn't even make sense to me. Again, his cock is fucking huge and juicy to the point that it's distracting. He reaches down to cup his balls, making it grow bigger, and I moan as my face floods with heat. Suddenly I'm not as brave as I thought, because *holy shit.*

"Spread," he demands and before I can even compute what I'm doing, I obey. This time I do hear the rip as the spikes of my heels dig into the comforter. Jesus, I have to pull myself together... but his cock *is pierced.*

He reaches down and wraps his large hands around my ankles. He's warm, and my skin feels sensitive to his touch. I blink up at him. I swear I see feathers now as he jerks me to the edge of the mattress.

Time and the world have stopped. The soft light from the fireplace fades away. Feathers dance around us. It's like we're in an enchanted world and he's a mystical beast sent to be my knight in shining armor.

Then he kneels. "Fuck, look at this pretty pussy." His thumb rubs my clit and I almost scream at how good it feels.

"I'm gonna eat this pussy." His thumb rubs back and forth on my clit causing me to grab hold of the comforter, and this time I do moan, loudly.

"Then I'm gonna fuck this tight cunt hard." I groan, horrified at how wet I am. I had no idea he could be so filthy.

"Oh. My. God." I lean up on my elbows, panting, then fall back as his mouth goes straight for my clit.

He wasn't kidding.

He's fucking sucking it as if it's nectar that he needs to survive.

"Rhys," I whimper as I grab his thick dark hair and spread my legs farther. Whatever he's doing, I never want it to stop.

Ever.

I'm climbing, literally. Lifting his head, he inserts two fingers and starts to fuck me again with them. Deep. Hard.

"This cunt. Goddamn, it's tight," he murmurs as I go over, splintering into blinding white lights as my body pulses.

Before I can focus, maybe even know my name, his giant, pierced cock is rubbing my clit and I orgasm again.

In one fast, blinding moment of pain he's inside me. I think I scream, or maybe it's just him cursing... but my head is no longer floating from pleasure. This freakin' hurts.

"You can't be a fucking virgin," he groans, holding himself still as if he doesn't trust himself to move.

I stay mute. Seems to have worked so far, so why start talking now? I'll only burst into tears. I want to scream the truth that I'm fucking on fire down there, and that I've been saving myself for him. But the more pain I have, the clearer I become. I should have told him the truth. His mouth takes mine and it's gentle, causing everything to fade but him.

"That's it, baby. Relax and let your body adjust and take me." Then he kisses me slowly as he pumps in and out.

"So tight." His voice, a gravelly melody that I love, makes my nails dig deeper into his shoulders.

I'm his.

As he moves in and out, his breathing is harsh. He pulls out and jerks himself off.

"Fuck," he groans as he shoots his wet, warm seed on my breasts, then covers my pussy with it, emptying himself on me.

"Stay here."

I almost say, "Where would I go?" But I'm tired. My eyes blink open when a hot cloth covers my breasts. I take a breath and realize I must have passed out and Rhys is cleaning me up. He's frowning. The light from the bathroom allows me to actually see him.

"Who are you?" His voice isn't mad, it's more matter of fact, as if he's going over everything in his head.

Our eyes lock. His narrow, and for a second I think I see him piece it all together.

"Nothing? Staying quiet?" He tosses the wet washcloth and reaches for my heels, which I'm horrified to find I'm still wearing.

Jesus, I must be way more intoxicated than I thought. I curl under the sheets and he crawls in.

I don't know what I should say, and I'm so tired, too tired to get into any of this now. He smells fresh, clean. I guess he took a shower while I slept.

"Keep your secrets, beautiful." He pulls me into his arms and I sigh, because all is well. He's not mad. If anything, he seems tired himself.

Tomorrow I'll tell him everything and we can start fresh. Everything will be wonderful.

Then I pass out.

CHAPTER 6

RHYS

Past — Twenty-seven years old
Seattle, Washington

"I'm gonna marry you." I can't see her because she's far away, but I know that voice.

"Gia?" It's raining. Why am I so dry?

"Gia?"

A flash of lightning makes me see silver. Then she's right in front of me, only it's not her. It's my goddess, with large cat eyes and cherry-stained lips. She's in the silver bubble with me.

"Rhys."

I need to get out. She's crying and I lift my hand to catch a tear.

"You need to protect us..." she pleads. *"Open the bubble. Something will happen to us if we stay in."*

I reach out to claw it open, but I can't. It's like I've been weighted down with sand and I can't move.

I'm dreaming.

Gia.

No, this is not Gia. Gia is a girl with braces and wild, unbrushed hair. *This is my goddess.* With long, silky brown hair and legs that never end.

"*Rhys...*" She's moving yet I can't. I reach for her but again, my arms are weighted down. The bubble breaks in two and she starts to float away. I yell for her, fight for her.

"*I'm going to marry you...*" She scratches at the silver bubble, her red lips tremble, but it's her eyes that bring me to my knees...

"Fuck." I bolt up and look around. Rain pelts the windows. The room is gray but not pitch black. It must be morning. I take a breath trying to steady my pounding heart. I glance over at the mass of dark hair on the white pillow next to me. The woman's back is to me. The covers have slipped down allowing me to see the crack of her ass.

"The fuck is going on?" I take a breath. Feathers rise and twirl. A sliver of sunlight streaks through the black and angry clouds.

I reach for my cigarettes on the expensive nightstand. I need to slow the fuck down. At this pace, I'll wind up in rehab. Leaning back, I rest against the headboard. My lighter flicks to life, and I let my sluggish brain try to recall the night before.

It's coming, rolling over me, like the feathers that are dancing around us. I bring the cigarette to my lips.

Inhale.

Exhale.

The nicotine needs to work. I need to stay calm and not overreact. The ominous feeling of doom weighs down on my chest. It's all there, bitch-slapping me awake.

The concert. We played like shit. That led to the club, cocaine, tequila, and *her*. I don't need to roll her over to know. I rub my chest, hoping to find some sort of calm. What has *she* done?

I look at her back, it's bronze from the sun and her Italian blood. She shifts slightly, allowing me to see a tease of a tan line. I take one last deep inhale and put the cigarette out as I wake up, cut through the cobwebs, and connect the dots.

My cock is hard. My nostrils twitch at the scent of us, of her. She tasted like fucking honeydew, with the tightest cunt I've ever fucked.

It can't be...

I throw off the white sheet, ignoring the barrage of feathers, and stand, staring down at the bed and my dick. The dried blood on both gives me answers.

A fucking virgin?

I rip the comforter off and my eyes rake over her body. "Brat." It comes out almost as a caress.

Green eyes blink open and up at me. A small smile graces her puffy lips, which is quickly replaced when she takes in my frown. The play of emotions on her beautiful face is almost laughable... if it wasn't happening to me.

"Motherfucker." I cover her mouth as she starts to scream. "Have you lost your fucking mind?" Rage that I didn't even know I had threatens to take over, and it's not gonna be pretty.

Gia fucking Fontaine.

The Brat.

In my bed. All grown up.

She stops struggling as if it's dawned on her that it's pointless. I have her pinned. Her eyes narrow and she sticks her tongue out to lick my hand.

"Scream again and I won't be held responsible." I lift my hand and get off her.

She bolts up, her fantastic tits heaving as she points at me. "You're the one who's lost your mind," she spits out, holding up her hands as if that could stop me from grabbing her if I wanted to. "I'm not the one who can't remember people." She looks fierce, yet her voice cracks as if she wants to cry. In a flash, she tries to bolt around me.

"You're kidding me?" I roar, grabbing her arm and jerking her to my chest. Her small gasp and firm tits make me bite the inside of my cheek.

I don't need this shit. My head is pounding, and not from booze and drugs. This is a Gia Fontaine headache.

"Take your hands off me. You've clearly become every pathetic thing you never wanted to be," she sneers.

"The fuck?" I stare at her, our breathing harsh. The room is charged with electric energy. I feel it; she feels it.

It's pure, sexual, almost an animalistic attraction, because Gia Fontaine is the last person I should put my dick into.

My eyes take in her face. How did I not recognize her? But then again, how in a million years would I have ever guessed she would show up, in a club... dressed like that.

I'm fucking livid, and the more I think about the way she looked last night in that scrap of a dress, the more I realize she knew exactly what she was doing.

I toss her on the bed. Grabbing both of her hands, I pin them on top of her head.

"What is wrong with you?" I shake her, causing the bed to move.

"Me?" she thunders, her hair wild, her lips red and swollen from last night and our almost violent mating.

"Why didn't you say something?" I shake the bed again.

"Because you would have stopped, and I wanted you more than anything in this world!" Her emerald eyes spill with angry tears.

I let her go. Her words burn into my soul. What the hell? This is wrong, so wrong, but knowing it doesn't change the fact that I want to lock her in with me and fuck her, over and over.

"This is wrong," I state. I need another cigarette, something to distract me from her vanilla smell. She's like a delicious, forbidden dessert. One you know you should never try, but when you do, you devour it.

My cock is rock hard. It doesn't seem to understand that she's off-limits.

Forever.

"You're right about that." She rubs her wrist. "God, I'm such an idiot because I believed in you. I freakin' saved myself for you. You jerk."

"I... how are you even here?"

"I thought you... Never mind. Get off of me. I was wrong." Her voice cracks.

My eyes sweep over her. Gone is the gangly girl with skinny legs and dirty feet. She's grown into those legs and is everything I always knew she would be.

Simply stunning. Unfortunately for either of us, she hasn't changed her ways. Instead of spying, she's somehow done the unthinkable and ended up in my bed. And now that I've tasted her, I want more, so much more.

Memories of last night and the way her candy cunt tasted make me snort in disgust that I was so fucked up I didn't even get to enjoy her.

And now I can't.

This was a mistake, a huge one that will never happen again. I need answers, even if they are laced with lies from that sweet mouth.

"Gia. I'm not going to ask again. What the fuck are you doing here?" She shuts her eyes and turns her face toward the pillow. Her teeth bite down on her bottom lip as if that will stop the tears that she can amazingly turn on.

"Get off of me." She turns her head almost violently. And there she is, magnificent in her anger and hurt as her eyes shoot me a death stare.

"Easy, Brat, you're the one who did this. Start talking." She opens her mouth, but the pounding on the door makes her scream.

"Goddammit, Granger. Is Gia in there?" Nuke's voice vibrates inside.

"Go away, I'm dealing with shit," I bellow. I'll take care of him later. I pull the cover up just as he storms in looking like a lunatic, eyes wild as he lunges for me.

"You fuck." His fist connects with my chin and I'm done.

Done with Gia, her drama, and whatever fucked-up shit she's got going on with Nuke.

I stand before he can get another punch in and go straight for his ribs, gut punching him until he bends over to catch his breath, wheezing.

"Nuke, oh my God." She jumps up and I grab her arm. Jesus Christ, she's truly lost it.

"You're fucking naked." I shake her, turning so I block her from Nuke. I'd rather him see my ass than anything on Gia.

"Let go of me!" she screeches.

My eye twitches. This is over. I grab my T-shirt, which is hanging on the chair, and drag her toward the bathroom.

"Get dressed, Gia, and then get the fuck out of here before I do something we'll both regret." I shove her stunned face in and slam the bathroom door.

"What in the ever-loving-fuck is happening?" Rafe, our manager, stands in the doorway drenched in sweat, completely out of breath. If his tone is any indication, he was interrupted before he could finish his daily morning run.

His blue eyes narrow on me. Arching a brow at my naked ass, he swings toward Nuke who is still slightly wheezing, hands on his knees.

"Tell him."

"Tell me what?" he roars, then holds up a hand as his phone starts vibrating.

"Fucking perfect." I brush past him, pull on some jeans, and stumble into the other room. The rain has stopped, allowing the rays of sunlight to streak into the suite.

Ammo lies on one of the couches, dressed in the same clothes as last night, hands crossed on top of his chest.

"What the fuck are you doing here?" I grit out, grabbing his pack of unfiltered Camels from the coffee table.

"I'm here for the family meeting." He opens one eye to look at me, then snorts, closing it again. "Although, I notice Cash is absent."

I drop down onto the stiff couch across from him and light up, leaning back to smoke and figure out what's the best move here.

"This is fucked."

"Yep," he says with eyes closed and a stupid grin on his face. I'm close with Ammo; he's like a brother. We fight, and half the time I want to put my fist in his arrogant face. But we're a great team.

He's a fucking beast of a guitarist. At twenty-six, Ammo has clinched his spot in rock 'n' roll royalty. He's that good.

He also can compartmentalize fame and success. Christ, he lives for it.

"You want food?" I grab the phone and dial room service.

"Yes, Mr. Tyler Durden, how can I be of service?" I glance over as Nuke's dark shadow leans over me. Grabbing his cigarettes, he glares at me. I almost gut punch him again, but I have the phone and cigarette in my hands. Ammo looks at both of us and starts laughing. I lean back and prop my bare feet on the coffee table, ignoring them.

"Yeah, can you send up a couple pots of coffee, some danishes, fruit, and five orders of bacon and eggs, scrambled?"

"Of course," the voice purrs. I know she knows who I am. We all use aliases, which is stupid. Somehow someone always leaks our rooms anyway.

"Anything else?"

A loud *goddammit* from Rafe makes me say, "Yeah, a pitcher of tomato juice and horseradish." I inhale and toss the phone back on the receiver, my eyes narrowing on Nuke.

"You need to explain what the fuck happened here." I point at him with my cigarette.

"You tell me," he fires right back. "All I know is Gia is my responsibility. She was supposed to stay with me." The hairs on the back of my neck stand up. Is he saying he wants Gia?

My feet drop and I lean over. *"Gia Fontaine* is not your responsibility. And where was all this concern last night?" My eyes zero in on his face. I need to see every expression because if he wants Gia... we're gonna have a problem.

"Are you kidding?" He scrubs his hands up and down his face, then drops them. "Look, last night I was high and drunk. Never in a million years did I think even you would fuck Axel's sister."

"I didn't know it was Gia," I state, getting madder as the seconds tick by. For fuck's sake, Gia is an adult. She needed to use her words last night.

Ammo sits up and looks over at Nuke, then me, and crosses his arms as if this is the best entertainment he's had in years.

"You can't be serious? You really want me to believe that you had no idea that was Gia?" Nuke stares at me, his brow furrowed, and reaches for a bottle of Jack Daniel's.

"Zero." I stare right back.

"I told you." He takes a step toward me.

"Like hell you did." My pulse is pounding. I haven't felt like this, ever. It was as if I finally found my muse, only to be slapped in the face.

"Granger." He looks up at the ceiling and turns to stare out the window. "This is Axel's baby sister we're talking about. He's gonna kill us."

"Fuck Axel. I'd like to see him try." Ammo stands and stretches as Rafe storms in. With a glare, he scrutinizes all of us as if we're his disappointing children.

"What does Axel have to do with any of this?" Rafe turns to look at me.

"I didn't know."

"Didn't know what?" he demands.

65

"How did you not know?" Nuke yells, then turns to Rafe. "That woman"—he points at the bedroom—"is *Gia Fontaine*. As in Axel Fontaine's baby sister. As in we are fucked because I'm sure she's called him, and the Disciples are now on their way."

"Christ." I stand and go straight to the minibar, saying over my shoulder, "Pull your shit together, Nuke. I'm not afraid of Axel or the Disciples." Grabbing a bottle of vodka, I figure screw waiting for the tomato juice.

"Okay. The last thing we need to deal with is a motorcycle club." Rafe's voice is calm—too calm. I glance over at him. Even without his suit he radiates control. There's a reason Rafe is the best at what he does. He's cutthroat. People don't fuck around when dealing with him. In his mid-fifties, he gets as many women as we do. Hell, he probably gets more.

He's also made us rich, along with himself, and he's the closest thing to a father I've had. Still, I'm not in the mood for any of his lecturing this morning.

"Just everyone relax." I look around at all three of them. None look happy. Even Ammo's smart-ass smirk is gone—he sits with arms crossed.

"Gia's not going to call Axel, and the Disciples aren't going to kill us. Stop acting like a pussy, Nuke." I take a big swig and breathe out fumes, instantly feeling better.

"Really? Well, I hope to God what I just heard is not true, because if it is, then we have a problem." Rafe holds up his cell. "That was Deborah." He waves his phone. "Apparently there's a video of you and *her* in the elevator last night."

My eyes bolt up to his face.

"I can see by your expression it's true. Deborah saw the tape. The woman is easily identified. What do you want to do?"

I put the bottle down and look up at the ceiling as I laugh at how in a matter of twelve hours the Brat has caused more drama than I've had in years.

"Pay them off and get it shut down," I snarl, replaying her face as she came.

"Goddamn, Granger, what do they have?" Nuke stares at me, his hand clenched, and at this point I wouldn't even mind if he comes at me. At least it would distract me from the repercussions of last night.

"Apparently, *they* have actual footage of Granger and Gia last night." Rafe says all this as he turns away to talk on the phone.

"This is unbelievable." Nuke comes at me, only for Ammo to stop him.

"Granger, this is unlike you. You need to clean up your shit." And that's all he says. I almost laugh again, like they're enlightening me on this. Of course, this is messy. Look who's involved.

I take a breath, blocking out Rafe screaming in the background about how much money they want, and that it doesn't matter how much *Entertainment Tonight* wants to pay. Rafe is the cheapest man alive, so having to pay people off is like getting fucked in the ass for him.

"Why is she here, Nuke? Tell me how it is that a girl I haven't seen in years just shows up fully grown, almost naked, in a club with you. *How?*" I demand.

"She's here to get a scholarship. I thought you knew." He sits down and looks out the window, shaking his head as he probably pieces together that he got played and outsmarted by one Gia Fontaine.

I roll my eyes. "Of course, she is." But before I can say more, I sense her. For some fucked-up reason, I'm connected with her. If the music that's playing in my head is any warning, I know I shouldn't turn around. This is what happens when I'm stressed and fed up. The music helps.

So, I turn and stare into the greenest eyes.

She's forbidden.

And devious.

I've never wanted anyone more.

CHAPTER 7

GIA

Past – Eighteen years old
Seattle, Washington

My heart races as I stare at the bathroom door, incredulous. I reach for the door handle but hear a loud "What in everloving fuck is happening?" and pull back as if I've been burned. Maybe I have with the amount of cursing going on out there.

This is a disaster. How did it spiral so fast? I mean, last night was not what I envisioned but still, he was connected, if a little inebriated, but whatever. Suddenly I don't feel well. I need to breathe, maybe take a shower. *What the hell?*

A door slams, causing me to scream and gag at the same time. The bile that's been threatening to come up is unfortunately doing its thing.

I reach for the toilet seat, barely making it before I heave, emptying my stomach. The smell of champagne and whatever I ate yesterday stings my eyes. I'm sweating, so I know it's not over.

Seconds that seem like hours tick by, my body stiff and frozen, praying for this to be over. This is absolutely the last time I drink. If I can make it through this, I'll never take a drop of—annnd here it comes again. I lean over and retch out the last of my hopes and dreams.

"God." I lay my head on my hand, which rests on the toilet, truly grateful that Rhys can afford five-star hotels with spotless bathrooms. At long last, the world stops spinning and I stand, feeling like I've just run a marathon and dehydration has set in.

I rest my hips on the cool marble sink, and twist my disgusting, puke-scented hair off my face. I feel like shit. *Why?* Why did I let Nuke talk me into those shots last night?

"Okay." I breathe out. This is not ideal, but not a complete nightmare. Now that I've eliminated all the poisons, I can somewhat function. My mind instantly reviews my options. One wrong move and I'll be kicked out of here.

I stink of sex and throw-up. A shower is a must before I can tackle all that's happening out there.

Stretching my hands toward the ceiling, I take another deep breath and feel remarkably better as I admire my surroundings. The bathroom is gorgeous. It's huge, probably the size of my dorm room. The white orchids and marble floors remind me how lavish he lives now. Rhys has come a long way from our little neighborhood.

My fingers drift over the numerous fluffy white towels rolled and placed perfectly in a wooden cubby. Too bad this morning is crap. I'd kill to soak in that large tub, let the hot water erase the truth that my heart hurts. I push all those negative thoughts aside, open the glass shower door, and blast the hot water.

What's my next move?

Lifting my face to the water, I close my eyes. It's pretty simple—I can grab my bags and run back to California.

Or I can stay and fight for him.

Now that I'm somewhat sober, I need to decide if Rhys Granger is worth the fight. This morning was not good. If that's a foreshadowing of the future, it won't be as easy as I thought.

Rhys is different. Maybe it's all the fame, being constantly surrounded by yes people, I don't know. But he's not the same Rhys Granger who lived down the street and slept in our garage.

It's like he has, in fact, become the Rock God. I came here to make Rhys fall in love with me, not realizing that ten years might have changed a few things.

Like, Rock God is fucking hot.

And used to getting his way. Case in point, grabbing me off the dance floor, not even bothering to find out my name. Butterflies flutter in my stomach at how exciting that was. He takes what he wants.

And he wanted me.

I turn my back to the pelting water and sigh. In hindsight, I probably should have told him who I was. I kind of understand his anger this morning. If I were in his shoes, I'd be pissed too.

And poor Nuke. The look of horror and guilt on his face as he stormed into the room trying to be my protector.

"God, I'm totally screwing this up," I groan into my hands, mortified. It's like I'm stuck in some endless film loop in my head showing the same clip of Nuke's face over and over as he lunges at Rhys.

"And I jumped out of bed *naked.*" My words echo around the shower as I grab some shampoo. This is almost cringeworthy. I need to call Julianna and tell her everything, but she'll be mortified for me.

Lathering up I close my eyes as the soap drips down my sensitized body. I breathe in some of the coconut-scented shampoo and decide to go with my gut.

And my gut says he wants me.

I'll let him calm down. Maybe everyone will be gone and I can distract him with my body. My nipples harden at that thought. I wish I hadn't been so drunk last night. It would have been nice to have a less fuzzy memory of my first time.

Yeah, I'm not leaving. I've come too far to give up now.

Turning off the water I breathe out. "Bold. Be bold, Gia." Then I almost laugh at how ironic it is. Rhys was always the one thinking my fearless attitude was great. Guess not so much now. I reach for a fluffy towel and crack the door open.

The room is empty, but I hear a loud voice. "Apparently, *they* have actual footage of Granger and Gia last night."

"Fuck." I shut the door and lean against it, my hand going to my chest since my heart feels like it just skipped a beat.

This is bad.

Beyond bad.

I drop the towel and spin around for something to wear. Of course, I have only the T-shirt he shoved into my hands, so I throw it on. Instantly I smell him, and for a second that calms me.

I love the way he smells: fresh, clean, with a hint of spice. Maybe it's smoke. I take a breath before I lose it. This is stupid. He's a freaking rock star, for fuck's sake. He must have people who specialize in dealing with things like this.

Rhys isn't stupid. He's not gonna let this get out. Because, if my mom sees it...or worse, *my brother.*

"Holy shit." I'm starting to panic as memories of last night return... memories of Rhys's fingers thrusting inside me, making me come over and over.

Axel can't see that.

He'll kill me. He'll kill Rhys. I throw open the door and glance around for my pumps. Freakin' fantastic. They're under an ornate chair, meaning I have to lean over and pray I don't puke again. I grab them, trying not to topple over as I slip them on, then march in only to falter at Nuke's voice.

"She's here to get a scholarship. I thought you knew."

"Of course, she is." Rhys snorts. Turning his head, he locks eyes with me as if he can sense me. I freeze and instantly regret not finding my dress from last night.

Up and down, he peruses my body, stopping to stare at the bottom of his T-shirt that comes to my midthigh.

Nuke's eyes follow Rhys's, then widen as if I have grown horns. "Christ, Gia." He shakes his head.

I toss my wet hair off my shoulder, trying to manage as much dignity as I can in heels, no panties, and an old black T-shirt.

"Hold on, Deborah." An older guy with piercing blue eyes, salt-and-pepper hair, and a beard to match points at me. "Gia Fontaine?"

I blink at him. He's a full-on silver fox. Unfortunately ,he doesn't seem friendly, if his eyes and tone are any indication.

"That's me." Puffing out some air, I try to smile, but it's tight, making my lips twitch.

"Okay, everyone out." Rhys stands and takes my hand. Silver Fox's eyes follow me.

"You're Axel's sister? The one who's in the elevator footage?" He barks out the questions but doesn't wait for my response. Just turns his back on us, continuing to yell on his phone at someone named Deborah.

Poor Deborah.

I'd heard rumors about their manager being an ass, but that was mostly from my brother, so you never know.

Rhys moves in front of me, his tall body a shield. "What the hell are you wearing?" he says, his eyes fixated on my boobs.

"I have no clothes. *This*"—I pull the bottom of his T-shirt—"is what you shoved in my face, remember?" I snap right back.

Ammo slaps his knees and stands as I peek over Rhys' shoulder to stare at the Ace of Spades.

That's what the tabloids like to label him, since each member of the Stuffed Muffins has a playing card tattoo. I know this because I've had a giant poster since I was thirteen on my ceiling with all of them looking like gods with their shirts off.

Ammo's the Ace. A gorgeous bad boy rocker, with blue eyes, honey-wheat blond hair, and hot tattoos.

"Gia." He sounds like he's saying it in Italian. "What a wonderful surprise and a pleasure to meet you. I know your brother." He smirks. And just like that, I don't think he's hot anymore, and his tattoos are stupid.

God, are all these guys assholes besides Nuke?

Ammo took my brother's place when he quit the original band, the Dicks. Needless to say, Axel has made fun of the Stuffed Muffins for years, especially Ammo. I used to think it was because of their success, but I'm starting to think it might be their personalities. My eyes widen at Rhys to see if he's gonna say anything. He has to know Ammo's trying to piss me off by bringing up my brother.

"I'm in room 318 if you want to look at my guitars or something else I'm really good at using."

"Ammo?" Rhys's voice is deep and kind of scary. Of course, my heart pounds and my stomach flips.

"Yeah?"

"Don't fuck with me." His eyes don't leave my face, and a shiver goes up my spine. My core clenches.

I want him.

I don't care if I've done everything wrong or if he thinks last night was a mistake. I'm caught in his sphere and don't intend on leaving.

"Interesting." Ammo's voice almost makes me jump. How could I have forgotten that he was still here?

Rhys Granger. It's like he dabbles in dark magic, the way his bourbon eyes with ridiculously long eyelashes make me speechless. He's pure perfection. I grow warm again. Maybe I'm hormonally off or something.

I have to pull myself together. I can't be this easy, obvious, whatever. I swallow and straighten my shoulders.

Geez, I'm breathless, slightly dizzy, and my nipples are hard and achy. I make myself break eye contact to look at Ammo's amused face. I almost roll my eyes at him.

But at least I can breathe again. Ammo doesn't make me feel like I'm on fire and in need of oxygen. He just stands there with a stupid smirk that I'm sure ninety-nine percent of women find sexy.

I don't.

I clear my throat and cross my arms. The cool air and Rhys's eyes alert me the T-shirt has risen. Whatever, I need to stay focused.

"Look—"

He grabs my chin. His fingers, rough from years of playing the guitar, slightly scratch my skin, and I hate that I have to swallow back a moan.

"Where are your clothes?" His voice is deep and gruff, almost like when he sings one of his ballads. My arms pebble with goose bumps.

"My suitcase is with Nuke." I turn my head away as I run a hand up and down my arm. I have to put some distance between us. When he's this close, it's impossible to think straight.

"What the fuck, Gia?" he says.

"I just—" I'm interrupted again by a loud knock. Clearly, I'm on edge more than I thought since I'm digging my nails into Rhys's forearm.

I hate him for making me feel like this—and his stupid guitarist. Also, why is Nuke sitting like a zombie drinking a bottle of Jack?

Ammo holds up his hand. "No, please let me get it." He opens the door to a guy in a white chef jacket who proceeds to roll in an elegant tray.

"Just sit." Rhys dumps me onto the couch.

"What is wrong with you? Stop it," I hiss, instantly pulling the shirt down and glancing at Nuke to see if he saw anything. Thankfully he's still staring out the window as if he can't seem to figure out the ABCs.

"I swear to God, Gia, don't move." Rhys crosses his arms and frowns down at me.

I despise him at this moment, but his commanding voice makes me squirm. *Am I getting wet?*

"Oh God," I whisper, my cheeks heating as I toss back a damp strand of hair and cross my legs, trying not to think about his giant pierced penis.

"Anything else?" the poor guy who's delivering the food shouts over Rafe's angry rant to poor Deborah.

I bite my bottom lip and try not to laugh. It's come to this. It's so bad that I'm going to start laughing. I do this when things are really uncomfortable.

I'll start laughing. I can't help myself, although something tells me right now, laughing would not go over well. So, I take a deep breath and look out the window. The view is amazing—it's so clear I can see snow covering the mountain peaks in the distance.

Maybe this is what happens if you hang out with them long enough. Look at Nuke. My eyes dart around, settling on the room service guy. He looks like he's ready to piss himself as he shifts nervously from one leg to the other.

Wow. We either look ridiculous or supercool.

"You want anything else?" Ammo yells, causing Rafe to raise an eyebrow at him and the room service guy to jump.

Jesus, this is a complete disaster.

"Knock it off." Rafe glares at Ammo as he walks over to the room service guy, causing him to take a step back.

"No, thank you. Now get out." He waits, hand on the door as the poor guy sprints out.

"Just pay whatever you need to get the footage, Deborah. I'll have the conversation before we can proceed past that. I'll let you know." He hangs up and sighs dramatically. His blue eyes narrow and find mine.

I stare straight back. The first thing I learned growing up with nothing but boys around is never show weakness. That said, I'm glad Rhys sat me on the couch because I need to look powerful. Like I own this room, and standing up with only Rhys's T-shirt does not scream power. At least sitting, I can use my long legs, if necessary, to distract.

"Let's take this from the beginning. And please, Ms. Fontaine, do not leave out any details." He walks toward me and sits across from me next to Nuke.

Rafe is by far the scariest out of everyone in this room. He looks like he wants to put a bullet in my head and bury me in a shallow grave. I know men like him; my brother's club is filled with them. It's in their eyes. They care about few things. But what few things they care about make them dangerous if you stand in their way.

"How can I help?" Sounding like a bitch, I smile at him. Which must surprise him because he raises an eyebrow at me, then sits back to look at Rhys.

"You can help me by explaining how and why you're here." He looks at his phone, which is blowing up with texts, then back at me.

I shrug. "I'm a photographer." Clearly that's not the answer he wanted.

"Bullshit, listen caref—"

"Just relax, Rafe." Rhys holds up a hand to keep him quiet, his eyes searching my face.

"Does Axel know that you're here?" He's like a king. I stare at him, almost speechless at how dominant he's become.

"Does he?" he demands.

"No."

"No?" His eyes narrow. I hear *goddammit* and *fuck* coming from behind him, but who cares now.

"Gia." Nuke comes into my view as he stands next to Rhys. "You told me that this was a scholarship opportunity... that Axel was the one who suggested you get in touch with me. Please tell me that wasn't a lie?" He looks so hurt that I almost come clean. But let's be honest—I'm too far gone for that.

Only the fearless one wins now.

I hold up my hands, trying to calm him since he's starting to look agitated, and the last thing I want to do is hurt Nuke.

"I am here for a scholarship." I assure him, opening my mouth to say more, but decide maybe less is more right now.

"Gia, Gia, Gia." Rhys's voice is like a caress. He's not buying it. Whatever, I'm not backing down.

"What?" I glare up at him. "I had an opportunity and I took it."

The room is quiet, almost eerily so. Only Rafe's phone seems to not understand what's happening.

"You want to take pictures of us?" Rhys's voice drips sarcasm.

"Yep," I snap. "I'm studying to be a *professional* photographer."

"And you expect me to believe that the university is going to give you a scholarship if we let you take these... photos?" He's trying to intimidate me, staring me down, causing me to rethink whether Rafe is, indeed, the scariest.

What has happened to Rhys?

Breathe, Gia. I swear I'm gonna pass out, but I'd rather die than look away from him right now.

"Yes." It comes out husky, and for a split second I think I see admiration in his eyes. It's gone too fast. Perhaps I'm just being hopeful.

"Okay." Rhys smiles but it doesn't reach his eyes. I think I might puke again.

"Ammo, Rafe, Gia's here to further her love for photography and education," he says. "She forgot to mention any of this before I fucked her."

I jump up and almost twist an ankle in my heels, but who cares. I could probably get hit by a car and not feel it right now.

I'm done.

He doesn't get to be an ass to me, not now or ever. He wants to make me look like the bad guy? Fine. I'll be the bad guy.

"I'd be careful, Rhys. I'd hate to tell my brother you took my *virginity* and called me a liar."

A loud *Jesus* explodes from behind us, I'm sure from Nuke, although at this point who knows.

He stands inches from me, so close I can smell the vodka on him. So close I can hear his teeth grind. So, I deal my last card.

"I want my pictures. And interviews with all the Muffins. In return, my brother, along with the Disciples, will never know *anything*." I place my hands on my hips if only to open my rib cage to allow air in.

One.

Two.

Three.

We're in a dead heat, both of us not blinking.

"You really want to play it like this, Brat?" he grits out each word.

"You leave me no choice," I fire right back.

"You think I'm scared of Axel?" His eye twitches.

"You should be." I spit it out in his face. As soon as it's out of my mouth I want to take it back. Because the look he gives me makes me want to run and hide.

How did this get so ugly?

"Wait, Rhys." I reach for him.

He looks at my hand, then up at my face, and for the first time in my life I'm actually afraid of someone.

"I'd take your hands off me, *Brat*. And stay away." He laughs, moving away, as if being close to me sickens him.

I think I call his name but can't be sure. All I hear is the slamming of his door.

Holy fuck.

"Are you out of your mind, Ms. Fontaine?" Rafe's voice makes me look over at him, rather shell-shocked, and for a second I almost say yes.

Instead, I straighten my shoulders back. "I need to talk to Rhys."

"I think you have done enough." Grabbing his phone, Rafe stands. "You can take the photos. I'll have contracts and numerous things for you to sign."

My eyes blink up at him. I wish he would leave. I wish they all would leave because I need to tell Rhys I didn't mean what I said.

"I'll get you a room. After all, we wouldn't want Axel Fontaine's sister to be uncomfortable." He laughs and I hate him.

Ammo walks over to stand in front of me. "Don't ever threaten my brother. I don't care who *your* brother is." He turns and leaves with Rafe, my eyes following them until the door shuts. I almost burst into tears.

"Gia." Nuke pulls me into his arms for a tight hug. "Come on, let's get your suitcase and a drink." He kisses the top of my head.

"What did I just do?" I mumble into his chest. His shirt smells like Downy. My adrenaline rush has vanished and I cling to him for support.

"You just made an enemy out of Rafe. And seriously pissed off Granger."

"I never meant for this... *oh my God.*"

"Yep." He sighs, holding me tight, resting his chin on the top of my head.

"I have to talk to Rhys." My voice sounds far away.

"Not now." My eyes snap up to his as he shakes his head. "Trust me."

"He needs to know tha—"

"That you lied to me and *Axel* to get to him?"

My face instantly heats up. "Nuke—"

"It's true. Gia, he needs time to cool down. Threatening to tell Axel wasn't your best move." He sighs.

"Are you kidding me?" I pull back. "He told everyone that we fucked." I whisper the fucked part.

Nuke frowns. "You don't think, Gia. You just go after what you want." He rubs the back of his neck as if I'm giving him a headache.

"Jesus." He laughs, then shakes his head, pulling out a pack of cigarettes. "Am I gonna have to defend your honor? Because you poked the beast, and I don't mean Rafe." He motions his head toward Rhys's door. "Granger is the fucking beast, babe. He's everything you should have stayed away from." He lights up and inhales.

I take the cigarette from him. I try not to smoke much since I quit a couple months ago, but I need one right now.

"No, you already defended my honor earlier." I grin up at him and allow myself to look at the room. The suite is impressive, bigger than most houses. All white walls with dark native wood. Gorgeous purple orchids surrounded by succulents sit on the tables.

"What the hell?" I look up at the tall ceilings. "It wasn't supposed to be like this." I shake my head, suddenly tired, as I close my stinging eyes against the morning sun.

"I'm sure it wasn't."

I sigh and cock my head looking at him. "You're a good friend, Nuke."

"Yeah, I am." He smirks, taking a deep drag of his cigarette and putting it out in his half-empty bottle of Jack Daniel's.

"So..." He leans against the back of the couch and looks at me. "What are you gonna do, Gia Fontaine?"

I inhale and drop my cigarette in the bottle, then look at him as I twist my wet hair back in a low bun. "I'm gonna win."

CHAPTER 8

GIA

Past – Eighteen years old
Scottsdale, Arizona

"Gia, meet me in half an hour at my room," Nuke yells across the lobby. I roll my eyes at him as I pass. He bursts out laughing. A long line of women has formed in front of him, all of them waiting to be in his arms. He pulls a random one and holds her close.

I'm hungover, depressed, and so tired I can barely wave at him. Instead, I push the elevator button.

"Rookie. Come on." He laughs at the face I give him. "If you change your mind, you know where—"

"I won't," I grumble. Sighing, I close my eyes and wait for the elevator. I'm not even fazed anymore by all the excited squeals and screams that follow the band everywhere.

I need a quick shower and sleep. After the awful events with Rhys two days ago, I've either been drunk or traveling. This morning I had to get up at 5:00 a.m. to shoot Cash working out. Rafe seems determined to make my life hell, and Rhys... I bite my lower lip, trying not to think about him. The doors to the elevator slide open and I wait for the five screaming women to get out of my way, pretending I didn't hear one of them talking about Rhys's pierced penis.

After I glance down at my keycard to check the room number, I push the button and watch the doors glide shut, snorting in disgust.

Two days.

For some stupid reason I allowed Nuke to get me drunk, and to be honest, I haven't been sober since.

Until now, and I feel like shit. But if I'm ever going to make this right with Rhys, I need to be at least somewhat on my game. The elevator dings, and I feel like I'm ninety as I drag my ass off the wall and pull my bag to the room.

I seriously don't know how everybody functions on tour. I've been here less than seventy-two hours and I'm about to collapse.

Opening the door, I relish the cool air in the room. Arizona weather is pretty much like California, so it's sunny even though it's December. Dumping all my stuff on the queen bed, I make my way straight to the shower. I can barely keep my eyes open as I scrub myself with the delicious-smelling coconut and vanilla gel. The shampoo is so good, I make a mental note to grab as many of them as possible.

Stepping out, I wrap a towel around me. I'm thinking room service. Can I order dinner this early? I'd love a hamburger with fries.

I'm about to pick up the phone when a knock on the door makes my heart leap to my throat.

"Shit." I look down at myself. Having tossed the towel seconds ago, I'm naked. And my suitcase is still shut. Maybe if I don't respond, they'll go away.

A louder pound on the door is my answer. "Damn it." I spin around and throw open the closet for a robe.

"What?" I snap as I peek out the door, my eyes narrowing on a tall, skinny woman dressed in expensive clothes.

"Granger wants to see you now," she snips. Heat floods me for numerous reasons. One, she said the magic word, *Granger*. And two, how dare he send a fucking whore to get me, like he's some kind of... king, god, rock star. Whatever, I refuse to participate.

"Who are you?" I open the door so she can get my full bitch energy.

"Sara." She straightens, and again I want to scream. Another fucking model?

"Well, Sara, please tell Granger I'm tired. If he wants to talk to me, he can come to my room."

She blinks at me then smiles. "Great, I will." Turning, she slithers back to the elevator.

I almost call to her, but what am I going to say? You'd better not be fucking Rhys? Clearly, she is. I slam the door shut, all my exhaustion gone. Now I'm pissed.

Asshole.

I've been feeling shitty about how it went down the other day and he goes and does something like this? He can't be that delusional, right? I mean he didn't think I'd simply jump at the chance to talk to him. Run to his room like what—a groupie? He has to know I'm special. I'm me.

Dropping down on the edge of my bed, I toss my suitcase off with a thud. I need my phone. Julianna will listen to me rant. As I stand, trying to remember where I left it, a loud pounding makes me scream. I cover my mouth, freeze, and stare at the door like it's going to magically open.

"Open the fucking door, Gia." His raspy voice goes straight to my core. I shake my head but realize he can't see me.

Actually, all of this is absurd. I told that dumb groupie to tell him. How did he get here so fast? Taking a glance in the full-length mirror, I almost laugh at how crappy I look. My face is fine only because I'm flushed, but I have black circles and haven't had a chance to brush my hair yet. It's a long, tangled mess. Since I don't have my usual elastic band, I grab a pen from the desk and pin my hair up with it.

Before opening the door, I stop to take a deep breath. I'm sober, thank God. Hungover, but that can work in my favor since I seem to always make an idiot of myself when I'm alone with him anyway.

Trying to get ahold of my racing heart and the butterflies in my stomach, I take one more breath. "Be bold. Only the strong win, Gia," I chant as I swing the door open.

CHAPTER 9

RHYS

Past – Twenty-seven years old
Scottsdale, Arizona

"She said what?" I snap at Sara, who can't even try to hide that she's thrilled she gets to tell me this.

"She's tired." She shrugs. "I have zero idea why she's such a bitch." She reaches for a bottle of vodka only to stop when I glare at her.

I took a private plane with Ammo, using the excuse I needed time to write. In reality, it was to decide what the fuck I'm doing.

I shouldn't go near her. But the bro code went out the window the moment my cock discovered her tight pussy. I'm not gonna broadcast that I'm fucking my friend's sister or anything, but I'm also not denying that I want her.

Is it wrong? Maybe, but fuck it, no one's perfect. Having Sara go get her was a dick move, but it's not like she's an angel. She wants to play dirty, then I'm the right man.

"What?" She licks her lips and stares at me. Doing one last pushup, I stand, ending my workout. I have an elliptical and a rowing machine that travel with me. In the old days, I'd box and work out with a trainer. Now I like a more traditional workout: heavy cardio and basic pushups and sit-ups, along with squats.

I open my door. This shit stops now. Gia's not in charge. I crack my neck as I walk down the hall. I had Rafe put her on the band's floor. He wasn't happy about it, not that I give two shits. I want her close.

"Granger?" Sara yells. "Should I wait for you?"

"No." I don't even bother looking back at her as I pound on the door.

"Open the fucking door, Gia," bracing my hands on either side of the doorframe.

She swings it open and I almost start laughing. Her green eyes, glistening with anger, widen as she greedily dips her gaze to my sweaty bare chest and basketball shorts.

"Oh." She reaches for her hair as if to make sure it's okay, then drops her hands and straightens her shoulders back. "What, Rhys?" Her voice cracks. She looks tired, almost fragile in the large white robe.

Pushing past her, I enter her room. Her unique smell of vanilla and whatever shampoo she's used makes me grit my teeth.

Christ, what is it about her that makes it impossible to get her out of my mind? Her smile, eyes, the way she moves and smells? Maybe it's just Gia. She ensnares you with her very being. It's a unique situation I'm in, because I can't stay away even knowing we're going to end badly.

I don't believe in destiny. But I do know the second I saw her something happened to me.

It's like I knew that she belonged to me. That's as much as I'm willing to examine right now.

I pull out one of the chairs and drop into it. She remains standing in the doorway, her eyes darting around, looking as though her mind's going a mile a minute. She's clearly at war with herself, but patience is not my strong suit.

"Shut the door, Gia."

Her eyes narrow, but she does and sashays over to the end of the bed. She sits, cross-legged, a hand on each knee.

Sitting up, I adjust my cock. Christ, I get hard just thinking of her, much less looking at those goddamn legs. I need a cigarette. Even though I try not to smoke after I work out, I need to get myself under control. The way I'm letting my dick rule me, I'm like a fucking teen.

"So." My voice makes her jump. Her eyes, which moments ago were staring at my chest, dart to mine. "Are you on birth control?" I demand, not caring that she looks like I slapped her. This is something I should never have let happen, but it did, so I need to clean up my mess.

"You've got to be kidding me?" She jumps up and goes to the mini fridge, grabbing a water. With a laugh, she points the bottle at me. "I should lie and say no because you deserve to fucking worry." She shakes her head. "But quite frankly, I'm the one worried. Clearly you don't care if you get a disease or give a disease." She jerks open the top of the water bottle.

"Gia, I always wear protection. I don't even fuck people without them signing shit. You were the exception."

She snorts. "I'm not seven, Rhys. Don't forget, I know all your secrets."

I take a breath before I lose my shit on her. "Careful, Gia." My pulse pounds in my temples.

"Why? Because you're the Rock God?" She waves her hands. "I'm not impressed."

I stand and laugh. "You think you can handle all this? Me? I mean, let's be honest, that's what you're here for, right?" I start to walk toward her. Now most women or men would back up. It's a commonsense reaction that ninety-nine percent of us have when someone invades our space. Not her though. She lifts her head, her green eyes full of battle.

"You want to play? I don't think you understand the game." I smirk, because as fucked up as all this is, I'm fucking turned on.

"I'm an expert at all games." She sticks her nose in the air. In an instant, all rational thought is gone. My fingers grab hold of the belt on her robe, and a small hiss escapes her as I pull her close.

"Listen carefully so you're not confused. I don't give a fuck about the past or who you are. My cock wants this tight pussy of yours, and rules don't apply to me," I grunt into her mouth as I guide her hand to my hard erection. She shivers but says nothing.

Fuck, if she's not magnificent. "On your knees," I demand.

Her eyes narrow but she drops down. Her hands jerk my shorts off, releasing my dick, which stands straight past my belly button—hard and hot, waiting for her.

She looks up, the anger in her eyes replaced by need. I get it. It's eating me up too. Reaching out, she grabs my hard shaft.

Then she smiles.

Our eyes lock as she glides her tongue to the top of my leaking tip, flicking my piercing up and down before she takes my cock and fucking owns me.

"Gia," I say, breathing hard. I'm ready to jet off already in her warm mouth, shoot my seed down her throat. My hands grasp her hair to guide her head.

"Relax your throat, baby." Fisting her hair tight, I thrust myself deep into her mouth.

"Goddamn," I grind out as she deep throats me. My eyes roll back in fucking pleasure. In and out, she sucks and takes my cock to the back of her throat.

"Yeah, that's it, Brat. Fuck my cock with your mouth." I'm thick, so she's only getting half of me. As she gags, saliva drips down her chin.

"I'm gonna come." I stop thrusting, don't move. My muscles tighten as I watch her take over. She sucks my cock like a fucking pro. The pleasure's so intense that when her other hand massages my balls, I let go. Fucking spiral, unravel, as my cock pulses and jerks in her mouth, filling it faster than she can swallow, and I watch it all.

"Yeah, that's it," I growl as my cock keeps pulsing in her mouth. She slowly raises her head and licks her wet lips like she had just sucked on a cherry popsicle.

My thumb rubs her puffy wet lips and her chin. "I take it that's not the first dick you've had in your mouth?" Now that I can see straight, the thought of Gia's mouth on another guy's cock is not making me happy.

She stands and shakes her head no. I should respect that at least she's not lying. Instead, I have to fight not tossing her on the bed and handcuffing her, only letting her up if I deem it. *What the fuck, Granger?*

"What are you expecting to happen with us?" I snap as I step back and pull up my shorts, trying to erase the irrational jealousy that's pounding through my head.

"Everything."

My eyes shift to hers and I shake my head. She can't be that naïve.

"I'm not what you need, Gia." It comes out harsh. My self-destructive demons are ready to take over.

"Maybe. But I'm exactly what you need," she states, her long, still-damp hair cascading over her shoulders. Her cheeks are flushed and her lips... her fucking lips that have wrapped themselves around numerous cocks...

"You're gonna get hurt," I say.

"I think you underestimate me."

I cock my head as I tell her the truth. "I will hurt you, Gia. It's what I do." I move past her stunned face and walk to the door.

"I'm not leaving, Rhys," she announces like a threat.

I hesitate, then open the door, saying over my shoulder, "You will." I shut the door, knowing that it's true. I'm not the kind of man who's going to be in a relationship.

I'm bad.

The man who makes all the girls cry. Only this time if I'm not careful, I might start believing her.

And then... I'll be the one who can't survive.

CHAPTER 10

RHYS

Past – Twenty-seven years old
Minneapolis, Minnesota

"Goddammit, BT. What the fuck is going on, man?" I pull off the piece-of-shit ear monitor that shot static into my ear, causing it to ring.

"Let me get the new ones," BT yells from somewhere.

"Watch your back." Two stagehands maneuver behind me, carrying one of our huge lights. The stage is a disaster. Equipment is scattered everywhere, and we're in Minnesota where it's a whopping seven degrees outside. Needless to say, I'm not happy.

The way this morning is starting off, I need a cigarette and maybe a bottle of Jack.

"Granger." Jerry walks up with a microphone. "I know we're waiting on the others, but if you don't mind."

Sighing, I rub the back of my neck. "I don't mind." I need to stop being an ass. It's not my crew's fault I haven't slept for days. I'm haunted by a pair of long legs and green eyes.

That and my music. It's loud, demanding to come out of me. I've given up worrying when I get like this. I just let the music tell me where I need to be, like a lover who can never hurt me.

"Testing…" I don't even bother saying more and shove the microphone back at him.

"Fix it, Jerry. We sounded like shit in Texas too."

He nods. "I'll reprogram again," he grumbles, talking to himself as he walks away.

Misty sashays past Jerry, shaking her head at the way he incessantly talks to himself. She steps up to me, saving me from all the dark shit I've been thinking about, most of it concerning the Brat. The way her lips felt taking my cock. Her tight, wet cunt that's made for only me.

"I thought you might need this." Her voice makes me focus on her as she hands me a large coffee. The smell of Irish whiskey filters out from the top of the plastic cup.

I grin. "Misty, you never disappoint." She smiles back as she bites her bottom lip.

"Nope, I never do. You need me to refresh your memory?" Her aggressive behavior is usually fun. I've fucked her numerous times. She's willing to do anything. Unfortunately, this morning it does nothing for me.

Wrapping my arm around her, I kiss the top of her blond hair, pretending I didn't get her blatant invitation.

"BT, how much longer, man?" I bellow, causing her to look up at me in confusion. Not that I blame her. I want to tell her I'm fucked up and to not take it personally.

"Arena's fault." BT walks up looking like a mad scientist. "It's a miracle we're doing as good as we are. The Wild played the Kings last night."

"Perfect, maybe I should hire their crew since they broke down an ice rink in a night, and my team can't seem to finish our rig." I remove my arm from Misty. BT laughs while he tries to wrestle open a box wrapped tight with clear tape.

"Jesus, Granger." Nuke walks by carrying a bottle of Jäger and it's not yet noon.

"Lighten up, Frances." He steps up to his throne and removes his shirt. "Misty." He motions for her to come to him.

"Nuke." She almost skips over to him. He takes a swig and hands the bottle to her. I swear I can smell the dark spice of licorice from where I'm standing. Nuke's getting worse by the day, but I have my own demons and shit to deal with.

"Where the fuck are Ammo and Cash?" I grit.

"No idea where Ammo is, but Cash's fucking Amanda. I saw his white ass on the way in." He says all this as he starts fondling Misty.

BT finally rips the box of IEMs open. "Here, brother, I'm sending that faulty box back. Fucking pisses me off," he grumbles. His hair is down to his ass and held in place by wires and two sets of headphones around his neck.

BT's been with the band for years, so bitching at him goes in one ear and out the other. He's either become immune to one of us being an ass or he just doesn't care.

"Let's go red for you, Granger." He grins, shoving the custom tiny ear monitor at me. I take off my electric guitar and hand it to Dallas, my personal tuner.

"I hope to hell this one works. My ear is still ringing." I put the tiny monitor in. BT's voice instantly becomes clear, along with Nuke's conversation with Misty.

"This one works," I say dryly, clicking it off.

BT gives me a distracted nod, glances down at the box, and walks over to Nuke.

One of our equipment trucks slid off the road last night. The teamster didn't see the black ice, and Nuke's drums were on it, so they brought in a new set.

"You want to give her a try?" BT hands him his sticks, moving Misty behind him. I'd laugh if all this wasn't so pathetic. Our head roadie is having to force us to do our jobs.

"Misty?" Nuke twirls his sticks, bringing them down in one hard, quick show-off solo.

"Yeah, Nuke?" she yells around BT's large frame and lets out a laugh.

"You. Me. Blowjob." He finishes off with a dramatic solo. Misty claps and BT shakes his head and hands him his IEM, telling him to focus.

"Cash. Get your cock out of Angela," I bellow.

"Christ, Granger, I'm here, you angry fuck." Cash walks out from backstage, zipping up his jeans. I don't even respond to him. He's right; I'm angry. His attitude isn't helping, or the fact that Ammo decided not to even show up.

"Dallas, call Ammo to see what the fuck is happening." Dallas stops tuning and reaches for his phone.

"And you got a cigarette, brother?" Misty's loud laughter makes me grit my teeth.

"Yeah." Dallas hands me his pack of cigarettes. He's old-school rock 'n' roll. Not that he's old, but he's got the eighties' Tommy Lee-look going on.

"I also got some serious hash if you need to chill out." He waggles his eyebrows, then talks into the phone. "Hey, man, just checking in. Everyone is waiting..."

Snorting, I light up and block out Dallas's conversation with Ammo so I can drink my Irish coffee and smoke in peace.

I should leave. I'm getting mean, and that's gonna end up with one of us having a black eye. I've basically done my sound check. If they don't give a fuck, why stick around?

Cash stretches his arms out and swings them back and forth, jumping up and down like he thinks he's the shit. I fight the eye roll. His ego is out of control.

Cash has nothing to be arrogant about anymore. He looks like he hasn't slept in days, wears his hair in his eyes half the time, and has a wardrobe of stupid clothes.

Today he's wearing a trendy red T-shirt held together by safety pins. I'd love to blame Cynthia for Cash's clothes, but he probably picked that shirt out himself.

I met Cash back in high school. He went to Harvard-Westlake, one of the most expensive private schools in LA. How he started hanging out with all of us is anyone's guess. I think it was David who found him. Anyway, his parents are big-time lawyers.

He had a BMW; I drove my mom's old-ass Volvo that was held together by duct tape and prayers.

None of us cared that he was different. He could play the fucking bass like Flea from the Chili Peppers. Also, his parents were one-hundred percent believers in us. They bought all our earliest equipment. I think half our early gigs were favors to his dad.

He didn't judge us. Even with half of us hanging out with bikers, it never fazed him. He was a cool kid who loved music and had big dreams.

That changed the moment we started to get popular. As soon as we made our first million, Cash started to distance himself. Suddenly, he was hanging out with other musicians, dating models, dressing like a douche.

"Okay, I'll tell them." Dallas's voice brings me back to the loud stage.

"He said he's almost here. Gia's shooting him." His voice cracks like a goddamn teenager mentioning Gia.

Which makes my head pound. He wants her, but I can't even get pissed since she seems to have enchanted everyone. Well, besides Rafe.

In the last week and a half, she's befriended my crew. Christ, I don't even know all their names.

But she does.

Taking a drag of my cigarette, I exhale and grind out, "You finish up for me, man." I jump off the stage and walk through the huge arena toward the doors, ignoring the numerous people calling my name.

"I need to take care of something," I yell over my shoulder.

CHAPTER 11

GIA

Past – Eighteen years old
Minneapolis, Minnesota

"You sure you don't want to come in?" Ammo inhales and hands me his joint. I wave it off as he exhales.

"Stop asking. The answer is still no."

He grins and opens the door that leads to the arena. "Come on, bring that camera, catch the magic." he winks.

"God, Ammo." I laugh, shaking my head. "I'll just wait out here or we can finish the shoot tomorrow."

"Nah." He rolls his neck. "I'm feeling good today."

God, I wish he had said tomorrow, but whatever. Maybe I'll try to take a quick nap. As usual, I'm tired. Partying all night and getting up two hours later to shoot the band is killing me.

Which sucks.

I'm young. I should be having the time of my life. I'm traveling with the Stuffed Muffins. Staying in luxury hotels, with chauffeurs, bodyguards, and people who will do anything just because.

And I'm not enjoying it. No matter what kind of happy face I try to put on, or how glamourous this world is, I came here to be with Rhys, not be uncomfortable, insecure, and exhausted.

Nothing has turned out like I planned. After that day when he came to my room, I've barely seen him. And if I do, he's surrounded by groupies or Rafe. Not sure whom I hate more. That's a lie—I hate the groupies. Rafe's just an asshole, but at least he's honest about it. The fucking groupies, on the other hand, are nothing but gold diggers trying to steal my man and my life.

Even Ammo is growing on me. He's arrogant, but I like that. He's also fun and extremely talented. God, if only I could turn off my feelings for Rhys and switch them to Ammo. So much easier, besides my brother killing him and all that.

I bite my bottom lip, my heart racing as I watch a couple of skanks throw me a dirty look, then laugh as they open the doors. I hear Nuke's drum solo and a bunch of yelling.

Fucking groupies or "models." I snort. That's what they call themselves since they post themselves on Instagram. I roll my eyes and concentrate my thoughts on the shoot I had this morning with Ammo and my masterpiece.

Sex, Drugs, and Rock & Roll. That's what I'm calling my book. Gone is the idea of selling it to *Rolling Stone.*

The photographs I've taken deserve to be in a book. My only problem is getting Rafe to agree. I might be forced to call in my brother on this one, but I'll wait until I have it ready. I bite my bottom lip to stop smiling at the visual of Axel, Blade, and Ryder making Rafe an offer he can't refuse.

It's too fantastic really. I grab the elastic from my wrist and twist my hair back into a low bun. Sliding down the concrete wall, I sit on the floor and pull my coat tight around my neck. It's not freezing in the concourse, but it's not warm either.

Cynthia, the band's personal stylist, dropped by my room last night with this fabulous black three-quarter-length Sherpa coat. I'm assuming it was from Nuke, since he was horrified when I pulled on my designer jacket before we landed in Minnesota. In my defense, I was born and raised in Southern California and have never experienced this kind of cold weather.

I should blow off Ammo, grab my bag, and go back to the hotel to sleep for a couple of hours before the concert tonight.

Or be brave and go inside to take pictures of the sound check. But the thought of seeing Rhys—and hearing him sing—makes my heart hurt.

Who am I kidding? I've parked myself outside the arena doors in hopes of seeing him.

Sighing, I let my head rest on the cool wall, my mind going a mile a minute. I've taken so many pictures that when I close my eyes, my brain still thinks I'm photographing. I've shot the crew, stadiums, fans.

Yesterday I got the band coming off their jet. It was like vintage rock 'n' roll. As if I stepped back into time and was photographing The Doors or The Beatles.

I captured everything that is purely the Stuffed Muffins: their charisma, the hysteria of the fans, and the wild energy that follows them with every step they take. It's what I love about being a photographer. *No one* can lie to the camera—it sees all.

My leather bag vibrates and I ignore it. I can't deal with whoever's on the phone bringing me down.

Eventually, I'm going to have to talk to my mom, but not today. And it might not be her anyway. That call feels like a Julianna call, and that's worse than my mom. I never should have told her the truth about what's been happening, but I needed her help.

Unfortunately, she's a literalist. I know this and *still* vomited out everything to her. But this morning I can't deal with her lecturing me about Rhys, lying to my mother, and how all of this is going to bite me in the ass.

Yeah, I can do without her caring-yet-harsh dose of reality. Instead, I'll people watch, hoping that will block out any negative thoughts.

The concourse is full-on happening. The smell of nacho cheese warming up makes my stomach rumble in protest since my main diet lately is Jägermeister, Jack Daniel's, chips, and the chocolate I grab from the bar in my room.

I look over at the concession shop. Too bad it isn't open yet. A pretzel sounds good right about now. I need to start eating better. Not that a pretzel is good for me, but at least it's substance. I grab my bag and retrieve my cigarettes. It's stopped vibrating, which tells me that call was definitely Julianna. Not only do I need to eat, but I'm also starting to worry that I might be a smoker. I knew I was in trouble when I bought a pack yesterday. Freakin' expensive.

And that depresses me. How am I going to pay Julianna back? I hadn't factored in Rhys's whole situation as... the Rock God. I know she would never ask for it, but that is not how I work. If I borrow money, I pay it back.

And thank God I did. Besides the hotel and transportation, I'm on my own unless I hang out with Nuke or the band.

Which I've been doing and look at me. I'm sure smoking is not allowed, but I need one. Also, the Xcel Energy Center isn't open yet, so maybe the *no smoking* rule isn't in effect? Whatever, if security stops me, I'll play dumb. I need something to settle me down right now.

I take a nice deep inhale, letting the nicotine calm my nerves as I try not to obsess about being a shell of my former self. I've allowed Rhys Granger to drag me down. Like an idiot, I can't even be mad at him. I'm pissed at myself for not being able to kick this crazy addiction I have for him. It's like we're both waiting, for what I don't know, but that's what it feels like.

At least I have my photography. If anything, I realize that college is a huge waste of time and money. If you want to make it in this world, you have to go out and do it.

My photos are art, history, they speak for themselves, and no matter what happens, he can't take that from me. No one can. I lean my head back and close my eyes, letting the slight heat from the cigarette warm my lips.

"Smoking? Nice." My pulse leaps into my throat and my eyes dart open. I almost drop my cigarette.

"Damn it, Rhys." I leap up only to grab ahold of him because my legs are slightly numb from the cold floor, and I guess I'm forgetting how to stand around him now.

"Let's go." He reaches for my bag, tossing it to me. I try to figure out if I should put out the cigarette or keep it on principle. Not letting go of my arm, he drags me with him.

"What are you doing?" I pull back, which does nothing except make me stumble. Never in my life have I felt less graceful, and that's ridiculous. After all, this is Rhys whom I've known forever. Yet, in reality, the man tugging me along is *the* Rock God—hot and strong and completely unpredictable. Merely touching him makes my arm feel like it's been singed, as if my body ignites as soon as I'm near him.

"We need to talk," he grumbles, ignoring the two men running behind us and calling his name.

"Rhys, I think they want you." I jerk my arm back, which does nothing, but he does stop.

"Dude, you can't leave, man." A dark-haired, thin rocker guy with a crazy mullet runs up panting as if he's finished a marathon.

"Dallas, I was there an hour ago. I don't want to be around them right now."

"But—"

"If anyone asks, Gia's with me." His hand slides down my arm and I shiver as his warm fingers take my cold ones. The poor guy looks confused as his eyes dart from my face to Rhys.

"You're really leaving?"

"Yep, see you tonight." Rhys takes the cigarette from me. I've been holding it like an idiot. He takes a drag and drops it, snuffing it out with his boot.

"I don't want you smoking." He looks down at me and my heart flutters. His brown eyes are almost black in this light. His hair is wild, and all I want is for this moment to never end. If I could stop time, I would.

Wait, did he just tell me I can't smoke?

"Granger? You need a coat, man. You'll freeze your balls off."

"I'm not afraid of the cold." He smirks, but they're right—Rhys is only wearing a faded black thermal.

"You need a coat. What are you do—" I say to his back since we're on the go. He bangs the doors open. A mob moves in, almost as if they're attacking us. It's the only way I can describe this madness. They're like a pack of hungry wolves, stalking him. Screaming at how much they love him, and can they have his autograph. People are taking pictures with their phones while I cover my face with my hand.

Usually, Rhys will talk to his fans. Not today. He maneuvers us forward, not engaging. His hand tightens on mine and I cling to him with both hands, giving up on hiding my face. Clearly my boots were not made for the ice.

"This is just fucking insanity," I yell at his back. My only answer is his hand squeezing mine as he leads us to a large, black SUV.

The celebrity chasers are screaming at us, so I bury my face in his shoulder. When he opens the passenger door, I jump in. Thankfully the SUV is covered in frost, so as soon as he shuts the door, no one can see inside.

Jesus Christ, they're ten times worse with Rhys than they are with Nuke. He gets bombarded.

I can't believe this, but I might actually feel bad for him. Which is ridiculous because this is what he wanted. This is what he's worked so hard for, dreamed of, but at what cost? Because what I'm seeing is a man who has everything, and yet he's drowning.

This is why my brother decided to leave the band. He knew what he wanted, and it wasn't to be a rock star.

Inside the SUV it's like a freezer. In all the madness, I barely registered how bitter cold it is outside. Rhys looks over at me, both of us slightly panting, allowing me to see our breaths.

"You okay?" His brown eyes sweep my face.

The craziness ceases, and it's just us. Suddenly I'm not cold anymore. Beneath his stare, I'm on fire.

"Yes." It comes out raspy.

His eyes dip to my mouth.

Oh God, this is it. This is when he kisses me. I can feel it, thick, powerful.

Rhys Granger wants me.

I lean slightly forward, forgetting that people are chanting his name. Not even caring that they're scraping the snow and frost off the front of the window.

Kiss me.

I close my eyes. His body heat caresses me as I wait.

Kiss me.

"Gia," his voice rumbles, forcing my eyes open.

What the hell? I'm almost too confused to understand that maybe I was reading him wrong. I stare at him.

"Put your seatbelt on." He turns on the engine. The defroster blasts on, causing me to jump. The warm air blisters my already-sensitive cheeks, which burn from humiliation. What is wrong with me?

He places a hand on my seat's headrest to look out the rear window, his eyes locking with mine for a second as my heart leaps to my throat. Then he looks back, and I turn to watch the sea of strangers chant their love for him.

God, I'm no better than the groupies. To be honest, I am a groupie. I'm following a man around believing that he's the one. With some difficulty, I try to buckle myself in, but my poor fingers are numb.

Warm hands push mine away. As if I'm an annoying child, he quickly buckles me in, then spits out, "Did Cynthia not get you gloves?"

Cynthia? Who's Cynthia? My brain is crazy right now. God, Cynthia is the band's stylist. I'm losing it. Wait, is he insinuating he was the one who got me the Sherpa coat?

Rhys glances at me, frowning. "Gia? Do you have gloves?"

"Did you have Cynthia buy me this coat?"

He ignores my question, lays on the horn, and puts it in drive. "Let me know if I'm going to hit anyone."

I put my numb hands under my legs hoping that he turned on the heated seats. My ass is starting to warm up, so I guess he did. People wave and surprisingly do move out of the way at last. Maybe they've figured out he's actually leaving.

"Holy shit." I stare in shock. "Oh. My. God."

A woman and her friend are jumping up and down. One pointing frantically at the friend who's *topless* with *Rock* and *God* tattooed, one on each breast.

"What?" He smirks at me. "You wouldn't tattoo my name on your tits?"

Rhys slows down and gives the girls a double honk, causing them to scream, "We love you!"

"Um. No. I would not have Rock God tattooed on my breasts. I don't even like tattoos," I grumble, gazing out the window at the gray morning. It looks cold, although the snow is white and pretty.

His mouth twitches. "Tell me something, Brat. This lying, does it just come naturally?"

My stomach flips, which bugs me because he's not being nice, but the way he says *Brat* makes me instantly wet, even if he is an egomaniac.

Arching a brow at him, "You're used to 'yes' people, Rhys. You've become a superstar. I told you I'm not impressed." I reach for my bag to get my sunglasses. Sure, it's gray outside and completely not needed, but whatever.

He turns and flashes me a grin, then throws back his head to laugh. My eyes hungrily travel down his neck, and I try to breathe.

It's been so long since I've seen him laugh, smile, or be interested in something.

"You're right." He nods and grins, gunning it onto the freeway.

I'm kind of surprised he owns it. Clearly all hope isn't lost on him, because what makes Rhys Granger incredible is not that he's beautiful; it's that he's got this charisma that makes people tattoo shit about him on their body.

He's gifted, brilliant, and imposing.

No wonder people worship him. He makes everyone want to be near his greatness, listen to his gift of music, and get caught in his sphere.

My stomach flips, and I bite my bottom lip so I don't scream *I love you.* Instead, I turn my head and pretend to watch whatever landscape is whirling by.

CHAPTER 12

RHYS

Past – Twenty-seven years old
Minneapolis, Minnesota

I glance over at Gia as she sits looking out the window. I know she's been hanging out with Nuke and my road crew, which I shouldn't care about, but I do. Jealousy. It's a new emotion for me.

"You're too thin," looking over at her. Her big eyes stare at me like I've insulted her, but it's true. She looks thinner than even a few days ago. My need to feed and protect her kicks in.

Christ, what's happening to me? I almost grin at my caveman thoughts. I need to feed my woman before we mate.

"You hungry?"

"I'm starving," she snips and takes her hair down, running her fingers through her long curls as she recrosses her legs. It's a simple thing; I've seen hundreds of women do the very same thing. But there's something about Gia, the way she moves. She's graceful and delicate, fierce and determined.

My hands tighten on the leather steering wheel. My chest almost burns for her, which aggravates me. And just like that, I hear music. It's like she's my muse.

I clear my throat. I'm acting like a fucking teenager excited to have a girl sit next to me, not a twenty-seven-year-old man who's a goddamn rock star.

I should have let Misty blow me earlier. That was stupid on my part. Could've taken the edge off.

But my dick wants only one woman, and I've got her sitting next to me. Let's be honest—I'm a depraved fuck, and I'm not ashamed to admit it.

I crave her. I'm ready to lock her in my room, eat her cunt, fuck her so hard she's raw, then turn her around and claim her ass. Maybe tie her to my bed, feed her, and bathe her.

I take a breath. I need to get off the freeway and find a place to eat. I can't believe I don't trust myself to be alone with her.

But I don't.

I make a U-turn and pull into a place called Bunny's. It's a big place and the parking lot is crowded. Fuck it, I'll take my fans interrupting me rather than have to fight myself.

Yeah, I need to get out of here. This energy that is *us* is suffocating. Christ. I'm like a dog that smells a bitch in heat.

I turn off the engine and look over at her. She sits, arms crossed, completely shutting herself off and staring out the passenger side window. It pisses me off.

"Look, Brat—"

"Stop calling me that," she hisses. She's wild, untamed. Again, my cock responds.

Mine.

"God, Rhys." She grabs her bag and throws open the door. "Do you even hear yourself?" She slams it before I can respond.

"Christ." I twist around to the back seat for the beanie I was wearing this morning. I take a breath before I vault outside into the fucking Minnesota winter.

Gia's already at the doors waiting as she jumps up and down, her hair falling around her shoulders like a waterfall of dark chocolate.

She's beautiful and she knows it. That's a dangerous combination. My cock throbs. I was hoping the frigid cold would make it calm down, but the thought of dominating her overrules even the weather.

Screw this. I should take her to the bathroom and fuck her in a stall. Slam my cock into her warm, wet cunt over and over.

Then we can enjoy breakfast, or is it lunch?

"You do know you're human, right? Like you're not really a god," she says tightly, dipping under my arm as I hold open the door. "You can't just demand and say rude things. I'm grossed out how much you've let fame—"

"Shhh." I grab her, causing her to gasp as we both look at the hostess.

"Two, please." I smile, using the waitress as an excuse to dip my nose into Gia's vanilla-scented neck.

"Welcome to Bunn... Oh my God. Ohmyyyygod." The hostess does what they all do and starts screaming, then covers her mouth as if that's gonna help.

"Dear God." Gia pulls away and rolls her eyes. "Can we sit in there?" She points at a room to the right. Looks like there are pool tables there, but no one is playing.

"Of course. Oh wow." She fans herself with a menu. "I'm your number one fan. This is so amazing. I'm going to the concert tonight. And... Oh my God, you're here." She looks like she might start crying, so I take pity on her and let go of Gia to take the menu.

"Do you have a pen?"

She looks at me, then grabs one, her hands shaking. Any other time I would talk to her. She's cute in a good-girl way. But all I can think about is Gia and the confused, almost sad look she's giving us.

Again, anger rises in my chest. What the fuck is wrong with her? Not that she has to be impressed, but she doesn't have to look like she feels pity for me.

"What's your name, beautiful?"

Gia huffs loudly, which I ignore and focus on the hostess.

"It's Teri. My name is Teri…" I scribble my standard autograph when I come to a bar and hand it back to her.

"Is there a bartender on?"

All she does is shake her head *yes*, clutching the menu to her breast. As I take Gia's hand, I walk us to the back area and nod at a stunned couple sitting on a bench as we pass.

It's dark, and it looks like this area doesn't get busy until later, so I pick the corner table and look for someone to get me a drink.

"I'll go get us some menus and see if I can ask them not to tell everyone you're here." Gia shimmies out of her coat, tossing it onto the other chair. As she goes to walk by, I reach for her delicate wrist.

She wears an oversized, soft gray sweater and dark skinny jeans. Again, that fierce protectiveness comes over me.

"I don't want you hanging out with Nuke anymore."

"What?" She puffs out as if she's having a hard time catching her breath.

"Just sit." I kick out the chair, tug her down, and scoot the chair close so that her legs are in between mine. My hands go to rub her legs up and down as I formulate how much I actually want to tell her.

"Rhys," she whispers, her lips parted, but her eyes dart around as if she doesn't trust me.

Wise. I wouldn't trust me either. She leans back to let the waitress set down the menus.

"Hi, I'm Dawn and I'll be your waitress." She waves her hand for a busboy to set down some waters.

"We're ready." I take the menu from Gia's hand.

"Rhys, just st—"

"Two bacon cheeseburgers, french fries for one, and onion rings for the other, medium rare and Tabasco."

"Anything to drink?"

"Bottle of Jack Daniel's." She's frantically writing but that stops her. "Oh." Her eyes dart to mine, then Gia's. "We can't serve the bottle, Mr. I mean... Granger."

"I'll pay extra." I flash her a smile. It depends on the place, but ninety percent of the time it works. Then again, this joint actually has people in it, so I put her out of her misery. "That's okay. How about four shots of Jack and the food."

The waitress, who doesn't even look like she's out of high school, sighs and smiles.

"I can do that." She turns, then comes back with, "Can I just say it's an honor to have you in he—"

"Stop, please. Look I'm a vegetarian," Gia interrupts her, causing the poor waitress to drop her pad as if Gia's the one who scares her. I lean back in my chair and smile. This is us: a constant push and pull.

"I'll have fruit and some sourdough toast."

"Just bring us what I ordered," I demand. The waitress looks over at Gia who glares at me like I'm a monster.

"*And* toast and fruit," Gia demands right back.

"Um. I'll go get your drinks." The waitress turns and almost bumps into a busboy. She tugs him along with her. Our energy is so volatile, even the poor waitress is running from us.

"Why are you acting like this? I can order for myself. I've been doing it my whole—"

"Why are you a liar?" That makes her eyes narrow.

"I have to use the restroom." She stands, grabbing her bag.

"Sit down. I have a few things I want to say." I jerk her back into the chair, our faces inches apart.

"I. Have. To. Pee. You lunatic."

"Hold it." I scowl.

She blinks at me, her face flushed with anger. "What's happened to you?" She stands again. "I'm going to the restroom unless you'd like me to squat right here." She kicks the chair back and walks toward the restroom sign.

"Fuck." I toss my cigarettes on the table, pick up my phone, and toss that too. I have zero desire to see what's going on. All I care about is the green-eyed witch I'm obsessed with. While I wait for her, I look around at the room, grinning at a random lyric that infiltrates my head.

Like a switch on the wall, you turn me on. A smile, a laugh, a wink and nod. And all the while you turn me on.

You turn me on.

"So here we go." The waitress comes by, jolting me out of Rhysland and back into the real world. She places what looks like two double shots in front of me.

"Thanks." I smile at her but get distracted by Gia coming out of the restroom. She slides her sunglasses on dramatically as she holds up her hands at a group of people talking to her. And I can't stop myself from smiling.

I like her *a lot.*

"God." She sits. Putting the sunglasses back on top of her head, she looks down at the massive glass of whiskey in front of her and wrinkles her nose.

"Can I get a cup of coffee, please?" She smiles at the waitress and the whole room lights up. I almost reach for my heart.

"You betcha." She rushes behind the bar area.

Gia pushes the whiskey toward me. She's put on makeup and smells like vanilla. I lean over to inhale her.

"Here you go, fresh coffee." The waitress dumps it in front of her and turns to me. "I hope I'm not bothering you and all... but can I get a selfie with you?"

"Of course." I stand as she squeals, then shyly moves toward me, but she's small and can't seem to get us in the shot.

Gia sets down her coffee. "Here, let me." She takes the waitress's phone. I sling an arm around her shoulder and smile and the waitress instantly bursts into tears.

Perfect.

I give her shoulder a squeeze. "I'm so embarrassed. But you're the Rock God." She laughs and cries at the same time, trying to smile at Gia.

"Nah, I'm just a dick. Ask her." I motion my head at Gia who is busy snapping photos.

"It's true, he's a dick." Gia smiles at the waitress. "Here, I got some great ones," she says, handing the phone back.

"Thank you." She turns as three other waitresses come in with our food.

"Can we—" I stop them because this is how it starts.

"How about you let me eat with my girl and I'll take pictures and sign shit on the way out."

"Thank you, Granger." They all start giggling and grab each other's arms as they walk out. A bunch of people peek in, but so far it looks like we might be able to eat without being interrupted.

I hold the chair out for Gia who has that look on her face again. "Let's just eat."

"Thank God, I'm famished." She sits and grabs an onion ring from my plate. "Shoot, I was going to ask for ranch dressing, but I can't handle any more of your fans."

"Agreed."

She completely ignores her fruit and toast and picks up the cheeseburger.

"Cured of your vegetarianism?" I raise an eyebrow at her. She's fantastic, even though I want to strangle her.

She waves her hand in front of her face. "Please. I would never be a vegetarian. I love meat." My cock jumps as she turns pink but continues, "I just hate you ordering for me, that's all."

For a moment, I let that register. I'm so used to doing things my way, but she's right. No one ever tells me *no.*

"You're right," reaching for the Tabasco to dump on my onion rings.

She stops eating for a second and picks up her coffee. "You know you could slow down, Rhys. Everything moves so fast with you." Her eyes dip to my plate, which now only contains onion rings. I ate the burger in three bites.

"And I get it, I really do. You're trying to stay one step ahead of all this." She motions to the room with her hands. "But if all you're doing is racing to get to the finish line, you'll only keep things growing bigger: your music, concerts, fans."

She sets down her coffee and leans forward, resting her chin on her hands. "Do you ever get to be you anymore, or are you really the Rock God now?"

I lean back as if she's gut punched me. I've never actually put into words how I've been living, because I thought it was way too complicated for anyone to understand. Yet she summarized it while sipping coffee.

"I've been running for a lot of years. I'd like to think that there is still a piece of the real me left. Having you here..." I pick up the highball glass and gaze at the amber liquor as my mind drifts. "Having you around centers me." I toss back the whole double shot of Jack Daniel's, barely even tasting it.

She takes a breath then picks up her burger. "Speaking of the real you, maybe you should call your mom?"

I lean back in the chair. "That's something that's not up for discussion."

"She's sick, but she loves you." She sets down her burger.

I shake my head. My mom and anything to do with her is something I try to avoid. "I give her money, bought her a fantastic house in Brentwood that she refuses to move into. I've had my fill of doctor calls and updates. So..." I grab the other shot and down it, breathing out the fumes as I look around for the waitress to get me another.

"Now I guess it's up to her." I slam the glass down.

"It's not your fault. There's no reason for you to pretend she doesn't exist." Her green eyes are filled with compassion, only she has zero idea what my mom was—*is*—really like.

She doesn't understand what it's like to be a child, scared and alone, watching your mom fall apart. The true hell of seeing her become someone you don't recognize. That is the real me. That is my pain. It's all consuming and rather unforgiving.

I was the child, yet I spent my first eighteen years taking care of her. Lived in fear, in *terror* of becoming like her. Christ, I'm happy when I wake up and find I'm still me.

Highs and lows, exhausting and painful. "Yes, she's definitely sick, always has been. It's too bad she won't stay on her medication." I stand up and grab my cigarettes. "I'm gonna go smoke, and we need to get back. You should take a nap."

"Rhys?" She stands also. "I shouldn't have—"

"What, Gia?" I lean down. "Drop it. I have a show in four hours." Then I leave her and walk into the main dining room.

"Granger. Dude, welcome to Minnesota." A couple to my right jump up with a pen and a napkin. I smile and start signing autographs. They love me, and I let them heal me.

Gone is the terrified boy.

In his place is a god. I laugh and take pictures.

This is what I do.

This is me.

How dare she remind me? I'm at peace not visiting my mom. The pain and emotional agony are too much to handle, especially because she *could* get help and won't. I've begged her so many times. Sent the best doctors to her house.

It's been five years since I've seen her. I went home to surprise her for her birthday. The house was a pit. No one should have to live in such filth, yet there she was, lying in bed with no sheets or blankets, unable to get up, and staring at a wall. The smell from her, along with the numerous drugs, was the last straw. I called

Rafe and he brought in the best doctors. I even stayed and missed things I had to do with the band to help her. But as soon as she was admitted to that hospital, she was complaining about how she hated the way the medication made her feel.

And that was the last straw. I haven't been back since. I pay people to come in and clean. I pay people to give her meds that she refuses. Some wounds are yours and yours alone. They own you, and you let them live inside you, fueling you, making sure you never have to see or be near that wound again.

"Rhys?" I turn and focus on Gia. She has her bag and holds my phone as she pushes her way to my side.

"I'm sorry." Her eyes blink back tears as if she understands my demons. She can't. No one can.

"Let's go." She takes my hand. She has the softest skin, like whipped cream. I almost laugh—she has no idea how deep my agony goes or what she's entering into.

Why do all the girls cry around you? At seven she knew. She should remember I'm no good. It's not like I've changed. If anything, I've only gotten worse.

CHAPTER 13

GIA

Past – Eighteen years old
Chicago, Illinois

I take one last look at myself, knowing tonight is *the* night. I've never looked or felt better. In the last week, they've included me in all of the band's meetings and sound checks. I've taken incredible photos of all the cities and numerous shots of the band.

I blink at myself in the mirror. I'm wearing a red silk halter dress, black leather jacket, and killer black heeled boots. I've pinned my hair back, and other than my red lips, I wear light makeup.

Taking a step back, I decide to add my large gold hoop earrings.

There. This has to do it. If Rhys Granger doesn't fuck me tonight, then I've definitely lost my touch. We landed in Chicago last night, and I thought for sure he was going to make a move, but he seemed perfectly happy laughing and listening to me tell stories.

What the hell? I know he wants me. His eyes devour me when I enter a room. He makes sure I'm not hanging out with anyone but him, but he hasn't touched me. He can't still be upset with me for confronting him about Christie, his mom, can he?

Frustrating.

I tried my hand at seducing him, but Rafe interrupted us right when I started. Maybe our timing is off.

Whatever, tonight is the night. It has to be. Because I'm pretty sure my mom is on to me. The only person I still need to shoot is Rhys. Maybe that's how I seduce him? That, and don't mention Christie.

God, that's absurd. It can't be because of his mom, right? It's almost like a control thing with him. I apply more lipstick and rub my lips together. Besides pinning a sign to my forehead with an arrow pointing to my lips saying kiss me, this is the best I can do.

Maybe I should bribe a hotel employee so that I can slip into his room and wait for him naked. Or maybe I'll do the *Pretty Woman* thing and wear a tie and heels. That way he'd laugh and fuck me.

"This is it," I tell my image. I've been touring almost three weeks with them, and my loan from Julianna is getting low, not to mention her constant phone calls reminding me that school starts in two weeks and that she's fairly confident he doesn't see me as anything more than a friend.

To add more to my plate, it's almost Christmas, and my mom is insisting I show up at her house for at least a day or two.

Pressure. Jesus, he's got to take the bait tonight. I'm becoming paranoid that pictures of us have been leaked and my brother is hiding, waiting to kill Rhys, which is stupid.

"Oh God," I groan. The loud bang on my door breaks me out of my funk.

Grabbing my bag, which holds my camera and pretty much all of my life, I sling it over my shoulder and take a breath.

Let's do this.

"Hey, Toby." I swing my hotel door open. Toby is Rafe's assistant. He's a great guy with bright red hair and cute freckles. He's around six feet and weighs maybe a hundred-and-fifty pounds, making him look like he's still in high school. The guy is freaking skinny, and I think he's maybe twenty-six or something, but every time we all go out, he's the first to get carded.

Whatever, he's great, and if he can survive Rafe, he's got to be amazing.

"So, Granger wants you."

My stomach flips and I clear my throat. "Fantastic." We head toward the lobby. Toby's easy to be around, another thing I like about him. He's always bringing me coffee when I'm shooting the guys. He doesn't have to, but still, I appreciate it since it's keep up or be left behind in their world.

"Oh, come the fuck on...really, Toby?" I almost drop my bag but it has my camera, so I stop and let it hang for effect. Rafe is standing at the exit in his stupid suit messing around on his phone.

"Sorry, Gia, he wants to ride with us to the United Center." His face turns red, so I don't say more. It's obvious he feels bad.

I roll my eyes and walk up to Rafe and stand there waiting. Like the arrogant ass he is, he keeps typing, ignoring us even though I've completely invaded his space.

"Hey, Rafe, haven't—" He holds his finger up and I swear to God, I want to kick him with my heeled boot. I look at Toby who is busy looking at his phone, so I swing my bag back onto my shoulder and start to walk out, only for Rafe to grab me.

"The car's over here." He keeps hold of my arm as if I'm a hostage or something. I don't even care. The faster I get into the car, the quicker I'll be at the concert.

A driver jumps out. Of course, Rafe would want a limo. I don't recognize this driver; he must be for Rafe only. He gives me a nod as I slide in.

"Wow," I say, looking over at three women with dresses so short you can see their crotches as they sit giggling with champagne.

"Gia, I want you to meet Vivian, Barbie, and Brittany." Rafe slides in. Poor Toby looks pale; his freckles are really popping in the limo's light. He sits next to the girls while Rafe sits next to me.

Fantastic.

I don't engage, but nod and put my big bag between us as the limo takes off.

"So, how are the pictures coming?"

I sigh. Whatever game he's playing, he's gonna be disappointed. I have a one-track mind tonight.

"Fabulous." Turning to look out the dark window, I watch as the limo speeds up to get on the freeway.

"I need to take a look at them since you'll be leaving us soon. I mean, you will be needing to go back to Berkeley, and with Christmas, I need to book your ticket."

My eyes narrow and I slowly turn to glare at him.

He sits looking like he might be a king or something. His suit is perfect, his beard, even his skin looks perfect.

We have mostly avoided each other, besides the one afternoon I begged him to let me take photos of him. Other than that, I like him best when I don't see him.

"Actually, I still have to photograph Rhys, and you don't need to worry about getting me a ticket home."

Prick, asshole... My mind gets cut off in the middle of its rant.

"No, I insist. You've had ample time to get Granger, so I'll be needing to see all photos. How does Thursday work for you? I'd let you have the jet, but we'll be needing it. So, Toby?"

"Yes, Rafe?" Toby sits up with his phone out.

"Book Gia on first class and send her the confirmation." He turns to me. "That will give you time to spend the rest of the holidays with your brother and mother." He smiles, turns to the champagne, and pours himself a glass.

"I'd offer you some"—he holds up the gold bottle of Cristal—"but of course, you're not of age and all."

I smile and reply, "What about Toby? He's of age?" If Rafe wants to be a fucking piece of shit, then I'll be the biggest bitch.

His eyes narrow. "Toby. Can I get you a glass?"

"I'm fine, thank you." Toby sits back in the shadows as one of the blondes slither over to sit on Rafe's lap.

Her perfume is like a flower garden was planted next to us. For the life of me, I will never understand why people douse themselves. "Relax, baby girl." He chuckles as his strong hand strokes her leg. "Save all this for Granger. You, too, Barbie. He wants both of you tonight."

My eyes dart to his, but he's sucking on the blonde's neck as if I'm not even here. I have to get out of this car. A wave a nausea comes over me. I can't lose it, or he'll know he got to me. Just because he says these skanks are for Granger does not mean it's true, I tell myself over and over.

I take a deep breath and try not to gag on all the perfume and stare out the window. I've never been more uncomfortable in my life. I'm also ready to cry, and I would rather jump in front of a train than cry because Rafe is a bully.

Actually, I wish he was a bully. Bullies are weak. Rafe is smart and calculating. He's mean, like a cobra waiting to strike.

"Do you, Gia?" My eyes jerk to Rafe's amused ones as if he knows that his diabolical plan is working on me.

"What? I'm sorry, I have a lot on my mind and wasn't listening." I stick my nose in the air, beyond grateful that my voice didn't crack.

He smiles and I see a flash of his eyes in the surrounding lights as the limo pulls into the United Center.

"Actually, it was Barbie who wanted to know if you like to party." His voice is dry, almost flat sounding.

"What?"

"Party. Of course, I'd need Toby to have you sign an NDA like they did if you want to join them with Granger tonight."

I blink at him as my eyes shift to the others. The girls look intrigued. Toby is the only one who rubs his forehead as if he wants to be anywhere but here.

I swallow, then smile. "Thank you, but no. I'm busy tonight."

"Ah. Well, then you have fun, Gia. You look stunning tonight." It's almost like he's got some weird way of controlling time. Because just as he says it, the limo stops and the door opens to a bunch of screaming people.

So, of course, he gets the last word.

"Think about it, beautiful," one of the girls murmurs. "Granger is truly a god in bed. He can take care of all of us. And when he's busy with one of them, I can make you see stars." She winks and slides out. Too stunned to move, I sit there.

Holy fuck.

I just got propositioned by a groupie... who fucks Rhys... and signed an NDA. I'm going to throw up.

"Gia? Sweetheart, we need to move." Rafe looks down into the limo at me.

He knows. I see it, feel it, he knows that he's affected me. "You go ahead. I have to make a call."

Please God, make this monster leave, please, I chant in my head.

"Gia?"

I look at him.

"You wanted to play, now let's go." He holds out his hand, and I stare at it. This is my moment—I can choose to fight or leave.

I take his hand and slide out. I have no choice.

I always fight.

CHAPTER 14

RHYS

Past – Twenty-seven years old
Chicago, Illinois

"Granger, you want some?" Nuke pounds his chest like Tarzan. "That, my friend, is good shit." He grabs a groupie and sticks his tongue down her throat.

I shake my head. As I bring the bottle of Jack to my lips, cold hands slither up my T-shirt and touch my chest.

"Rock God." Fumes billow from her mouth like a Harley starting up.

"I will suck your cock so good. Ask Nuke about me and my deep throating," Tea says, her voice sultry. Her enlarged lips look like she recently got a fresh dose of collagen.

"Wipe your nose." I mutter. She pulls back.

"What's your deal, man? Do you like dick or something?" She stomps her high-heeled foot. I couldn't care less.

"Yep, you found me out, Tea." I refuse to engage with junkies. The truth is, a month ago she would have worn me down and I would have let her blow me. Now I only want Gia.

"God, you're an asshole!" She spins around, I'm sure looking for Nuke, but Nuke's moved on. It might not be nice or even healthy.

Fact.

We all move on. None of us can stay in any sort of real relationship. Actually, that's not true. My brothers—that's who I'm in a relationship with. Which is why the Brat should never have shown up.

She's crashed her way into my life, no hesitating.

Fearless.

She gets what she wants. What I didn't factor in was that she was right. Gia makes me feel. When I'm with her, I'm me, the good and the bad.

I take a swig from the bottle. Why am I worried about her? I'm the one who will be destroyed when she walks away.

And she will.

This is the time where I should actually take Tea or any groupie and fuck them. Just be done with this song and dance we're playing. Strike first, fast, and lethal.

Instead, I'll feed my craving, this insatiable hunger that grows every day.

The green room door swings open and my eyes search for her, disregarding Rafe and the trail of girls he has with him.

"The fuck? I asked Toby to bring her. Where is she?" I say to no one.

Cash is in the corner lifting weights. He does this before every show. Ammo stands strumming his guitar, laughing at something a girl said.

The large flatscreen that displays our opening act reads *Five Minutes.* Then the camera pans to the mass of people stuffed into the United Center.

My cock hardens. This is my church, my one true love. The music I hear in my head, put on paper, and record.

For some crazy, fucked-up reason, people buy it. I never set out to be famous. I wanted it, but I was happy to be able to touch one person.

Playing in front of twenty-six-thousand loyal fans is a high like no other.

Reaching for my guitar, I ignore the hopeful faces of women who seem to all blend together now. I step toward Rafe who's deep in conversation with Devon, one of our PR agents.

"Where is she?" I don't care if I'm interrupting. I have to go on stage in under five minutes and I want her.

Rafe frowns and stops talking to Devon but doesn't answer me.

"Gia, where is she? I told Toby to bring her."

"Excuse us, Devon." Rafe walks a few feet away from a confused Devon who instantly pulls out his phone.

"What's going on, Granger? Need I remind you who her family is? We don't need this," he gripes.

I shrug and stare him straight in the eyes. "She's my muse."

Turning to Ammo, I say, "Let's do this... Cash, Nuke." I take another swig of Jack and nod at our cameraman, Bobby, who films us as we walk down the long corridor and out onto the stage.

"Turn on the cameras."

I hear Rafe cursing. Doesn't matter. I'm in my zone.

"Yeah, let's do this." Nuke jumps up and down cracking his neck. The intro music is at a level that no one should be near without earplugs, yet that's nothing compared to the roar and energy of the crowd.

The door opens and we start to walk. BT and our road crew follow close, along with Fred helping Bobby not trip over anyone, since he refuses to use a dolly. He insists he likes the look of the camera moving along with us.

Screaming, stomping, it all vibrates through my chest. Nuke's already on stage, the roar alerting me. As I turn, I see her. Christ, she can't be real. My eyes travel up and down her body.

Gia Fontaine knows how to own a room as she walks straight up to me in a red slip of a dress, her hair up, allowing me to feast on her stunning face.

Hunger.

I lift her chin so I can see those eyes of hers. "I've been waiting for you." I don't yell. It's not necessary. Even with the noise, Gia gets it.

"I'm here."

"Granger? Man, you ready?" BT hands me my ear monitor, though my eyes never leave hers.

I want to fuck her, bury myself so deep inside her that we stay locked away for days. Grinning, I put the piece in my ear and walk out onto the stage.

The crowd erupts, like it's just been recharged.

Not gonna lie. I love it.

"Merry fucking Christmas, Chicagoooo." And like I'm some fucking god, my followers scream and feed me with their love.

I close my eyes and open them as I give them what they want. Me. All of me.

The lights zigzag into lasers and smoke fills the stage.

I sing the words that at one time seemed powerful but now feel like a lie. Empty words that rhymed. What I feel now is real: alive like a spark that ignites and bursts into flame. My arms tingle and my chest burns.

My goddess.

My muse.

This hunger that I have for her might never leave me, but tonight I'm fucking feasting.

CHAPTER 15

GIA
Past – Eighteen years old
Chicago, Illinois

I can't look away. He owns the stage, ensnaring me with his voice. I reach for my camera. Tonight is different and I want to capture every moment of *him*.

Rhys is different. I look through my lens and zoom in so that all I see is him as he does what only a handful ever can.

He loves them. It's in every note, every word he sings.

This. His music: that's his real love and he adores it. My body feels as if I might have a fever even though it's freezing outside.

"Ms. Fontaine." I bring my camera down slightly so I can turn to Rafe, but before he can spew anymore of his bullshit, I snap numerous shots.

"Are you done?"

"With you? Yes." I turn back to the stage. BT walks up with headphones for both me and Rafe, and Rafe, of course, waves his off.

"I'm not the enemy, Gia. In fact, if these last couple of performances were brought on because of you..."

I turn to him. "An hour ago, you bought me a plane ticket," I yell over Nuke's drums. It's so weird that Rafe never seems to yell but you can always hear him.

125

"Yes. Keep that." He brings out his phone and starts typing. I guess he's done. Such a shame he's a complete ass. He is fucking hot in his own way.

Not hot like Rhys, but hot. I see him with a ton of women, but same as the boys in the band, he seems to have a new one at every stop.

"Why do I need to keep the ticket?" And I want to kick myself for playing right into his game. *God Gia, you're slipping. Never show weakness.*

"For when all this comes to a brutal and ugly end." He motions with his phone to Rhys.

I straighten my shoulders. "And what if it doesn't? What if Rhys and I are actually happy?"

He looks up from his phone, his blue eyes pinning me to the floor.

"This will end. You will not be able to live the life that he needs, and he'll not be the man you need."

If he had slapped me, I think I would have liked it better. No matter what Rafe has achieved or whatever his goal is tonight, those might be mere words, but they sting, and my chest hurts as if I'm already preparing myself.

Bad juju.

"I guess we'll see," I say and aim my camera at the crowd, completely putting up a mental shield against this man. He's testing me, waiting to see if I'll falter, or at least stumble.

"Yes, hold on to that ticket." I don't see him walk away but know he's gone by the way my body relaxes.

"Fucking asshole."

My eyes pass over the horde of groupies drinking with the roadies. It's a whole family in a fucked-up way.

These people spend more time together than they do with their spouses. I look back at the stage and my heart skips a beat.

He stands with a spotlight on him, and I reach for my chest as he sings my favorite song of theirs. It's a ballad and Rhys's gravelly voice makes goose bumps travel down my arms and my legs.

As he lets the words flow out of him, not just singing them, but feeling them, he's breathtaking. Cash walks up and takes over as he lets his bass sing.

When Rhys looks over at me, suddenly I can't breathe. I may pass out because he's coming for me. Like a dark god he moves, determined and fierce. His energy is electric and so intense that I take a step back.

Breathe.

I need to breathe because he's coming for me. *Holy fuck.* I might pass out at the way his eyes look at me.

One.

Two.

Three.

He doesn't stop. There's no hesitation. He takes my face with both hands, and then he kills me.

I'm lost as his mouth claims mine. I cling to him as I let his fierceness consume me. This is not just a kiss; it's raw and primal, stealing my very soul. My lips are tender. Groaning into his mouth, I allow his tongue to twist with mine.

"I'm gonna fuck you *now.*" He lifts me up. My legs wrap around his waist and I lean into his neck. He's sweaty, and I want to suck and lick it off of him. His body heat seeps into me and I barely recognize my own voice.

"Yes," I groan. I'm spinning. My back hits the cold concrete wall and he takes my lips again.

This is insane.

I try to look around, but his hand is already lifting my dress, and before I can even mention that we might get caught, his fingers are inside my panties.

"Fuck yes, Gia, look how wet you are for me." It's a growl but he's right. I'm soaked as he finger fucks me hard, rough.

"Rhys," I murmur, digging my nails into his neck.

"Spread your legs wider." I do as he rubs my clit hard, and I'm gone, soaring as I come.

I open my eyes. He's not holding me anymore. My hands slap the concrete as I watch him undo his jeans and push them down. Grabbing my left leg, he thrusts himself deep inside me.

I think I scream but can't be sure. All I hear is music. I have no idea what happened to my headphones.

"Christ." He freezes, letting me adjust to his giant pierced cock. "Fuck. This tight cunt is mine," he rasps into my mouth.

"Yes," I chant.

He pulls out and thrusts in again as I claw at his chest. He grabs my chin roughly. "I'm gonna fuck you hard."

I can't respond as his tongue fills my mouth and I taste the Jack he must have been drinking earlier. His other hand holds my legs so I don't fall over as his cock pounds in and out of me.

"Fuck," I snarl, reaching up to bite his lip. He ruts into me as my body contracts.

"Who do you think is watching me fuck you?"

My eyes jerk open as my core pulses. I try to stop it, but I'm gone, soaring as I cling to him.

"Yeah, that's it. I'm gonna fill this cunt up." He thrusts into me hard, then stops as his body jerks.

"Christ." He kisses my forehead. "I couldn't wait." Our breathing is harsh as if we're in sync.

I nod, trying to piece together that I just got fucked, standing up in the middle of his concert.

"You're so cool." He looks down at me and raises an eyebrow as I laugh, our mouths inches apart.

"You have to get back onstage," I say, trying to sound fierce as he pulls out of me, then buttons his jeans.

I straighten up, only to discover my panties are soaked. I should probably take them off, but I'm trying to get my mind and legs to work.

"You stay where I can see you at all times." He takes my lips again.

Unsure if I can stand alone, I hold on. Somehow I put one foot in front of the other. He leads me back to where I was standing before he wrecked my life. Because after that, I'll never be the same. After that, I know for a fact that I'll love him till the day I die.

My bag is on the ground, along with my headphones, but that seems like a lifetime ago. In seconds, my world has changed, and I'm never going back.

CHAPTER 16

RHYS

Past – Twenty-seven years old
New York, New York

"Rhys, honey, I need you to sing for Mommy."

"I'm tired. I need to sleep. Why can't I sleep?"

"Don't be silly. You can sleep later. We need to get you ready. You and Mommy are performing tonight." My mom spins and spins as she picks up a feather boa, a white one, and drapes it around my neck. It tickles my nose and I hate it.

I hate all of it. I need to find my grandfather. He'll make her stop.

But my grandfather is gone, and I'm hungry.

"Mommy?" I yell, but no sound comes out. "Mom?" She's gone and I'm alone, always alone.

I bolt up. The room is dark. Taking a breath, I try to figure out where I am. My hand reaches for her, but she's not there.

"Gia?" I swallow down the remaining hangover I have after having that dream. "Brat?" Standing, I don't bother with jeans and walk to the bathroom.

"The fuck?" My mind instantly wakes up enough to figure out I'm in New York and Gia's not in my bed.

Where is she? Goddammit. I storm out of the bedroom and into the main area of the lavish suite.

I grab my phone and am about ready to call when I see her. "Fuck." I throw my phone back on the coffee table and lean against the wall to catch my breath and watch her.

She's on the balcony, smoking, in what looks like one of my black T-shirts. The fluffy white robe hangs open. My eyes trail down her form and my chest burns as I take in the sight of her wearing my black combat boots.

If I live to be a hundred, I don't think she'll ever be more stunning than at this moment. She looks up at the dark, early morning sky and the moonlight kisses half her face along with the smoke. Her steamy breath circles her as if it knows she's the beauty it seeks.

I push myself off the wall, grab my aching cock, and stroke it as I open the glass door. One of the best things about having money is that you can step out onto a penthouse balcony equipped with heat lamps to warm you.

Don't get me wrong. The Christmas night is almost magical with all the lights of Manhattan, the horns, and the excitement of the city.

"Looking for Santa Claus?"

She smiles and turns, her eyes going directly to my cock, which stands straight as I stroke it and slowly rub the precum all over my piercing. "I'm hoping I've been a good girl." She licks her lips and smiles.

"Eyes on me," I command and watch her battle with wanting to do her own thing and listening to me.

It's irrational, this sense of possession I have with Gia. As soon as I stopped fighting my conscience about fucking my childhood best friend's baby sister, I went all in.

Sometimes when I'm with women, I dominate them. Not full-on, but I can get into spanking and tying them up. It's fun and an adrenaline rush to have someone at your mercy.

But with Gia, it's altogether different. I need her. I want her to be as addicted as I am. The more we explore, the more it turns me on.

Tomorrow is Christmas, or maybe it's already Christmas. Whatever, I plan on spending it balls deep inside her all day.

This is the first Christmas I've celebrated in years. Fuck, it's definitely the first time I've ever bought a woman a present.

I reach for her neck and wrap my hand in her thick hair. "I guess we will have to see if you're a good girl." I bite the bottom of her puffy lip. She moans as I suck it and taste a slight hint of blood. The metallic taste makes my cock throb. Letting go of her, I trail my hand down her neck to the collar of the robe and pull it off her shoulders. It flows to her feet.

We both look down at it and I glance at my boots, which are ridiculously big on her but sexy as fuck.

"Nice boots."

"You like?"

"I do. Give me the cigarette." She does and I put it out in a large plant.

"Take off the shirt, Gia." My voice sounds harsh in my ears. My nostrils flare as she slowly lifts the shirt, allowing my eyes to feast on her waxed pussy.

"I can't decide if I want to shove my cock down your throat or suck on your cunt," I husk.

"Rhys," she whispers, glancing around as if someone can see us. I grab her hips and bring her chest to mine. Her full tits and fucking hard nipples make me groan.

"Take it off."

Her breathing is harsh. Licking her lips, she slowly removes my T-shirt. And there my pretty baby stands, fucking naked in the New York winter, wearing only my boots. I have to fight myself not to make her kneel while I jerk myself off on her tits and face, claiming her over and over.

Fuck that. That can come later. Right now, I'm gonna eat and suck on her wet pussy, then fuck her. After that, maybe I'll jerk off on her tits.

"Sit on the couch, Brat."

I smile as her ass drops right down. "Open those fucking long legs." She does and I sink to my knees, pulling her to the very end and slinging both over my shoulders.

"Now we shall see if you're a good girl." I go straight for her plump clit and suck on it hard.

"God," she pants out, her hands slapping the metal base. She arches her back like a cat.

I'm about to command her to spread wider when she moans and shoves her cunt deep in my mouth. Her slick juices drip onto my tongue, and I greedily use it to fuck and lick her. I'd love to finger fuck her ass, but not tonight.

Gia has zero patience and it's my fault. I fuck her hard and fast, becoming borderline obsessed with her magical pussy. I want my cock inside her twenty-four seven.

As soon as I let go and stopped fighting myself, things became clear real fast. Gia, on the other hand, is so caught up in her lies that she insists she have her own room. Not that she's ever in it.

I know it's because of Axel. She's paranoid. I've humored her the last week or so. But it's getting old fast. I'm not scared of Axel. I'm sick of hiding her when we leave, worried photos of her face are gonna be in *The Enquirer*.

Fucking come clean. I intend to deal with all this shit. We have a week off before we play Madison Square Garden on New Year's Day.

Hunger.

It's not abating. If anything, I'm like a man who has been given his favorite meal and allowed to feast.

I lightly bite her clit and feel her start to contract. She's slick and wet and fucking perfect as I send her over the edge. Her hands grab my head while she whimpers and pulses in my mouth.

Lifting my head, I gaze at her. She's fucking magnificent: legs spread, lying back spent on the recliner. The moonlight and lights of Manhattan kiss her skin. I crawl up her body as she smiles and reaches for my cock, jerking me.

I take her mouth, wanting to savor her, not rush this time. She tastes like mint and delicious smoke.

Thrusting my tongue deeper, I want all of her. Always wanting more—that's me. Forcing her for more. I'm a greedy fuck, and I want her soul.

I want her to breathe only for me.

Think only of me.

I slide inside her honey walls and my eyes roll back in my head at how fucking amazing she feels. Her tight cunt squeezes my cock and I try to go slow, letting my body have this moment.

This is fucking ecstasy.

In and out, I torture us. Music floods my head as I take her ragged breath and inhale it back inside her. Our bodies are in sync, and I'm ready to blow my load.

Fuck that. I pull out as she gasps her protest, then screams as I take my slick cock in my hand and rub my pierced tip on her swollen clit.

"Shit. I'm gonna come." She sits up as if it's happened so fast she can't handle it.

"That's it. Come for me, Gia. Come, baby." I push her back, my hand wrapping around her neck to hold her still.

Her eyes blink at me wide as I watch her come apart, fucking explode. Holding for one more second, I let go and slam my cock back inside her.

"Fuck," I grunt. "Christ, it's good with us." I'm done. I'm not holding back. She can take it and then some.

My balls tighten as I pound into her tight cunt. I'm so close but not ready for it to end. Her nails claw my back as her pussy clenches tight, like a vise, milking the cum out of me.

And I'm soaring, free, as my body jerks. I fill her warm cunt with my seed. Wave after wave of euphoria flows through my body.

I look down at her, and as our breathing calms, I slowly pull out. Brushing a strand of hair off her neck. "Come on, baby." I stand and bring her relaxed, almost drugged body with me.

"I can't move," she mumbles.

I grin and carry her into the suite, straight to the bedroom. When I lie her down on the bed, she curls into a ball and reaches for me.

"Where are you going?" She pouts as she watches me head to the bathroom. Flicking on the light, I almost do a double take at my reflection.

Christ, I'm smiling like a fucking lovesick idiot. It's pathetic, but for the first time in my life I'm happy.

I grab a washcloth and wait for the water to get hot. I can't seem to let myself have this. Peace is fleeting to me; I'm always trying to stay one step ahead. The problem is I somehow have forgotten what that one step is.

The truth is, I can't believe I'll get to have her, this. It's always in the back of my mind that something bad will happen.

I turn off the sink with way more force than necessary and bring the washcloth over to clean Gia up. She sleeps peacefully. Her easy breathing almost makes me jealous. I never sleep that well; insomnia is not unusual for me.

It's fucked up.

Clearly this is because of my dream.

I take a breath and close my eyes. *Enjoy this, Granger.*

Enjoy us.

Trust that it won't be taken away, or that I'll fuck it up. I toss the washcloth aside and climb into bed. The crisp, cool sheets feel perfect.

The heat clicks on, and I pull Gia into my arms. She groans, turning her face toward my neck. I grin, thinking about the morning and the tree I have coming.

I haven't had a Christmas tree since my grandfather died. I don't know why, but on a spur of the moment, I had Rafe arrange for someone to have a real tree fully decorated when we wake up, which is another reason Gia needs to not be roaming around anymore.

"Was I good? Is Santa coming?" She snuggles in closer, lying on top of me.

I kiss her forehead. "I guess we shall see in the morning."

"'Kay," she mumbles. Her phone on her nightstand lights up with a picture of her mom.

Yeah, that headache is going away tomorrow. I owe Janet more than that. The woman practically fed me every night for years. She was more a mom to me than mine.

I'll be dealing with all this shit in the morning, I'm sure that's why Gia was up. She feels guilty about lying to her mom and not spending Christmas with her.

I close my eyes, needing to sleep, but music fills my head. I embrace it, let the words swirl around me, memorizing them so I can write them down later.

A deep sigh brings me back to her. I tighten my arms. Her full breasts and warm body rise and fall as I inhale her scent and let my body relax. In and out, her chest rises and falls.

She sighs my name, and I grin again. Gia makes me want to be better. A better man, a better musician. We can have it all, and I need to know that. You can't control who your heart beats for, who touches your soul.

I sigh as I match her breathing, letting it slow my pulse and rest my mind.

For this moment, I'm at peace.

CHAPTER 17

RHYS
Past – Twenty-seven years old
New York, New York

Warm, minty breath tinged with vanilla and coffee tickles my ear and I smile. Rolling over, I prop one arm behind my neck.

"Merry Christmas." Gia is straddling me on her knees. Her hair is wet, falling around her breasts, and she has that goddamn camera in my face.

"Smile." She laughs. My eyes feast on her tits. Her fucking rosy nipples are hard.

"Put down the camera," I command, grabbing her hips. She ignores me, laughing as she snaps photos.

"Brat, if you want to keep that camera, I'd put it down."

She gasps when I jerk her hips to my face. "Rhys, you're such an ass sometimes." But she wisely sets her camera down. I pull her legs toward me, positioning them on either side of my head.

"Grab hold of the headboard and sit on my face." She tries to scoot back, but there is no way—I'm gonna eat this cunt for breakfast.

"Rhys, stop." Her voice is breathy, and I smile at her shyness. Gia likes to act all worldly, but she's innocent on pretty much

137

everything but blowjobs. I'm not going to think about that right now.

"Come on, baby. Spread your legs and fuck my face." Puffing out some air, she grabs the headboard and I guide her honey right down onto my mouth.

"That's it." I lick and suck her clit, then grab her ass. "Relax." I bring her down and shove my tongue inside her.

"Oh my God." She throws her head back and closes her eyes. I guide her hips up and down on my face.

"This is... Rhys," she whimpers and grasps my shoulder, digging her nails into it. She lifts up, almost as though she's horrified she loves this. "Wait. I need to..." She looks down at me, her lips red, her nipples hard, and her cunt wet.

"Gia. I'm not playing." I grab her wrist with one hand and shift the other to her ass. "Now make yourself come."

She instantly tries to pull her hands away, but I'm ten times stronger. Smiling, I lick my lips and taste her. Her eyes flash with defiance. I'm taking away her control.

"Can I at least have my hands—"

"No, fuck my face." She closes her eyes. "Eyes on me. You watch me eat your cunt," I growl as she tries to break away one more time. Her eyes lock with mine and I grin at her distress. She lowers her pussy to my face and rubs herself against me. Fascinated, I watch her come to life and let her slick arousal saturate me.

Her hips grind, her chest is flushed, and she's panting like she's on a treadmill.

"I'm gonna come," she says, her voice ragged. I let go of her hands and hear her claw the wall while I suck on her clit, my thumb reaching to stroke her folds and move to her rosette hole.

As soon as my thumb rubs it, she goes off, pulsing and coming in my mouth. I grab her and flip her over. Spreading her legs, I thrust my cock deep inside her.

"So fucking tight." I pump into her and hold her ass. Our bodies slap together almost as if we're making music.

My nostrils flare as I inhale our scent and rub my hand up and down her back.

"God, you're beautiful." I pound into her.

"Rhys," she says, her voice husky with need. Her pussy latches onto my hard shaft; my thumb rubs her hole.

I pull out and she yelps in protest. "Shhh." I slap her ass, causing her to turn.

"Lie facedown and keep this ass up," I demand. Her long, sooty lashes bat at me, and for the first time since I've known her she looks at me unsure.

I cock my head at her, pissed. "What the fuck? You don't trust me?"

Her eyes dip to my wet cock, then up to my face. "I do… but you're huge and I don't think…"

"You either do or you don't?" I cut her off, gritting my teeth. I have no idea why this is pissing me off so much. She should know how I feel, that I treasure her. Fuck, I'm risking a lot having her with me.

"Gia?" I growl, my cock throbbing. I'm seconds away from standing up and jerking myself off.

"I do. I trust you, Rhys. You know I do," she retorts and flips over to stare at me. "What's happening?" She reaches for my cock and I slap her hand away.

"What the hell? Are you kidding me? I was seconds away from coming," she exclaims.

I chuckle. Leave it to Gia to be greedy.

"Never mind. I'll do it myself." She spreads her legs, moving her hand toward her clit.

I straighten, watching her hesitate.

"Perfect," I sneer. This has somehow gone to shit. It's Christmas and I'm standing with my cock in my hand instead of in her cunt.

Slowly I stroke myself, pulling on my piercing. "Do it," I demand. "Never mind, Gia." I jerk myself off fast, hoping to finish in a rush.

"Why are you acting like this?" she fires right back, eyes narrowing as she looks at my face.

"Squeeze your tits. I'm close," I rasp. "Or do you want me to get a groupie in here to help? They have no problem spreading their legs. That way, I can come and you can learn." And there's my self-destructive behavior. My ugly words just hang in the air, smothering us.

She gets up on her knees. I fully expect nails in my chest or ugly words in return.

"Go ahead, Brat, tell me I'm shit. Remind me how I'll never be happy or have true love," I grind out.

She cocks her head and slowly reaches for me. I flinch, as if her touch has burned me, and to be honest, maybe she has because my heart actually burns.

Her fingers trace my lips as if she can magically heal me and she shakes her head. "I refuse to let you do this." Her beautiful eyes shine with tears. I grab her wrist and hold it tight.

Our eyes lock.

"You want to know if I trust you? *I love you.* Is that enough trust for you?" Her voice is strong and confident.

Time stops.

She loves me. I let go of her wrist.

She puts her hand on my heart, as if she knows that's what needs to heal the most. I reach up to take it away, but instead I jerk her into my arms, burying my face in her neck.

She smells like vanilla and me and I like it. Need it. I pull her head back and thrust my tongue into her mouth. Somehow, she's become my everything, and I'm too raw to speak it. Her tongue twists with mine and we fall back onto the bed.

"I need to be inside you."

She opens her legs and I thrust in. Her slick walls take me; her words float around my ears like a symphony.

I love you.

In and out, I thrust into her slowly, kissing her mouth, her eyes, then back to her lips. I make love to her with my body because I can't say the words.

Her nails dig into my ass, and her honey core grabs my cock. "I love you, Rhys Granger." She goes over, her eyes turning almost black as she arches her neck. I latch onto it, sucking as I let myself come inside her. Releasing all my poison, I soar with the sound of her harsh breathing.

"Fuck." I pull out and roll onto my back. As we let ourselves recover. Throwing an arm over my eyes, I attempt to digest what just happened. I sense her getting out of bed and I grab her, rolling on top of her.

"You know you're fucked, right? You think I was obsessed before? You've woken the beast."

"I'm counting on it." She smiles and wraps her arms around my neck.

I'm not sure she gets it: I *am* obsessed. She's mine.

I have no intention of ever letting her go.

CHAPTER 18

GIA
Past – Eighteen years old
New York, New York

Oh God. This is it. This is when he actually tells me that he loves me. I can see it in his eyes, sense it in his body. This is... what is that freaking noise?

I close my eyes and count in my head for my phone to stop ruining my life.

I know it's crazy, but every time Rhys gets close to uttering those coveted words, my mom calls.

It's unbelievable. I wait while the ringing continues, my breaths coming in short bursts, and I shudder, knowing that when I open my eyes, all we experienced moments ago will be lost. Gone, evaporated into thin air. I swallow, but my throat is dry. That was intense and scary. I took a big leap, and now the phone interrupts me like an annoying fucking hornet.

At last, the vibrating stops and I crack my eyes open and stare up at him. He's grinning and I almost burst into tears. Maybe the moment isn't lost.

"Trying to block her out?" He kisses my mouth, which has formed a stunned "O," and reaches over me to grab my phone. He hands it to me. Excitement followed by fear fills me. Why is he handing me my phone? I'm not calling my mom. I'm already filled with guilt about lying to her and not coming home for Christmas.

Rhys and I are only now finding our way. He needs to know I'm one-hundred percent in. He comes first. If I leave, even to go visit my mom, that will leave him available to the numerous fucking women, and that's not something I can risk.

My mom will have to understand. She was young and in love at one time, I think. I mean, she despises my dad now, but I'm sure at some point in their relationship she would do what I'm doing. At the end of the day, she will get over it. I'm definitely needed here more.

If only Axel would show up at least with a gift or something. I know he won't. He probably isn't even in town, and you can't get ahold of him unless he wants you to, which bugs me. Why is it always my job to make sure Mom is not alone on holidays?

'Cause you always do.

Axel has no clue what's going on. If I told him he needed to be there for Mom, he would, but that can't happen either. I'll call her tomorrow and tell her I had food poisoning. That I was so sick I didn't even remember it was Christmas, and now I'm super busy and will check in soon.

I mean, that could happen.

The flick of the lighter brings me back to Rhys. He's leaning back on the headboard smoking and watching me. It's relaxed and my heart aches. I almost blurt *I love you* again, but that might be a bit much. He looks okay with me saying it. Actually, he looks happy I said it, so I'm gonna leave it at that.

I smile at him and sit up, bringing the white sheet with me. I have no idea why I do this. Rhys has seen every inch of my body and then some, if me sitting on his face this morning means anything.

"You need to call her, Gia." He pulls me so close that his strong heartbeat vibrates through my back. His tan, tattooed arm holds me tight. He's so hot, dominating, and nasty that it's hard to breathe.

As if he can read my thoughts, he brings his cigarette to my lips. It's such a simple thing to share a cigarette with someone, but with Rhys it's like foreplay.

God, my face is getting hot. I'm mortified that I can't seem to get enough of him. Sitting with him makes me want to climb on top of him and rub my clit on his giant, pierced penis.

I sigh as smoke escapes my mouth and deal with one thing at a time.

"I will tomorrow." I cross my legs and look down at his dick. It's hard again, and I'm ready to lean down and take him in my mouth.

"No. Call her now. Tell her we'll be there for dinner." He puts the cigarette in his mouth and swings his legs over the bed, reaching for his own phone.

"What?" I'm so stunned I sit motionless and stare at his back, focusing on the tattoo of a large black raven sitting on a guitar.

He turns and grins, causing my heart to flutter. "And Merry Christmas, Brat." He stands and my eyes trail down his perfect body. Michelangelo would have begged to sculpt him. I need to shoot him naked.

"Call her. Have her set the table for three." He turns, taking a long drag from the cigarette. Something has to be wrong with me. I'm losing it and staring at him like a complete idiot.

My mom. "Wait, did you say three?" He rubs his chest as he looks out the window. It appears to be gray and snowing slightly.

"Make the call. I need a shower." He inhales and my gaze drifts to his hard cock.

"Gia." My eyes dart up to his amused face. "I'm not hiding us anymore. I owe you and your mom more than that. Also, she should not be without you for Christmas."

I nod because he's right, I know he's right, but this could be a terrible mistake.

"The..." My voice cracks, so I clear my throat and sit up straight. "The thing is, Axel *could* show up. And I've been lying for almost a month. Can't we spend Christmas alone?"

"Call, Gia. We're having dinner with Janet. Unless you want to surprise her." He laughs. "And try to focus on something other than my cock right now."

"Oh my God. You're unbelievable." I throw a pillow at his retreating back. "I'm not thinking about your..."

But he disappears into the large bathroom. The sound of the shower tells me he's serious. If he wasn't, I'd be in the shower with him.

"God," I groan and bring the sheet up while reviewing my options. Should we surprise her?

No, that would be bad. I'm gonna have to call and stop acting stupid. Once she sees Rhys, she'll know that what I did was right and all will be forgiven. Also, I need to break it to her that I have no plans of returning to college. My life is with Rhys now, and he's a full-time job, along with my photography.

What am I, crazy? She's gonna freak. I can already hear her tell me no man is worth dropping out of college for.

Rhys is though. He needs me. All that fame and money can't buy him happiness, but I can make him happy. I love him and I know he loves me.

I'm a little disappointed he didn't say he loved me back. But he does. I can feel it. If he didn't love me, there's no way he'd be getting on his private jet to Los Angeles to have Christmas with my mom.

I pick up my phone and look at the numerous missed calls from her and Julianna.

I take a deep breath and let it out slowly as I push on Mom's number.

"Hello? Gia?"

"Hey, Mo—"

"Oh my God. What is wrong with you? Didn't you see the 911?" She sounds like she's been crying, and my mom is not a crier. She also uses 911 a lot so, no, I did not take it seriously. I sit up and start to sweat.

"What's happened? Is it Axel?" I can barely breathe. My brother is a dick, but I love him, He's my rock. Being in the Disciples means things could happen to him, more so than with a regular person. I'm always worried about getting *the* phone call.

"What?" Her shriek is so loud I have to move the phone from my ear. "No, your brother is fine. I just... where are you? I called the cops to try to locate you." This time she blows her nose loudly.

"Mom," I yell, flopping back. "You scared me. And please tell me you did not call the cops?"

"What are you talking about? Of course, I did. I called Julianna's father and he had absolutely no idea where you were, but he did know you were not working with him or staying with Julianna. I demand to know what's going on. You're making me sick."

"Okay, calm down. I'm sorry. I should have told you, but I didn't want you to be mad or tell Axel." I bolt up. "Wait. You didn't tell Axel any of this, did you?" I'm freaking out. I can deal with her calling the police, but not Axel right now. The door to the bathroom opens and Rhys walks out wet with a towel wrapped low around his waist. Taking one look at me, he frowns.

"Of course, I told your brother," she retorts as I fall back onto the pillows again and cover my face with my hand.

"No, God no. Why, Mom? *Why?*"

"Well, I think you're in luck because he hasn't called me, which means he got another new phone," she huffs. "I don't understand why he's always getting new phones."

"Stop, Mom." I blow out air and slap the bed. "You do, you just don't want to admit it." I take a breath and look over at Rhys who stands, arms crossed, in his signature black jeans watching me.

"Anyway, I'll be home for dinner and I'll tell you everything." My eyes trail from Rhys's chest, which has *TSM* tattooed on it. His muscled arms are covered in tattoos, but I think my favorite one is the microphone on his forearm or maybe it's the king of hearts. I should get the queen of hearts tattooed on me.

"Gia Ana Fontaine, you've done something I never thought possible. You have disappointed me. I trusted you." She sniffs again, but I can tell she's calming down since she's starting to get mad.

I sigh and break away from Rhys's penetrating stare. "I'll be home soon and I'm bringing someone. Axel is not coming, right?"

"He's not. Like I said, I haven't been able to get ahold of him. Unless he just drops by, which would be wonderful—"

"Okay I have to go." I hang up because this is bullshit and it's Christmas. I drop my hands dramatically on the bed and turn on my side to look at him. His hair is a black, wet mess; As he gazes at my body, up and down, his bourbon eyes seem almost golden.

"Why don't you come see if Santa came." His raspy voice makes my core pulse. Even though it's sore, I would love if he'd fuck me again.

"What do you mean?" I slowly sit up and let the sheet slide off me. I know what he means, but it's a kick to play Santa with him.

His full mouth twitches. "You didn't tell your mom that it was me coming. That's not being a good girl."

I smile. "I thought I'd make you a surprise. I mean it's not every day a girl gets to bring the Rock God home." I gush out Rock God.

"Hmm. On your knees," he demands.

As I crawl to the end of the bed, his eyes darken with every move I make.

His hands fist my hair and I swear to God, I almost come. I don't know why I like when he gets all caveman, but I do.

"Unzip me." He guides me to the floor and holds my hair tight as I reach up and unzip him slowly.

"Take him out," he says gruffly. I lick my lips and smile that we call him, *him.*

"Now I'm gonna fuck your mouth and you're gonna spread your knees apart and get yourself off. After that, if you were a good girl, we can see what Santa left you."

Jesus Christ, he's filthy, so fucking filthy. But this time I feel my power. Gone are his mean insecurities or his threats of groupies. He wants me, and I'm going to make sure he's never the same again.

I spread open his jeans and *he* comes out. Thick and strong with a drop of precum already on the tip and on his piercing. I wrap my mouth around the tip and suck.

Hard.

My eyes aim up at him. Opening my knees, I rub my clit.

"Fuck yeah, that's it." He holds my head as he watches me. "Brat," he says, his eyes fierce, and I almost come—not from my fingers, but from the look on his face.

"You're in charge. Make us both see stars," I murmur.

His breathing is harsh. Nostrils flaring, he guides my head. I open my mouth and gag, taking him as deep as I can. My fingers speed up as my mouth follows the same rhythm. My eyes stay on his as he watches, my clit so sensitive I'm ready to go over. But I need to wait.

His hands tighten in my hair. "Come, Gia," he demands, and I do, going over while he holds my head. As he empties himself, my mouth fills with hot sperm and I try to swallow it all.

He pulls me off and jerks the last of it onto my breasts, then lifts me under the arms as if I weigh nothing. He thrusts his tongue in my mouth.

It's hot.

Nasty.

With a moan, I cling to him, my mind spinning.

"I had no idea I would feel like this." I sound out of breath. Everything is moving so fast. I didn't factor in that I would feel this overwhelming, consuming love. I didn't understand what loving the Rock God meant.

But I'm starting to figure it out real fast.

CHAPTER 19

RHYS

Past — Twenty-seven years old
Burbank, California

"**G**ia." I take her hand and her eyes dart to mine. We landed about a half hour ago. I don't think she sat still the entire flight. I finally ate her cunt and fucked her to calm her down enough to sit and have champagne with me.

Christ, now that we're pulling into the old neighborhood, with Gia's nervous energy along with my mom's house looming ahead, I realize we should have stayed locked up in our suite.

"Babe, what are you looking for? Do you seriously think your brother is following us?" I'm trying to be patient since I think she might actually think that. Which pisses me off. This is exactly why we're doing this. All this sneaking around stops today. Axel doesn't like it, I guess we can fight it out. Won't be the first time I've punched his sanctimonious face.

I take her cold hand and rub my thumb back and forth where my Christmas gift dangles on her wrist. I got her a diamond Rolex. Diamond is her birthstone. I wanted something special, something she can have forever, pass down to our kids if we get that far.

I was feeling pretty good about mine until she gave me hers and that made me falter. Because the thing about gifts is how the right one can touch you, make you feel all sorts of emotions.

Gia gifted me with a glimpse inside her head and heart. She made me a book with her photographs, starting with the present and going back to when she was a brat in dirty clothes taking pictures of us in her garage. I've been blessed to win every type of award imaginable. But holding her gift brought home the reality that she's the one.

For the first time in my life, I'm thinking about my future, and it has nothing to do with my career. I'm seriously thinking about taking some time off after this tour.

Maybe I'll take Gia to Italy or southern Spain and lock us away, just fuck, write music, eat, and drink. Lie in the sun and let her tell me all the wonderful things she sees out of that lens. From the second I saw her dancing with Nuke, I knew she was it for me. I've been self-medicating myself as if I was waiting for her to grow up. And now that I have her, I have no intention of letting her go.

She's my muse.

My life.

My anchor. Gia, who keeps me sane when my world wants to fuck me up. If I was good, I'd encourage her to finish college. But to be honest, I'm a selfish fuck, and with my connections, school is foolish. Especially with her talent. It's raw and unique. Going back would only stifle her creativity. She needs to travel, continue developing her own style, not be molded into something someone else has already perfected.

"I'm being ridiculous, I know. I have no idea what I'm looking for." She takes a deep breath. "I love you, no matter what happens today, and I'm sure nothing will, but if something does, I love you." She tries to smile but it's strained. She looks down at her new watch as if it'll calm her.

My lips twitch. She's adorable. "Gia Fontaine?" I say as the SUV pulls into her mom's driveway.

"Yeah?" She leans into me; her green eyes blink and I know she desperately wants to hear the words. And I will say them, but not in her mom's driveway.

I reach over and rub her lips with my thumb. "I'm crazy about you." That will have to do for now. Her eyes reveal hurt and confusion, but we have all the time in the world. I'm not rushing it.

A cough from the driver interrupts us. She pulls back as if she's only now remembered we're not alone.

"Sorry to interrupt, but are you going to need me to wait, Mr. Granger?" He turns to look at us.

"What do you want to do?" I ask.

She puts a hand through her hair then rubs under her eyes. "Um. Dinner and that's it. I don't have a good feeling about any of this." She points at her mom's house, then digs in her bag, retrieving some lip gloss.

"Do I look okay?"

I grin at her. "Relax. You look like my girl. Now, let's do this."

"Yes, let's get it over with." She flings open the door as I lean forward to the driver.

"Give us a couple hours and then we will head back to the tarmac."

"Yes, sir."

"Thanks, man." I open my door as he jumps out to finish opening it for me. I hold up my hand.

"You don't have to do that." I glance around the old neighborhood. All the yards still have green lawns. Most are decorated for the holidays.

"I just want to say it's an honor to meet you. Huge fan." He nods at me, then Gia. "The *TSM* and *Humanoid* albums are my all-time favorites. They kind of changed my life." He nods.

"Thanks, brother." Sadly, I'm jaded. I will not be surprised at all if tonight or tomorrow I'm all over *ET* or the tabloids. I can see it now: Has the Rock God finally found his goddess? Is it true love or another notch in his belt?

"Gia?" My eyes turn to the old couple on the sidewalk.

"Hi, Mr. and Mrs. Dorsey." Gia smiles but her tone is clipped. I don't blame her. It's been years, but Mr. Dorsey never has been the cliché old man. I can't remember how many times he called the cops on us for noise pollution.

"Gia, darling. Thank goodness you're alive." Mrs. Dorsey glares at us.

"What?"

"Your mother has been sick with worry. We thought you were kidnapped." Mr. Dorsey zeros in on me.

"Oh God. No, I was not kidnapped, it was a misunder—"

"You look familiar." His old eyes shift up and down, taking in my appearance. Clearly, he disapproves since his wrinkles deepen.

"Merry Christmas, Mr. Dorsey. It's Rhys Granger." I hold out my hand knowing he recognizes me, but he's old so I'll humor him.

They both stare at me, their little dog running around barking at us as I put my hand down and turn to the driver.

"You can go get some food. I'll text you if I need you sooner." My voice gets louder as I try to speak over the loud growling and high-pitched barking from their little rat dog.

"Okay well, Merry Christmas." Gia waves at them and I smile, placing my hand on her lower back to get us away from them.

"Boy." That stops me. I lift an eyebrow at his gall. I'm not a boy, nor am I in the mood for what I know is coming.

"You hold up. I have things I need to say to you, and I don't care one bit that you're some hotshot singer." He snorts, contempt oozing from his mouth. "Your mother needs you. She's sick, and with all that money of yours, you'd think you could do better by her. I'm done calling 911 all the time." He points an old arthritic finger at me, then takes his wife's arm to continue walking down the sidewalk, their football dog still barking at the air.

"The fuck?" I mutter, my face flooding with heat. My head pounds and my pulse feels like it will bust out of my temples.

Last report on my mom was that they were changing her meds and a new doctor was needed. I turn as if I'm in a tunnel. My eyes focus on the house three doors down across the street.

The grass is green and flowers are blooming. I've hired people to fix it, paint it white with cute yellow shutters. Red roses climb and drape around the top of the archway joined with red and purple bougainvillea.

It sure as hell looks like a dream house compared with the run-down mess I grew up in.

"This was a mistake." I stare at the house. I thought I was beyond this. But no matter how big I get, all I am is a fucked-up kid running from the past, staying one step ahead of my demons. This place lets them free. They can swarm and infiltrate my brain here. After all, this is where they live.

"I have to call Rafe. Do you see any paparazzi?"

"Rhys?" Like a soothing warm blanket, she touches my hands, my face.

"You don't need to call Rafe." Her voice brings my eyes to hers. Her green eyes are clear, holding no judgment. Gia understands my pain, always has, yet never have I felt shame about my mom with her.

"You want to go?" My eyes look down at her hopeful ones.

I grab her, pulling her tight. "I need you," I say, my voice rough. Taking her hand, I glance around for a spot where I can fuck her. Maybe her body will take my mind's poisons away.

She nods, her eyes reflecting that same pull, craving, our own personal hunger.

I turn, only to halt. Janet Fontaine stands watching us, her eyes narrowed almost to slits as she shades her face with a hand.

"Rhys." She sounds shocked as she drops her hand. She'd be beautiful like her daughter if she didn't always look like she had the weight of the world on her.

"Oh, Gia. I just can't believe this." She holds open the door and steps aside rather dramatically, but whatever. Let's get this over with. Gia was right. This was a mistake, but we're here, and hopefully I won't have to come back for years.

"I now understand why you don't want my son over for dinner," she snips as I step inside. I bite the inside of my mouth to stop from snarling that I'd fucking love to beat the shit out of her son right about now.

"Take it easy, Mom. I can explain everything—" Gia's voice trails off as we both take in the inside of the house.

It looks like Janet has decided to move to the North Pole and become an elf in Santa's workshop. I shit you not, there's fake snow, a long wooden table with wooden toys, paint, glitter, and fucking elves everywhere.

"Oh my God...wow, Mom." Gia looks around as Janet walks by and grabs her glass of white wine.

"I had to do something or go mad with worry." She says all this as if it's normal to make your living room look like this.

She sits on the white couch, which has a blanket saying *Santa's*, and I wonder if she thinks she's Mrs. Claus as she reaches for a red-striped pillow to put behind her back.

"What is happening?" Gia mumbles as she tosses a few elves aside so we have a spot to sit.

"Janet, I'm sorry if Gia scared you." I lean forward, my hands resting on my knees. "I'm assuming you have pieced together that Gia is with me—"

She holds up her hands. "When you say with you, like *with...* you?" She looks like she's swallowed a bitter pill. "Or do you mean with the band? Taking pictures for the scholarship?"

"Oh God, really, Mom?" Gia's eyes are huge as she stares at her mom.

I sit back. Christ, the way her disapproving eyes look at me, it's like I'm ten again, begging her to let me stay for dinner since my mom has been gone for days. It's fucked up. All of this is fucked. I'm one of the biggest musicians in the world. I work my ass off to be the best at what I do, and the way Janet is acting, it's as if Gia and I are Bonnie and Clyde coming to dinner.

"Both." My voice is clipped because I'm done. "There's no scholarship. As for our relationship, that's private. All you need to know is that I'll take care of her." The room is silent except for the soft sounds of Bing Crosby and reindeer bells that seem to be on replay.

"Jesus, Rhys," Gia whispers. "Let me handle the rest." She sits up and tosses her hair off her shoulder.

"Look, Mom. I..." She motions with her hand in a circular motion almost as if she's strumming a harp. "I saw a fantastic opportunity and I took it." Her cheeks turn red instantly. "Wait. That came out wrong."

I frown and look at her. "What are you doing?"

She goes to open her mouth, but Janet jumps up. "Rhys Granger, don't you dare snap at my daughter. You're not the boss of her."

Gia lets out a loud groan and I stare at Janet. I take a deep breath, smelling the ham cooking in the kitchen. If Gia doesn't do some fast talking, I'm not even gonna make it to dinner.

"Mom, I've been lying from the beginning. I made it all up. There never was a scholarship." She shakes her head. "I made that up because I knew you would never say yes to me touring with the band." She holds up a hand. "Although, two of my professors are insane fans of Rhys and The Stuffed Muffins."

She clears her throat. "I wanted Rhys. I wanted him and I was willing to lie so I could get to him."

Janet sinks back down onto the couch. "Please, tell me you're on birth control."

Gia cocks her head at her. "Yes, Mom. I'm on birth control." Her hand reaches for my leg and her mom's eyes follow.

Janet takes a huge sip of her wine. "How do you think this can possibly work? He's a star, Gia." She laughs as she puts her glass on the coffee table. There's a whole train set on it. Thankfully it's not on, or I might toss it out the window.

"You're coming back to college in two weeks. I don't understand what you want me to say. I'm glad you finally caught Rhys's attention. We all know you've been seeking it since you were a child. But"—her eyes drift toward me—"that's all this is, a fascination with a hero that morphed into a young girl's fantasy about a rock star. And since you knew him, you think he's what you want. He's not." Her voice is flat. "Trust me."

"Huh. Thanks for psychoanalyzing us, but you have zero idea what you're talking about." Gia leans down for her purse, grabbing her cigarettes. "I was gonna try to sugarcoat this." She flicks the lighter as Janet looks like she might faint. "I'm not going back to Berkeley. I'm going to stay with Rhys because he's my man." She blows smoke up to the ceiling and my cock hardens. I'm a sick fuck, I guess.

Janet looks as if she might throw up. "You're kidding me."

"She's not. I told you I'd take care of her." I stand. This is about to get ugly. That, and it's uncomfortable to sit. I'm not going to fight with Gia's mother. This is her cross to bear. She's disapproving, controlling, and judgmental. It's why Axel was never close with her.

As a kid, I was jealous because at least she cared enough to be critical. But he was right—Janet hated the band. Always said we were average, at best, and needed to spend more time studying. And she really despised the Disciples. God, the first time she met Jason and David, I thought she was going to have a stroke.

"So, you're engaged?" she says in a raised voice, her face going from sheet white to red and splotchy.

"Mom, relax. I understand that you're in shock, but you need to stop. Don't you want me to be happy?" Gia jumps up and goes to her mother.

"Happy?" She laughs. "You can't be that stupid. Look at him. He will cheat on you, Gia. Drag you through things you can't even imagine."

She covers her mouth and shakes her head. "He says he'll take care of you. Look at how he takes care of his own mother. When was the last time he checked on her? When?" She turns to me.

"I pay people an enormous amount of money to take care of her," I say.

"Mom! How could you say that? You know Christie's illness has nothing to do with Rhys."

Gia looks at me, her eyes filled with tears, and there it is. *Pity*. I can take anything but having my girl look at me like that. My head is heavy, as if my neck can barely hold it up. *Look how he takes care of his own mother...*

"Rhys?" I walk past Gia, who tries to grab my arm. I need to get away or I will say something we all will regret.

"Rhys, I'm coming with you." She lets go to get her purse. I turn to tell her to stay but her pain makes me stare, as fat tears spill down her cheeks. I catch one and take in her beautiful face.

Pain and tears.

Why do you make all the girls cry?

"I need some air." She nods but digs her nails into my arm as I try to leave.

"You're okay, right?" She's borderline hysterical as her mom stands there and drinks.

"I'm fine. You stay and work this out with your mom. I have things I need to do." I hadn't planned this, but we can't escape who we are.

"Not without me." She shakes her head, panic in her eyes. "You need me," she croaks.

"Let him go, Gia." Janet's voice makes me grit my teeth.

His own mother.

"I need to be alone, Gia." I remove her hand. This time she doesn't try to grab me again as I throw the door open.

She screams at her mother. I tune it out, letting it be my background music, angry and alive.

The sun is going down. Reaching into my pocket for a cigarette, I notice our black SUV and the driver sitting a couple of houses down. He waves. I light up and inhale.

Music fills my head; the tempo is set as verses write themselves.

Why do you make all the girls cry?

Nuke's drums will take over, angry and powerful.

Ammo will make his guitar scream.

I bring out my phone and start to type as I sit on my grandfather's porch. Like magic, the words appear:

Drops on the tile. Tears of red. Not good enough, that's all she said.

All she said.

Take that muscle from my chest. You had it in your hand. In the year of the snake, you pounded it like dough.

Drops on the tile. Tears of red. Not good enough, that's all she said.

My fingers can barely keep up.

An hour, maybe a minute, has gone by as I let myself purge. I reach for my cigarette, but it's burned out along with the sun.

A car drives by, its headlights making me stand. It's Christmas and I'm coming to see her, with nothing but a pack of cigarettes and my phone. I take a breath and knock on the door.

CHAPTER 20

RHYS

Past – Twenty-seven years old
Burbank, California

I roll my neck and it cracks as I wait. The camera that hangs in the top right corner blinks red as the door opens. A woman in blue scrubs looks confused, her mouth hanging open.

"Mr. Granger, I... no one told me you were coming." Her hand goes to her hair, which is pulled up into a knot on top of her head. It seems to be all the rage with women lately.

"I'm sorry. It was spur of the moment." She nods, then steps aside as I walk in. My eyes scan the room. The large flatscreen I bought her is on the wall. The house is almost unrecognizable.

Jesus, it really has been years since I've been back here.

"Call me Granger." I'm not sure I even said that out loud as my eyes sweep the large room.

It's spotless. The walls are painted a pale green, almost celery color. Black-and-white photos of me and my old band, the Dicks, hang on the walls. On a separate wall hangs my first platinum record: *TSM*.

I vaguely remember having one of Rafe's assistants deliver it to my mom for her birthday. Or maybe it was Mother's Day. The hardwood floors are new. That was one of the first things I insisted on when she refused to move. I agreed but had the carpet removed and added a new kitchen, along with the two bathrooms. I would have done more, but apparently the more I changed, the more it upset and caused anxiety for my mom.

I stopped the construction after she disappeared for four days. They finally found her in Las Vegas, in some sty of a hotel, fucked up on heroin and cocaine.

"I'm Lisa." She smiles, looking at me like I walk on water.

"She in her room?" I don't know why I ask. I know the answer, can feel her depression, her fucking agonizing mental pain from here. And just like that, I have to grab the back of a chair as I hear my grandfather's voice.

"Rhys, make sure you got them all. My eyes aren't good enough to see them all. She hides them, you know."

"Yes, I hope I got them all. I think I got them, Grandpa." My hands open revealing the razor blades. He pats my shoulder and wipes the perspiration from his forehead, then holds the garbage can for me to dump them in.

"Why does she do this, Grandpa?" I whisper. One slices me and some blood spills from my palm.

"Rhys, I told you to be careful. I have enough to deal with," he snaps. Grabbing my hand, he squints to see how deep it is.

"Sorry, Grandpa. I was super careful." I watch as the blood drips down my arm. My grandfather tries to move without groaning. He has a bad back and he's old.

"Here, wrap your hand." He hands me a tissue. "Now you go watch TV, or maybe do that music you have such a gift for. Your mommy needs to sleep."

"I will, Grandpa. Do you want me to start dinner?" I jump at the loud scream and the sound of things being thrown in my mommy's room.

My grandfather looks pale and worried. I bite my lip to not cry. I'm a big boy. I just turned six, and my grandpa says that's big enough to not cry. That I'm gonna be the man of the house, so no crying. But she scares me when she's like this. She scares me a lot of the time. I go to hold his hand, but he's holding both of his together, praying.

"Pray with me, Rhys." I close my eyes and try. I try to say the words my grandpa says all the time. Instead, I ask God to make sure my grandfather lives forever. We need him. I need him.

"You go now. Do your music, Rhys. Lock yourself in your room until Grandpa says to come out. Go." He pushes me toward my room.

The door flies open and my mommy stands in almost no clothes.

"You go, Rhys. Go to your room, son." I can't move as I stare at my mommy. She looks wild, and she's covered in brown stuff. Maybe it's red?

"Now, Christie, you be a good girl and give Daddy that razor. You don't want your son to see you like this...

"Mr. Granger? I mean, Granger, are you okay?" I blink at her, trying to breathe. I look around the room. Jesus Christ, how old was I? Six? I was six years old, running around trying to get the razors before she did.

I clear my throat. "I'm fine. Why haven't I been notified? Clearly she's not doing well." I turn and look at her. She's probably late twenties, but who knows these days.

"They tried... the doctors. After this last time, they wanted to put her in the hospital, but she refused. They left messages with your assistants." She looks over at my mom's shut door, much like I used to do worrying at any moment what would emerge. The sad, loving mom, the wild and fun mom, the angry, bitter mom... on and on.

"She's down, I take it?"

The nurse nods. "I think she definitely should be hospitalized Mr.... um, Granger. She doesn't eat. She can't get up to use the toilet. You're spending a fortune on nurses, but in my opinion, she needs a doctor to watch over her, or at least help with her meds."

"I pay for the best doctors." Because I do, and heads are gonna roll if they have been billing me and not treating her.

She takes a breath. "I'm sorry. I just can't believe you're here. I'm such a fan. Do you think you could take a picture with me?"

My eyes dart to hers. She must understand her mistake by the disgust on my face. What the hell is wrong with people? My mom is a fucking train wreck, a woman who can't take a shit or piss by herself right now, and she wants a selfie with me?

"Get her doctor on the phone. I don't give a fuck that it's Christmas." I walk past her and don't bother knocking. I know what I'll see. The room is dark, save for a small glow from a light in the corner.

My eyes adjust enough to see that in her large room, all the walls are bare. There's nothing but her bed.

As I enter, I see a small lump. The bed looks to be made, except for the lump.

"Mom?" I take a breath, amazed at how clean it smells. At least it appears they're keeping the place, and her, clean.

I walk around. I know which wall she will be staring at. It's the same wall she always picks. Once, when I was angry as a teenager, I taped a picture of a naked woman over the spot she always stares at to see if I'd get any response.

"Mom." I sit and pull the comforter down to see her.

She lies on her side, her hair pulled back in a ponytail. Her temples are tinged with gray. Her skin is pale as if she's been locked in this room for a long time.

"Fuck." I close my eyes and let this sink in. Let it all sink in. I reach into my pocket for my cigarettes and light up, inhaling deeply as I look at her. She pulls herself into a tight fetal position.

Her movement doesn't change, and she remains staring at that spot. "So, here's the deal, Mom. It's Christmas and I came to see Janet because Gia, you remember her, the Brat..." I inhale again. "Yeah, the Brat fucking showed up and rocked my world, just tore it up. I wasn't gonna come see you because I knew this is what I'd find." I lean forward, my thumbs touching together, and decide to keep going and voice it all. She's not hearing me anyway.

"So, you'll be shocked to know that Janet hates me. Well, maybe not hates, but certainly doesn't want me with Gia. And I was sitting in her fucking crazy house as she told her daughter what scum I was, and all I thought was I don't belong here."

I look over at her. She blinks but there's no other response. "Yeah, it sucked. It hurt, and all of a sudden, I wanted you." I take another inhale because no matter what, I do want her.

"I knew you'd be like this. But that's okay, Mom. Because there's one thing about you. No matter what I do, how bad I fuck up, I know that you'll understand." I look out her window. It has bars on it, but the shades are slightly open.

"And that's good. Because it's a crazy fucking world out there." I nod as I look down at my hands. One holds the cigarette; the other reaches out to touch her hand, which hangs at her side.

"I'd have liked to talk to you sometime." My chest is tight, as if I have the flu and I can't get a good breath.

"I'd have liked to tell you things. Instead, I left you. And look at you. You're alone in this room staring at that goddamn spot again." My vision is blurry. "I wish I was a better son. I wish you had been a better mother, but I get it... because every day I live with the fear that one day I'm gonna wake up and be staring at a spot, not wanting to move." Something wet is on my jeans. I can't be fucking crying. I don't cry, ever. And I certainly don't cry over her.

"Fuck. I'll see you around, Mom." I go to take my hand away, but she holds it.

I freeze.

"Mom?" I let the tears come. I let all of it come. Like a raging storm it pours out of me, and I weep for the first time since I turned six.

I weep for her, me, Gia, because deep down Janet is right. I am my mother's son.

"I'm sorry." I lean down to kiss her cold cheek as she keeps staring at her spot. If my hand wasn't warm from hers, I'd think I imagined her giving me that.

I turn and *she* stands in the doorway, her eyes a mess, her mascara and tears running down her face, her lips red and puffy. This is when I should make her stay with her mom. Fuck, everyone is right. She is light and doesn't need all my shit.

"Gia."

She moves toward me. Her hands, which always seem to take my pain away, touch my face.

This is when I walk away from her. Her hands reach for my cheek, trailing down to touch my lips as if she knows I'm going to speak something she can't hear.

"I'm not good." I'm raw. This room is like a death chamber, sucking the life out of me, yet I can't seem to move.

One of her hands goes to touch my hair. She stands on her toes to look me in the eyes.

Hunger.

It crawls through me as I lean into her touch.

"You're good and kind. You're the one, Rhys Granger." Her eyes look like giant pools of green water as her hands soothe me.

"Fuck." I pull her tight, nuzzling her neck as I give in to my famine.

I'm not good.

My brain is at war with my heart. But there is no war with the heart. It's strong, and powerful.

And mine beats for her.

CHAPTER 21

GIA

Past – Eighteen years old
San Francisco, California

My eyes blink open and for a second, I'm confused as to where I am. I reach for him, but he's not there. Sitting up on my elbows, I look around. Yet another hotel room. This time, we're in San Francisco.

"Rhys?" I yell. "How long have I been sleeping?" The room is silent. I flop back onto the pillows and wipe my hands up and down my face, then lean over and grab the pack of cigarettes and light up.

San Francisco, only fifteen to twenty minutes away from Berkeley. It wasn't that long ago that I was sitting in my dorm room plotting with Julianna on how to get to him.

Now I feel ancient compared to that girl. I cross my legs, prop the pillows behind me, and look around the room. We need the maid, but Rhys is writing so, no one but us is allowed in.

Leaning my head back, I close my eyes and mentally prepare for tonight. It's the last concert of the tour.

My mind wanders to how I need to call Julianna and tell her I'm not coming back.

I miss her. She's the only thing I do miss about my old life. After the fucking nightmare with my mom and dealing with Christie, yeah, Julianna is definitely the only one I miss.

Rhys ended up firing his mom's doctors. He then put her in a private hospital in Malibu. It sounds as if she's making progress, and her medication is stabilizing her. I know she's been calling, but he's been writing music.

Watching Rhys write, create, seeing the way his mind works... God, I'm in so deep with him, nothing can tear me away.

He's my everything, my fucking world.

He's beautiful, a musical genius, and he can fuck like a god. My face turns pink and my nipples harden. I want him, twenty-four seven.

I'm starting to worry I have a real problem. All I have to do is think of him and I'm wet.

Damn it.

I need a shower and have to get up. I almost reach down to take the edge off. But why bother? It's never as good with my fingers anymore.

It's like he's trained my pussy to crave his thick, pierced cock, and nothing else will do. Except for his fingers and tongue. Leaping out of bed, I put the cigarette out and march into the bathroom.

Rhys is probably doing a sound check, or did he miss that this morning? Where the hell is my phone? Not that he's gonna answer. Most of the time, he forgets it. Although, with his mom in the hospital, I think he's trying to be better.

My eyes longingly shift to the giant tub. Screw it, I have time. The concert is not for a couple hours, and soaking in the tub will do wonders for my body.

I turn on the gold faucet and reach for the pretty bottles laid out on a gold tray. They all smell delicious, so I dump in the one that smells like a combo of vanilla and lavender.

Turning, I look at myself in the large mirror. I look like a different person. My lips are swollen from constantly being kissed; my nipples are dark from being sucked. I'm flushed.

Jesus, I look wild. I definitely have lost weight, but who cares? I have full breasts, so it balances it out. Trying to shake my unease, I grab my toothbrush and brush my teeth.

It's weird that he hasn't called or left a note. I take a deep breath. I'm being absurd. He hasn't left the room in days, and he has to perform tonight. I'm sure he's with the guys. Maybe he's showing them his new stuff?

I spit and rinse. "Everything is okay," I tell myself. Exhaling, I sink into the hot tub. But now I'm getting paranoid. I can't enjoy this. I need to wash up and go find him. I'm just reaching for the gel when I hear the door click open and I freeze.

"Rhys?" Nothing.

"Rhys?" I shout, standing. "Rhys?" I reach for a towel, glancing around for a weapon. What if it's a crazy fan who's somehow gotten in and is going to kill me because I'm not Granger?

"Brat?"

I scream as I reach for the edge of the tub. "What the fuck? You jerk." I throw the towel at him. Of course, it misses him, not even getting close. He looks at it, then leans against the door. His dark eyes inspect my face, and he smirks as he stares at my breasts.

"Stop it." I sink back down. "I thought it was a lunatic fan coming to kill me," I huff, leaning back until the bubbles are up to my neck.

He watches with his arms crossed, his hair a mess, the dark strands making my fingers itch to run through them.

Pushing off the doorframe, he enters, stopping at the edge. "Why are you all flushed?" His voice is deep, gravelly, and of course my nipples harden and my clit throbs.

"What do you mean? I'm taking a hot bath," I snip. He leans down, his hands on both sides of the tub.

"Let me see," he says, and I can smell the bourbon from here. My eyes narrow. "Where were you?"

"Out." He grins as his hand reaches into the tub and wraps around my ankle. "Rhys, stop it. I'm not in the mood." I try to jerk my ankle away, but he holds on as water splashes up to my face.

In one quick jerk, my ass slides toward him and he holds both my ankles. "Now, beautiful, let's try this again. Show me." His nostrils flare as he watches the bubbles around my breasts.

"Show you what?" My voice tight. I have no reason to be mad at him, other than that he left to go drinking without me, and now he wants to get all domineering.

He does nothing but smile as my heart flutters. I hate him right now. It's not fair for him to be this perfect.

"I want to see your cunt. Did you touch yourself?"

"No." That was way too fast. Now he's gonna think I did. "I didn't," I say to his raised eyebrow. "I thought about it, but I didn't." I bite the bottom of my lip as his hand slides up my wet legs.

"You look like you're lying, Brat." I gasp as he slides one arm through the water and stops *right there*.

"Talk to me, tell me." His voice makes me arch up, but he takes his hand out and I almost scream, because now I'm needy as hell.

"I didn't touch my—"

"You didn't touch *my* pussy." He corrects me. "Now say it right." He sits on the edge of the tub, his wet hand playing with the bubbles around my breasts.

I take a breath. "I didn't touch *your* pussy." I whisper the pussy part.

"Nah." He grabs the back of my hair so that my head is held tight at the base of my hair. "This is my cunt," he says, and my eyes grow wide.

Blinking at him, I wonder if he's been drinking tequila instead of bourbon.

"Now, say it. Tell me what's mine." He brings my head up as the water drips down my chest.

"I'm not saying the C word." I'm trying to be outraged, but my breathy voice gives me away.

Kneeling, he whispers, "Say it and I'll give you what I trained *my cunt* to need."

"What the hell is happening?" I try to slap his hands away, but he's already rubbing one of my nipples, his eyes like dark orbs.

"These are my tits also." His calloused hand and fingers caress and squeeze it. As I swallow back a moan, he smiles at me.

"I want to pierce this nipple." Leaning forward, he takes it in his mouth.

This time I do moan as he sucks it almost raw, my core clenching.

He looks over and bites it.

Hard.

"The fuck, Rhys?" He leans up and silences me with his lips and my sore nipple tingles as his hand leaves my breast to travel down to my clit.

I'm spinning, trying to keep up, then let go because I'm coming.

Hard.

Before I can recover, he pulls me out, carrying my wet, slippery body to the glass shower door. I wrap my arms around his muscled shoulders. His mouth attacks mine as our tongues twist, and I definitely taste the bourbon.

I feel his hand unbutton his jeans and my feet help push them down past his ass. In one fast thrust, he's inside me.

He doesn't move, only pulls back to look at me. Our eyes lock and I see everything I will ever need.

"I love you," I murmur into his mouth as I kiss him. His hands move to the top of the glass door and he thrusts into me fast and hard, his piercing rubbing me over and over as my back slides up and down from the water, and now, our sweat.

He's not even trying to hold back. He needed me. I throw back my head and he bites my neck as I shiver and moan loudly.

He's inside me, and I never want it to end.

"That's it, Gia. Talk to me, baby." He grunts his approval and my core pulses and contracts as his hips slam into me.

He's primal, almost intimidating. I'm climbing, my core contracting, and he doesn't stop. My eyes close, but dots still appear as I orgasm. I think I scream. My pulse races and I see stars as wave after wave of addicting pleasure fills me.

"Whose cunt is this?" he hisses in my ear, still fucking me hard while I scream his name.

"I'm gonna fill my sweet cunt up." His body jerks and he comes undone.

Steadying our breaths, neither of us moves. Finally, he pulls out and backs up. My legs shake and I grab his arm.

"Take a shower and get ready." He kisses me.

"Aren't you going to join me?" I look down at his wet, slick cock that still stands proud. I almost tell him to sit on the toilet so I can ride him, but he's right—I need to get ready.

"No. I want to smell us and *my* cunt when I play tonight."

"God, Rhys, you are so... vulgar." He grins, then throws his head back and laughs.

"Vulgar?" He rolls the *rrrr*. "I like that. Hurry up." He slaps my ass and I roll my eyes, stepping into the shower. There goes my relaxing bath. The way my legs feel like rubber, I could use it.

Sighing, I raise my face to the water and try to figure out what's going on with me. It's not like I'm in a bad mood. How could I be? I've had numerous orgasms already today. It's more an unsettled feeling.

I grab the shampoo. This has to be because we're in San Francisco. I wish I could skip tonight's concert, snuggle in bed wearing one of his black T-shirts, and wait for him to come home.

Yet I can't and I'm being ridiculous. Just because he hasn't said what we're doing next, doesn't mean I should get weird. I hurry, washing and turning off the shower. I need to look fantastic, especially tonight. No clue why I feel this way, but I do.

CHAPTER 22

RHYS

Past – Twenty-seven years old
San Francisco, California

I take a deep drag off my cigarette, barely registering that it's raining. Leaning forward, I let the rain soak my head. Some asshole paparazzi is probably zooming in on me but fuck it—I need some air.

I look up at the sky. It's gray and dark.

Angry clouds.

I haven't gotten the phone call saying we're postponing, so I assume this will let up. Not the first time I've gotten wet playing outside, but it always casts a strange unease over the band.

My phone vibrates, and my heart races so fast my temples pound.

Rafe: We might have to postpone until tomorrow. This fucking rain.

Me: Do you want me to wait here?

Rafe: No.

I pocket my phone and breathe out deeply, letting my heart rhythm return to normal. A woman I dated almost a year ago called Rafe yesterday demanding I pay her money. She claims she's pregnant and that I'm the father. The chance that this is real is zero. This happens all the time, women saying they're pregnant. It's always some desperate groupie looking for a handout.

But this time, I have Gia. Something tells me this would not go over well.

Renee.

I shake my head. Can't even remember her face. Nothing but a name. I've racked my brain trying to remember. I recall a Renee, but her face blends in with the faces of countless women I've fucked.

Taking a deep drag, I close my eyes and let the rain soothe me. If I had anything to worry about, Rafe would have found out. The fact that he hasn't mentioned it and is concerned about the rain makes all the drama go away.

I open my eyes as a zigzag of lightning streaks across the sky. Maybe I need to buy a house. Living out of hotels is getting old. And now I have Gia to look after, care for, and we need a home base. Fuck, we can have houses all over the world for all I care.

I always see myself in Los Angeles. It's home, and I need the warm weather, but can I deal with my mom? We can always buy in Malibu, or the Palisades. I'll let Gia decide. I take one last drag of my cigarette and put the butt out in a potted plant.

Time to go. My cock is getting hard.

"Gia?" I look around, making sure I'm not forgetting anything. "With the rain, traffic might be shit, babe."

"I'm ready." I look up and freeze.

There she stands. My goddess. My heart aches at the fear that this thing we share can be ruined by any bad mistake. She sashays by me. Her vanilla perfume fills me, calms me as I watch her get her bag.

My eyes take in her body. Black skinny jeans and high-heeled boots showcase her long legs. Her see-through sweater leaves little to the imagination.

"You're fucking stunning." She smiles as she lifts her arms to pull her hair back in a low bun.

My hand goes to rub my burning heart.

Hunger.

Grabbing her, I pull her into my arms. She bats her long eyelashes at me. She's got the smoky-eye makeup thing going on that makes the green of her eyes look like glittering emeralds. Her bag falls to the floor with a thud, and she wraps her hands around my neck.

"Have I told you that I *really* like you?" I say, my voice low.

She laughs. "You have." She purses her red lips.

My nose dips to her neck. "Have I told you you're my life?"

She leans back to look at me. "Kind of."

I straighten and take her hand and put it on my chest. "Feel that?"

"Yes," she whispers, her chest rising and falling in perfect rhythm.

"That's my heart beating for you." I have no idea why I'm doing this now. Maybe it's because of the phone call earlier, or maybe it's time.

"What's wrong?" Her eyes search my face.

"I want to tell you." I cup her face. "You need to know how I…" My phone interrupts with a loud buzz. She looks down.

"Ignore it," I demand. "Fuck the rest of my world, Gia. I love you." It's raw and not smooth, but it's the truth.

"Rhys," she whispers, blinking back the tears as she laughs, her whole body shaking.

"I should have told you earlier. I thought it was clear." I frown. Why am I stumbling like this? She places her fingers on my lips and cocks her head as she watches me.

"I love you, Rhys. I've loved you forever."

I stare at her. She's fearless, always has been. It rolls right out of her mouth. I can write the fuck out of a song. Perform in front of thousands of people. But she knows me, sees past all the fame and wealth. Gia sees the man that I am. She knows my demons, has seen me bleed.

She traces my lips and I lightly bite the tip of her finger and suck it. When she smiles, my heart squeezes.

"We need to go, Rhys." The room is thick with all our emotions and things that need to be said. But that can wait.

"You ready?"

She leans down for her bag. Wiping under her eyes, she smears her eyeliner, so now she's got the Cleopatra look going. I take her hand and open the door. Ace and three other bodyguards wait.

I wink at her and the madness begins.

"I've got Granger. We're on the move." Ace speaks into his earpiece. I squeeze her hand as we take the stairs, trying to avoid the crowds that must be waiting for me.

"Get the limo. We're coming in three, two, one." Ace throws open the door that leads to the lobby.

"There he is." A man tries to block our way, his damn camera in Gia's face. I fucking know this scumbag. He stalks me all the time.

"I'm warning you, Bob, get that camera out of her face." He swings it toward me right as Ace pushes him back.

"Granger, man. Who's the beauty with you?" He laughs as we pass and ignore him. "You gonna reschedule because of the rain? Granger?"

I flip him off. He keeps smiling the whole time. The crowd that was waiting at the lobby entrance and elevators runs toward us.

"Granger? Rock God, can you sign this, please..."

"Granger, I heard the concert is postponed until tomorrow... Granger?

"This is insane. Get more guys and clear them out," I tell Ace who is talking into his earpiece.

"Rock God... I love you!" A woman grabs ahold of my shirt.

"What the hell?" Gia explodes as Ace calmly removes her hand and pushes the crowd back. Jesus, this a big fucking mess, and the rain seems to have picked up. It's pouring and still, people are outside waiting.

I hold up my hand as I plow through. *Rock God, I love you. Rock God, over here. Granger, I'm pregnant...* the words just blend together as I hold up my hand and go straight for the limo.

"Christ." I shake my head, water dripping down my face and neck. Leaning back into the leather seat, I pull a wet Gia next to me.

Ace slides in and slams the door. "Move," he yells at the driver.

"What the fuck, man? Who leaked that we're staying here?" I glance out the window, then over to Ace.

The limo pulls out, horn blaring.

"Cash was at the bar last night, and Nuke stopped to sign autographs earlier." Ace looks out the window, then back at me as we glide down the street slowly, the wipers going at full speed.

"You can't play in this rain, Rhys," Gia says, almost dazed as she looks out the window.

"Pull over." I tell the driver, raising my hips to get my phone out of my pocket.

"Christ." There are at least twenty missed calls from Rafe. The last one reads *911*. "Did you hear anything about tonight?" I look at Ace as I push on Rafe's number.

"My main priority is your safety. I haven't checked my phone," he snaps, which is very un-Ace. He always stays cool and collected, but even he must feel the ominous vibe.

I rub the back of my neck waiting for Rafe to answer as I kiss the top of Gia's head.

"Hand me that bottle of Jack, brother."

Ace grabs it, passes it to me, and pulls out his phone.

I'm almost ready to hang up when Rafe answers. "You still at the hotel?" Loud noises filter through.

"No, we just left."

"Go back. I'm already at the hotel. Meet me in my suite. The show has been postponed for tomorrow. It's not safe."

"The fuck, Rafe! You could have told me earlier." My head pounds as I crack open the bottle.

"Bring Gia." The line goes dead. I take a breath, because I'm getting ready to lose my shit, and that's not gonna help anything right now.

"Rhys?" Gia looks up at me, confusion on her face.

"It's not happening tonight. Go back." I bring the bottle to my lips and drink, swallowing the spicy burn like it's water.

"Concert postponed, and Rafe wants to talk for a few minutes in his suite." I spit it out as I take another swig.

"Why?" she demands.

"I guess we'll find out." It comes out harsh, causing her eyes to narrow as she looks at the bottle and leans her head back on the seat.

"God, please tell me it's not Axel. Do you think my mom told him? Or worse, he saw a picture of us?" Her leg starts to bounce. I look at her. I'd fucking give anything for it to be Axel.

"I told you I'm not hiding."

She rolls her eyes at me, then looks out the window as the limo pulls up to the hotel again.

"Okay, I've had my guys clear most of the crowd out. Let's go nice and easy." Ace is back as he opens the door and I climb out, holding my hand to Gia.

Two cop cars are parked on the side, and people are still yelling and taking pictures, but the crowd has definitely thinned out. We head toward the stairs.

"Are you gonna drink the whole bottle before we even find out what's happening?" Gia exclaims, passing me as she takes the stairs like a pro. Her ass looks amazing. I must be feeling no pain as my cock hardens and I'm almost ready to blow Rafe off. He can deal with whatever shit this is. That's what I pay him for.

"Fuck this." I stop at the third floor and open the door leading to the rooms and elevator. "Rafe can handle whatever it is."

Gia and Ace stop mid-climb.

"No, we're going to Rafe's suite." She puts her hands on her hips, barely out of breath. I grin at her as she shakes her head. "Whatever, you stay here and finish the bottle. I'll take care of whatever drama is happening." She leaves me, her boots clinking as she takes the stairs two at a time.

Ace nods approvingly. "Gia kicks ass, man." He follows her while I watch, knowing I need to follow.

It can't be. I would never fuck without a rubber. Aside from Gia, it doesn't happen. I bring the bottle to my lips. The few times the rubber has torn on my piercing, the women have taken the Plan B pill, right?

I stumble out the door into the lavish hallway and push on the elevator button. Clearly, I'm not gonna catch up with her, but at least I should make it to Rafe's suite first.

CHAPTER 23

GIA

Past – Eighteen years old
San Francisco, California

I'm fucking out of breath, but my nerves feel better at least. Ace and the other two security guys are with me as I walk down the end of the hall to Rafe's room.

"Do you know what this is about?" I whisper to Ace, who's a big guy, so he's still catching his breath.

"No clue. But the vibe is not good," he mumbles. I stop and wait for him as I take my hair down. The low bun thing is making my head hurt. I run my hands through it and straighten my shoulders.

"Gia, you're not gonna wait for Granger?" Ace laughs and shakes his head like I'm either a badass, or have lost my mind.

"I have you. Let's get it over with." I start to walk.

"I'm not going into that room," Ace responds.

I ignore him. As my bodyguard, he has to, right? Jesus, I'm freaking out now that I'm staring at the ornate door. I should wait for Rhys.

I turn to Ace. "Listen. You know who I am, right? Like you know about my brother?" I shake my hands because they feel numb.

"Yeah, I know Axel, Gia."

I sigh in relief. "Okay, good. So, he might be in there and he doesn't... or didn't know about me and Rhys—"

"I know all this. Wait for your man, Gia," he warns as he texts.

"My man is drinking a bottle of Jack. Look, you don't understand. Rhys is not afraid of Axel." I look at Ace, but he keeps texting, and the other two simply stare at me.

"God, if Axel is in there," I whisper, pointing at the door. "Maybe I can calm him down before... Screw it." I pound on the door, taking a deep breath.

"Granger is on his way." Ace says this like I'd better be scared or something. What is wrong with them? My brother is ready to kill Rhys, and all he is saying is wait and let it happen? The door opens, and Rafe looks at me, then over my shoulder to Ace and his team. His arrogant face morphs into a frown as he pushes the sleeve of his starched, white dress shirt up.

"Where's Granger?"

"He's coming. Is..." I clear my voice and straighten my shoulders back. "Is Axel in there?"

His eyes narrow on me as he slowly brings the crystal tumbler of brown liquid to his lips.

"Not yet." And I almost sag with relief as warm hands grab my hips, jerking me back to his hard chest.

"Brat, let me take care of this," Rhys says tightly in my ear, causing me to shiver.

This is bad.

Something bad is about to happen. Rafe swings the door wide open so we can enter. I dig my nails into Rhys's arm. If it's not Axel, then... I walk forward almost as if I'm having an out-of-body experience. One foot in front of the other I move, my fingers laced with Rhys's as I blink at the large silver and gold room. It's decorated like we're back in France, and Napoleon might step out at any moment.

A woman sits with a man in a suit. And I know this is going to hurt me. And not just a small prick. Whatever is about to happen is going to rip me open and make me bleed.

"No," I whisper and stop moving.

Rhys turns and his eyes... oh my God. This is happening. It's in his eyes—he knows.

The man next to the woman stands and comes forward holding out his hand, which Rhys ignores, instead looking at me.

She heaves herself up to stand also, a gloating smile on her pretty face.

She's tall, like six feet, in jeans and a tight pink sweater, with pale skin and pitch-black hair cut in a bob. Jesus, is she pretending she's Uma Thurman in *Pulp Fiction*?

My eyes fill with tears and I look up at the ceiling to stop them from falling.

I'm Gia Fontaine.

My brother is Axel Fontaine. We don't cry or show weakness. But this... this bitch is pregnant, and everything that I've dreamed of did not include this.

"Baby, it's okay." Rhys hasn't even looked at them. Does he not see her fucking stomach? I take a breath and blink away the tears as I look at him and smile. Turning, I shake the man's hand. "I'm Gia, and you are?" That makes the room almost crackle with tension. The man hesitates and shakes my hand. His is cold, almost clammy.

"Yes. I'm Mr. Daniels and this is my client, Renee Abbott." My eyes meet hers, and she somewhat falters beneath my stare.

"Yes. So, unfortunately, our lawyers have to be involved also, but Renee requested a friendly meet and greet," Rafe says. "Gia, something to drink?"

"Sure." I reach for Rhys's bottle of Jack as he takes over the room.

"Look, I'm not even going to humor you two. This is not mine." He motions with his head to her stomach. "I barely remember Renee."

I take a swig and swallow the burn of liquor. It slides down, then threatens to come back up.

"Yes. Ms. Abbot thought you would think that as you always use condoms. You have a piercing on your genital?"

I'm going to puke. I never should have taken that swig on an empty, anxiety-laced stomach. I'm starting to sweat as I hear my life being torn apart and snagged away from me. I want to scream that it can't be.

I'm the one.

Me! I'm supposed to be first. I'm supposed to have his babies. Not some pale-faced, skinny model.

Rhys takes the bottle from my hand as if he can feel and know everything I'm thinking. For one horrifying moment, I wonder if I said all that out loud.

"It's none of your business," he grumbles.

"Granger, the baby is yours. The rubber tore on the piercing." Renee speaks for the first time, and she has an accent. It's not French. Maybe Scandinavian? "You fuck like a beast." She turns to me. "It happened more than once."

"If that had happened, I would have made sure you took Plan B," he says.

"You did," she replies and sits back down. All eyes stare at her and I start to back up, because this is when I need to leave. Run, hide, curl into a ball and try to make this not be happening.

"My lawyers will be in touch. This is not my kid." He grabs my hand as Renee shrieks at our backs.

"It *is* yours. You'll see when you take a paternity test. I intend on my child knowing his father. I'll use everything in my power, and that includes the press, to make sure you're on board."

He swings around. "If that kid is mine, I'll be the one making sure he understands that the mother is a gold digger who purposely got knocked up. Go to the press. I couldn't care less." He takes my hand and we're out the door.

One foot in front of the other, I chant as Rhys drags me along. My legs feel like lead. I'm sure it's from all the steps, or else I'm in shock. He must get sick of it and sweeps me into his arms, carrying me to our door.

"Don't. Please don't do this to yourself. She's lying. That is not my kid." His voice is soft, soothing, and I cling to him, knowing that everything from this day forward will change.

Inhaling, I breathe in his clean scent. I'm addicted to that scent; I'm addicted to him. It's gone beyond loving him. I need him. He's my everything. Without Rhys, I'm not sure I know who I am.

I had a goal. It was clear: I was going to marry Rhys Granger.

I guess I'm weeping. I didn't think I was crying, but he's setting me on the couch and kneeling between my knees, and I don't even remember getting on the elevator.

"Gia." His voice is demanding, but his touch is gentle as his thumbs wipe away my tears. The tears that signified what made me, *me*. The very tears that are forcing me to grow up. Not everybody gets what they want no matter how hard they fight, claw, and try.

The tune "You Can't Always Get What You Want" bursts into my head as I look at him. My hands run through his thick, wavy hair, and I let him take away all the shit his dick has gotten us into.

His full lips kiss my eyes with soft, light kisses that make me cry harder. Is he trying to get me to forgive him? I haven't even comprehended that this is happening. The damage is in play, and even if she's lying, it'll be months before we find out.

Months of her hanging around making us miserable.

Fucking months.

"It's not mine. She's trying to get money and fame by saying it's mine." He pulls back. "This is not the first time this has happened, Gia. It sucks, but we'll get through it."

I nod because when he says it like that, it sounds right. "Yes. I'm sure it's not yours." I sigh into him as he takes my lips gentle and slow, so different from our usual kisses.

"I need you." His hand drifts to my neck as he holds me still, allowing his tongue to lick and suck at his leisure.

I can't seem to stop crying. Rhys is being gentle, loving. Like he worships me. Any other time I would love it, cherish it, but right now it makes me feel like he's apologizing and *guilty*.

"Christ, Gia." His tone holds a warning, all the gentleness melting away. He stands, anger flashing in his eyes, and my core becomes wet. *This* is what I want, need. I can't handle tender right now. I need... I don't know what I need.

My head is throbbing as if I've just been knocked awake with a brick. He may be a father. And then Rhys will be connected to that woman *forever*. He'll experience one of the greatest things in life: having a child.

And it will be with *her*.

I'm devastated. God, I'm so pathetically naïve. I truly believed Rhys was everything—everything but flawed.

"Was this what you were dealing with today?" I raise my chin.

He ignores my question, which makes me assume it's a silent *yes*. He reaches into his pocket for his cigarettes and sits down. The elegant, giant wingback chair makes him look like a king or a god. As he lights his up, he narrows his eyes on me and inhales.

Goose bumps cover my skin. The look he gives me is almost contempt, like he's the one who's been burned instead of me.

"Clothes off," he says. His full lips latch onto the tip of the cigarette so he can unbutton his jeans.

I lick my lips. Rhys has been demanding and domineering, but this is different.

"Clothes off now, Gia," he commands. His tone is so cold. Kicking off my boots, I can barely get a full breath in as I toss off my sweater and bra, then shimmy out of my jeans. I look at him and almost sink to my knees. He's so beautiful, and for a moment, he was mine.

"Take your panties off and *crawl*," he demands. I freeze, then slowly let my G-string slide down my legs and step out of it.

"What?" I croak, wiping away my tears.

"Crawl. To. Me." He leans forward, resting his hands on his knees. Slowly I lower myself to the ground.

My nose is stuffy, and I'm sure my face looks scary with all the crying I've done. Yet the way his eyes change as I start to crawl on all fours, naked, makes me scared that we're entering a dangerous game.

A game I know nothing about. A game that might break me, but I obey and crawl to him anyway.

"Look at me, Brat." My eyes jerk to his and I arch my back, watching his nostrils flare as if he can smell my arousal.

"You want me to fuck you, don't you?" he says, his voice thick.

I move in between his legs and nod.

"Use words, Gia. Tonight you might need them." My heart leaps.

"Yes," I snap. "I want you to fuck me hard." He grabs my chin and I almost whimper. The tears have finally stopped. Only our rage fuels the room. My hands fall forward on his thighs.

"Get up." He pushes my chin away, putting his cigarette out on the glass table before he jerks off his T-shirt.

He's intimidating in his anger, and I bite my tongue not to scream that this is his fucking fault, not mine. Lifting his hips, he kicks off his jeans.

His cock stands hard and thick up to his belly button.

"You want rough, I can do that." He grabs me and spins me until I catch myself and rest my hands on the couch cushions. His hand holds the back of my neck still.

"What are you gonna do?" A shiver of fear goes up my spine.

"I'm gonna fuck you rough."

"Let go of me, Rhys." I try to jerk away, but he's already spreading my legs with his feet.

"Careful, Brat. You sure you want me to stop?" He knows I don't. I bite my lip as my nipples rub against the couch's silk upholstery.

"I wanted to love you, but this is what you want." And in one fast thrust he slides deep inside me.

"Yeah, your cunt is wet. You like it like this." He pounds into me from behind, lifting my hips so that he's so deep, his piercing hits my cervix.

I moan and claw at the end of the couch.

"This cunt is mine. You're mine."

I moan as if I'm possessed.

"You want rough?" He slaps my ass and I scream. *What is happening?* He spanks the other cheek and I moan with pleasure. I'm climbing, and everything but him, his cock, and my warm ass fades away.

"I can feel you getting my balls wet. You want more," he says as he roughly slams in and out and his thumb rubs my other hole.

"Relax." He swats my ass again and I start to contract. I'm going to come, fucking explode. He slows, and his thumb slowly goes into my ass.

"Rhys..." I groan, my voice hoarse.

"That's it, Brat. You like my cock fucking your cunt and my thumb in your ass." He picks up speed and I'm gone, floating in mindless bliss. My body is his, as he grunts out a "Fuck you, Gia." Then he jerks, and I feel the warm pulse of his seed filling me up.

And then nothing. Coldness is all that remains. I hear the rustle of him grabbing his jeans. The slam of the door makes me finally turn.

He's gone.

I stare straight ahead as the tears spill down my cheeks. *Why do all the girls cry around you?*

Because I'm bad.

Bad.

I bring my hands to my face, pull my knees up, and let go. Just scream out my grief. I get it now.

I understand everything that Stephanie was crying about years ago.

I get it and hate him for that. I despise that he's human and not perfect. I hate that he's famous and gifted, beautiful and strong... *I hate.*

"I hate you," I whisper into the silent room. He did exactly what I wanted. He fucked me and now he's gone, barely staying with me long enough to get dressed. I glance at the coffee table where he's left his phone, along with the cigarette he put out.

Standing, I make my way to the bathroom. The water from earlier is still in the tub. After leaning down to let it out, I twist my hair up.

He's gone, just fucked me and left, kind of like Renee. He's fucked so many women, he doesn't even remember her.

"God." I look up at the ceiling, needing Advil and sleep. I was going to take a shower, maybe a bath, but I'm tired. So tired.

I barely pull the covers up when my mind goes blank.

CHAPTER 24

RHYS

Past – Twenty-seven years old
San Francisco, California

"**B**rother, we need to get the fuck out of here." I stare at Ammo, and for a second I see two of him. With a grin, I bring the warm bottle of Jack to my lips.

"What time is it?" I look around. We're in a seedy, downtown strip club.

"I fucked Lacey and it's time to roll."

I snort. Leave it to Ammo to blow his load and hightail it out of here.

"Come on, man, I called Ace to come get us. We need to get to the stadium." He rolls his neck as I slowly sit up.

"Christ." I look around again, trying to forget the last twenty-four hours.

"Did Gia call?"

Ammo reaches over for the bottle, his blue eyes narrowing. "No." He takes a swig.

"Call Rafe and have him check on her," I say gruffly. Ammo raises an eyebrow, then dramatically sets the bottle down so he can lean forward like he's about to reveal the secrets of the universe or some shit.

189

"I'm gonna try real hard to put myself in your position, because I feel for you."

I reach for my cigarettes. "What the fuck are you talking about?"

"I'm talking about you. *Gia.* You're fucking obsessed with her." He looks around, then back at me. "But the fact is, you knocked up another woman and you need to figure out how you're gonna deal with this."

That sobers me up. I open my eyes wide, needing Visine. And here it comes. Like dominoes, every piece starts to topple on me. Gia, Renee, pregnancy.

"I didn't knock that bitch up. I don't even remember her. Wasn't she with Cash?"

"You fucked her. I remember. Wait, was she with Cash? Look, it doesn't matter. She's saying you're the dad, and until that kid comes out and we can get DNA, you need to figure out what you want to do."

I scrub my hands up and down my face. The sting of Gia last night not trusting me, believing the worst... Actually, it was more than that. I fucking needed her. We are supposed to be a team and she fell apart.

"She's eighteen."

Ammo looks at me "Are you telling me this or telling yourself? Because I love Gia, she's got fucking balls, but this? Can she handle our kind of life?"

"I left her. Just fucked her, picked up my clothes, and left." I lean my head back on the leather booth.

"You need a bump." Ammo takes a snort, then hands me the vial. My head rolls to the side. As I take it from him, a couple of haggard-looking dayshift strippers stumble over.

"You want to party?" They smell like stale cigarettes and knockoff perfume. Rather than smell them, I snort the coke. *There we go.*

I blink as my eyes water for a second. "Fuck." My heart pounds and I can't see straight. All I smell is vanilla sun-kissed skin.

Ammo smirks. "Hello, Sunshine. Ready to rock and roll?"

"Fuck off." I shake my head and run my hands through my hair. He laughs and turns his attention to the strippers.

"Thanks, gorgeous, but we've got to go. You gonna dance for us while we wait?" Ammo slaps the heavier one's ass as she laughs and winks.

"I need to piss." I stand and stretch. One of the numerous things I love about strip clubs is the anonymity. No one makes a big deal about who we are. They seat us in the corner and let us do anything.

"Granger."

I blink over at the front door, squinting to make sure I'm seeing correctly.

"Axel." I hold up my hands, my fingers almost beckoning him. The light from outside fades as the door closes.

"You motherfucker." He charges at me. "You really thought you could fuck my sister and live?"

I don't even get the chance to hold my hands up before I'm lying on the stale, crunchy carpet, while Ammo and a bouncer pull Axel off me.

"Take it outside," the bouncer yells, picking me up as I smile. Yeah, this is what I need. I've been waiting for this.

I spit blood and shake off Ammo. "She's mine, Axel, so fucking deal with it." What few customers there are in this joint start yelling and filming as Ammo pats my shoulder and pushes me toward the door.

"Hey, Axel," the bouncer says as he escorts him outside with me. "You give my best to Blade, man." He lets go of Axel and walks back inside.

We stare at each other. "Look, I should have told you."

"Are you kidding me, Granger? You fucked my sister, then knocked up another bitch?" he explodes. "You just don't learn, do you? Gia's coming home with me. Forget you know her, or I'll kill you."

"Axel, do you think you scare me? I don't give a fuck," I yell at him as the limo pulls up. "Gia's an adult. She can make her own decision—" The sting of his punch makes my head swing to the right, and I wonder if he broke my nose. I don't care. Physical pain always feels better than watching Gia cry.

"Goddammit, Axel, watch his face. He's got to perform in an hour." Ammo stands to my right smoking a cigarette, holding up his hand to stop Ace from interfering.

"That's it, Axel?" I pound my chest. I need this, want this. My fist makes contact with his eye.

Rock God Twins is what they used to call us because we used to look alike, but as we beat the shit out of each other, I realize we look nothing alike. Axel is changing. His eyes have seen and done shit that I don't understand.

"Enough." Ace grabs my arm.

"She's my sister, you fuck," Axel bellows. "Have some respect. I should put a bullet in your head."

"You're so full of shit, Axel. You're gonna put a bullet in my head because I'm in love with Gia?"

We're both panting as he sneers, "Love. You don't even know what that word means. You can't make her happy. You must know deep down that all you'll bring is misery, and I can't have that."

He shakes his head and scowls at me. "Dude, you and I both know you're like Christie." I take a step forward, but Ammo holds me back.

"Come on, brother. We have to go. We're gonna be late."

"You know nothing, Axel, because you're a sociopath," I spit, rage radiating through me as I shake Ammo off. "And if you mention my mother again, I'll put a *bullet* in your ignorant head."

All he does is smile and take a step forward. "I know you, man. Those demons run deep. You don't want your mom brought up, then stay the fuck away from Gia."

I can't hear anymore. I'd rather we beat the shit out of each other than this, the reminder that he's right.

My hands open and close. The skies open and rain pours down on us. "Gia, is *mine*, Axel, and you know it."

Axel snorts. "Oh, really? Let's see how accepting she is when you've got a kid you want her to help raise. That's not her thing, brother." He's not even yelling anymore just stating all this as if it's a fact.

"If you try to take her or tell her lies—" I lunge for him as Ace and Ammo hold me back. Axel stands there, shaking his head, laughing. And all I can think of is if I had a gun he'd be dead. I'd beat that smirk off his face and pull the trigger.

His eyes narrow as he stops laughing. "She's coming with me. Forget you know us." He turns to get on his black Harley.

"Come on, Granger. Let's go, man." Ace pushes me back and opens the limo door as I watch Axel, his hair already dripping wet, start up his bike. He's texting someone.

"Where's Gia? I need a phone." I get in, the adrenaline rushing through me. Ammo and Ace follow and the limo pulls out.

"I took her to the stadium. I'm not gonna lie, she's pretty upset about all of this." Ace's voice is calm, as if he can help me extinguish the murderous rage that runs through my veins.

You can't make her happy... you're just like Christie. I run a hand through my wet hair and realize I'm bleeding. Who cares? He knew exactly how to come at me, exactly how to take me down. This is not about my external bleeding; this is about him threatening my very existence if he gets to her and takes her.

"A phone. Give me one," I bellow. My energy is so off-balance Ace holds up his hands as if that will stop my hemorrhaging.

"Here, man, take a breath." Ace hands me his phone, and for a second I see myself through his eyes, as if I'm in a tunnel. All I see is pity. He thinks I'm nothing but a fucked-up rock star.

I stare at him as he cocks his head at me.

Dismissing me.

Axel, Ace, Ammo the three A's, all of them dismiss me. Staring at me as if I'm crazy. Just one breath away from the psych ward.

Leaning back in the seat, I exhale. I'm calm now. I toss the phone back to Ace, who looks shocked, but catches it.

And I face the truth... *I did this.*

Axel's not gonna take her away. Gia will willingly want to leave me. I thought I was worthy of her, that I could love and be loved. But the universe always reminds me, slaps me in the face and tells me that it's not the case.

My path is alone.

"Granger?" Ace's concerned face comes into focus.

"Fuck it." I turn and look out the window as Mother Nature weeps for me.

CHAPTER 25

GIA

Past – Eighteen years old
San Francisco, California

"Ace, what the fuck are you saying?" Rafe yells next to me on the phone.

I'm wet and cold, and to be honest, I've never been more miserable in my life. Rhys didn't come back last night. My mind was my only company, and it's an awful friend. Every horrible scenario played over and over in my head all night. I might have dozed off around 4:00 a.m., but let's be honest—my nightmares might've been worse than being awake.

I can't eat, and if those fucking groupies shoot me one more dirty look, I will not be held responsible for my actions.

I pull my hand through my long hair trying to keep it out of my face as I hear Rafe saying, "You've got to be kidding me. Does he need a medic?" He looks around, his frown landing on me, and I know something bad has happened.

Is happening.

"Oh God," I whisper, and for the first time in my life, I wish I was religious and believed because it's time to start praying.

My eyes veer back to him. With his tall frame and expensive black suit, he appears strong, confident, and perfect. I barely put on makeup. I've cried so much my eyes are swollen and my cheeks are flushed. I might have made myself sick. My skin's so hot, it's as if I have a fever.

I think I slathered on some red lipstick before I left the hotel. I was going to stay, wait for him to finally come back. But my mind wouldn't stop. I kept imagining Rhys with one of the band's many groupies.

It would help if I could stop crying. But I'm biting back tears while I watch everyone else getting pumped up—all but the lead singer and his guitarist.

Rafe breaks our gaze but continues to yell out demands on the phone and at the road crew. Shivering, I bite my bottom lip.

It's coming.

The final straw. The nail in the coffin. The *thing* that's gonna send me over and make me start screaming and never stop.

Cash is jumping around, stretching in a silver Adidas sweat suit. Thankfully, the rain isn't getting worse. It's sprinkling, and the stage is wet. Numerous guys are on their hands and knees with bar towels trying to make sure no one slips.

Rafe looks down at me, his arms crossed. "How you holding up? You look a little pale." His voice is almost kind, but I'd rather he were a dick.

"I'm fine," I snap at him. Rafe has never been my fan, so being nice tells me it's bad, whatever *it* is.

I point at Renee. "Why is she here?"

Only women who are getting fucked by someone in the band are allowed backstage. I guess since she's telling everyone she's Rhys's baby momma, she thinks she's Queen Bee. Either that, or Rafe is behind it.

"Gia." He looks down at me and sighs. "Look. I told you from day one, something like this would happen. I warned you, did I not?" I go to speak, but he holds up his hand. "This isn't the first time, nor will it be the last." He looks back at the stage. I grab his forearm, his suit feeling like silk, as I fight my need to beg him to help me.

"She's lying. Right?" I need him to say yes, say everything is okay, that whatever *it* was on that phone call is not as bad as I think.

Just help me.

He frowns at me. "I have no idea, Gia. Rhys fucked her on and off. I'd prepare myself that it's his."

The floor rumbles as the crowd becomes electrified, but all I want is for it to open up and take me with it. Swallow me into the earth, just disappear, because my lack of sleep, no food, and fear that I've lost him is making me break.

The crowd roars again, causing me to jump as Nuke walks onto the stage. Strobe lights flash on and off and I think I might puke.

"Then it's true. He fucked her?" I yell at Rafe who's right next to me, his knowing eyes boring down into my head.

"Oh, sweetheart, yes, he's fucked all of them."

"I can't do this." I back away as again the crowd goes wild.

He nods and looks to the stage. "I know you can't."

"Rock Godddd. Aaaccce of Spades. Rock God. Ace of Spades!" they chant.

"Don't make yourself any more sick. You look like you might pass out. I have someone who's going to help you." He speaks to me soothingly like I'm a wounded animal or hurt child.

I nod like a zombie, not understanding anything he's saying except that Rhys fucked her and that he warned me.

"It was nice meeting you, Gia Fontaine." My eyes dart to him, watching as he walks away. And I'm alone.

Alone with forty-thousand adoring fans.

"Gia." I take a breath because this might be when I really do snap. His whore can't really have the gall to speak to me. I turn and stare at her stomach as though I'm watching a car accident and can't look away.

"I thought you might want to see a picture of his son?" Her fucking accent makes me grit my teeth as I look up at her pretty face. Glancing over her shoulder, I see her posse of bitches behind her.

It dawns on me that I never fit in. The whole time I've been on tour, not once have any of them ever smiled at me or said hello.

"What?" I yell, barely able to hear. Cash has taken the stage. His bass guitar is so loud my ears are ringing.

"Our baby. Mine and Rhys's. I have my latest ultrasound photo, and I figured since you might be like his second mommy, you and I should become friends." She shoves it into my numb hands as I stare at a black-and-white picture of an ultrasound, I guess.

Tears fall, and for the first time in my life, I couldn't care less that I'm showing this woman my pain.

"Look, I'm going to be honest since you look like you're... not well. I'm not going away, Gia. I'm having his baby. It's only a matter of time before I'm back in his bed. Having a child with someone creates a bond that can never be broken."

"Get the fuck away from me," I yell, dropping the picture.

She cocks her head as if she's trying to decide if I'm gonna fight, and like a dumb bitch, she has to have the last word.

"I will, but your days are numbered."

I almost start laughing, because *numbered*? My days are done. He's stripped me of my dignity. I don't even recognize myself.

Except that I can feel him. He's coming. No matter what logic my head tells my heart, it still beats for him.

Only him.

I watch as he and Ammo enter. He's everything, a god surrounded by mere mortals. I wanted so badly to be what he needed. I believed that I could be enough for him.

My eyes move to Ammo who drinks from a bottle of Jägermeister and strips off his wet shirt. He slings his guitar over his neck.

I back away, wanting to run, but can't because no matter how much he hurts me, he is and always will be my soul.

He holds up a hand and takes a towel to wipe his face, then looks up, his eyes searching for me.

Everything fades.

Time stops.

Voices, music, the crowd gone.

He looks at me, and my heart, which I didn't think could break any more, rips in two as I watch him come for me.

My throat tightens and it's hard to breathe. I barely notice that his nose is bloody and his lip is swollen. He looks like he got hit by a truck, but I know better.

"What happened to you?" The hurt that's been piling up seems to reflect in his eyes.

"Everything." The crowd roars as Ammo takes the stage, and I can tell I'm losing him. I can't share him anymore. He wasn't mine to begin with; he was always theirs.

Rhys belongs to his fans, the nameless masses that adore and worship him.

"If this baby is yours, do you plan on being in its life?" He cocks his head as his eyes caress my face.

"All I do is make you cry." He frowns as he reaches to touch me, but I back away. His hand drops and his eyes change.

And I know that he's guilty of all his sins.

"I have to go."

I nod *yes,* then fight myself and almost grab his hand. Almost beg him to reassure me about way too many things. Because in twenty-four hours, everything has changed.

He starts to walk to the stage, and I yell. "Yes or no?"

He looks up and his eyes mirror my pain. A knife twists deep in my heart as I wait for him to make me bleed.

"If that child is mine... Yes. I will raise it."

I choke back the lump that seems to want to strangle me, and nod again as I watch him walk onto the stage.

The floor seems to be alive with their excitement. Only a few lead singers are great. Rhys Granger is one of them.

This is our goodbye. I allow myself this last bit of love, knowing I will never listen to him again.

"Gia." Slowly, as if in a dream, I face my big brother. He takes one look at me and pulls me into his arms, shielding me like he always has from any pain.

But he's too late. I'm bleeding like someone has opened a vein and I'm drowning in blood.

"This hurts," I cry into his shirt.

"Fuck him."

I close my eyes as Rhys's voice ricochets around the stadium. Burrowing my head in Axel's shirt, I finally let it out in loud, gut-wrenching tears. His arms hold me as I sob and try to talk, knowing he can't hear me with all the noise. It doesn't matter. I don't even care that I can't seem to stop. It doesn't matter because Axel is here and I'm not alone.

"Piece of shit." Axel strokes my hair. "I'd kill him, but by the look of things, I think you did the job for me. He can fucking wallow and slowly die in his own misery," he snarls.

I shake my head as I gasp for air. I've cried so much, I'm forced to breathe through my mouth.

"I love him."

He takes a deep breath and releases it. "You're eighteen," he grits out, as though trying not to lose patience. "You'll go back to college and find someone else. Fucking Granger will be nothing but a bad memory."

"You think he got her pregnant?" I say to the air, since I'm holding onto his T-shirt, staring blankly at all the insanity happening around us.

Axel snorts. "Of course, he did. This is his pattern, Gia. Why would you want to surround yourself with this shit? You'll be miserable. Look at you already." My heart squeezes. He's right—I know he is.

"He's my everything. You don't understand what that means, that I'm not me without him." I pull back so he can see the truth. The music is so loud it's vibrating through my chest.

"He's not good. He's not the man for you." I stare blankly as his words almost take me down.

"He's good," I yell.

Axel stares at me as if I'm lying. My mind battles my heart. Can I really live with all this? Can I let him destroy me with other women and being a father to babies that are not mine?

I can't.

But thinking that and actually making myself leave him, giving up on everything that I dreamed about? That's the crazy thing about dreams—they can turn into nightmares real fast.

"I'm gonna get my bike. If I stay any longer, I may get violent. The decision is yours."

I back up and wipe under my eyes as I try to smile reassuringly at him. If I don't want him to kill Rhys, I need to go.

"Give me a second."

He looks down at me, then over at the stage. "Make it fast." His blue eyes hold mine, and that's the last of his patience. He's done.

Nodding, I turn to watch Rhys one last time. He's mesmerizing. Beautiful and not mine.

All I do is make you cry.

One foot in front of another, I walk. Passing roadies that give me sympathetic nods. Passing Rafe and Renee as my face burns with humiliation.

I. Don't. Belong. Here.

I push back my hair, vaguely caring that I'm leaving without my suitcase. All it would do is remind me of him anyway. I have everything I need in my bag.

I start to run and nearly trip down the steps leading to the parking lot. Stopping, I look up at the dark sky.

"Why?" I scream as the rain picks up and my body shivers. I want to sink to my knees and let the water sweep me away.

"Why?" I scream again, this time turning, knowing that he's here. My heart races as an angry zigzag brightens the night and I see Rhys's beautiful face. He stands in the rain, his dark hair wet, his eyes full of pain. I open my mouth to scream my rage at him, wanting to beat on him, scratch him, make him bleed like me.

He looks over at my brother's bike. Surely, he'll stop me...

He doesn't.

Pain. It's agonizing, almost as if I can't survive another moment. But I do. I breathe in and out as I make my way over to Axel.

I hesitate. He said he loved me... he made me believe. Yet Rhys stands in the rain, the concert raging behind us.

I get on the bike, wondering how I will live with this agony.

He was the one.

My heart beats for him, and now it's over.

It will never beat the same again.

PART 2

CHAPTER 26

RHYS

Present – Thirty-five years old
Paris, France

"**W**hy?" *she yells at me. Her long, wet hair sticks to her face. This is the moment I die and become reborn.*

Her grief will heal; mine will fester and ooze its poison, growing stronger each day until my heart will not beat for her anymore.

She is, was, my anchor. My fucking lifeline to the real me.

I watch her beautiful face in the moonlight, her pale skin never looking more striking at this moment. She backs away from me, taking my soul with her.

Agonizing pain seizes my chest as I let her.

I don't reach for her.

I don't stop her.

"Granger?" Rafe's voice brings me back to the large, private room at Hôtel Ritz Paris. Five suits sit with Rafe and the band. My eyes go back to staring out the window and the wet streets. Rain, always rain.

I clear my voice as I get my head back in the game. I'm not the same man who let her ride out of my life. It's been years, and still a day hasn't gone by that I haven't thought about her, wondered if I'd see her in a crowd.

So seeing her laughing with some man was a bit of a surprise. I lost my shit on him. The thought that he's been inside her... Fuck it, no one's perfect. Least of all me.

I turn to the conference table. Cash is on his phone, Nuke is nodding off, and the only one who looks interested is Ammo.

I lean forward and reach for a pack of cigarettes, not caring that I'm invading a producer's space.

A loud snore comes from Nuke's mouth. His head bobs up and he straightens, blinking as if he's confused about what's happening.

Life has been tough for Nuke. He's my brother. I tried to be there for him. He's been in and out of rehab, and if his nodding off is any indication, I'd guess he's using again.

I light my cigarette. It's fucking amazing that we're still together. Cash looks at Nuke and rolls his eyes. If any of us has completely pulled away, it's Cash, but that was after the bomb was dropped. Meaning, I got the paternity test back and Cash was the father of Chase, not me.

Yeah, my life was destroyed, and he never once spoke up, never once said, "Hey, I was fucking Renee too." I lost Gia over that shit. But I moved on and tried not to hold a grudge. Cash shows up and he's a beast on the bass. As for everything else? We don't talk about it.

Professionally, we're thriving. Success seems to favor us, even when our personal lives tank.

The Stuffed Muffins rise no matter what. I turn again and lean my hand against the glass window. Paris, Fashion Week—I came here because I've gotten back with my on again, off again model girlfriend.

I'm trying to be supportive and show up when she walks the runway. I guess you could say Paulette's the closest I've come to having a relationship in all these years. I'm thirty-five, our last album *Untouched* went platinum and stayed number one on the charts for months.

"Is there anything you want, Granger? This is going to be a major motion picture, a gritty look at the band, your pasts, and your future in the rock and roll world," Stanley announces. He's the bigwig at Weddington Studios.

I know I shouldn't do it. I need to leave her alone. She's successful and seems happy. But my heart still beats for her. Or maybe it's just my cock that beats for her. Whatever, I can't seem to find peace. I'm obsessed with a green-eyed goddess.

She's my muse... *Goddammit*.

"Yeah, I do want something. I pick the DP and the photographer, or I walk," I state, causing the whole room to stop what they're doing and stare at me.

Someone clears their throat, and I grin at the stunned executives and Rafe who looks like he's ready to lose it. He's not stupid. He knows.

The execs glance around at the band. Ammo leans back in his chair with his arms crossed behind his head.

"Who'd you have in mind, brother?" He smirks.

Stanley clears his throat and leans back in the leather chair. "The thing is, Granger, production has started. We have an award-winning DP, and he has his crew. As for the photographer, we thought we would hire a few to give the band that gritty look. You can't be serious. We're paying you a small fortune." His eyes narrow and he reaches for a Fiji water.

I nod. "I'm dead serious. I have more money than anyone should. A movie about us does nothing for me. I can't speak for my bandmates. They can do whatever they want, but I don't allow the cameras near me unless you use who I want." I put out my cigarette and move toward the door as Stanley stands.

"Who do you want?"

I smile and walk back over, pulling out a chair to drop into. "Gia Fontaine and Sebastian Knight."

"You got to be shitting me?" Cash looks up from his phone and shakes his head.

Stanley leans back to look at me. "Unfortunately, Gia Fontaine has passed on our offer. We wanted her first. She said for the right price she'd consider selling some early pictures of the band, but to go on tour and be our visionary, she declined."

"Well then, I'm not available." I hold up my hands and look around the table, first at the suits who seem uncomfortable, and at Ammo who throws his head back and laughs.

"Fuck it." He stands. "I'm with you, brother. He's right. Gia Fontaine is the only one who truly knows this band, so make the magic happen."

Stanley looks stunned and aggravated. "I... is this what you all want?" He looks at Rafe as if that's gonna make me change my mind.

Cash stands. "Get Gia or I walk also." He nods at me as he walks by.

I knock on the table. "There you have it. The Stuffed Muffins have spoken. Make it happen, Stanley." All eyes turn to Nuke who still sits passed out.

I almost snort, but I'm not that dick anymore. I can't point fingers. Nuke is dealing with things the way he does. I'm no better.

"Now if you'll excuse me, I do need to go watch my girlfriend walk the runway in thirty minutes. I leave you in the capable hands of Rafe." I stand.

Stanley looks down at the papers in front of him as his assistant types on his phone and shows it to Stanley. "This is the Sebastian Knight you're talking about?" He holds the phone out, and there's the motherfucker's face on IMDb.

"Yep, that's him. An up-and-comer. You'll love him. Very production friendly," I say over my shoulder. "Go after him first. You get Sebastian, you'll get Gia."

Rafe stands as I pass. "Gentlemen, excuse me. I need a moment with the Rock God." He walks next to me as I exit the room.

"What are you doing? *Gia?* And Sebastian Knight? He's threatening a lawsuit against you."

I look down the elegant hallway and back at him. "I'm sure he'll drop the suit. We're offering him a chance to go from a nobody to an actual DP. What time is it?" I smirk. "And if you're worried about it, make him sign something."

"Fuck you, Granger. Why now? After all these years you really want to put yourself and her through this?" he sneers. "You see her one time"—he holds up a finger—"for a few minutes, and you're bribing her with her boyfriend?"

A couple of girls are giggling and watching us about ten feet away. I smile at them and wave. "We love you," they say as they film me, then bolt down the hall.

"That's exactly what I'm doing. Make it happen." I start to walk.

"Just tell me why," he calls after me.

"Because I've been dead inside, and spending that one moment with her"—I turn to look at him—"made me feel alive."

Rafe shakes his head. "I don't like this."

I nod. "She's my muse."

"Shut up with that muse shit, Granger." He rubs the back of his neck. "Fine, I'll get it done. What about Axel?"

I laugh. "Axel loves us." I start down the hall. "Make Gia an offer she can't refuse."

"And Paulette?" he yells.

"She's not my muse," I yell back into the large hallway, smiling as I hear him curse.

CHAPTER 27

GIA
Present – Twenty-five years old
Paris, France

My phone is ringing *again*. With a sigh, I roll over and push my eye mask up to look at my phone.

"Jeff, I hate you." I'm tempted to block him and his numerous missed calls, but he's such a lunatic, he might just get on a plane. So I text, *Sleeping,* then toss my phone back on the nightstand. I pull my eye mask down and turn to my side. If I can get another hour, that would be amazing. I take a deep breath and let it out, trying to relax my mind, but all I see are bourbon eyes, full lips, and dark, wild hair.

"Goddammit." I roll to my back. The room is silent, save for the gentle click of the heat turning on. I hate feeling like this, and by this, I mean remembering. Thank God I have my job to distract me. Fashion Week turned out way better than I expected.

I worked all day, came back to my room, ordered room service, and watched *Jeopardy*. Sebastian did the party scene, so that kept everyone happy and took away the stress of running into *him*.

I sigh. Clearly, I'm not going back to sleep. Sitting up, I toss the eye mask and glance at my surroundings, not really seeing them.

I need coffee and a cigarette. I lean over to dial room service and pick up my iPhone to translate that I'd like coffee, eggs, bacon, and a bagel with cream cheese.

I love this feature on my phone. They probably think I'm crazy, but whatever. I lean my head back and try to figure out what I'm gonna do. I'm supposed to return to LA for a quick job, but I might cancel it since New York is starting to look good. It has Julianna and no Jeff.

Great, I'm in another shit mood. This is becoming my new norm lately. Where's that pack of cigarettes I bought the other day? I bite my bottom lip. I'd quit until the run-in with *him*.

Asshole.

I haven't said his name once since I got on the back of my brother's bike that rainy day. I basically considered him dead... until he became alive again.

I grab my hair and roughly put it into a messy bun as I remember...

Everything.

Not being able to function and locking myself in Axel's room *for days*. Fucking pathetic. No man is worth that.

I try to block out that time of my life since all it does is piss me off. I wasted so much heartache on him. Didn't eat, didn't sleep. God, I think I dropped ten pounds, and I was thin to begin with. Poor Julianna had to come and get me. Otherwise, there's no way I would have made it back to school that semester.

Then dealing with my mom flip-flopping between sympathy and her I-told-you-so crap. That's what made me get my ass into Julianna's BMW and go back to Berkeley with her. The thought of having to live with my mom in that neighborhood and looking across the street at his mom's house was not an option.

But I survived. Standing, I stretch to get all the kinks out. Might as well pack since I'm heading back to the States in the morning. A small tap on the door alerts me that room service has arrived. That was fast, or I've been so caught up in the past I don't even realize how much time passed.

"Coming," I yell, which is stupid because most rooms are pretty soundproof. Thank God my coffee is here. I'm completely jet-lagged. I feel like I could drink a gallon, that's how sluggish I am. I grab a robe and open the door.

"Good morning, gorgeous." Sebastian winks at me, leaning against the doorframe, wearing a black beret.

"Jesus." I roll my eyes at him. He's ridiculous in all the right ways. I also know him—he's either plotting or wants something. I step aside, letting the room service guy in. He sets the large silver tray on the table.

"Grumpy bear." Sebastian grabs me and picks me up as I scream and laugh.

"I am. So don't bug me. I need coffee." I shake my head and slap his chest as I smile at the room service guy. As I sign the check, I try not to tumble out of Sebastian's arms.

"Merci," Sebastian says to the retreating back of the poor service guy as he dumps me on the bed.

"Oh my God, what's going on?" I sit up, feeling Sebastian's eyes travel the length of my legs. He turns to look at the room service tray. I know Sebastian still thinks he has feelings for me. I catch him staring at me sometimes and pretend I don't see it. Like right now, I focus on how excited he is rather than the fact that he was staring at my legs.

"Do I need coffee first?" I reach for the silver pot.

"I need you to do this for me. This is me calling in my best friend card or old lover, partner, whatever-you-want-to-call-us favor."

Christ, he's still hoping. I sigh as I pour myself a cup. "You know I'll always say yes to you." Sitting on the end of the bed, I cross my legs, making sure the robe covers them.

I need to get better about this. We're so close that sometimes I forget he's a straight man. I mean, I don't, but we used to fuck, so I'm comfortable around him. Lately he's been hinting that if I need him, he'll be happy to take the edge off for me. My sex life is so bad that it's a bummer I can't accept the offer. Sebastian is fantastic at making a girl come.

I can't though. I need his friendship more than an orgasm.

"Wait, what's going on?"

"They haven't contacted you yet?" He sits down in the big arched chair. Stretching his long legs out, he crosses them at the ankles, then takes off his beret and runs his hands through his curls.

My eyes narrow on him. "Is this what Jeff is calling nonstop about?" I sip my coffee and open the top of the container for my eggs and bacon.

"You want some? I'll never eat all this. And they only gave me one coffee cup, so get a glass from the minibar area." I pick up a piece of bacon.

"Gia."

"Yeah?" I say, almost choking on the bacon with the way his face is looking. "What? Clearly you have good news. Why are you dragging this out?"

"Because I thought you knew." His eyes find mine. Again, the bacon kind of gets caught in the back of my throat as I swallow it down.

"I've been offered to be director of photography on a major motion picture," he yells.

"What?" I shout, because are you kidding me? No one works harder than Sebastian.

"Oh my God, I'm so happy." I drop the bacon and throw myself into his arms. "I knew it was only a matter of time until the world saw how amazingly talented you are."

He smiles, and for a split second I see Rhys's smile instead. Goddammit, why can't Sebastian be the one my heart beats for?

"They offered it to both of us." He laughs.

"What?" I pull back as dread, or adrenaline, makes my stomach flip. All of a sudden, I can't breathe.

"As a team. I'm the DP and you're the photographer." He motions with his hands, and suddenly it all falls into place. I rub my temples.

"Please tell me this is not The Stuffed Muffins movie." My chest tightens.

"So, they did ask you?"

"No. I mean, yes, they did, but I said no." I start to pace. I do this when I get nervous or pressured.

"Sebastian, I can't be a part of it. You take it though." He simply stares at me. "Stop it," I continue. "They don't need me." I point at him, but the fact is they do. No one has more photos of that band than me. I have pictures back from when I was seven, eight years old with my first Nikon.

"I already passed on this. What the fuck?" I look up at the ceiling and shake my head. "Who asked you?"

"The *head* of Weddington Studios. This is a once-in-a-lifetime opportunity for me. I need you to say yes." Gone is my playful Sebastian. He's full-on asking me to do this as a favor to him. How can I tell him no? He's been there for me through everything, unknowingly keeping me going. But what he's asking for is not the end of the world. Rhys Granger is my past. I need to think about my future, and this would be amazing on my résumé. In reality, I'll hardly deal with him. It'll be the director and me, along with Sebastian.

"Fine. If you need me, I'm there for you." I smile at him. It's either that or burst into tears that he's throwing me into the lion's den.

Because I'm lying. Rhys is the only person who's dangerous to me.

"Gia. *Gia*." He grabs me and hugs me again. "Do you realize what this means? I don't want to jinx us, but with this kind of budget to work with, and our creativity and the popularity and allure of The Stuffed Muffins..." He pulls back and I look into his brown eyes—they're full of excitement.

Sebastian is passionate about his craft. He loves making the magic happen so much that you can't help but get caught up in his enthusiasm. Spinning me, he tugs me close to slow dance and murmurs in my ear, "Hunter Falcon's directing it. We're gonna get an Academy Award. I can feel it. My cock is getting hard."

I pull back again, choosing to ignore the last comment, and focus on Hunter. "You're kidding?" Hunter Falcon is fucking huge.

He smirks. His split lip from Rhys is only now starting to heal. "Apparently, he's a huge fan of The Stuffed Muffins. He was the one who approached them about a behind-the-scenes movie. Just get in there with them, see the real band. I already talked to him on the phone. He's beyond excited to be working with us."

I raise an eyebrow at him. Clearly, he knew he would wear me down and I'd agree. It kind of sucks that I hate *him* because Hunter Falcon is a big deal. The prospect of working with him is exciting.

"So, I take it you're not suing him anymore?" I turn back to my breakfast that suddenly holds no taste.

"Gia, sit." He takes my hand and brings me to the silk couch. "Tell me the truth. What's the history between you and Granger?"

"Why? Are you going to say I shouldn't worry about doing the movie with you?" He frowns and sits back as I jump up for my bag and cigarettes.

"So he's the reason why." He looks down at his shoes, not asking the question.

"What are you talking about?" I snap. "You have been given an amazing opportunity and I'm thrilled for you. But I can't deal with all the psychoanalyzing me and shit." At last, I retrieve the pack from the bottom of my giant purse.

"Huh," is all he says as I roll my eyes and light up.

"Don't, please, not right now." I sit next to him, blowing smoke at the ceiling.

"Well." He slaps the couch and stands. "I know two things, my beauty." He leans down to kiss the top of my head as I stare straight ahead, smoking.

"One, you should not be smoking. And two... you need to do this movie." My eyes shift to his. "Good, bad, or ugly, you're finally gonna be free, babe."

"I'm already free." I recross my legs and tighten the top of the robe around me, as if that can shield me from his knowing eyes.

"No. You're locked in a cage of your own doing. Maybe Granger can wake you up." He smiles and heads for the door, taking a piece of bacon with him. "And if he doesn't, you're gonna make enough money to hire the best psychiatrist. Look at it that way."

I cock my head, my eyes narrowing on him.

"Oh, and Jeff wants you to call him," he says over his shoulder.

The door shuts and I take a breath, my leg bouncing up and down. What the hell? Sebastian did not at all get the fact that I'm sacrificing for him. In fact, he's acting like this is good for me.

Screw this. I jump up, clamping the cigarette in my teeth and throwing the closet door open to grab my huge suitcase. I'm not one of those people who unpacks when they travel, so my suitcase is a mess. Whatever. I'll organize later.

I drop to my knees and fish around for Rip's latest and greatest strain, which he gave me a few weeks ago to try.

Rip is partners with my brother and part of the Disciples. They own a bunch of cannabis dispensaries in Los Angeles.

Smoking weed is not really my thing. It's Axel's drug of choice, but I ran into Rip at the supermarket of all places, told him I was dreading coming here, and he insisted I take some of his stuff, stating that if anyone needed it, I did. I probably should have been insulted, but it's Rip, so whatever. He did give me a prescription note in case customs stopped me.

Well, today's the day. I was going to walk around Paris and enjoy my last day, but maybe I'll get high and go back to sleep.

I dig around, finding all kinds of film cannisters but not the one container I'm looking for. I'm about ready to give up and order a bottle of Cristal champagne and bill it to Sebastian's room when I find it.

Three joints. I take one out and toss the container back into my suitcase. Using my cigarette, I light it up, inhale, hold, and inhale again, then slowly let it out. Hmm, kind of citrus flavored. Leaning back on my suitcase, I inhale again and raise one leg, wondering if I should get a tattoo on my ankle or maybe my foot.

Loud pounding on the door makes me drop my cigarette on the floor. Thankfully, the joint is in my mouth. I try not to scream and drop it also. What the fuck?

"God, Sebastian." I pick up the cigarette and use my foot to rub the carpet as the black soot turns gray.

The pounding continues as I march over to the door, joint in one hand, cigarette in the other.

"Sebastian. What now? I'm trying to meditate all my negativity awa—" I swing the door open dramatically.

Only it isn't Sebastian.

Holy fuck, it's Rhys.

CHAPTER 28

RHYS

Present – Thirty-five years old
Paris, France

Why I'm standing outside her door pounding on it instead of making an appearance at the runway show is beyond me. I can't even remember the designer, but Paulette is in it.

I said I'd show up. I should. I owe her that, I guess... even if it is only for show.

It's been time to break it off with Paulette for a while. And since I just spent ten minutes flirting with a receptionist, taking selfies with her and fans, all so she'd give me Gia's room number, I'd say Paulette needs to go.

I almost get my phone to text it to her, but that's a dick move, and I don't do dick moves anymore.

So here I stand outside room 696.

Needing to break up with Paulette, but so obsessed that I have to see her. Call it unhealthy. I don't care. I just want to be near her, even if it's for two minutes.

I pound on the door more forcefully than I need to. Adrenaline pumps through my veins.

Christ, I didn't think this through. I want her, so here I am. Unfortunately, if Sebastian is with her in her room, I might lose it again. Which would be unfortunate since I've made him the DP.

I take a breath and wait to pound again, not trusting myself, though at least I'm acknowledging it. The other day filters through my mind. I should have been fine. It's not like I haven't run into plenty of women I used to fuck yet didn't look twice.

But none of those women were Gia.

She's mine.

I knew she was in that restaurant the moment I set foot in it. Because I can *feel* her. What I didn't factor in was Sebastian. Seeing her with him set me off. For a split second, all the rage and pain brewing inside me for almost seven years came out.

All I heard in my head was *he's been inside her.* I wanted to kill him for being able to touch what's mine. I take a breath. If he's in there with her... I pound again and hear a squeal.

"Sebastian. What now? I'm trying to meditate all my negativity awa—" The door swings open.

Gia Fucking Fontaine in all her glory.

I almost reach to rub my chest because just looking at her hurts. *She thought I was Sebastian.*

I want to wrap my hands around her beautiful neck. Bring her ripe lips to mine and fuck the thought of any man out of her head. Go all caveman and shit and keep her with me twenty-four seven. That's the thing about obsessions. They grow and snake their way inside your head until you're consumed.

She stands in a white hotel robe, her naturally tan skin glowing with health. My eyes trail to the V of the robe, which is open enough to allow my eyes a glimpse of her full breasts.

She's fucking magnificent.

My cock bulges at the thought of her hard nipples.

She's also holding a joint in one hand, and a cigarette in the other. My mouth twitches, this ought to be interesting.

"Rhys," she states. Her eyes narrow, and for a split second, I see her pain. It's gone as fast as she tries to slam the door on me. I stop it easily with my hand and walk in.

"Excuse me? Get the fuck out. *Granger.*" She sashays by me as I catch a whiff of her scent. Vanilla beans, coffee, and whatever shit she's smoking.

Jesus Christ, she's high as a kite.

"You've got some nerve. I knew you were an egomaniac, but using Sebastian to get me to do your movie is fucking—"

"Watch it, Brat. I'm giving your boyfriend a career and you know it," I snarl, my blood pumping. I haven't felt this good, this interested, in years.

For a second, she blinks at me as if she's trying to come up with something to say but can't.

I grin at her. She frowns and walks over to the phone. "Do I need to call security?"

I sit down on her couch and prop my hands behind my head. "Why would you do that? I'm not gonna bite... yet." She slams the phone down.

"Look, I don't want to fight. I agreed to do the movie so get—"

"You gonna share that or just wave it around?" I interrupt her as I motion to the joint with my head.

"Wait, what?" I can tell she wants to go off but can't do it justice. I smile. Can't help

it.

"Sit, Brat. The least you can do is share what I'm assuming is making you feel pretty goddamn good. Then we can hash it, you can have at it, tell me how I hurt you—"

"You didn't hurt me," she says. "You destroyed me." She drops down onto the couch. Her words are fierce, yet her body heat radiates off her and into me.

She needs to be fucked and hard. I take the joint from her and it's like a fucking electric volt zaps us with that single touch. She feels it also—her lips puff out a little air and her chest becomes flushed.

Her eyes trail down my body, and I lift my hips to pull out my lighter.

"Axel's latest strain?" My voice makes her eyes blink back up to my face and she leans back and smiles.

"No, Rip's."

I almost demand, *Who the fuck is Rip?* but I light the joint and inhale deeply, then take more as I hold, feel the magic, and slowly exhale.

"This is good shit, Brat. This Rip's a dealer?" She smiles, and again my heart burns, aches as I bring the joint back to my lips.

"He's partners with Axel, not that it's any of your business."

I lean my head back and inhale again, then hand it to her as my eyes watch her every move. Blowing the smoke at the ceiling, I say, "Axel's done well for himself. Twins, marriage…"

"They're not married yet," she retorts. "He saved your ass, so yeah, Axel is doing amazing."

I roll my head to look at her. "What are you talking about?"

"'Untouched.' It put you guys on the top again, and that was all my brother." Venom drips from her pretty lips.

"Huh." I nod. "Say it, Gia. Let out all the anger that's eating you up."

She leans on her elbow. "Fine." Her eyes narrow on me. She hesitates as if she's almost startled by the way I look, then licks her lips… as if my dick isn't hard enough.

"I don't know why you want me on this job. It's shitty that you're using Sebastian and my love for him to get to me. But most of all, I can't stand you. Everything I thought you were was a lie. I loved you and you betrayed me." Her chest heaves and her eyes swim with angry tears. But all I hear is love and Sebastian, and I'm glad the fucking man isn't here. I should get up and leave. This is going to get ugly, but ugly is how she left it.

Unfinished. So, I guess today we finish it.

"Brat, the fact is, you couldn't handle this life. You didn't trust me. You left me. You believed everybody but me about that fucking pregnancy. I told you that baby wasn't mine." I sit up, my hands clenching as I try not to throw something.

"I waited for you, thinking you'd come back after it was all over the news that the kid was Cash's. But nothing. So fucking hate me, but at least get the facts straight, baby."

"Oh, trust me, I'm not your baby, and I don't hate you, Rhys. I *loathe* you, despise you, my skin crawls if I hear your crappy, sellout music on the radio. I used to think you were a musical genius." She snorts. "You're nothing but a mediocre musician, at best."

My nostrils flare as I watch the play of emotions on her face. I can sense her need, almost smell her fucking wet cunt.

"Admit it, *Granger*, you sold your soul to be a fucking star." The room is silent besides our breathing. My eyes caress her face and lying mouth, which is almost trembling.

"You need to be fucked, Gia," I grunt into her shocked mouth. "I wanted to kill Sebastian, fucking beat him until he couldn't ever touch you again, but looking at you makes me actually feel sorry for him."

"Get out," she pants as my hand wraps around her neck.

"I'm not going anywhere." I take her mouth. I'm not being gentle because she doesn't need gentle. It's rough and deep. Her tongue twists with mine. She tastes like fucking coffee and maple.

I open her robe and almost fucking come. She has her right nipple pierced. It's then that it all falls into place for me.

She has and always will be mine. My muse. Sinking to my knees, I go straight for her wet cunt, sucking on her clit hard as my thumb rubs the gold hoop on her nipple back and forth.

"Oh fuck," she groans and spreads her legs wider.

I latch onto her pink clit and suck as she tugs on my hair. Unbuttoning my pants, I grab my cock, ready to jerk it. I can tell she's close.

She freezes as her body jerks and pulses in my mouth, her face thrown back, and I give her one more suck, watching all the emotions play out on her face. I stand, towering over her as her eyes lock with mine. It's all there, her anger at letting me make her come, her pain, and most of all, her hate.

And I fucking love it. I kick my shoes off and jerk my jeans down. Grabbing my cock, I start to slide my hand up and down, jerking my hand on my piercing.

"That's it, Brat." I don't think my dick has ever been this hard. There's something intoxicating about being this connected with someone because she's fucking primal, wild right now. She's at war with herself, and that turns me on.

Power. It flows through me as I sit, spread my legs, and grab her hips so she can straddle me.

"Now, fuck me hard. I want to feel how much you despise me." With eyes like glittering gems, she takes over. Nails dig into my chest, and she drags them across my abs. The sting makes me growl as her lips hover over my mouth.

She wants my soul.

The truth is, I gave it to her years ago.

"Fuck me, baby," I demand as she grabs my cock, impaling herself on it in one fast thrust.

"I do hate you. I fucking hate you more than you can imagine." Her tight cunt is so wet and hot that I grab her hips, needing her to move.

She smiles and her lips take mine, her tongue twisting as we fall back into our own rhythm. Her hands reach around for mine and she removes them. Then I'm gone. When she stops kissing me, her hands move to the back of the couch on both sides of my head and she raises herself slowly off me, then thrusts down hard as we both groan.

"Jesus." My nostrils flare as she fucks me. Her full tits hit my face. As I bite and suck on the piercing, she rams her wet core up and down on me.

"I hate you," she hisses like a feral cat, nails digging into the couch as she pounds herself on me. Her head is thrown back, and if I died right now, I'd be fine. I'll never have this connection with anyone but her. It's raw and powerful, fucking ecstasy. She jerks her hot, slick cunt greedily on my hard cock. Thrusting and rubbing her clit on me, she works us into a frenzy and I let go. Fucking soar as I call her name. My hands grasp her ass, and my piercing hits her G-spot. Her cunt grabs my cock and we both go off together.

"Fuck," I say hoarsely as my cock fills her cunt. She collapses on me, her lips and breath cooling my neck. Our bodies are slick with sweat as we both try to come back to earth.

Slowly she lifts her head and we stare at each other, her finger tracing my lips as she lets me stay inside her. Be with her.

She seems calm, connected.

"Gia."

Slowly, she lifts herself off me. And I know that we are not over, that she will and always has been mine.

My muse.

She stands, her hair having come loose in our primal fucking. It flows in wild disarray around her face.

She says nothing but turns and walks to the bathroom, slamming the door. What the hell just happened? I look at the closed door and smooth my hand up and down my face. Christ, that was more than casual fucking. Neither of us expected something that intense.

I jerk my jeans up and put on my shoes as the shower turns on.

"Fuck." I grab my cigarettes, lighting up as I make my way to the door. I'm not sure what I expected to happen, but mind-altering fucking was not it. I bring the cigarette to my lips and smell her on my fingers, my shirt, *goddammit.*

I've got to get out of here. I don't trust myself to stay. There are things I need to clean up in my life. And we both need time to cool down and process what just happened, because now I want more.

Fuck that, I want all of her. I pull out my phone and press on Rafe's number.

"What?" he snaps.

"Get her to sign the contracts and tell them I'm ready to start filming. *Now.*"

I hang up before he can respond. Rafe will get her to sign. She's in too deep now not to. We both know it.

Good or bad, it's time.

CHAPTER 29

GIA

Present – Twenty-five years old
On the way to London, England

"Granger, I love you." "Ammo, I want you." "Rock God, Cashhhh, over here." Their screams make my already limited amount of patience drop to zero.

"Nuke, Cash, remember me? Rock God..." I stand patiently and watch all the usual chaos. This is the madness that happens whenever you travel with them. Yet today, I'm not in the mood. We're preparing to fly to London, but the fans essentially attacked us when we made our way across the tarmac. Thank God they have Ace and his crew. I know Rhys hates having security but they... he needs it.

"Hunter, what's it like hanging out with The Stuffed Muffins?" I roll my eyes at the kiss-ass paparazzi.

Hunter either is a pro at working the room, or he loves them. God, he's almost as coveted as all The Stuffed Muffins combined. They have that in common. Every member of The Stuffed Muffins is to-die-for hot, and Hunter Falcon fits right in with his California surfer boy look.

He's also a machine. I don't know how he does it, but he never gets tired. He's probably ten years older than me, but the man can shoot all night, get three hours of sleep, then text me because he came up with a great idea about following Cash around as he goes on his morning runs.

That might be why I'm so burned out already. Because I don't care that Cash runs every day.

I almost told him that this morning. But knowing Hunter, he would have had Sebastian turn the camera on me.

That's another thing I'm going to have to deal with. Not only is Hunter a consummate flirt, he desperately wants to interview me. I have declined that along with a lot of dinner dates.

I look down at my white sneakers. I rushed to get ready, so my hair is piled on top of my head in a messy bun and I'm wearing light makeup: mascara and red lipstick. Which is stupid since everyone is always late. I lift my camera and snap some shots of Nuke. He's laughing, and even though it's freezing and slightly raining, he's still shirtless. It works for him. His body is all muscle and lean. But I can't remember seeing him in a shirt in the week that we've been filming.

"Stop it." Sebastian smirks at me. I look up at him. I guess he saw the eye rolls.

"What? I'm tired," I groan as he wraps an arm around me.

"Do you need a Valium? I can feel your energy." He looks concerned. I wish I could reassure him, but honestly, the lack of sleep and being around Rhys is messing with me.

"If they'd get their asses on the jet, we'd be there in no time," I grumble, ignoring the throngs of women surrounding Rhys.

"Why can't I just take the train?" I look up at Sebastian's handsome face.

"Because you can't." He digs in his pocket.

"Here. Take this *now*." He hands me a yellow pill with a V on it. I take it without water and reach into my bag for my cigarettes.

"I thought you were stopping."

"I am, just not today." My eyes narrow as I light up.

He holds up his hands like I'm robbing him. "I'm not gonna bitch while we're filming. Also, Hunter loves your photos. I heard him bragging to someone on the phone yesterday about you."

I roll my eyes. "You do know he wants to sleep with me," I mumble, blowing the smoke out into the gray, rainy atmosphere.

"You said no. He's been respectful, right?"

I smile at his protective side coming out. "Yes, although I have a feeling he thinks he can charm my panties off me." I roll my neck, hearing it crack. I need a freakin' chiropractor.

"He's a creative genius. And completely self-absorbed. I mean, for him not to have picked up on the sexual tension between you and Granger." He turns me so that I'm facing the action as he massages my shoulders.

My eyes go straight to Rhys. As if he can feel me, he looks over. "There's no tension," I say automatically as I try to look away from his intimate stare but can't.

"All right, we are cleared to take off. Let's go." Rafe walks up. He pats Sebastian like they're pals while he grabs my arm, forcing me to speed walk with him toward the jet.

And here it comes. I shouldn't get on this plane today. I'm ready to freak, and all I'm doing so far is climbing the stairs.

"Stop pushing me," I say to Rafe who's ignoring me.

He puts a hand up, blocking a couple of groupies from climbing the steps. "Sorry, my loves. We need to see how many we have before I let more on."

I almost say you can have my spot, but like a nitwit I keep climbing until I stop at the entrance. The jet is amazing. It seats close to twenty-five people with a massive bar in the back, which is where the cool kids—meaning the band members—get to sit. It's decorated in white and black, as in the seats are white, buttery leather, the carpet is thick and black, and the tables are black, along with all the sleek, voice-activated TVs that slide down when needed.

God, what is wrong with me today? My flying phobia hasn't been this bad in a while. Sebastian and I flew back to LA, and I was shockingly calm. Might have been because I was running away from Rhys and what happened in my room. Whatever, I made it.

We got in on Monday. I packed, paid my bills for a couple of months, and signed my contract all that day. Then I fired Jeff, telling him to take his commission and not call me again.

Tuesday I had lunch with my mom, Axel, and Antoinette. Three hours of hell, listening to Axel bitch at me about Rhys, like he was educating me on the fact that he's a fucking rock star and incapable of love. I almost went off on him. Clearly, he thinks I'm stupid. If anyone knows exactly what and who Rhys Granger is, it's me.

I simply smiled and assured him he had nothing to worry about. It's not like I'm perfect. I did fuck him and then basically ran. The only positive thing to come out of that lunch was Antoinette excused me from being a bridesmaid.

I kind of felt guilty. But I know my limitations, and being around all the Disciples' wives, with their kids and happy marriages? Yeah, I can't handle that.

"Gia, let's go, hustle, hustle." Rafe moves me in and out of the way of the entrance. I'm ready to tell him I can't fly today, but Hunter enters, laughing with Sebastian, riding the high of the adoring fans.

All the chaos that was outside starts to trickle inside as I sink into a seat and try to breathe.

"So, Gia." Hunter drops his giant leather messenger bag on the table.

Shawn, one of the flight attendants, slithers over. She's my least favorite. Pretty much rubs me the wrong way with her fake boobs and fake-looking flaming-red hair.

"Can I get you anything, Mr. Falcon?" she purrs at him.

Again, I roll my eyes. I'm sorry but she bugs me. Maybe it's because I suspect the entire band has fucked her. That includes Rhys.

"Yeah. Martini, Bombay Sapphire or Hendricks." When he stretches, his honey-wheat blond hair falls over one eye.

"Gia, baby, anything?" I sit up, gritting my teeth. I hate the baby thing. I should say something, but I'm trying to fight a panic attack, so who the fuck cares. If he were anyone else besides Hunter Falcon, he'd be looking at a lawsuit. You can't call women *baby* or *honey* anymore and he knows it.

God, even the hair and makeup folks are taking offense. Apparently, they don't appreciate people calling them Glam Squad or Vanity. They prefer people call them hair stylists and makeup artists.

"No, thank you. Water, please." Shawn doesn't even acknowledge me.

"Make it three. Sebastian needs one." Hunter drops down into the seat and looks at his watch and phone.

"Tomorrow in London, I want to film the morning interview with *Shredder Monthly* and the guys."

"Yep, already scheduled it." Sebastian sits and rubs my shoulder as if he's trying to give me support.

"Gia, I need you there also." Hunter winks at me, then looks over at the back of the jet where the band is.

"Sebastian, get the portable." He smiles and says pointing, "Film it all."

Nuke is pounding on his chest as he grabs a groupie and throws her onto the couch.

The captain comes on, but Cash is playing his bass, so I assume he was trying to tell us we are taking off. Apparently, when you're a rock band, you don't have to follow rules. Because as usual, I'm the only one who's buckled in. Sebastian opens his backpack and pulls out the camera. The studio spent a fortune on it. Both Sebastian and Hunter threw a fit, stating they needed to be able to film anytime any place.

"You okay?"

I look at Sebastian, then over at Rhys who is laughing with Ammo and a couple of groupies.

"No."

"Okay, well, I need to work. Why don't you grab your camera? It will take your mind off things." He turns on the camera.

Fucking nightmare. How long is this flight?

"What's wrong with you?" Rafe's demanding voice makes me jump.

"Jesus Christ, you scared me." My hand goes to my throat, and I can feel my heart pounding and that's all it takes. Why didn't I take more Valium?

Rafe sits down where Sebastian vacated his seat and straightens his tie as his eyes scan my face.

"You're pale. What's going on?" I almost grab his hand because maybe he'll get the plane to land, and quite frankly I'm freaking, so Rafe is better than nothing.

"Here we go." Shawn comes back and drops off three martinis and no water.

"Can I have a water?" I say, my voice tight. As the jet dips, my eyes snap to Rafe who looks like he's making a huge decision.

"Shawn, water, *now*, and Granger?"

"I... we need to land. I can't..." I shake my hands as I try to take in breaths.

"Christ." Rafe grabs my head and puts it between my legs as I hear Sebastian calling me. Hunter asks if I get air sickness, and all the while, I'm about to pass out if Rafe doesn't let go of my head.

"I need to get out of here. I can't breathe." I try to sit up, knock away Rafe's hands, and run.

"Gia." His gravelly voice almost makes me burst into tears because as much as I hate him, I love him, need him.

Suddenly I'm free as he picks me up and sits down, holding me in his lap.

"Breathe. I got you, Gia. In and out," he whispers in my ear.

I cling to his shirt, listening to that voice I've loved forever, my hand on his chest where his strong heartbeat thumps beneath it.

"I have Valium," I hear Sebastian say.

"She'll be fine," Rhys responds, and the whole plane disappears. It's just him and me. No more screaming or guitars, girls, and cameras. Only us and his strong heartbeat.

"That's it, baby." His hand is in my hair as I lean into him and breathe in his scent. Fresh rain and clean, spicy skin with a touch of smoke.

"I hate being like the—"

"You're fine. Listen to my heart." I close my eyes and match my breathing with the strong thud. Right now, I don't care that I need him, or that he makes me feel secure. All I can do is breathe.

"Are you getting this, Sebastian?" Hunter's voice breaks into our world, and I lift my head, but all I see are amber-colored eyes.

I blink at him as he lowers his lips to mine. It's slow and calm, almost as if we're still in our own bubble. I cling to his T-shirt and our tongues dance together. My head falls back, and I let him take me away. If I live to be a hundred, I will always remember this moment when we soared above the world, Rhys and I.

He lifts his head, his eyes caressing mine. "You feel my heart?"

I nod. "I love it," I say, not even caring what I say or do. Reality can slap me awake when we land, but right now I'm right where I need to be.

He pulls me in tight and I listen to his heart. I survived the panic attack, but the real question is can I survive him?

I should pull away.

He will hurt me again.

"It beats for you," he whispers.

I can't look at him. He'll see all of me right now, and that can't happen. I burrow my nose in his neck while he strokes my hair. When the noise of the jet returns, he lowers the seat, yet all I hear is the slowing of his heartbeat. I sense his body relaxing, which is a little surprising. Rhys is always on the go, his mind rarely at rest. Even when he was young, he never really rested.

You feel my heart? It beats for you.

It rings in my head. I know I'm going to be mortified later. But right now, I'm tired. I listen to his heart and let myself drift away with him.

CHAPTER 30

RHYS
Present – Thirty-five years old
London, England

"Hey, Granger? They're ready for you...been ready. You're late," Pam yells for me from the other room. She's Rafe's latest assistant. He's gone through two on this tour so far.

I walk out of the bathroom, grabbing my phone, feeling better than I have in years. That's no joke. Waking up with Gia curled in my arms did something. I got a solid three hours of sleep on the plane, and woke up to Rafe, Hunter, and Nuke staring at me.

After I told them to fuck off, Gia woke up and bolted to the bathroom until we landed. I was going to demand she come to my suite, and nearly picked her up and carried her. But I didn't. Instead, I let her go and figured she knows where I am.

I want to do this right this time, and if giving her space is what she needs... Actually, I'm full of shit. I'm not giving her space. I let her have last night to herself, but tonight she's in my fucking bed.

The view out the window is amazing. There's so much history here. Maybe I'll kidnap her after the interview, go crazy, and take her out to dinner.

"Okay. So, the woman who is interviewing you is Dorothy Ames, and the photographer is"—Pam looks at her phone—"Lacy

Burton." She rattles off all this shit like I need to know or even care. I glance over my shoulder to see her running to keep up with me, which can't be easy in her heels. I smile at her. She's petite, maybe five two? And she probably weighs all of ninety-five pounds, so I take pity on her and slow down.

"Pam, I need a word with Gia first." I know I should get the interview done but screw it, I want her.

"Oh, um." Pam's cheeks turn pink again. I like her; she has a nice personality. Unfortunately, if she lasts through today, it will be a miracle. Having to deal with Rafe is not easy, but when you add all of us to the mix, you've got a real handful. She pushes up her stylish, black-rimmed glasses and clears her throat.

"What?" I exclaim, causing her to jump.

"Rock God, hiiiii," a bunch of girls at the end of the lobby scream and wave.

"Sorry, I didn't mean to snap at you." I pull us over to the private conference room. Ace stands outside in a black suit, waiting for me and looking like he's guarding the president. He looks ridiculous standing there surrounded by dozens of ornate pots holding what looks like thousands of flowers.

"No need to apologize. I need to stop being a mouse." She smiles, but her eyes have tears. Where did Rafe find her? Whatever. I'm late.

"Gia, I mean, Ms. Fontaine is running a bit late." She almost runs into my back as I stop and turn to her.

"Unacceptable. Get her."

"But Sebastian and Mr. Falcon are in there." Her eyes widen at my stare, and she nods. "I'll go get her, Mr. Granger."

"Thank you. And it's Granger, please." I smile at her because I don't want her to quit. At least not until she finds Gia.

"Ace." We fist-bump and he opens the doors to the room. It's all set up for the shoot. Barely any outside light filters in through the large window, thanks to the gloomy London weather, and I almost squint at the tons of lights they've set up. The photographer is busy snapping pictures of everyone but me.

"There he is." Lacy, Lucy? I can't remember her name. She's tall and thin with long blond hair, baggy slacks, and a tank without a bra. It's white and basically see through.

Nuke is already drinking straight from a bottle, twirling his drumsticks. Cash is on his phone, and Ammo is smoking and strumming on Black Beauty, his guitar.

"Ammo, the lighting is perfect on you. Do you mind?" She walks over and takes off her hat, which looks like a cross between an Indiana Jones hat, and something Janis Joplin would have worn.

He leans back as she smiles and puts it on him. "Yes, that's lovely." She brings her camera to her eye and starts shooting.

"Care to join, Rock God?" I ignore her. I almost feel disloyal having anyone but Gia take my picture, which is irrational, but that's the way I roll these days.

My eyes scan the room. Sebastian and Hunter are in the corner talking to Dorothy Ames, I assume.

I walk over to the large catering table. Rafe appears behind me and fills his coffee cup.

"I sent Pam to get Gia, if you're wondering where she is." I lift a silver platter to see bacon. "And go gentle on Pam. I like her."

He raises an eyebrow. "Really?"

I look up at him and grin. "Yeah, she's way too sweet to be around us." I shake my head at him. There's something going on with him and her, but I have my own shit to deal with.

I load a plate up with French toast, an omelet, and some sausage. I'll come back for the pastries. There're croissants, biscuits, scones, and strawberry jam all stacked on a silver platter.

I pour myself a cup of coffee, then look around for the booze.

"Hand me the Jameson. It's behind you." I motion with my head.

"Granger?"

"What, Rafe? I'm not into your little pixie, okay? So, save the lecture. I'm actually in a good mood today." I smile and look over at the door, but it's just a couple of staff members carrying more flowers and food.

He takes a sip of coffee, his blue eyes narrowing on me.

"Rock God, we need you," the photographer calls out.

"In a minute," I yell back, taking a huge bite of French toast. It's fucking good. The buttery, soft bread mixed with cinnamon is perfect.

"Try the bacon. It's that maple shit you like," I tell Rafe.

He sets down his coffee and straightens his sleeve under his suit jacket. "So, here's what's going on. Gia wants to quit."

I freeze midbite. "The fuck?"

"She says she has taken enough pictures, and that her contract is fulfilled. Of course, that's bullshit, and I told—"

I toss my plate down and go straight for Sebastian, completely ignoring Rafe's cursing behind me.

"What's going on, Sebastian?" I demand, walking past both the women and Hunter to shove him up against the wall.

"The fuck, Granger?" He pushes back and that's all I need. Gut punching him, I watch in satisfaction as he drops to his knees.

"I'll tell you the fucking facts. You're here because of Gia. No Gia, no Sebastian," I snarl.

"Jesus, Granger, what the hell, man?" Hunter grabs me as Rafe tries to block me from kicking Sebastian in the face.

"Security!" Dorothy calls. I look at her as she stands there, watching, and I know she's one of those we have to pay off.

Sebastian gets to his feet. His hands rest on his knees as he sneers, "This is why she wants to quit. You're a fucking piece of shit, Granger. A jealous, entitled, *prick*. I should have let her leave instead of talking her into staying." He lunges at me as Dorothy shrieks and Rafe holds him back.

"The hell is going on?" Ace yells. I shake loose from Hunter. But Ace's big body is now in the way of me kicking the shit out of Sebastian for no reason other than the fact I know he's been inside her.

"So, she's staying?" I demand.

"Fuck you, Granger." Sebastian straightens up, still wheezing. Clearly his anger is more powerful than the lack of oxygen in his lungs.

"Okay, let's all cool down." Ace lets go of Sebastian, who turns and goes to the window.

I look at Dorothy, who again looks way too interested. "You want that interview? Let's do it now." I sit in a chair as she looks at me, then sits, crossing her legs, a smirk on her lips.

"Christ, Granger." Cash saunters over. The adrenaline still pumps through my blood as I turn to look at him. To be honest, I should beat the shit out of him. This all started with him. Had he come forward years ago and said that he had fucked Renee, Gia would never have left.

"Shut up, Cash. Just sit and lie like you always do." The room goes silent, save for Hunter talking to Sebastian. I grab my cigarettes from my pocket and light up.

"Excuse me, Mr. Granger." A man dressed in a suit walks over and waves his hand for attention.

"There's no smoking in here; actually, in all of the hotel. I see that some of you have cigarettes. I'm going to need you to please put them out. We also have a no-fighting rule. I'd hate to have to ask you all to leave—"

The sound of my lighter makes his face turn red. He glances around as if someone in this room would actually help him.

"Fine me." I inhale and look at Dorothy. "Better start asking questions."

She looks around as Nuke pulls out a chair and lights up a joint. Ammo saunters over wearing that stupid hat, while the photographer smiles and continues taking pictures.

"Before we start, none of what you just saw goes in the story. If you can't agree, then no interview." Rafe is in full damage-control mode.

I look over his shoulder as the door opens.

One.

Two.

Three.

I know it's her before I even see her. I can feel her, my muse. I want to grab her and shake her for making me crazy enough to punch Sebastian, then fuck her for days. My hand rubs my chest as she comes closer.

She's dressed all in black. Skinny jeans, a long-sleeved shirt, and ballet flats.

Her eyes scan the room, taking in the bad vibe, but I couldn't care less. She's here. I'm ready to bolt out of my chair, but I'm gonna do this fucking interview and lock us in my suite once it's over.

"Granger?" Nuke hands me the joint. I take it and inhale.

Dorothy turns her head to look at Gia, then back at me. "All of you have been linked with numerous women, yet none of you have settled down. Why is that?"

"What kind of question is that?" Cash demands.

My eyes laser in on Dorothy. She must be feeling all powerful since she saw me lose my shit. Hunter and Sebastian stand a few feet away with the camera, filming all of us. I feel like I'm on trial.

"We're on the road a lot. This life we live isn't great for relationships," Ammo answers.

"And you?" Dorothy turns to face me. "What about you, Granger?" Her eyes shift to Gia.

"Yeah, I've been in love."

"Is this Paulette? I know you guys have been on and off for a while." She smirks, and I wonder why people are the way they are. Like does she go home after trashing people and feel good about herself?

"Paulette and I are better as friends."

She nods. "She has been quoted as saying you were the love of her life, but unfortunately, you can't keep your dick in your pants. Any comment?"

My eyes narrow on her. I take a hit off the joint, handing it to her as I blow smoke in her face. "Nope, no comment."

She glares at me for a nanosecond, smiles, and turns to Cash. "What about you, Tommy Cash? You have a child?"

"Christ." Nuke rubs his shaved head. It seems Dorothy has been snooping around in places that are better left alone.

I look around the room. Rafe is on the phone in the corner. Ace is standing next to Gia.

"Yeah, I have a son."

"Correct me, but wasn't the mother saying it was Granger's? I'm only asking because it was all over the tabloids, and I thought since you are all together you could clear up the rumors. Did you take a paternity test?"

And I'm done. She's a bitch, and I have other shit to deal with.

Cash leans over the table so that she has to sit back "That's *my* son."

I'm about to stand when she says, "What about the Disciples? You all are connected to the notorious MC club, right? Axel Fontaine is the other Rock God. Is that correct?"

"The fuck are you doing?" Nuke stands up.

Dorothy grins. "My job." She glances at her phone, which is blowing up. Pursing her lips, she flips it toward us, eyes twinkling like she's won the lottery.

"This was just announced. Look who's the sexiest man alive this year."

"Stay on Granger," I hear Hunter tell Sebastian, and I'm ready to punch him.

"As a band, it's got to be hard that Granger seems to always steal the spotlight. Now he's the sexiest man alive."

I stand and reach for my cigarettes. "Go fuck yourself. We're a band, and they're my brothers. Write whatever shit you want." My eyes follow Gia as she shakes her head and turns to leave.

The room explodes with Cash going off on her along with Nuke. Rafe moves in.

But I'm done.

I don't look back and slam open the door. "Gia." I reach for her and swing her around. "What the fuck is happening?"

"Everything, Rhys. Jesus Christ, it's insanity being around you." She starts to speed walk.

I grab her arm and move her toward the elevator.

"Just stop, Rhys." She sounds tired.

I maneuver us past the stunned faces. People point and whisper excitedly. Pushing the elevator button, I ignore the animated crowd. Thankfully, the door dings open as a couple of guys exit.

Gia stays quiet as we ride up the elevator, my hand sliding down to her cold one.

"Let's go." I pull us into my suite. Leaving her, I head straight for the elaborate bar and pour us bourbon in large quantities. Grabbing the glasses and bottle, I step over to where she stands staring out the window.

"Here." I shove it into her hands.

She turns toward me, and there's my girl. Her eyes sparkle with anger. When she shoots the whole glass, I raise an eyebrow. Her eyes water and she starts coughing.

"What the hell are you doing?" I can't help but laugh because what the hell? I pull her into my arms and rest my chin on her head as she wheezes, her forehead resting on my chest.

"Another?"

She pulls back as I shoot my full glass, barely feeling the sting.

I look down at her and pour myself another. "Why are you running again?"

"Because I can't do this. I hate feeling... like this." Her green eyes are watering from the residual coughing and bourbon, but her honesty makes me bring the glass to my lips and throw back another shot. Taking her glass and mine, I set them on the table but keep the bottle.

"You have to know you can't leave."

"So they say," she says dryly.

"Not because of the contract. I couldn't care less about that." I wrap my hand behind her neck, bringing her close. My eyes caress hers.

"I need you to stay." My lips hover around hers. "You're my muse, you know." My thumb rubs her lips.

Her eyes close as if my words are too painful for her to hear, but she was honest, so I'm gonna give her my truths.

Trust her.

"Open your eyes, Brat," I growl into her mouth.

She does, and all I need is in her eyes. My hands tighten on her hair, and I take her lips. I want to be gentle, to cherish her. But the moment her mouth opens, and my tongue finds hers, I'm lost.

Suddenly it's different, frantic, as if we're both scared to stop for fear it will end. Dropping to my knees, I push her back against the glass window. The bottle hits the floor with a thud.

"I need to be inside you." I grab her delicate ankles and toss off her ballet flats. Christ, my hands are shaking as if she's my drug of choice and my body is going through withdrawal. Jerking her jeans down, she lifts her leg so I can toss them behind me. My hands scan her flat stomach.

"Open your legs."

She obeys me, then shivers as she runs her hands through my hair.

"Your ass cold, baby? Or are you just aching for me to fuck you?"

She looks down at me. "I want you to fuck me."

When I stroke my thumb against the flimsy fabric at her crotch, her head thuds against the window.

Slipping her panties aside, I push her legs farther apart and suck her fucking nectar. She's slick and wet. I insert two fingers deep inside her, causing her to moan.

"I'm gonna finger fuck you hard and fast." I stand and start to fuck her deep with my fingers, then pull them out to rub her swollen nub hard. Her hands grab my forearm, and as she looks at me, her eyes change when her cunt pulses and jerks. She clamps onto my two fingers and orgasms.

Pulling my fingers out, I unbutton my jeans, kicking them next to hers. She opens her eyes to watch.

"Take your shirt off, baby. I want those fucking tits."

She tugs it off and gasps, covering herself when she looks down to the sidewalk below. "Holy fuck, I can see them. If they looked up they would see us—"

Grabbing her shirt, I toss it to the floor. My hard body rubs against her soft one. I take her mouth, silencing her, my tongue going deep, my cock throbbing. My balls are tight, and I haven't even entered her yet.

Rubbing my chest on her, I say, "Take your bra off."

She looks at me as I lift her up, ready to impale her with my cock. She reaches behind and tosses her black bra to the floor, her nipples standing erect as if begging for me to fuck them. That can come later. I'll slide my thick, hard cock between those full tits and come all over her, mark her mine forever.

When I lift her ass, she wraps her legs around me and I thrust into her slick, wet cunt—all moist and ready to fucking come already. Like a goddamn teenager, I have to breathe through my nose while I rut inside her. Her nails dig into my shoulder. The window supports us, allowing me to move her up and down on my dick.

"Open your eyes, Gia, and look down. Do they see you, baby?" I whisper in her ear. They can't—we're too high up, and even if they could see, they can't see our faces.

"Oh my God," she whimpers, turning her head and gazing down below. Her head falls back and my mouth attacks her neck, biting and sucking, marking her in the most primal way.

"I'm going to come, Rhys," she moans, grabbing hold of my neck as her body contracts.

"I'm going to..." Her eyes flutter. She whimpers in my mouth and her cunt pulses and contracts over and over on my cock. She cries out my name while I keep fucking her deep and hard.

"Watch me," I snarl. Her eyes meet mine. "I'm gonna fill this cunt of mine up." I thrust deep inside her tight, slick walls. My cock jerks as I let loose in gripping, pulsing, mind-blowing waves.

Euphoria. So intense I feel it all the way down to my toes.

"Fuck, it's good with us," I say. She's almost limp. I hold her still, letting myself jerk out the last of my seed inside her. Slowly, I slide out of her.

"I can barely stand." She places her hands on the window to steady herself.

Grinning, I lift her into my arms and kick the bedroom door open. "You're tired. I'm exhausted."

All the craziness of my world is gone. My head is surprisingly quiet as I slide into the large bed. She rolls to her side, and I pull the sheets over us, grabbing her tight so we can spoon.

"What are we doing?" she whispers.

With my eyes already closing, I tighten my arms around her. "Sleeping," I say, inhaling her scent. It wraps around me, almost lulling me to sleep.

"It's just us, Gia. Relax and sleep."

CHAPTER 31

GIA

Present – Twenty-five years old
London, England

"Ihave to use the bathroom." I look around and see him grinning at me. His dark hair is wild, his tan, tattooed body almost glistening.

"Gia, come here." He motions for me. I look around. We're at the beach. He takes my hand as we walk to the ocean. It's foamy, the water rolling up to my toes. I look at him and his eyes are like brown bourbon.

"Okay, go pee," he says.

My eyes pop open. Holy shit, I really do need the bathroom. Thank God I didn't listen to Rhys in my dream. I almost I giggle, which is absurd because I don't giggle.

"Rhys," I whisper, trying to escape his arms that seem to tighten as I move. Finally, I escape and make my way into the bathroom. This might be one of my favorite hotels. I stayed here a couple of years ago. Not in a suite like this, but everything in this hotel is gorgeous. I quickly use the facilities and wash my hands. Looking up at the mirror, I almost laugh. I look like Spot the dog. My mascara is a mess, and my makeup from earlier is probably all over the pillow.

I can't remember sleeping that well in years. Turning the faucet, I attempt to fix my eyes. I'm probably delirious because I have zero to be happy about. I need to get out of here, run away as he likes to call it. But let's be honest—he's right. I do need to run... guard myself from the eventual pain that's going to crash down on me.

I'm too old for this crap, and I promised myself I would not get into any more unhealthy relationships.

Rhys is not relationship material, but he is, without a doubt, the best fuck I've ever had. No matter what I say about him, Rhys Granger can fuck like no other. Maybe I should stick around a bit.

I run my hand down my neck, noticing the tiny bite marks. My core clenches. Christ, I'm like a junkie and he's my crack. Would it be bad to stay in here all day and let him make me come numerous times?

"Probably" I say to myself. I know I need to leave. Slip out without a backward glance. I thought I could do this. Be professional and leave. But Rhys wants more, I can feel it, and as much as I am able to logically say my heart is detached, I'm not sure that's the case.

With a sigh, I grab his toothbrush. The truth is, I can't trust him and can't forget that he let me go. Meaning, I guess I can't forgive him. As I brush my teeth, my mind travels back to that day—that fucking awful day in the rain.

I broke that day. Although I recovered, here I am, brushing my teeth, trying to talk myself into leaving when my body wants me to stay.

That's what all this is: sex. I want him, and you know what? That's not such a bad thing. I put his toothbrush back and turn off the light, returning to the bed. I have no idea what time it is, but clearly I'm not leaving since his cock seems to be awake even if he's still asleep.

For a second I falter, as if a neon sign saying *Danger* is going off in my head. He's so beautiful. But it's more than that. He's talented, so fucking talented. He's done what few can only dream of.

How does he handle it—the grueling schedules, and the mental and physical wear of a world tour? I'm exhausted and I've just started.

When I crawl back into bed, he instantly tugs me back into his arms. His warm, delicious smell of freshness and spice makes my heart race.

I'm not as tough as I think. All my talk about how this is just sex might be bullshit. Because all he has to do is touch me, and my heart breaks into little pieces, scattering all over.

What the fuck am I doing? I move to sit up, but he rolls over, pinning my hands above my head as if he knows...

Knows that I'm fighting myself. Knows I'm considering leaving before we both get hurt. I might not survive. Last time, I became a bitter bitch. This time, I can't become a broken one.

"Brat," he says, his voice raspy. His long, black eyelashes blink open, taking my breath away as I stare into his dark eyes. "What's going on in that beautiful head of yours?" His eyes search my face. He's not haunted; he's present, and that seems almost worse.

My hands tingle and my nipples harden. I'm close to bursting into tears. I can't do this. He's going to hurt me, and yet I can't leave.

"I should go." My voice cracks.

Again, his eyes peruse my face. "Not an option."

"Rhys, I—" His mouth crashes down on mine, and he holds me possessively, as if he means it. I open, letting myself have this, because I can't walk away.

Our tongues twist as his hands tighten on mine. He bites the bottom of my lip, then sucks on it. Lifting his head, he looks almost as tortured as I'm sure I do.

"You're fucking mine. Do you hear me?" He lets go of one of my hands to grab the back of my leg. "I hope this cunt is ready because I can't wait." And in one amazingly forceful thrust, he slides deep inside me.

"Fuck. That's it, baby. So wet." He plunges into me hard. My eyes roll back in my head at how good it feels. My body betrays me with need, which isn't fair. Then again, life isn't fair.

In and out he thrusts, his piercing rubbing me as I start to climb. His mouth hovers over mine; his eyes bore into me. Our breathing is in sync, and for as rough as he fucks, there's an intimacy we've never had before. My legs wrap around his ass. His hand travels up my torso, pulling on my pierced nipple, and that's it. I'm going over in fast, pulsing waves of pleasure.

"Rhys," I cry out. Blinking away the dark spots, I peer up at him. It's that intense. When he pulls out, he grabs my hips, and his mouth goes straight to my clit. I haven't even stopped coming. Pulsing, contracting, I let out a scream of pleasure. He lifts his head. His two fingers rub hard on my clit as I buck up, then fall back onto the bed.

"You're mine. Say it." He jerks his slick cock. "Say it." He straddles me, his muscled legs strong. He jerks his cock hard. I lean up and pull on the piercing.

His hand goes to my throat. "Say it," he grunts.

"I've always been yours," I whisper.

His eyes shoot to mine and he comes undone. His beautiful stomach muscles tighten, and his seed spills onto my tits.

He looks down at me as we both try to catch our breaths. The warm liquid drips down my side, but I can't move.

This is the moment. He's either going to pull away or...

He takes my hand in his tan, rough fingers and places it on his chest. "This beats for you."

Holy fuck. He's not pulling away; he's bringing us to another level.

"I can't fight this hunger for you anymore, Gia. Don't want to."

My eyes fill with tears. For a second my heart fluttered. For a mere moment I had *hope*. But that's the one thing I'll never allow myself to indulge in.

Hope.

It's a beautiful word, yet it causes unlimited damage. I lived with that word my whole life. Hope took me down once. I can't allow it to again.

If he notices I haven't responded, he's hiding it well. He pulls me up, and his jizz drips down my stomach.

"You want to order dinner, or go out?" He brings me into the bathroom and starts the shower. I'm almost too stunned to respond at first. Does he actually think we are going to continue?

He steps in and reaches for me as I'm trying to make my brain work. I should go, but let's be honest: I never should have come with him to begin with.

The hot water pelts my body. He grabs my chin almost roughly. "I'm done playing. I know how you feel. You don't have to say it. *I know it.*"

Then he grabs the shower gel and starts to wash himself in angry, fast movements. By the time I get the shower gel in my hands, he's moving me aside to rinse and opening the heavy glass doors.

"Rhys?" He stops but doesn't turn. "I can't commit to anything right now." It sounds strained and pretty pathetic as I swallow back the words that I should say. I should tell him that he let me leave. That he hurt me and now I'm not the same. That because of him I make bad decisions, all so I never have to feel that burn in my heart again.

He grabs one of the white towels and wraps it around his waist. Looking at me through the mirror, he shakes his head as if he can't understand me.

"Relax, Gia. I asked you to dinner." My eyes hungrily watch him leave. As he runs his hands through his wet hair, his broad shoulders and back look truly spectacular.

I take my time in the shower. What the hell am I doing? Rhys is starting to seem like the normal one here. I wash my hair and grab the body wash for the third time before I feel stable enough not to humiliate myself. My emotions are all over the place. I'm terrified he's gonna hurt me, and I can't even enjoy the moment. The only time I'm completely free is when his pierced cock is fucking me.

This is absurd. I have to get out. Wait, did he say he's taking me to dinner? I turn off the water and almost laugh because did Rhys Granger just ask me out on a date?

I step out, and the large bathroom looks like a sauna. That's how long I stayed in the shower. Wrapping a towel around my wet hair, I grab some moisturizer and freeze.

I hear his guitar, but this is not a song that I know. He's creating. Goose bumps cover my skin and it's all I can do to breathe. After reaching for a robe, I slowly open the door.

I have known that Rhys is a musical genius from as early as I can remember. I used to sneak out of my bed as a kid and spy on him. He basically lived in our garage his senior year, sleeping on that old mattress and writing.

I'd go through the kitchen and sit on the steps that led down to the garage. It was then that I knew he was the perfect man. His words and voice moved me even as a child.

I lean against the doorframe and listen as he sings and plays. Fuck, I need a cigarette. This song is about me.

She's a hunger that I've come to need. I've never been good with words, but that's all right because my heart. My heart beats for hers.

My heart beats for hers.

And this is when I fall. I'm no better than his crazy fans. In fact, I might be worse because I've been loving him since I could feel what love is.

My heart beats for hers.

Somehow I'm in front of him when he looks up and flashes me the famous Granger smirk. He's shirtless. His arms flex and his hand travels up and down the neck of the guitar.

After a dramatic strum, he says, "You're my muse."

I look at him, wanting this to never end. "That is... Rhys."

He puts the guitar aside and pulls me in between his legs. As his hands untie my robe, he brings me close. My hands weave through his thick hair. And that's it—the tears fall.

"Why didn't you come for me?" There. I asked the question that's been like an albatross around my neck.

He doesn't let go. If anything, he pulls me tighter. His breath kisses my flat stomach.

"Why didn't I come for you?" he repeats slowly. "You were eighteen. I guess I felt that you'd be better off without me. I had all that shit with Renee and my mom to deal with. And you didn't trust me."

I pull back so I can look at him, see him. "Why would you think anything changed?"

He leans back and cocks his head.

"Hasn't it?"

I shake my head *no*. "I waited for you like a fucking..." I throw my hands up, searching for the word. "Like a stupid girl who sat and cried in the Disciples' clubhouse because I couldn't get up and I couldn't bear to... go on."

"You needed to go to school." He pushes me back to stand, but fuck that. He doesn't get to walk away. He thinks he can simply write a song and that makes eight years just vanish and everything's all right?

I grab his arm and he turns, his brown eyes filled with a pain no one wants, one that's hard to get rid of.

"Don't you ever tell me I run. Look at you." The tears that I've been holding back seem unstoppable, but I couldn't care less.

"What the fuck do you want me to say, Gia?" he yells. "I fucking love you. Always have. But that day, I begged you to trust me. I told you that kid wasn't mine."

"You never came for me. You let me go," I yell back. "And you're right. I was only eighteen. I still believed in love and soulmates and all that crap. But beyond that, I believed in you."

He looks down at my hand that won't let go of him. If I do, that will be it. I'll leave this room and won't come back.

"That was mistake number one. You, out of everyone, know I always make all the girls cry." My hand drops as his words float around the room.

"You gonna run, Gia?" His voice is like a caress, but I know better. We're just getting warmed up, and this hasn't even started to get ugly. I turn and look around for my clothes.

"Yeah, I'm going to save us both and get out now." I turn but he grabs me, bringing me to his chest.

"Careful, Gia." He shakes me. "Do you really think that's how this works?" His hand tightens on my arm. "Do you?"

"I don't know how any of this works. All I know is that—"

"Exactly. We can't know our future. We only have now. This second. Goddammit, Gia, I choose this moment to be with you."

"You scare me."

"That's probably the most honest thing you've said to me." He holds me close, the robe falling to the floor. "Tell me what you want, baby."

My head is spinning as I try to breathe. My eyes feel like someone tossed sand in them and my skin is on fire. When my head falls back, his mouth hovers at my lips.

"I want..." It sounds like a growl, but I've lost all sense of anything as he kisses my eyes and licks my tears.

"Talk to me," he coaxes.

"I want... *you*," I whisper as hot tears spill down my face.

"You got me." Our eyes lock, and in this moment I believe him.

I believe him.

He cups my face, his thumb wiping away my tears as his mouth dips to mine. His kiss holds everything I could ever want.

"My heart beats for you," he whispers, lifting me up. I wrap my legs around his waist. For now, this seems like it's enough. I close my eyes. I'll let him make me forget. As soon as his body connects with mine, he'll take away my pain, my doubts. So I close my eyes and let his mouth take away the pain.

CHAPTER 32

RHYS

Present – Thirty-five years old
London, England

As we enter the O2 Arena, I squeeze her hand. It's fucking raining again. I'm so fucking sick of rain.

"We're going to the south of Spain after the documentary," I grumble.

"Let's just go to Hawaii." Gia sighs as she looks around at the multitude of fans rushing toward us. Ace and his crew instantly shield us as we walk in and make our way to the green room.

We haven't been out of the suite in two days. I've fucked us raw emotionally and physically. But now that we're out, it's business as usual and by that, I mean, anything goes.

Gia must sense it too. Her beautiful green eyes are back to being cautious, almost resigned to the fact that something's going to happen. Good or bad, this is our life. We'll power through it.

"You look beautiful," I tell her, stroking her hand with my thumb. Her hair is down, her green eyes pop since she did that smokey thing, and her fucking lips... like ripe berries. If I were anywhere else than here, I'd suck on them, throw her up against the wall, and lose myself in her.

She smiles back and my heart burns. *Need.* That's all I feel. God, I'm in so deep. We need to talk, really talk, but that will have to come later, I guess.

Rafe stands waiting at the door of the green room along with Hunter.

"There he is—the sexiest man alive." Hunter laughs and puts his hand out for a fist bump, but his eyes are on Gia.

I stare at him; he's pushing it. The adrenaline's already rushing through me, and it's not because I'm getting ready to go on stage.

Hunter needs to back off. I've been ignoring a lot of his shit because he's a younger version of Quentin Tarantino. He's out for number one, and I can respect that as long as he doesn't look at my girl.

He's a pushy fuck, using his looks and charm to his advantage. He tried to invade our space yesterday, knocking on the door saying he needed a quick word with Gia.

I texted Ace to get rid of him and asked him to have one of his guys guard the door. It doesn't help Hunter's cause that I know he has a thing for Gia, not that I blame him. All men have a thing for Gia—she's gorgeous and has a personality. A fucking fire that draws people to her. She's always had that. *But she's mine,* so he can either respect that or I will lay him out. Fuck the film.

Gia's not dumb, and she knows what Hunter is. Which is the only reason I haven't punched him when I see his eyes travel up and down my girl's body. Like right now.

So I fist-bump back with so much force I hear his knuckles crack. He cocks his head and nods as Rafe opens the door allowing Gia to go first.

"You okay?" Rafe says under his breath.

"Fine. Why?" I walk into the usual chaos.

"Hold it together, Granger. I can feel your energy." He walks by me.

Ammo looks over at me as I put a protective arm around Gia. "He lives."

"Knock it off," I say, looking over at Cash who shakes his head as if in disgust.

Nuke calls for Gia, motioning for her to come sit with him on the couch. She laughs and throws herself on his lap as he hugs her. Christ, Nuke is a mess. We're gonna have to deal with it soon. I watch as Gia rubs her hand on his forehead as if to see if he has a fever. If anyone can motivate Nuke to get help, it's Gia. I know he's stayed close with her. It used to make me crazy, but now I'm happy he has her. For Nuke's sake, I can share Gia.

"You okay, brother?" Ammo's voice brings me back to the loud room.

"I'm fucked."

He glances at Gia soothing Nuke whose head is on her shoulder. The two groupies who were sitting next to Nuke are taking pictures or shooting video of it. I grit my teeth and motion to Ace.

"Just fucking relax. You got Gia. Look, Granger, shit has been going on since your outburst the other day." I'm barely listening. Of course, everything is a shit show. That's our lives.

"Jesus Christ, just try to get through the show," he snaps.

I look around the room. It's the same as all the others. Different size and color, but all the same shit. We have everything: money, success, all the things people dream of, yet all of us are miserable. A fucking waste of talent.

Gia. She's my lifeline. My key to happiness. I need her to make me whole.

"I'll be back." I leave him, knowing he's staring at me like I've lost my mind. I'm done caring. I need her.

Now.

She stands as if she knows I'm coming for her, even though she looks down at Nuke. She feels me, senses my need. My cock hardens as I breathe through my nose to steady myself. It's not like I can pull her dress up and fuck her in the middle of the room.

"Hey, brother." Nuke smiles at me. His bloodshot eyes shine as if he's in his happy place. Of course, he is. He's on fucking heroin again and his demons are asleep.

"Nuke." I nod, pulling Gia with me toward the door where groupies keep emerging.

"Five minutes. Let's start getting up," someone yells as I pull the door open. Two groupies look over at us.

"Hey, Granger, want to party?" They break away.

"Out," I snarl. They both look at us and walk around me as if confused. I kick the door shut and grab Gia, setting her on the sink, my mouth taking hers in a hard kiss.

She matches me as if her need is as desperate as mine. "I need to be inside you," I say gruffly. Leaning back, she spreads her legs open. I shove my jeans down and she reaches for my cock, jerking me off fast.

"I need you." I take her mouth again and grab her legs. She lets go of my cock and lifts her hips, pulling her dress up. I rip her panties off.

"Fuck," she hisses, leaning into me. I thrust inside her fast and hard, pushing her back until she leans against the mirror. My eyes watch my pierced cock gliding in and out of her wet pussy.

"Rub your clit, baby," I grunt.

She reaches down and roughly rubs on it as I feel her start to pulse. Someone bangs on the door, but I'm fucking coming, losing myself inside her magical, wet cunt that makes all my demons go away.

"Fuck, Gia," I rumble, pounding into her. Our bodies slap together as she shouts my name. Her juices run down my balls, and my stomach muscles tighten as she arches her back and comes.

I watch her die a little, then come undone, as I jerk into her in deep, hard thrusts.

"Jesus Christ." I look at her. She's spread out for me. I need to go. Someone's banging on the door again, but all I want to do is turn her around and fuck her ass, be in every single hole I can.

"Rhys." She touches my lips. "You have to go." I blink at her as the world comes in loud.

"Granger, you need to go now, man," Rafe yells. I pull out and cup her face.

"You stay where I can see you." It's irrational, but I can't shake it. She nods as I grab a paper towel to clean her up.

"I'm fine. Besides my underwear. Rhys." She dips down to grab the torn material and tosses it in the garbage. I back up and almost shove my wet cock in her mouth. She must know because she reaches over and gives it a quick suck before standing.

I grin and pull up my jeans. Grabbing her hand, I open the door. Rafe stands, arms crossed like a fucking disappointed parent.

"Watch her." I walk around him, ignoring everyone who is staring. By the sounds of things, Nuke and Cash are already on the stage.

"Oh my God." She almost bumps into my back. "Sebastian, turn the camera off," she says as we start to walk. Ace is screaming for everyone to clear. Dallas hands me a bottle of Jack Daniel's. I look over at the camera and grab Gia's chin.

"You stay here. I'll be right back." I lower my head and grin at her. "I like you a lot."

She looks out at the crowd, the numerous fans who love us. Amid the deafening noise, she looks back at me and stands on her toes. "I like you more. Go. They're waiting for you."

I look out at the enormous arena and grab her hand, placing it on my hard cock.

"Oh my God." She looks at Sebastian who, like the dick he is, happens to be right there as she takes her hand away.

"I'll be back." I kiss her, then walk up the stairs. BT waits next to the entrance with my IEM, which I put in my ear. Lifting my hand, I walk out into the lights.

CHAPTER 33

GIA

Present – Twenty-five years old
London, England

As Rhys takes the stage, the crowd goes into a frenzy and my arms get goose bumps. He's awe-inspiring. When he lifts his arms, the crowd comes alive—like a fire that's found dry brush, it ignites into an inferno.

They all rise and chant, "Rock God, Rock God," their shouts echoing around the venue.

"Hello, motherfucking London," he yells, and I jump at the response. It's wild and strangely intimate. No wonder his cock gets hard. Merely watching him makes me wet.

I reach for the camera in my bag, wanting to let it describe what I feel as I see him. But for the first time, I lower it and simply watch. People stand smashed together, singing and crying because Rhys has smiled and said hello.

"They worship him." Sebastian stands next to me. He lowers the large camera from his shoulder.

"Jesus, you scared me. And fuck you for filming me." I turn back to watch Rhys perform, the crowd a sea of lighters and phones.

"Do you?"

"What?" I yell, looking at him. Something is wrong, and suddenly I don't want him near me. For the first time ever, I'm terrified at what Sebastian is about to tell me.

"Do you worship this prick?"

"What's wrong? Why are you looking at me like that?"

He grabs my arm and pulls me to the far corner. "Gia. What the fuck are you doing? You, out of everybody, can't possibly think he's the one for you."

"Don't you dare. I told you I didn't want to do this. You fucking begged me, basically bribed me with our friendship. So back off, Sebastian. This doesn't concern you." My head is throbbing. Sebastian wouldn't act like this if something wasn't wrong and he believed I needed his help.

"He's a ticking time bomb. He attacked me because he thought you left. The man is obsessed and yes..." He holds up a hand, his handsome face fierce. "Yes, I admit I have a past with you, and you know how I feel about you, us... But Gia, this?" He looks around. "This is the kind of future you want? Always looking over your shoulder, or pretending not to see when he comes out of the bathroom with another woman? Because he will, Gia. He's a *fucking rock star*."

I shake my head and try to move past him. He grabs my arm. "Just wait." He takes a breath. "I'm having a hard time believing that the confident, vibrant woman who is my best friend would lose herself to him. You heard about Nuke, right?"

I look up at him. "Well, I can tell he's on something." The crowd goes wild as we stare at each other. Sebastian, my best friend besides Julianna, hates Rhys, and I can't deal.

"Another woman has come forward saying he's the father. But that she fucked the entire band." I back away. He's lying. *Not again.*

"Is there a chance it's his?" I scream, causing a couple of roadies to look over at me despite the noise of the crowd.

"She says no. That she went from one to another and then stayed with Nuke exclusively for months. But Gia, who cares? If it's not this one, it will be another and another. He's a star. Fuck." He runs his hand through his hair. "I can't even blame him. If I had this much pussy in my face twenty-four seven, I'd fuck behind your back too." He holds up a hand at Hunter who walks over, looking concerned.

"Everything okay over here? I'd like to get the band and crowd, Sebastian."

I can't speak because I'm numb.

"Gia, are you okay? What's happening? You didn't tell her, did you?" Hunter looks at Sebastian who stares at me.

"Of course, I did. She's what matters, Hunter," he grits out.

"Perfect." He shakes his head. "I disagree. She was hired to do a job and so were you. Do it." He turns toward Rafe who stands still, arms crossed. His knowing eyes watch my nightmare come to life.

"Why are you doing this, Sebastian?" My voice cracks and my heart starts to shatter. It burns so much I want to double over, because this is a pain I thought I could avoid.

I thought I had kept myself distanced enough so this couldn't happen.

I lied.

"Because I couldn't live with myself if I didn't at least ask you what the fuck you're thinking. Because you would do the same for me."

"I love him."

He looks like I just stabbed him. "I know. And if he is truly what you want, then I will walk away and give you nothing but my love. But he will fail you." He grabs his camera and walks out on the stage to do his job.

I swallow—I might throw up if I don't. The people who seemed so far away tilt and swerve in front of me as I wipe my eyes.

"Goddamn you, Rhys." I walk up to Hunter and hand him my camera.

"I quit."

"You've got to be kidding me! What the fuck, Gia? So the guy fucks around. Who cares—it's not personal," Hunter yells at my back. This isn't even about the other women. That hasn't even sunk in because I've been locked in his room for days with his cock distracting me. This is about the fact that deep down, I was waiting for this to happen.

Sebastian is right. All of what he said is right. But God, it hurts.

I take one last look, knowing I need to go.

Now.

If I stay, he'll seduce me with words that will eventually ring hollow, and then where will I be?

"You running, Gia? I'd think about this." Rafe stops me as I start to walk away.

"Why are you talking to me, Rafe? You should be happy I'm done." I wipe under my eyes, refusing to cry in front of him, in front of any of them.

"I thought maybe you might want to take a moment and talk to Granger." His eyes seem genuinely compassionate.

I switch my bag to the other shoulder, smile, and look up at the top of the arena, then shake my head as I scream, "He's the Rock God, Rafe. The crazy, fucked-up thing is all I ever wanted to be was his." I don't wait for him to respond. I've said too much already. Pulling out my phone, I bang out the doors and lift my face to the dark sky. *What the fuck am I doing?*

"Can I help you, Gia?" I turn to face Ace, his kind eyes sad. "Rafe said you might need a ride. Please, let me help." And for some reason, that kindness does me in. My legs give out and I fall to my knees as I acknowledge the pain: I really am leaving him.

Ace's strong, dark hand reaches for me, and I take it. He opens the door of the black SUV for me and I slide in.

"Where to?"

I reach into my bag for my cigarettes and remember Rhys took them. "Do you have a cigarette?" I sniff, not caring that I've completely humiliated myself in front of this man. He opens the glove compartment and hands me a pack of Marlboro Reds. My hands shake as I open it.

"Here, let me, Gia." He rips open the plastic wrapper and hands it back to me, and my eyes get blurry again.

"Thank you." I shake my head, trying to stop crying, as I fish around for my lighter. "Can you take me to the airport, please?"

"You sure?" I can't look at him. I'll start to doubt myself, or feel worse, because somehow, I've started to grow fond of him. Christ, even Rafe looked sad.

"Yes." Grabbing the lighter, I finally lean my head back and watch the rain on the windows, wondering if that's an omen. It seems like Rhys and I are always in the rain.

I can't go back to Los Angeles. It's a week until Axel's wedding. He might try to kill Rhys.

I sit up and text.

ME: I'M COMING TO YOU

Three dots appear.

JULIANNA: THANK GOD

I toss my phone back into my bag, light my cigarette, and let the lights of the passing cars lull me into knowing that this is right.

CHAPTER 34

RHYS

Present – Thirty-five years old
London, England

"We love you, London!" I look out into the adoring crowd. Thousands of fans singing your music is something I will never get used to but am always grateful for. I'm sweaty and fucking amped up as I make my way off the stage. I'm taking Gia, and we're locking ourselves in until we fly to Berlin tomorrow.

Everyone closes in on me. BT takes my earpiece and Dallas hands me a towel as I pull off my T-shirt, looking for her.

"Rock God, I love you. Can you sign my tits?" A woman who is clearly British, along with her leggy friend, have somehow gotten backstage and she tears off her T-shirt.

They both squeal as she hands me a marker. I barely register as I write Rock and God on each tit. It's been a thing I've done for years. I feel Sebastian and Hunter following as they zoom in with the camera.

"Have a good one, darling." I turn and take the bottle of Jack that Fred, one of our roadies, hands me.

"Where's Gia?" I look around, then straight at the camera, because out of anyone, Sebastian would know where she is. "Gia. Where is she?" I yell at him.

Hunter walks over to Rafe. He's deep in conversation with Ace who has a bunch of extra security on hand tonight.

I look over my shoulder at Ammo. He's giving the leggy one his number on her tits.

The crowd still roars their appreciation as Rafe walks over. "Let's move," he says.

"What the fuck, man? Where is Gia?" Cold dread, like someone dumped a bucket of ice water on me, makes me almost grab my chest. He looks me in the eyes. That's Rafe—he never looks away. I wonder if I look as crazy as I feel, because the look on his face makes me turn.

Ace grabs me, but I have rage on my side as I lunge for Sebastian. "What did you do, you fuck? Where is she?"

He drops the camera just in time to save his eye as I take him to the ground.

"What did you tell her?" I slam my fist in his face, and the satisfying crack of his nose breaking makes me only want to hurt him more.

"Fuck, Granger. Dude." Hands are pulling me off him. He sits up and smiles. Fucking dick has a broken nose, fat lip, and blood everywhere and still, he fucking smiles at me.

"I'd start talking and stop smiling," I spit at him.

He doesn't engage, only puts his head back and pinches his nose.

Hunter, who's holding the camera and filming, looks around the lens at me, then at Sebastian. "Jesus Christ, Granger, you fucked up his nose."

Ace and his team are moving me toward the back exit. "Fuck you, Sebastian."

"I'm suing your ass, Granger. You don't deserve her." And I snap. See red. Growling like a caged animal, I try to break free.

"Granger, we need to get you out of here, man." Ace pushes me back as I hear people scream, or maybe it's me as I try to fight my way loose.

Sebastian takes a towel wrapped in ice for his nose. "You think I'd let her end up with a prima donna like you? Think again, *Rock God*."

"Motherfuck—" I lunge again as Rafe steps in to push me back.

"Get him to the hospital and fix his fucking nose," he says to one of the medics who's trying to help Sebastian sit. I have no choice but to move backward.

Ace pats my chest. "Brother, you need to cool your shit. She's okay. I took her to the airport."

My eyes dart to his. "The fuck you say?"

"She was borderline hysterical," he says as we bang open the heavy door and go outside into the rain. I'm like a man possessed. Whatever she heard must have been bad. Bad enough that she fucking ran.

She ran from me again. Just like I knew she would, just like my mother did, just like anyone I love.

"Where'd she go?" My voice is almost hoarse. I need to find her, tell her none of this shit matters, that it's only her and me.

Goddamn her for not trusting me and running after everything we've been through. Ammo and Nuke are waiting for me outside by the limo.

"I don't know where she was going. They wouldn't let me past the gates, even with my badge, man." He opens the door of the limo. Ignoring the paparazzi, we all pile in. I lean back and try to breathe. I need to form a plan. I sit up and get my phone out of my pocket. Of course, it goes straight to voicemail.

"Gia, I don't know what happened..." I look over at Rafe and Ace, both not even trying to pretend they're not listening.

"Just come back." I hang up and fight the urge to throw my phone.

"I asked Desi. She said she saw Gia crying with Sebastian," Ammo says as he looks out the window.

"I want that piece of shit fired. You know what? Fuck this, I'm done with the whole thing. They have enough footage." Clenching and unclenching my fist, I examine my swollen knuckles.

"You're all under contract," Rafe exclaims. "I'm going to have to work something out with Sebastian since he's threatening to sue. As for Gia..." He leans forward. "Granger, I told her to wait and talk to you. She said no."

The limo glides down the road as I turn to him. "You let her go?"

"I did."

"I told you to watch her. This is a fucking betrayal." I'm ready to attack Rafe, and that's never happened.

"Pull your shit together, Granger," he says dryly while typing on his phone. Reaching into his suit jacket, he pulls out another phone.

"Find her. Trace her fucking phone if you have to." I reach for my cigarettes, only to hear Nuke snort. I look over at him.

"You got something you want to say?" I sneer.

"You're unbelievable, man. The great Rock God has finally fallen. She's too good for you. You ain't gonna be faithful to her and you know it."

"What the fuck, Nuke?" I snarl.

He looks at me, his eyes almost slits as he lays his head back. "And you wonder why she left?" His voice sounds bitter. "The sexiest man alive and look at you." He laughs. "You don't give two shits about Gia."

I lean forward. "You need to get off the smack. You don't have a clue about Gia."

He snorts again. "Like you're a saint. What're you gonna do? Beat me up?" Wiping his nose, he sits up to stare at me.

"Nuke, shut the fuck up." Ammo lights a cigarette and hands me his bottle of Jägermeister. "Listen, Bianca is pregnant. It hasn't been a fun couple of days. She went and sold her story to *People*. It's coming out tomorrow."

"Bianca?" My mind goes back. "That was months ago. Did that fuck tell Gia that?" And it's all making sense. Of course, she wouldn't handle it well.

I take a large swig of the Jägermeister. Christ, I don't know how Ammo can stand drinking this shit all the time. "If she is pregnant, it's not mine. I didn't even fuck her. She blew me a couple of times—"

"The kid's mine," Nuke snaps, the most animated I've seen him in a long time, other than when he's onstage. I almost say I'm sorry, but screw him. Nuke is one of my oldest friends, but he's letting drugs take him down. He also sounds like a jealous dick. Like I would ever want to be the sexiest man alive.

Rafe glances up as the limo pulls into the hotel. I almost demand a new room. The thought of being in that suite without Gia makes me hold on to the bottle of shitty Jäger.

I turn to Ammo. "Let's go to the bar."

"Absolutely." He takes a drag of his cigarette. I don't wait for someone to open the limo door. My shock is wearing off.

I'm fucking livid, and strangely numb. She just fucking ran. Didn't try to talk. Didn't give me a chance. Fuck that. She didn't give *us* a chance! She's been holding back since I saw her a month ago. To be honest, she never trusted me.

I take a swig as Ammo walks next to me. "You might want to take it easy, brother." He eyes me.

"Nah, not tonight. Tonight, anything goes."

He tosses his cigarette and opens the door. "After you."

CHAPTER 35

GIA

Present – Twenty-five years old
Manhattan, New York

A bare foot jabs me in the ribs. "Gia."

"Oh my God, what?" I sit up and blink at Julianna, who stands over me looking perfect. Rolling my eyes, I fall back onto the incredibly comfortable mattress.

When she sits, the bed dips and I open one eye. "Go away with all your beauty. It's bugging me."

She starts to laugh, taking her blond hair down as she lets it cascade over her shoulders. She's like a porcelain Barbie doll.

"Stop it. I only wish I was you." She crosses her long legs in some incredible, form-fitting black slacks.

I sit up and the room spins slightly from last night's tequila. Also, I'm kind of off balance, lying here in my darkened canopy bed.

"God, my life." I rub my head and try to swing the heavy canopy open to give me a little more light. "Did I miss something? Are we going out?" Pushing the rat's nest known as my hair out of my face, I blink a few times.

She sighs dramatically as I crawl over to reach for my cigarettes. "No. I had to meet with my lawyer. Then Matthew showed up. I just can't."

I barely get the cigarette lit when she takes it from me.

"Oh God. Shit, the lawyer," I groan, now remembering that appointment. "I'm sorry. Why didn't you wake me up?"

"I tried." She shoots me a glare and I burst out laughing as I lean back on an ornate pillow, taking the cigarette back.

"So, what happened? Are you keeping the apartment?" I look around in distaste. I'm trying to be positive because Julianna is kind of fragile right now, but God, I don't care that this place is worth millions; you couldn't pay me to live here.

Her eyes look up at the red and gold canopy with gold tassels hanging down, and she shakes her head. "I gave it to him. I mean, come on, when he wanted to decorate all the bedrooms like Versailles, that should have been one big fat red flag," she mutters, reaching for the cigarette again. A pang of guilt runs through me. I haven't been the best influence on her lately.

I showed up a fucking mess, crying and doped up on Sebastian's Valium, which I found in my bag, and the gin I shot on the plane. We haven't exactly been sober since, and I think that was a week ago.

Julianna had *really* quit smoking and look at her now. Sheesh.

"I just." She looks up at the ceiling, then swings her hair over her shoulder and looks at me. "My dad is all over me to make him pay, and all I want to do is sign the divorce papers and forget this nightmare ever happened."

I nod, trying to be supportive as I attempt to detangle myself from the ornate bedspread.

"Agreed, sign the papers." Jesus Christ, I need a lady-in-waiting to help me out of this bed. Her eyes follow me as I try to get out.

"Are you okay?"

"Yes. Why?" She rolls her eyes. "Margaritas?"

"Um." I'm finally free of the bedding. "Is it noon yet? What day is it?" I say over my shoulder, trying my hardest not to look at myself in the large gold mirror in the bathroom. I'm holding on by a thin thread; hence the massive quantities of alcohol so I can pass out and not think about him.

"It's Thursday the twenty-first!" she calls out as I use the toilet. "And it's noon somewhere."

I grin because it's better than crying. I have completely lost it, holed myself up with Julianna for... "Wait. What is today?" I jump up and frantically finish doing my business, then stumble to wash my hands.

"The twenty-first," she yells again. "How about we do Irish coffees? That way it's like breakfast."

"Julianna, stop it." I march out and stare at her.

I must look bad because she says, "Are you going to take a shower, or should I just call and have all the stuff deliv—"

"Oh my God." I grab her arm, looking at her. "Holy fuck, I'm dead."

"What? What now? I can't take anymore, Gia. What have you done?" Letting go of her, I cover my mouth before I start screaming. I need to think.

"I need your phone." I motion with my fingers for her to hand it to me. She looks at me and frowns as she goes to her cute Chanel purse and hands me her phone. I take a breath. "Shit. I need alcohol and give me a cigarette."

She runs over to the nightstand and grabs the pack. "What is happening? I haven't seen anything on the news." She hands it to me.

"Axel," is all I say.

"Yes?" She looks confused.

"What the hell, Julianna? The wedding is in two days. In Los Angeles. We're in Manhattan." I sit down in a gaudy, high-backed gold chair. "This is bad, so fucking bad. I... we have to go. Do you think your dad would let us use his private plane?" I lean back and light up as she stands there staring at me like I'm growing horns.

"I can't go to LA." Her face is pale.

"Um, as my best friend, you ha—"

"Sebastian is your best friend," she states and leaves the room.

"Fantastic," I groan, looking at her phone. Leaping up, I follow her to the only normal spot in this monstrosity of a kitchen. It's state of the art, but it has stuff that would be better suited to some creepy French castle.

"What the hell is wrong with you?" I scream because she's dumping ice into a blender.

"Nothing." She grabs the Jose Cuervo Gold.

"God, no, not that." I take the bottle away from her and hand her Cazadores.

"Whatever," she mumbles.

I'm wearing one of her cute little silk pajama shorts sets and leaning against the marble island. It's freezing against my bare legs.

"Julianna, I can't deal with this today. Do you understand that—"

She turns on the blender and my mouth drops open. She might be snapping, which is pathetic. She couldn't stand Matthew. He was a balding gay guy she married because he was rich. Not wealthy, but rich, and he had a title. Oh, and her dad loved him. I begged her not to marry him, but did she listen? No.

So this crazy behavior is throwing me. During one of our drunken rants, she confessed about the cringeworthy sex they had, but I'm the one whose life is ruined. I'm the one who's nursing a broken heart. Who can't seem to move, breathe, eat, sleep without feeling his touch. I'm madly in love with a man who has completely destroyed me twice, or maybe I fucking left prematurely. It doesn't matter now. I'm gone and he's fucking other women, if the Internet can be believed. And let's not forget that I've been so self-absorbed, I completely forgot about my brother's wedding.

I suck.

I take a deep breath and wait for her to finish. As soon as her finger is off that blender's button, she says, "No."

"What has happened? Because I—" Droplets from the wet, freezing margarita hit my hand while she dumps it into two glasses.

"Julianna, are you okay?" I walk over to the sink to rinse my hands.

"I can't go." She brings the margarita glass to her lips and starts downing it.

"You have to, I need you. I can't go by myself. Everyone in that wedding party is happily married. I'm calling in the best friend card," I announce and proceed to chug my margarita, only to get brain freeze. I'm blowing out air to stop the pain when her phone rings on the island where I left it.

"That's stupid. What does that mean? Best friend card?" She rolls her eyes and grabs her phone.

"It's Sebastian. What do you want to do?" I look at her and mime *no* by shaking my head.

"Hey, Sebastian," she answers, looking straight at me. "Yep, here she is." She hands me the phone.

I glare at her. "You're going with me," I mumble, grabbing the phone. "Sebastian." I clear my throat. My voice is raspy from too much crying, along with all the booze and cigarettes.

"Gia? What the hell? I've been calling."

"I destroyed my phone," I snap, still on the fence about my feelings toward Sebastian. I'm starting to worry I overreacted.

He sighs. "Look, I'm sorry about what happened. I probably could have handled it better, but seeing you walk out of that bathroom with him... and hearing about the groupie getting pregnant."

I take a breath. "I don't understand. Do you know how many times I look the other way when it comes to your... shall we say, bad behavior?"

"You bitch at me all the time," he says. "Have you forgotten Jenny?"

"She was insane. Whatever, it's done." I rub my forehead with the icy glass.

"You need to get your ass to LA. Axel has been calling."

My eyes snap open. "What? Why would you talk to him? Where are you? You need to come back and go with me." I sound crazy, but at this point I don't care.

"Christ." He sighs again and I grit my teeth because I can just see him shaking his head. "You're a fucking mess, aren't you?"

"I can't deal with you right now, Sebastian. I can't turn off my heart like that. *I love him,* always have. So excuse me if I'm not perfect at this moment."

"Then you shouldn't have left. I'm not having you put all this on me," he says tightly.

"I'm not putting anything on you. That's your own conscience talking," I retort.

"We're in Rome. Take Julianna. I'm sure you've dragged her down to your level anyway. Call Axel and tell him you can't get your shit together to go to your only brother's wedding. That ought to go over well."

"Sebastian, I swear to God—"

"I have to go. We're filming." The line goes dead. I look at Julianna.

"Well, that went well." She reaches for the blender to top off my glass.

"You have to go with me. I can't do this alone." And I'm actually serious. I don't think I can handle flying for six hours alone.

She shakes her head. When her phone rings and it's an 818 number, I grab her hand. "Don't answer." I squeeze her wrist.

"Ow, stop it." She takes the phone as I back away, knowing who it is.

"Hello." Her face pales and I want to scream, *Who did you think it was going to be?*

"Oh my God, Axel." She looks at me, her eyes the size of giant blue saucers. "Hi, congratulations... Is Gia here? Um..." She reaches for me, but I step away, shaking my head.

"You have to go with me," I whisper.

"Gia. Take the phone." She hands it to me as we both jump at Axel's voice coming through the phone.

"Give it to me." I grab it.

"Hey, I'm on my way—"

"You've got to be fucking kidding me. I have to have Sebastian track you down?" I attempt to talk, but what can I say? So I let him go off. "Do you have any idea what is going on over here? *My wedding*. That's what. Now I have no fucking idea what you're doing in New York instead of being here with Antoinette and the girls like you promised. But I do know you're getting on the plane *today*."

"I had to stop and get Julianna. She's coming." I ignore her choking on the margarita.

"Great, I'll let Rip know to get both of you. Call me with your flight, and Gia?"

"What?" I cringe.

"I'm only saying this once. Do not disappoint me."

"I won't. We won't. I can't wa— Hello?" I look at her screen. It's gone black. When I peer up at Julianna, her eyes are watering, and she continues to cough.

"How could you?" She wheezes.

"Stop it. It will be good for you to get some fresh air, get out of New York and all the grayness—"

She grabs her phone and holds it up. "Call him back and tell him I'm not going."

"You call him." I motion to the phone. "He's crazy right now. He told me to tell you not to disappoint him." So, I'm twisting the truth. It's actually true—Julianna does need to get out of this apartment.

"I... Gia." She takes a breath. "I can't go to a Disciples wedding." Her eyes are filled with tears.

"Stop. I know what you're thinking, but this is going to be a super nice wedding. Like Antoinette has spent a fortune on it."

"That's not why I can't go," she says quickly, picking up her margarita. "I'm insulted you would think that's why I can't go."

My head is pounding, so I either need to sober up and take Advil, or I need to keep drinking, and since I need to fly, I guess I'll keep drinking.

"Then why? Because I shouldn't have to beg you. This is fucking pathetic. Do I have to go tit for tat with you? Remember when I rescued you—"

"It's Ryder, okay? I can't go because of Ryder." She blows out air as if that's been hanging over her for years.

"What?" Trying hard not to freak, I blink at her. Holy fuck... Ryder? And how is she only saying something now?

"It's not that big of a deal, but I don't want to see him." She rubs her face, and all her perfect makeup is not that perfect anymore. Dropping her hands, she looks at me.

I set down my glass and walk to her. "Julianna, I... what is going on? And how is it that this is the first that I'm hearing about this?"

She holds up her hand as if to stop me from getting too close as tears fall from her eyes. I'm floored. In all the time we've been friends, I've never seen her cry. I've cried, but not Julianna.

"Gia... I just... couldn't tell you. It was a long time ago and... he didn't..." It's like the flood gates have been opened and she's full-on hysterical. It's hard to understand her.

"Come here." I hug her. Julianna, the perfect one, the one who's always sensible, is a fucking mess. And I had no idea.

I grab the blender, forgetting the glasses as I guide us to the kitchen nook area and sit her down, placing the blender in front of her. She looks up and starts to laugh, then cry again, as I take a drink from the side of the glass blender.

"Okay." I pull out the other antique chair. It's uncomfortable, but what in this place *is* comfortable?

"Did something happen when you came to the compound to pick me up?" My voice is gentle, almost coaxing as I put this all together. She nods.

"And you have kept this inside for eight years?"

She nods again.

I take another sip from the blender, starting to feel the wonderful tequila take away my pain. Unfortunately, it also takes away my filter.

"I just... I have to be honest. This is rather shocking. I mean, I know I was a mess, but how... what is wrong with you?" I stand and start to pace.

"Not everyone is you, Gia. I can't vomit out all my shit all the time," she yells, then looks horrified. "I'm so sorry." She wipes her runny nose. Her mascara drips down her cheeks.

As I stare at her, tears form in my eyes, and I drop back into the seat. "You're right. It's not easy being my friend, but come on, I love you. Why wouldn't you say anything?"

She sniffs loudly, tosses her blond hair off her shoulder, and reaches for my hand.

"It happened when I came and got you. I thought he was everything, and you were in such pain I couldn't tell you. Then he vanished. It was like he dropped off the earth and I... was so humiliated. And my dad..." She sighs, trying to get a good breath. "I couldn't tell him about Ryder. I mean, could you imagine?" She shakes her head. "Then I didn't hear from him. It went from one day, to a week, then a year, and now here we are."

I bite my top lip while still piecing this together. "So. Ryder was your first?"

She nods.

"And you haven't seen him in eight years?"

"Exactly. So you understand why I can't go." She takes the blender that I was preparing to drink from and starts to swallow the contents in big gulps. Thankfully the ice is melted, so hopefully it's watered down. Standing, I take it away.

"Well, that definitely explains a lot of things."

We sit in silence as we both let everything sink in. At last, Julianna says, "I feel so much better letting that out."

I nod. "I bet. So what time should I book our flights? I need to do it before I'm too drunk." I reach for her phone.

"What?" She jumps up.

"You're coming. Fuck them. I had to deal with Rhys. You can deal with Ryder. Call it closure. Trust me, this is meant to be... for you." I start searching for flights. "We're going first class, unless we can use your dad's plane?" She only stares at me.

"I'll take that as a no." I start booking us on American when she stands and straightens her shoulders.

"You know what? You're right," she says.

I glance up at her, my brain somewhat sluggish, but I'm not going without her. Sure, Ryder has some weird thing going on with Cindy, but if Julianna is his soulmate it needs to be explored. Also, one of us needs to be happy.

"I know I am."

"Fuck him. I need to go to at least tell him what I think."

I glance up. "Well, maybe don't tell him off right before the wedding. That's why we should get there today because tomorrow is the wedding. There." I smile at her, trying not to look at her puffy, splotchy face. Not that I look any better, but I still had to remind her to hold off until afterward.

"We're booked for six p.m. We should be able to get our shit together in four hours, right?"

"We need showers, and I'll get Dean over here to do hair and makeup. I don't care that he might have fucked Matthew. He's the best." I nod supportively. Either she's in shock or completely smashed.

I stand and make my way to my horrible bedroom to shower. "I need to raid your wardrobe. Actually, just pack for both of us."

"Already on it." She waves me off, causing me to frown. God, I hope she's not going to make a scene. She's acting weird.

Screw it. My brother is far from perfect and has caused numerous scenes. And fuck Ryder. How dare he blow off my best friend. She deserves answers.

Screw all of them.

CHAPTER 36

GIA
Present – Twenty-five years old
Los Angeles, California

"Ladies and gentlemen, welcome to Los Angeles. If you have checked luggage, please go to carousel three, and thank you for flying American Airlines." I blink my eyes open and look around. Thank God we made it.

My mouth is dry. I lick my lips and clear my throat; I've got to quit smoking. I passed out about twenty minutes ago—enough time to screw up my neck, but not enough time to sleep off my hangover. I blink again and look over at Julianna. If I look as bad as she does, we might be in trouble.

"Hey, we landed. They're getting ready to open the doors." Her eyes pop open and she groans as if it's only now dawned on her where we are and what we're doing. We got fucked up with Dean while he did our hair. Of course, we missed our flight and had no choice but to take the redeye. Now we're landing at 9:00 a.m. on the day of Axel and Antoinette's wedding.

I grab my bag, praying I kept that bottle of water I bought at the duty-free store. I need Advil and a large black coffee.

"Oh shit." Julianna stares at the woman across from us in first class who's reading a magazine. And there he is on the cover in all his glory.

I want to throw up.

People magazine's sexiest man. I should try to be happy for him, because if there's one thing he is, it's sexy. But I'm not happy at all. Everything is crashing down on me. I need to get through this wedding and hold it together until I can lock myself in my bungalow. Julianna will have to stay with me.

My heart pounds as I stare at the magazine. His signature smirk haunts me. I should have taken the picture—mine are so much sexier. Except I gave my camera to Hunter, and I need to get it back.

Standing up, I sling my bag over my shoulder. "Let's get this over with."

She nods. I reach up to open the overhead bin to pull down our carry-on but a man in front of us takes pity on me.

"Here, let me." His voice is deep, reminding me of Rhys, and I want to burst into tears.

"Thank you," I mutter as I take in a breath. I'm about to smile, but freeze when I stare into green eyes and a fucking gorgeous face.

Holy shit, he's one of the Saddington twins. It has to be Jax; his hair is longer. Why the hell is he flying commercial? The Saddingtons are billionaires. I've been trying to get a photo shoot with one of them for years. David, who's like a second brother to me, is best friends with Reed Saddington. I tried to get him to call Reed, but he kept coming up with excuses, so I just dropped it. That and Axel said over his dead body, which is absurd. I photograph many big names.

I need to say something, grab my opportunity. I mean, what are the chances?

"Excuse me." He looks down at me, his muscled arm on display as he brings out my carry-on.

"I'm Gia Fontaine. I'm actually good friends with David McCormick. He and Reed—your brother—are good friends."

He grins. "I know David."

"Yes." I smile back. "Anyway, I'm a freelance photographer and I would love to photograph you sometime. I... shit, let me get my card." I drop my bag back on the seat and fumble around for my wallet to give him my card, almost hitting my head on his arm as I stand back up.

"Oh God. Sorry." My face heats up as he cocks his head, his eyes caressing my face.

"Thank you. Let me check my schedule and I'll be in touch." He takes my card, looks at it, and flashes me a smile that should make me wet.

"You two need a lift?"

"No," we both say at the same time.

He raises a dark brow and laughs. Jesus, this man is beyond beautiful. He's also looking interested. I should say yes and get in his car. It's Jax fucking Saddington. If anyone can make me forget about Rhys, it would be him. Unfortunately, I feel zero. Nada.

"Well, it was a pleasure meeting you, Gia Fontaine." He hands me my carry-on and starts to walk out. The flight attendants look like they want to faint, and one of them is a man. He smiles as Jax passes.

"Just walk," Julianna says under her breath because I'm not moving. I'm just sort of shell-shocked that in this moment, I finally admit to myself that I'm full-on fucked.

And in love with Rhys Granger.

She pushes me and I start to walk, not even looking at the flight attendants as they wish us a good day.

"I'm in love with Rhys," I say to Julianna under my breath as we walk up the ramp out into the madness of LAX.

"Of course, you are. Keep moving. You hired us a car, a limo, right?"

I look at her. "Did you just hear me? I felt nothing for Jax Saddington. I'm doomed to be alone for the rest of my life. At least last time I rebounded with Sebastian. This time..." I grab her arm to stop. "This time I don't want anyone but him. Oh my God. I'm never gonna have sex again." Stunned, I wonder what the hell I'm going to do.

"Car? Where are we going?" she demands. Her slacks and white button-down shirt are a wrinkled mess.

"Axel sent one of the guys to pick us up. He didn't trust us after we missed the flight yesterday." She freezes.

"Relax. It's not Ryder." But what if it is? Yesterday, bringing Julianna seemed like a necessity. Now that we're walking out into the hot morning sun of Los Angeles, I'm rethinking everything.

A black SUV honks and maneuvers into a spot a couple of cars away. A blond woman jumps out. "Gia." She waves.

"Who's that?" Julianna stares at Eve.

"Eve, Blade's wife. I know, she's gorgeous, right? Welcome to my world. Wait until you see the others." I start to pull my carry-on over to her, and thank God it's Rip who gets out of the driver's side.

I'm not even at the SUV, and Eve throws her arms around me. "You're in soooo much trouble." We sway back and forth as my eyes pool with tears. I love Eve. I'm actually super close with her, and she's one-hundred percent supportive.

She pulls back and her blue eyes look at me, shift to Julianna, then back at me.

"Oh wow. Um, Rip." She snaps her fingers. "Get their bags."

"Eve, this is my best friend, Julianna." I'm wearing Julianna's clothes, which are ten times more conservative than any of mine. But when I left London, I only had my purse and what I was wearing. It's not like I've had time to shop. Besides, I have a closetful at my house.

"I'm so happy to finally meet you, Julianna. Gia talks about you all the time." She smiles and I want to put my head on her shoulder and sleep. I'm fucking depressed.

"Okay. Well, let's get going." She looks at me rather unsure.

Rip walks over and hugs Julianna. We all go way back. He used to be my pot dealer at Berkeley.

"Did you finally realize that we're meant to be?" He kisses the top of her head. Secretly I think Rip has a thing for her. Too bad she can't like him instead of the six-five, dark-haired enforcer.

"Ripper, you never change." She smiles up at him. He takes a step back as if her appearance surprises him. His blue eyes laser in on me and he scowls.

What the hell? I know we look a little haggard, but our hair is still holding up well.

"Okay, Eve's right. We need to get going. They moved the wedding an hour earlier because of the heat."

"What?" I climb in as Eve gives me an encouraging pat on the shoulder. He slams the door on my question.

The SUV has the air on, thank God. As Rip pulls out, Eve turns to me. "Listen, it's been a little tense lately."

I look out the window as we pull onto the 405 North. "Do you have a cigarette, Rip? My head is pounding."

He looks at me through the mirror and hands me the pack laying on the console.

"Thanks." I offer Julianna one, but she shakes her head no.

"What's the drama?" I light up and roll down the window slightly, making it sound like we're in a wind tunnel.

"Just club stuff, so they moved the wedding to a secret place. Dolly and Doug are doing our makeup at the clubhouse."

I turn and look at her. "What the hell, Eve?" My heart starts to race in fear. Ever since the day Axel said he was getting patched in, I've hated this feeling. I'm always on edge, worrying something bad could happen.

"Don't panic. They're just being careful. No one wants unexpected guests today."

I rub my forehead and try to let the nicotine calm me. "I can't really handle anything, Eve. So if you need to tell me something, spit it out."

She looks at Rip, then back at me. "Axel's not happy for numerous reasons. So maybe wait until after the wedding to like, hug him."

I blink at her. "Aren't we doing pictures before the wedding?"

She just stares right back. "Do you need to borrow a dress?"

"Julianna packed me one." I wave my hand, then glance over at her. "Maybe. What time is the wedding? I need a nap."

"Three hours." Rip looks back at us. "And what Eve's not telling you is that Axel is pissed about everything. Starting with you, and ending with the fact that Eve and Dolly got Antoinette a stripper for the bachelorette party."

I'm not exactly listening because I'm either getting car sick, or everything is catching up with me. I need to sleep or drink because I'm starting to sober up. Julianna must feel the same way because she takes my cigarette.

"Three hours?" I take off my seat belt and slide to the middle so I can talk easily to both of them. "What happened to a dusk wedding? What's going on?"

"Relax, Gia. Everything is fine." Rip holds up his hands. His mellow pot-grower attitude is getting on my nerves right now.

"It's been a fucking nightmare." Eve turns sideways. "Something's going on. None of them will talk about it, but at the last minute, everything changed. Then you, and whatever is going on with Granger..." She points at me, and I slap her hand down.

"Sorry. Anyway, I thought it would be fun for Antoinette to have a stripper. Sue me."

She looks at Rip who shakes his head. "Don't bring me in on this."

"You would have thought I had murdered someone. They freaked." Eve rolls her eyes.

"Knowing how my brother is with Antoinette, he probably would have been happier if you had murdered someone." I sit back.

"Probably," she huffs. "And Jason went all Blade on me..." Her face starts to flush as a small smile crosses her lips, and I think I might throw up. This is why I need Julianna. I'll never make it through today without her.

"Anyway, I just texted Dougie. He'll fix you both up." She smiles and continues texting.

Eve is gorgeous. With golden-blond hair, blue eyes, and legs that seem to never end, she commands the room. She also did the impossible. She got Blade McCormick to fall for her *hard*. I remember my brother feeling so sad for him. Jesus, look at him now.

I lean my head back on the cool leather seat and close my eyes. They're so swollen, even shutting them hurts. I have to pull myself together. I've cried myself and drunk myself into an emotional mess. Considering how physically exhausted and torn up I am, a short nap or a moment to rest my eyes might help.

"Eve, what the fuck? Who is with her?" I groan at the deep, angry voice that dares to wake me.

"Jason, I'm at a loss. Look at her. Our beautiful Gia. Fucking Granger, that's it. I'm no longer a fan, no matter how much I love The Stuffed Muffins."

"This is fucked. Axel saw the article on them today."

I blink my eyes a couple of times and sit up as Blade comes into focus.

"I'm jet-lagged," I say, turning to wake Julianna. Her spot is vacant.

"Where's Julianna?" Jumping out the open door, I look around the clubhouse and cringe as the sun bounces off the shiny bikes.

It looks pretty much the same. Grass and play area on one side, gravel and firepits on the other. Lots of bikers walking around, but no Julianna.

"Give me your arm." Blade and his large body tower over me, his eyes going straight for my veins.

"What are you doing?" I pull my arm away. "What is wrong with you?"

"Nothing. You look like shit. I'm taking care of my family, and that includes you."

I'm completely mortified. "So, you're saying I look like a junkie?" This week has been hell, but Blade checking my arms for needle marks might be my breaking point. He cocks his head at me, his green eyes dissecting me.

"Christ." He grabs me for a tight hug. It's strong, warm, and secure, and, of course, I start to cry.

"It's okay, Gia. Just get it out. Fucking piece-of-shit Granger. I should put a bullet in his head," he growls as he strokes my hair and I try not to get snot on his cut.

"Sorry." I wipe it, the smell of leather strangely comforting. "I'm just tired. I hate to fly." I shake my head and reluctantly pull away as I wipe under my eyes and try to laugh. When I glance over at Eve, she looks concerned.

"This is not because of Granger." I motion to my face as I take the elastic from around my wrist to pull my hair back into a low bun. "Where's Julianna?"

"Gia, do you think I'm stupid?" I shake my head no at Blade.

"I never forget a face. Especially when one belongs to the woman who fucked with my enforcer's head," he says. "Why would you bring her?"

I sniff. "I have zero idea what you're talking about," reaching back inside for my large purse.

"Wait. Please tell me you're not saying that Julianna has a past with Ryder?" Eve looks at Blade who simply stares at me.

"Oh God. This is bad." She swings around to look at me, her long hair hitting me in the face. "Do you get that Cindy is... Cindy is here. She's supposed to be with Ryder," she whispers as if we're passing around CIA secrets.

I sling my purse onto my shoulder. "Well, if we want to get technical, Julianna saw him first."

"What?" Eve's voice rises.

"Just take her inside, Angel. Get Dolly to work her magic. Axel will lose his mind if he sees her like this." Blade stares at me, along with Eve, both of them seeming to forget that I'm standing right in front of them.

"And, Gia?"

"What?" I snap, over this already, but that seems to be my new normal.

"This is Axel and Antoinette's day. I don't want drama." He nods at me. Fantastic. That's code for I shouldn't have brought Julianna. They want Cindy. She's part of the group, or at least the old lady group.

Screw it, Julianna's part of my group. That being said, I'll try to seat her in the back. Eve loops her arm through mine as we start up the stairs to the clubhouse.

"You need to tell me everything," she whispers as a prospect opens the door for us.

"I need booze. I'm never going to make it through this. And stop looking at me like that. Ryder is a grown man, and I have a feeling about them."

"Do not, under any circumstances, tell anyone any of this. If Cindy finds out, even gets a whiff of this, I can't be sure what she might do."

I look over at her, and she looks serious. "Are you being honest? I thought they weren't together?"

"They aren't technically. But with the wedding, it hasn't been easy for her." Great, now I feel bad for her. I can relate to not wanting to be around them. Jesus, even Doug is madly in love.

"Julianna is not a threat to Cindy. I think they had a small fling years ago. If it was going to go anywhere, it already would have. I needed her to come. I've had a rough week."

She smiles and rubs my arm. "Do you love him, Gia?" God, leave it to Eve to just come out with it.

"I do. But I can't handle the women. Constantly looking over my shoulder. Now another groupie says she's pregnant." My stupid eyes fill up with tears. I try to move around her, but she stops me at Blade's door.

"We read the article. But it's not his kid. Does he fuck around on you?"

"What?"

"Does he? Because I'm trying to figure out what you're crying about? He's a rock star who looks like a god. What the hell's wrong with you?"

I'm about to open my mouth to defend myself but close it because I have no answer for her. When Sebastian said all that stuff, it sounded right. But now?

She shakes her head at me. "You need to make this right. You want him, then do what you've always done. Make it happen." She throws the door open.

"Finally." Doug grabs me for a hug. I look over his shoulder as Dolly looks up from doing Cindy's makeup.

"Hey, Doug." I smile up at him.

"Jesus Christ." He looks me up and down. "They weren't lying. You look like shit. Go take a shower. And Eve, get her your red strapless dress."

"Thank you, Doug," I state dryly. "I need to find my friend."

He arches a dark brow at me. Whatever, Doug has zero filter.

"She was here. She had to make a call," Cindy says. Her eyes are closed while Dolly applies her eye shadow.

"Oh, thank God. I'm exhausted. Where's Antoinette?" I go over and hug Dolly. Eve trails behind me as if I'm on suicide watch.

"She's with Charlie." Dolly puts her hands on her tiny hips. Everything about Dolly is small—she truly does look like a doll. She's fucking fierce though. A couple of years ago, she stabbed

Edge. Tried to slice off his dick because she thought he was cheating. Crazy, yes. Unfortunately, I understand how that could happen. It's one of the reasons I don't own a gun.

"Go. Take a shower. I'll get coffee." Doug shakes his head. He's already dressed in a conservative black tuxedo, which is very un-Doug. But Antoinette made it clear that she wanted an elegant wedding.

Besides me and Julianna, everyone is a bridesmaid. Their beautiful lavender gowns hang on a rolling garment rack to my right. A pang of guilt shoots through me. I should have said yes. She wanted me, and I used the tour and film as my excuse. I'm a shitty soon-to-be sister-in-law.

"I'll be back." They all nod. What the hell? Something is up, but I need to get cleaned up. Julianna will need the shower after me, and I'm determined to sober up at least enough for the wedding.

Yes. This is about my brother and Antoinette. I flip on the bathroom light, strip off Julianna's clothes, and step in.

This is it. I'll shed no more tears for Rhys Granger.

CHAPTER 37

RHYS

Present – Thirty-five years old
Rome, Italy

"Five minutes," Rafe announces as I sit in the corner, feet propped up on the table. We're in Rome getting ready to play the Stadio Olimpico, an enormous venue. I should be joining in with my brothers and preparing to bring down the house, yet I sit alone. My bottle of Jack Daniel's is my faithful companion as I close my eyes and smoke, hearing music in my head.

It's been a week since she left. A week of shit. Like the fucking dick that I am, I've had woman after woman brought to me, maybe to remind me I'm fucked. One after another they come to me as I try to use them to block out her smell, the taste of her lips.

But your heart knows the truth. It knows when it beats for another, and my heart has been taken by Gia. Torn out of me as it hemorrhages on the floor, yet somehow it continues to beat.

A loud scream should make me open my eyes, but I don't. I ignore the mayhem and stay where I am.

"Granger? Let's do this, brother." I open my eyes to see Ammo, Jägermeister in one hand and his guitar in another.

I drop my feet with a loud thud. My limbs feel weighted, as if cement has been poured on them. "Fuck it." Tossing my cigarette onto the floor, I step on it and run my hands through my hair.

While I walk toward the stage, BT is by my side, along with Rafe and the fucking film crew. This will be the last concert on the tour. After this, it's a lot of interviews. I have nothing left to say. I can barely stomach Hunter and his pushy attitude, and fucking Sebastian is lucky he can walk. His sanctimonious attitude makes me want to beat the shit out of him over and over.

Rafe worked it out. Sebastian's not suing, but he gets to finish the film. I don't give a shit. My interest is at zero. All the gossip rags want are details about whom I've fucked. The sexiest man alive has only added more to the hype, and since I'm not talking, they find a story no matter who they dig up.

Our boots pound the long hallway as we head out to the arena. The noise of the crowd filters in as I hold out my hand for my ear monitor.

Nuke is always the first to go on, but again, I give zero fucks. My fans, this crowd is my lifeline. So I take the stage.

The noise and love that vibrate out of them as they see me makes my cock come to life. Stepping onstage, I motion for a confused Tim to hand me a bottle of Jack. Nuke's drums come to life.

"The fuck you doing, Granger?" he yells. I laugh at his pissed-off expression.

"How you all doing out there?" I walk up to the microphone and crack open the bottle of Jack. The thousands of adoring eyes stare up as if I truly am a god.

"Yeah, that's it. The Rock God is here." I lift my hand, step back, and take a drink as I let the world call out my name.

"Rock God. Rock God," they chant and I smile.

"Ammo? Ace of Spades, you here, man?" There's a loud weep from his guitar while he walks up to me, and the crowd gets louder. I'm numb.

Cash's bass follows suit as he walks out, and the band is complete.

We're four guys who started out in a garage and did the unthinkable. Yet with the whole world in our hands, all I can think about is her.

My muse. Nuke pounds his drums, and Ammo and Cash start to play "Untouched." The words that never desert me pour from my lips. I used to question how that is. How half the time I can't remember what day it is, but every word, verse, or tune I've written or sung is like a faithful lover.

Always with me, never gone.

Our hits flow out of me as if I'm crossing off a to-do list. The only difference is the crowd's worship and enthusiasm.

Dallas walks on and hands me a towel and my guitar while I tug off my shirt. The sounds of crying and screaming make me smile as I scan the sea of faces. "Don't mind these cameras." I motion at Sebastian and the other guy they brought in to shoot the crowd's reactions. "We're doing a movie, but pretend they don't exist." I snicker as I look down at the screaming masses.

There, in the front row, is an angel with long, dark hair. Could she be my muse? She looks up at me adoringly. Her big brown eyes are full of tears, pouring out love.

She worships me.

I motion for them to bring her onstage. The barrier that keeps them away, blocks her, but she claws and tries to reach for me. The tips of our fingers touch, and I motion for Sal, one of our roadies, to bring her up as the masses go wild.

Nuke's drums start to beat almost menacingly, and I grin as she at last gets on stage and launches herself at me.

I hold her close, almost swaying with her.

Her heart beats for me. Rapid, frantic, excited pounding, it seeps into me as does her own smell. Not unpleasant but not what I crave. I kiss her lips, wanting to feel anything, wanting my heart to beat.

I back up and she cries and speaks. It doesn't matter that I don't understand her words. I know what she's feeling as I replace her face with another.

Then I hold her hand up and let my addicts adore her. She trembles as they take her away and I grab the bottle, waving my hand for my brothers to stop playing. The lights and smoke fade as I drink and tell them all my truths.

"You ever been in love?" They answer with a loud rumble. Ammo walks over, his face filled with concern as I continue. "My brothers are thinking I'm gonna go all cowboy on you guys. But I know you all understand me." The answer is a loud, pulsing roar and I nod.

"That's the thing about love—fucking *amore*. It comes at you like a bullet ripping into your skin and can take you out." I laugh. "There're all kinds of love." I take a swig of Jack and pace the stage. "Good, bad, toxic, exciting. The kind that comes at you and you know it's unhealthy, but you do it anyway, right?" I lift my hand, grasping the bottle, and they scream that they understand.

"How about the ones who leave and run away like a fucking rat? They take a part of you with them. Yeah, how about those?" I nod as my eyes see double and I reach for the microphone to stabilize me.

"How about the ones who turn your love ugly?" I scream, and they answer me. It vibrates loudly in my chest and I reach for my heart.

"This next song I wrote as a love song, but I'll let you all decide." I take a drink and turn to look at Cash who shakes his head. I ignore him and tell Ammo to follow. As I let my guitar scream, Nuke picks up the tune and Ammo joins in.

"There's been a lot of talk lately about my personal life. Shit that means nothing. But this meant something. I wrote it for another, but it belongs to you." I nod at the crowd. The earth pounds as they chant, showing their gratitude with lights from phones and lighters.

"Fuck you, Gia." The words vibrate around the arena. Suddenly I'm not numb. I'm alive and angry and so fucking in love with her it hurts.

One.

Two.

Three.

Four.

Baby, I don't want to see you cryin'.

But I can't live without your love.

This hunger that eats me up, only your lips can cure.

I make everyone bleed.

But that's nothing compared to my heart.

It bleeds for you.

It's strong and powerful. And mine beats for yours.

It beats for you.

Let me match your breathing; let me steal your breath, rest my racing mind.

For this moment, I'm at peace.

I can't make you love me. I can't control your heart.

But baby, mine is yours.

It beats for you.

It beats for you.

"Thank you, my friends." I lift my hand. "Rome, you rock. I love you all. Good night!" I leave without a backward glance. I know they want an encore, but I'm too raw right now. I sense Sebastian following me as I head to the green room.

"Granger? Hold up." I stop and look up at the fluorescent lights as our team runs past. Ammo is playing a solo for the encore, I guess.

"Stay away from me, Sebastian. If you want to live, stay the fuck away." I start walking again.

"I don't like you and you don't like me, but I fucked up. I'm a big enough man to acknowledge it."

"What?" I turn to see the camera off and hanging by his side.

"I'm not in love with you, so I see things differently. But Gia is." He shakes his head, almost like he can't quite believe it.

"She ran from you also?" I laugh, but it's bitter and hollow.

"She never runs from me. Her heart was yours from the day we met, and I don't think I really acknowledged it until right now." He nods at me, a shine of tears in his eyes.

"Look, man." He runs a hand through his hair. "I can't tell you what to do. But I can come clean for my own self. I wanted Gia away from you. I pushed her to leave. I thought you would hurt her. But the thing is, I'm the one who's hurting her, and I can't live with that. She deserves the world. And it's not my place to pick who she shares it with."

I shake my head. "Don't beat yourself up. She's never trusted me. She would have left sooner or later." I turn, needing a fresh bottle of Jack, a cigarette, and some Italian pussy.

"She loves you, Granger!" The sharp echo of his voice is like a knife stabbing me in the back. "She always has. There was a ghost in our relationship and that was you. I thought eventually I could make her forget. But that never happened. You deserve to know the truth."

My hand stops before I open the door. "You talk to her?" I close my eyes against opening up more pain.

"I have. She's in LA at Axel's wedding." I nod, then swing open the green room door as I hear my brothers riding the high that only our fans' love can give us.

I take a breath and turn as I pull my phone out. Ignoring the whispers, I pass everyone and keep moving. Someone calls my name; it sounds like Ammo.

But I'm done with all this shit.

I'm done running.

CHAPTER 38

GIA

Present – Twenty-five years old
Los Angeles, California

"I can't believe you." I look over at Julianna. Wearing an incredible pink chiffon halter dress and heels to die for, she looks like an angel. But clearly Julianna has become a devil since she came strolling in right when I was getting ready to call Blade and tell him one of his guys kidnapped my friend.

Thank God I didn't because she's glowing. "I was worried," I say quietly.

"You were passed out. I thought you needed sleep," she whispers back.

"I... how did this happen?" I smile as Bear and his old lady sit down next to us. We're in a giant air-conditioned tent in the middle of one of those huge horse estates down the street from the clubhouse. And I should clarify—when I say tent, this is like lavish celebrity stuff. It had to cost my brother a fortune.

"Bear." I nod. He looks uncomfortable in his dress slacks and black cut. He's been around since as long as I can remember. I think he has a daughter my age.

"VP gone crazy." He looks up at the chandelier hanging from the top, and the thousands of little sparkling lights glittering around the tent.

I can't help but grin. "Guess so."

"I love it," his old lady says, her bloodred lipstick a bit distracting. "Big Bear here is just ornery because he had to get dressed up. Don't he look handsome?" Julianna and I look at Bear whose stomach is almost bursting out of his black T-shirt. His beard is combed and his hair's slicked back, all for my brother. That makes my heart ache.

"You both look gorgeous," she adds.

I nod, tears already stinging my eyes, and lean back toward Julianna. "I'm losing it."

She looks at me, then at my dress, and shrugs. "Well, at least you look good."

"What has happened to you?" I mumble.

"I'm sorry I disappeared, but I had business to take care of." She crosses her legs.

"Business? I had to sit in utter torture waiting for you while I got my makeup done, and I couldn't say anything because apparently he's with Cindy."

"He's not." She smirks and I'm stunned.

"Are you high? What is happening?"

"Excuse me, Gia?" I jump and look over at a prospect who looks about as uncomfortable as Bear.

"Yes?"

"The VP said get your skinny ass... butt in the family section." He straightens.

"Oh, yes. I was just..." I stand and look over at my mother who's glaring at me. So much for hiding. "I'll be right there." He backs up but waits, which makes me grit my teeth.

"Just lay low," I grumble, forcing a smile.

"What?" She looks confused.

"Stay here." I slap her legs so I can shimmy out and try to walk straight. I had to have a couple of glasses of Cristal champagne because my head was pounding. That and my nerves were shot from worrying about Julianna.

The tent is filling up. I take in the multitude of flowers and the sight of Doug sitting and talking with my mom. Something is up. I mean, I know I'm going on very little sleep and all, but it seems like everyone is looking at me. Maybe it's because I'm Axel's sister, but that's stupid. It's not like they haven't seen me before.

"Hey, Mom." I brace myself against Doug's shoulder as my mom looks up at me. Her knowing eyes don't miss a thing, so I sit. Why pretend I'm good? It seems everyone knows already.

"Doug, please stay with me." I grab his hand.

"Gia Ana Fontaine, do you have any idea how worried we've all been? Your brother has had enough to deal with, having to be all secret, and now all the press. Doug, tell her." She looks over at Doug, who squeezes my hand.

"We're not gonna worry about any of that right now, Janet. Gia's here. I've fixed her up." He turns to me. "You look amazing." He runs his hands through my hair. "It's all going to be fabulous."

"Do you have any Advil? My head is pounding." I feel bad, but my mom's energy is not great right now. "What press?" I sigh, almost bracing myself.

"Nothing," she snips as Doug sits back, wrapping an arm around me.

"Where's Robert?" I lean into him.

"In the back. He gets nervous, you know." I look back and blink at how many bikers and their families are here.

"You can bring Julianna up with us," my mom says primly.

"What is wrong with you, Mom? I'm not in the mood. I'm here, the whole club is fixed up for your son, and he's spent a fortune. Look at this tent. What can you possibly be unhappy about?"

She looks at me, and for the first time I can actually see tiny wrinkles under her eyes. She appears tired and worried, but I guess that's our theme.

"You've been missing. You should have been a bridesmaid, not sitting in the back like a stranger. You missed all the parties, and you've hurt Antoinette, not to mention the twins, all so you can follow Rhys Granger." She looks straight ahead.

And I'm done.

"Excuse me." I stand as Doug pulls me back down.

"Let's all just get through this day. We can get fucked up after pictures. Hold it together, Gia."

"I'm not going to fight with you, Mom. But I will say this: I'm almost twenty-six years old. I refuse to let you take out all your shit on me. I have enough of my own." This time my eyes are getting teary from anger, which, let's face it, is better than a broken heart.

"Okay, let's take a little walk." Doug stands, takes my hand, and we head to the side of the tent.

"Talk to me," he demands, his brown eyes looking around before he takes us into the corner of the tent.

"I'm holding on by a thin thread, Doug. I already have enough guilt, and don't need my mom and all her shit." I point at her.

He brings my hand down as I straighten my skintight red satin dress. It's strapless so it's a good thing I have great breasts. Otherwise, I would have spilled out of it already.

"That's not what this is about." His eyes caress my face. "Gia, Gia, Gia." He pulls me into a hug.

"I'm almost numb, Doug. Yet my heart still burns. Why does it hurt so much?" I stare at the vast array of flowers in front of me.

"If it didn't hurt, baby girl, it wouldn't be worth it in the end." I pull back.

"What does that mean?"

"It means the wedding is starting. Do you want your friend?" he says tightly as we both glance over at Julianna. She's watching something on her phone. Then I glance over at my mom who looks pitiful sitting alone.

"God," I groan and take his hand, returning to the chair I just vacated. "I'm sorry, Mom," I whisper. It's curt, but at least I did it.

She nods as the music starts to play out of the speakers and we all turn. All the guests in the tent, even the roughest-looking bikers, smile at them.

"Oh my God." My hand goes to my chest as my twin nieces stand at the opening and stare at us. Juliette starts to walk, tossing rose petals, but Michelle stands there looking like she's gonna cry.

"Oh dear." I stand, ready to help, just as she sees me and throws the basket screaming, "Giaaa!"

I catch her right as my brother enters the tent. I laugh and squeeze her and kiss her fat cheeks. She squirms, but whatever, I need her right now. As my eyes lock with Axel's, he must be satisfied with my appearance because he laughs as my other niece throws herself around my leg.

I hand Michelle to my mom and grab Juliette. We all turn to watch the wedding party walk down the aisle.

Eve smiles up at Blade. They're all so beautiful and so in love, it almost makes my knees give out.

Charlie and David, Edge and Dolly, followed by Ryder and Cindy make their way to the assigned spots.

"I got you." Doug stands behind me. He gets it, understands, and thankfully doesn't say I'll get over it. Because I won't.

Never will be. I've loved Rhys Granger for as long as I can remember, and I will love him until the day I die.

It doesn't matter if we never see each other again. This is my truth, and I need to make peace with it.

"Mommy." Juliette points and my eyes drift to the tent's opening. Antoinette stands in a white lace dress that has the most incredible train I've ever seen. She also has a veil I could only dream of wearing.

She's beautiful, breathtaking. Guess I'm not the only one who thinks so, considering my brother, one of the club's most-feared bikers, blinks back tears. Not waiting for her, he meets her halfway, taking her hand.

It's then that I realize my niece is wiping my tears away. Why am I crying? Because he loves her so much. Axel never wanted this, and yet here he is. I look at his brothers standing next to him, smiling at him and at their own wives. It's a family, a band of brothers who would die for each other.

Chairs creak as we sit and listen, but all I can do is cling to my niece who holds me back. Her chubby little hand plays with my hair as her parents say their vows.

"I never thought I'd see the day." My mom reaches for my hand. I wonder if my dad was invited.

Why do you make all the girls cry? It spins in my head. I should have listened to Stephanie all those years ago. But as I look at my brother, I know that I regret none of it.

I love him, and no matter what the future holds, I know he loves me. And I wouldn't give any of that up, even knowing how we've hurt each other, and despite the pain I'm in.

Some people are born to love many times. Others love only once.

Axel kisses Antoinette. Everyone cheers, and I smile, walking over to hug and laugh with my new sister-in-law.

Smiling for the camera as the photographer takes pictures. Laughing with Dolly. I do all these things, while in my head I'm counting the moments until I can hide in a corner and fucking sob and let out all of today's joy. Because as happy as I am for my brother, I'm still human.

"You okay?"

I look up to see Edge. How long he's been standing next to me is anyone's guess.

"Edge, how are you?"

His blue eyes focus on me, and he wraps an arm around my shoulder. "Better than you." He grins. "Come on, let's get fucked up."

Laughing, I let him steer me into another large tent with tons of decorated tables. I almost groan. I didn't know we were having a sit-down dinner, or I guess brunch, in this case.

He walks me straight up to Axel who's laughing with Blade and David, his arm planted possessively around Antoinette. I could have sworn I saw Julianna come in here. We need a plan. I figure we let everyone start drinking, then call an Uber and have them take me to my house in Venice.

He looks over at me and brings an arm around my shoulder but keeps talking. Again, I have this odd sensation like I'm missing something, but quite frankly, I'm too tired to care.

"I need to use the restroom." Axel looks down at me, frowning, but lets me go. Stepping back out into the afternoon sun, I head into the massive, ranch-style house for the bathroom.

"Oh my God, in a way it's fucking hot," I hear Dolly as I turn the corner. She and Cindy are watching something on her phone, and I know this has something to do with me, or Rhys.

"It's hot. Even the *fuck you* part." Cindy bites her lip, watching the screen.

"Especially the *fuck you* par—" I walk straight up and hold out my hand to Dolly. She purses her red lips, and she glances at Cindy who looks a mess already. Her big boobs are almost falling out of her dress, and her eyes are slightly glazed. I almost ask her what she's taking because whatever it is, she looks comfortably numb, and I could use some of that right now.

"Gia, I'm not supposed to show you this." Dolly looks at me and suddenly it all clicks.

"Is this why you guys are all acting weird around me?" I almost stomp my foot, but I'm in five-inch Jimmy Choos, so I flop down on the couch.

"Just give it to me. I don't have a phone anymore." I put my head back. I'm so tired I could probably fall asleep, but that can wait until I see why the whole world seems to be looking at me like I'm some kind of different species.

Dolly flops down next to me and holds the phone away from me.

I sit up. "What? And who told you not to show me?" I reach for it, but she has speed on her side right now.

"Everyone." She waves her hand. "I wasn't even a Granger fan, but fuck, Gia." She winks as a wave of adrenaline flows through me.

"Give me the phone."

Dolly smiles and hands me the phone as she digs in her bag for her cigarettes. Her screensaver is Edge and their baby, Gunner, who has red curls and fat, rosy cheeks. Dolly and Edge need to have more babies. He's incredibly cute.

"What's your password? And I love this picture." She smiles and lights up, taking the phone back so that her face can unlock it as Cindy sits on the other side of me, fixing her dress. Maybe she's not as numb as I thought since her energy is rather aggressive.

"What's the deal with your friend?" she says curtly.

"Why?" I may sound defensive, but fuck it, my life is out of control, and I need to watch the video. Her eyes laser on me.

"Cindy. Do I need to slap your tits?" Dolly leans over me to give Cindy a warning stare and hands me her phone.

"Is this going to upset me? Because I can't—"

"God, Gia, really?" Cindy rubs her head. It's kind of harsh since I don't know her all that well. She's close with Charlie. Dolly and I stare at her.

"I'm sorry. I'm a bitch, but come on. The fucking Rock God is singing about how his heart beats for hers, and she's sitting here crying."

"She doesn't know any of this. And you're cut off," Dolly snaps right back as Cindy stares straight ahead. The only thing moving is her heeled foot, bopping up and down.

Suddenly I want to hug her. I've seen that look in so many women's faces. Desperation, it takes over. You're consumed with a person who you know, deep down, has moved on, but you can't accept it.

"It's okay, Cindy."

She looks over at me, her blue eyes full of tears, and I nod. I want to say I get it, but the way she looks at me makes me think I should watch the video. Dolly takes her phone and presses play as she shakes her head and rolls her eyes at Cindy.

"This is actual footage of the Rome concert yesterday." She sounds bubbly, excited.

"How is this up?" I say, because seriously this looks like Sebastian's stuff. It's up close and clean, not gritty like a fan shot it from below.

"Shhh, you're gonna miss the best part." Dolly cuddles up with me as my heart skips at what I hear next.

"Fuck you, Gia."

Dolly pauses it. "I've got goose bumps." She lifts her arm so I can see them.

I have to hear it again.

"Fuck you, Gia. One. Two. Three. Four."

I bite my bottom lip as the dreaded tears I've been holding back spill and I hear his voice sing.

Smoke and whiskey, I can almost smell him as he grabs the microphone.

Baby, I don't want to see you cryin'. But I can't live without your love. This hunger that eats me up, only your lips can cure. Ammo's guitar comes in hard and fast as it builds. *I make everyone bleed. But that's nothing compared to my heart. It bleeds for you.*

It's strong and powerful. And mine beats for yours. Nuke's drums add the beat, and I'm mesmerized as I watch the magic.

It beats for you. Dolly's hand takes mine, hers warm, mine cold as I watch him fucking destroy me with his voice and words.

Let me match your breathing; let me steal your breath, rest my racing mind. For this moment, I'm at peace. I can't make you love me. I can't control your heart. But baby, mine is yours. It beats for you. It beats for you.

The crowd starts chanting "beats for you." Like someone addicted to pain, I swipe my finger to go back to the beginning.

"There's been a lot of talk lately about my personal life. Shit that means nothing. But this meant something. I wrote it for another, but it belongs to you." I jump when another video comes on of him. And I hand the phone back to her as I sit and smoke, the room filled with his black magic as all three of us can't help but hear his voice in our heads.

"Well?" Dolly says.

"Well, what? That video means nothing, except that he's drunk and wrote a song to me, then gave it to his real true love: *his fans.*"

"Snap out of it." She claps her hands in my face. "You love him, he loves you." She holds the phone up. "That was hot, and you know it."

I clear my throat and wipe under my eyes. "He's a rock star. I will agree he's beautiful, but it's way more complicated. I can't always be worried he's cheating or getting someone pregnant or dealing with his fans and the band—"

"Please. Welcome to our world. Why do you think I fucking stabbed Edge?" Dolly waves her hands, then leans back and crosses her legs like that's a normal thing.

"Dolly?" We both jump as Eve walks in and looks at all three of us.

"You showed her?" She puts her hands on her hips.

"Of course I did. It's freaking hot," Dolly retorts.

"Are you okay, Gia? We all agreed to let you see it after the wedding." Her eyes narrow on Dolly who answers for me.

"She's fine." Dolly turns to me and frowns. "Well, she will be." She rubs my shoulder as I shake my head and stand.

"At least I know why you guys were looking at me weird."

"We were not looking at you weird," Eve says, shaking her head at Cindy who keeps staring at the wall in front of her.

"Let's go. They're ready to make a toast, and brunch was already served, plus they'll be cutting the cake soon." Eve motions for us.

"Let me fix your eyes." Dolly stands and grabs my hand.

"Cindy? You coming?" We all look down at her.

"In a minute," she says to the wall, then turns and looks at me.

"Stop it, Cindy. You're definitely cut off. I'm serious." Dolly frowns at her, then pulls me as we follow Eve.

"We need to get Charlie to handle Cindy," Dolly states.

"Agreed. What is she on?" Eve hesitates. "Which one is the bathroom again? This house is huge."

"That's it." Dolly points to the far door. "I know she's on a new antidepressant. You think it's that along with the alcohol?" she whispers, already digging inside her giant purse. She pulls out her makeup bag as Eve opens the door.

Only it's not the bathroom.

We all three stop in horror. I think I scream, or maybe it's Eve, but Julianna's eyes pop open. Her blond hair and pink dress are like a flare alerting us. That, and their loud groans, along with her legs wrapped around Ryder's waist as he fucks her against the bedroom wall.

"Holy fuckkk." Dolly drops her bag with a loud thud.

Julianna screams.

Ryder doesn't even seem bothered. He keeps thrusting, snarling for us to get the fuck out. I go to back up only to bump into a pale-faced Cindy.

"Oh. My. Fucking God," she explodes. I try to grab her, but she's already lunging at his back. "I'll kill you!"

If I thought my life couldn't get worse...

It just did.

CHAPTER 39

RHYS
Present — Thirty-five years old
Rome, Italy

"**H**ey, brother, wake up," Ace's voice vibrates in my sluggish brain. I open my eyes and try to remember where I am. Sitting up, I reach for the bottle of Jack, tossing the cap on the floor. I shake my head as I let the warmth travel down my throat.

"You got Visine?" I say, looking at the tarmac and our jet waiting for me.

Ace opens up the glove compartment and tosses me some. I saturate both eyes and lean my head back, trying to let the sting subside before I get out.

"Mr. Granger, we have the G6 ready. We should be in Los Angeles in about eleven hours." Tim, our pilot, walks over to me as I slam the SUV door.

"Perfect." I pull out my cigarettes and turn to watch the limo pulling up and stopping right in front of us.

"Fuck you, man," Ammo says as he gets out with two groupies.

I light up and smile. "What are you doing?"

"I don't know. What the hell are we doing?" He points at me with the bottle of Jägermeister. Rafe steps out on the other side as Hunter and Sebastian come out with the camera on.

Inhaling, I shake my head. "This is a personal trip. No cameras."

"Relax, Granger," Hunter says. "Think about how you can always have this moment recorded for your kids. Pretend we're not here." He takes the stairs to the jet.

Sebastian walks up, turns off the camera, and we stare at each other, both of us in love with her, but I'm the one who owns her heart.

Rafe walks over. "I'm counting on you to do the right thing. If it's personal, I don't give a shit what Hunter wants. Turn that thing off."

Sebastian nods at me and turns to Rafe. "You have nothing to worry about. I edit everything." He shakes his head and laughs as he runs a hand through his hair. "So, you got a plan, Granger?"

"I'll think of something." I toss my cigarette and stomp on it, moving toward the stairs only to see Cash and Nuke step out of the limo.

When I raise a brow at Cash, he smiles, reaches in to grab his bass, and walks by saying over his shoulder, "You didn't think I'd miss out on this, did you?"

Nuke, who's shirtless, as usual, hops around from foot to foot. I snort. "You gonna make it?"

"I'm fine," Nuke says. "We need to go home and you're my family. If you're gonna go get Gia, I'm coming with you."

I motion for him to pass. Even as fucked as I am, I'm not gonna lie. Having my brothers with me calms me.

He takes the stairs two at a time while Ace stands talking to Rafe. I look around wondering how it went from me and Ace to my whole family, because like it or not, that's what we are. In a way it's not bad having Sebastian with me. At least if she sees the camera, she'll have to let me in.

Not that I've forgiven her.

But I can't seem to live without her, so we can fight later. Get into all the shit we should have hashed out earlier. I climb the stairs and enter the jet, and for the first time in years, I have absolutely no idea what I'm gonna do, but I'm not alone.

They didn't leave me.

Ammo hands me his Jägermeister as the doors close. Rafe sits down next to me as Hunter walks over with a joint and hands it to him.

"You want to get into the studio. We need to record 'Heart Beats for You' as soon as possible. I don't want it pirated any more than it already has been."

I lean my head back and close my eyes. I've been running for so long, the thought of staying put sounds really good.

"Yeah, I like that. I have a bunch of songs I'd love put down in the studio."

Rafe nods and inhales, eyes narrowing as he offers me the joint. I take it. Maybe I can pass out and wake up with some incredible idea about how to get Gia to move in with me, rather than picking her up and forcibly taking her with me.

"What time is it gonna be when we land?" I mumble before I inhale and hold.

"Probably around eight a.m." Rafe smiles at something on his phone. I exhale and lean forward.

"You got something going on that we should know about?"

His blue eyes look at mine. "I never tell my secrets. You know that."

I recline my seat all the way back, smiling. "Wake me when we land."

"Granger, man." I crack my eyes open to see Ammo laughing with a groupie on his lap and drop my feet to the carpet with a thud.

Scooting up, I look around the jet. Everyone seems to be up already, besides Cash who's still lounging on the couch. This was actually one of the better flights. I slept.

"I'm gonna take a quick shower. We almost ready to land?"

"Thirty minutes," Sebastian says as he passes.

I turn the water on and take a quick rinse-off in case others want to use it. I rub my hands across my scruff. I need to shave but fuck it. I slather on some deodorant, brush my teeth, and open up one of the cabinets where we keep clothes. I've probably spent more time in this jet than anywhere else lately.

I pull on a black tee and some jeans and run my hands through my hair. Exiting, I go straight for the bar and a bottle of Jack and drop into a chair, seeing Sebastian out of the corner of my eye. He's filming already.

"Hey," I yell at him.

"Yeah?" He lowers the camera.

"I'm thinking of a concert outside her place. How big of a deal would that be?" He brings the camera back up.

"So, what? You want to start playing a concert in the middle of Venice Beach, California?"

"Yep." I crack the bottle.

"Excuse me, what did you say? No fucking way, Granger. We need permits and all kinds of shit." Rafe looks like I've asked him for a million dollars.

"Nah, I'm doing it. Even if it's one song, that's enough." I take a swig.

"You're gonna get thrown in jail," he threatens as if I'm five and he's trying to have patience with me.

"Get her flowers, show up on your knees. But you're not serenading her."

"We need to have you *Say Anything* her," Cash says from the couch, not even removing his arm from his eyes.

"What?"

"*Say Anything.* The movie. John Cusack stands outside the girl's bedroom window with a boom box playing Peter Gabriel's 'In Your Eyes.'" He sits up.

Ammo glances behind him at Cash. "I had no idea you were a Cusack fan."

I can't help but fucking laugh. Cash, of all people, watches eighties' romantic comedies? It's perfect. I bring the bottle to my lips.

"Refresh me, did he get the girl?"

"Of course." He lights up a cigarette, lifting his hip to pull his phone from his back pocket.

"We're going to jail," I say to Ammo.

He throws his head back, laughing and bringing the Jägermeister to his lips. "It's been too long. We need a little jail time. Make us mean again."

Rafe brings the phone down and his eyes narrow. "You two are getting too old for jail, and it's bad press. This is *not* happening."

I grin at him. "Hey, Ace?"

"Yo?" His voice comes from somewhere behind me.

"We're gonna need equipment," I yell.

Nuke stumbles over and I almost tell him we have a shower. I don't think he's been out of those black leather pants in a week.

"Why don't we have a bet on how many songs it takes for Granger to get Gia?" He grins as he sits down next to the other groupie who's snorting cocaine. He holds up his finger, bends down and takes a bump, then looks at us, eyes wide as he laughs. "Or we can bet how many songs it takes before we get arrested." I have to bite my tongue not to say, *You'd better hope we don't get arrested. Detoxing in jail is a bitch.*

"Here." Cash sets down his phone, bringing my attention back to him as he hits play. "In Your Eyes" by Peter Gabriel starts up on a YouTube video. "See, the boom box."

I look up at him. "Yeah, man, I see the stupid boom box and a girl who can't seem to sleep. What the hell, Cash?"

"Just watch." He nods.

I take a breath, and the video ends with John Cusack standing alone by his car, playing the song. "That's it?" I rub my face. "That's what you think I should do?"

"Yeah, it's perfect. We play 'In Your Eyes,' and you'll get Gia."

"Jesus Christ," Ammo says.

"Cash, he didn't get the girl." I motion to the phone, laughing. It's so fucking absurd, I'm tempted to do it.

"Fuck you, guys." He sits down. "Cusack gets the girl later. You have to watch the movie, assholes."

Leaning over for the pack of cigarettes, I look at him then Ammo, trying hard not to laugh again.

"Trust me, if you want to be romantic, this is the way," Cash says with conviction.

"All right, any other tips?"

"Fuck off. I'm giving you great advice." He grabs his phone.

"Why can't I just play one of our songs?"

Cash sighs as if I'm not right in the head. "It's the whole production, Granger. 'In Your Eyes,' it's—" He searches for the word only to have Rafe interrupt him.

"You can't be thinking of listening to him, can you?" Rafe says wide-eyed. I grin. "Jesus Christ. You're all fucked in the head. We have no permits. This is going to be chaos," Rafe says all this as he texts.

Looking up, he snaps, "Ace, beef up security."

"We all know 'In Your Eyes,' right?" Cash asks as Ammo chokes on his swig of Jäger.

"What the fuck has happened to you?" Rafe snarls, shaking his head in disgust.

I stand and hand him the bottle. "Drink up, Rafe. Looks like we're going to jail."

CHAPTER 40

GIA
Present – Twenty-five years old
Venice Beach, California

I hear music. Loud music, like it sounds right next to my head. Groaning, I roll over and blink at the morning sun shining into my room. And consider the fact that I wasn't dreaming about hearing music.

"Who's playing Peter Gabriel at shock volume?" Julianna grumbles next to me.

My heart leaps to my throat as I slap her awake and bolt up. "Holy fuck." My stomach flutters and my face heats up as I hear it.

"Gia. Gia Fontaine?" It vibrates around my small bedroom as I try to breathe.

"Oh my God, Julianna. It's him." My hand goes to my neck. I try to swallow.

"Wait. What's happening?" She sits up on her elbows. Her mascara and the residual makeup we forgot to remove last night makes her look a bit like Harley Quinn.

"Gia Fontaine, please come to the front of your house." His gravelly voice is loud and clear as Julianna grabs me.

"*Oh. My. God.* It's Granger. Outside your house playing 'In Your Eyes'!"

I blink at her because *holy fuck*. What do I do? I might have said that out loud because she yells, "Get out there."

"I'm going to throw up." I slap her hand away as she tries to fix my hair. Taking a deep breath, I open the door.

And there he stands like the Rock God he is. He can't be real. He's so beautiful my heart aches. Our eyes lock and I shiver at the intensity I see. Goose bumps trail down my arms and my nipples harden as his eyes dip to them.

I can't think straight. I can't breathe right. All I can concentrate on are his full lips that I wish were on mine. And his big, pierced cock that I need inside me.

Jesus, what's happening to me?

"Come here, Brat." The rumble of his voice brings me back to the now and the fact that he's actually here.

In my front yard. Playing "In Your Eyes."

I stare at him greedily. He looks tired, but it works for him. Nothing has changed. It can't change. He will always be the Rock God. But somehow that doesn't matter anymore.

Ammo stands next to him playing the guitar. Nuke is pounding on his drums in my next- door neighbor's yard as Sebastian walks around filming all this mayhem.

"What are you doing?" I yell.

Cash is on the keyboards. I almost do a double take. Is he actually smiling? I think this might be the first time I've seen Cash smile in ages.

"Come over here and find out," he demands into the microphone.

"Gia, honey? Are these men for you?" Mrs. Darcy yells at me from her porch as Nuke pounds on his drums, tossing his sticks in the air, though he doesn't miss a beat. And I almost start to cry, and I have no idea why, except that Rhys is here. All of them are.

He came for me.

"Are they?" she yells again, forcing me to break Rhys's hypnotizing stare. She's wearing one of her homemade tie-dyed dresses. Mrs. Darcy, or Sunshine as she prefers to be called—but she's in her mid-seventies so I feel uncomfortable calling her that—is the best neighbor. Peace, love, sex, and drugs is her motto. I think she used to be seriously into selling LSD, and has lived in the same house for over fifty years.

"They are." I smile at her. Behind me, I hear Julianna talking on the phone. More than likely it's Axel, since yesterday was a shit show. But that's Julianna's problem.

"Well, what are you waiting for? Go to him." Mrs. Darcy's hands shoo me away.

"Holy shit, it's The Stuffed Muffins." People start to run up to see them. Most have their dogs out for their morning walks as they start to film them.

"Granger, Ammmmo, Nuuuke," a surfer screams as he walks by in his wetsuit, a surfboard under his arm.

"Brat, if you don't want me going to jail, I'd get over here."

Licking my lips, I close my eyes, and suddenly I'm free from all the self-doubt. I know where my destiny lies. Have always known but lost sight of it for a while. He is and always will be my one true love. For as long as I can remember, I've known that I belong to him.

One.

Two.

Three.

I breathe in and out, then run to him, throwing my arms around him. He drops the microphone with a loud screech.

"Took you long enough." His voice is rough as his eyes caress my face, which I'm sure looks like shit. But whatever. He thinks I'm beautiful.

"You fucking ran again. Left me when you knew I couldn't stop you." His strong hands hold my face.

"I'm sorry." My eyes fill with tears, but I blink them back and tell the truth. "I was going to come back."

"Fuck that. I came for you." He fists my hair and brings my lips to his. "What do I have to do, Gia?" He shakes his head. "Don't you get it?" His mouth claims mine as I lean into him and let him carry me away.

"My heart beats for you." I blink at him through my tears.

This is our moment.

I groan and let his tongue take mine in a kiss that leaves every other one lacking. Our tongues twist and join as I taste bourbon and my own salty tears. Excitement snakes down my stomach and I cling to him, digging my nails into his neck.

He lifts his head. His eyes, like deep amber crystals, make my breath stutter as he allows me to see his pain.

His voice cracks. "Don't leave me again." His hand tightens around my hair.

"I won't." I tremble beneath his lips.

He's a man, not a god. He bleeds like all of us. Somewhere along the line, everyone lost sight of that. He's a master at verse, turning words into magical rhymes. But he's also the scared boy searching the streets for his mother. The musical genius sleeping in our garage. The boy who makes all the girls cry.

"Rhys?" I place my hand on his heart. It's strong and fierce and *it beats for me.* "I love you. I've loved you forever."

"Let's go," he says softly as Ammo starts playing "Untouched." All I can do is hold on to his warm, strong hand while he reaches down and scoops me up in his arms.

Helicopters circle around us. The crowd seems to have multiplied. Sirens fill the air as Ammo's guitar and Nuke's drum drown it all out.

"This is the LAPD. You all need to go home," a voice says over the police department's microphone. "This concert is over."

A loud roar of "No" is the crowd's answer. People are running toward us. Cars are honking. Crowds of people stop and abandon their vehicles. I look up and see that one of the helicopters is KTLA

News. Great, that ought to go over well with my brother. I tuck my head into Rhys's neck as he walks.

"Rock God, can I have your autograph?" They circle around us until he stops. And I slide down his hard body as he tells Ace to go. I slide in, watching the small mob scream, "We love you!"

They do, and they should. He's given them his life up until now. He slides in next to me, pulling me onto his lap. "Take us to the Four Seasons." Then he pushes the partition closed.

"Fuck me." His rough hands pull the bottom of my dress completely off, then snaps my string panties off too. I grip his shoulder as the limo starts to move.

Sinking to the carpet, I grab his pants and unbutton them. Jesus, my hands are shaking. He lifts his hips as his hard cock spills out. I pull down his jeans and freeze at the sight: My name is tattooed on his thigh. Thorns and roses snake through the letters.

"Not now." He fists my hair. "Suck hard," he grunts, filling my mouth with his thick dick. My eyes instantly water and I gag, taking him in as far as I can.

"Fuck, I missed you. That's it, Gia, baby, suck the tip." With my hand, I pump him while I pull and suck on his piercing.

He jerks my head off him and lifts me up and onto the seat. "Spread those legs." His mouth goes straight for my clit as I moan and scratch the leather seat. He pulls me to the edge and lifts me up so that both his hands are holding me open. Looking up at me, he grins.

His tongue goes straight for my ass and twirls around my rosette hole, making me moan.

"Why does it feel so good? I'm getting ready to come," I whimper.

He moves up to my clit, licking and sucking while his finger goes into my ass. I start to pulse as he sucks my clit hard, his middle finger going in and out of my ass as my orgasm builds. I grab his hair and prepare to ride the wave.

Then I do. My body contracts and pulses in his mouth and on his finger. He lifts his head and reaches for my pierced nipple, tugging as he rubs it.

Sitting, he spreads his legs, his velvety cock standing hard and thick. I don't wait for him to tell me. I straddle him and in one fast, exquisite thrust, I impale my wet pussy on him.

"Fuck," he rasps. While he watches me, his nostrils flare.

I'm beside myself. Don't even think I know my name. All I know is he's inside me. And that I love him.

"That's it, Brat, fuck me." Up and down I pound as he slaps my ass, the sting making my core grab hold of his cock. While his piercing rubs inside me, he shoves my breast into his mouth.

"I'm gonna fill this cunt of mine up. I want you off the pill," he growls, and I'm so consumed, I chant, "I love you" and "Yes" as I ride him hard.

"Yeah, baby, ride me. Rub that clit on me." His thumb flicks over it.

I thrust against him so hard I can feel the piercing on that tender spot.

"I'm..." I hiss, my body is climbing as he grabs my ass with one hand, holding me still, his cock so deep inside me I throw my head back and convulse. Pulsing pleasure makes me scream his name. While he holds me still, I watch him come undone.

He's beautiful, hips jerking as his thick cock pulses and fills me. When he pulls out, I can barely move.

Our breathing is harsh. He pushes my sweaty hair, which is stuck to my face, out of the way.

"I love you," I moan.

He leans down, his tongue swirling around my clit, and I groan because I'm so sensitive but it also feels so good.

"Gia." I sit up. His mouth takes mine and I can taste us. My hand snakes down to his rock-hard cock. *What the hell?*

Rhys can stay hard but not this hard. Usually, he just stays inside me and grows as he slowly fucks.

"I'm sensitive." I groan as his fingers take my wetness and rub it slowly on my clit.

"I know, baby. But I need the truth."

"What?" I try to shut my legs.

He stops me with his hands. "Why did you run?" I close my eyes, and he inserts two fingers inside me, letting his fingers go deep, slowly pumping. When I arch my back, his mouth hovers around mine.

"Look at me."

Slowly I open my eyes and tell him the truth. "I didn't want to lose myself completely, and I was scared." I grab ahold of his wrist. His fingers go deeper, fucking me.

"You were scared that I wouldn't take care of you? Protect you? What?" He watches me as I lean my head back and open my legs farther. If he thinks this is torturing me, he's sadly mistaken. I'm getting ready to come.

And just like that, his fingers are gone. I sit up almost dazed as he pulls his jeans up angrily.

"Don't do this. Are you kidding me?" I yell.

"You fucking left me. I love you. I needed you, and you ran. That woman is after Nuke. It has nothing to do with us. What the fuck is wrong with you?" He reaches into his pocket and pulls out his cigarettes as my mind tries to process everything he said.

"This. Rhys." I turn toward him. "All of it. I left because I was scared. I left because the thought of you tiring of me and being with another makes me physically ill."

He shakes his head as if I'm a crazy person, so I fire right back. "Don't look at me like that. You fucked her. You act like I'm insane because I don't want to stick around while you put your dick in anything that's warm and wet."

"That's not the issue, Gia." His voice is quiet, and for some reason that makes me shiver. "You don't trust me. If you did, you would have stayed and we could have saved ourselves a lot of regrets and agony."

That makes me falter. "I... I knew you would touch me and then I'd start rethinking everything." I can't get a good breath as we stare at each other, our desperate energy bouncing around us like recycled air.

He nods and his eyes narrow while he lights up the cigarette. "Babe, I'm not gonna lie to you and say I haven't fucked a lot of women." He brings the cigarette to his full lips as I watch.

Consumed. That's what he does to me.

"You can't possibly hold that against me. This life that I'm so fucking blessed to have is not perfect." He motions at us. "We're not perfect."

I take a deep breath. "I was scared, Rhys. I didn't think I could survive you getting tired of me. But if I'm honest, I was scared of what I felt for you," I whisper.

His eyes caress my face. Inhaling deeply, he lowers the window enough to toss the cigarette out before turning to me. "Do you think I'm not scared, Gia? I get up every day *terrified* that this is the day I go insane. And when I don't, it's in the back of my head that it will be tomorrow, or the next." He leans back against the seat, his dark eyes holding mine.

"*That* is my world," he continues. "I hear music in my head. I can play any instrument because I can hear it in here." He motions to his head. "But when I'm with you..." He looks out the window, then back at me, his eyes almost black with a fury that ensnares me as my heart starts to bleed. "When I'm with you, it's gone, baby. I know you love me, Gia." He rubs his heart as if it hurts. "That's why I got on the plane. You're mine. My muse, my fucking lifeline. And if I wake up one morning and I can't get out of bed, I know you'll be there to hold me through it."

I cover my mouth and nod, realizing how strong and tortured he truly is, how me leaving him brought up all his abandonment issues with his mom.

"I will always be there." I don't care that I'm crying, or that I'm still naked. I climb onto his lap and straddle him as I kiss his face, his eyes, his mouth.

"I love you. I always have." I smile at him, not caring that I can barely see him through all my tears. "And if you go crazy, Rhys, I'll go crazy with you."

He grabs my face with both hands. "You're gonna marry me." When he brings my lips to his, I cling to him, letting his mouth and love pour into me.

"Of course, I am," I say into his warm lips. "I told you that when I was seven."

He frowns as I watch the play of emotions on his face.

"Christ, you did, didn't you?" He laughs and slaps my ass just as Ace's voice carries back to us.

"Granger, we're here. I'm gonna try to clear the lobby."

"Thanks, brother," he yells as I crawl off of him to grab my red dress, slipping it over my head.

"Feel better?"

I nod. We both look like we've been through hell and back.

"You need to trust me. I want it all with you. But right now, I want to order room service, fuck, and sleep. Can we do that?" He pulls me onto his lap again, and I rest my head on his chest.

"I can feel your heart beating." I look up at him.

He flashes me that grin that I've decided is only mine. "Of course, you can. It beats for you."

He opens the door and I step out. We both look down at my bare feet, and I squeal when he lifts me into his arms. He smiles at the small crowd of paparazzi waiting for us. Snuggling against his neck, I let him carry me inside.

He's tortured, talented, and fierce. And I will love him until the day I die.

EPILOGUE

RHYS

One year later
TCL Chinese Theatre, Hollywood, California

The limo stops and we wait for the valet to remove the cones so the driver can drop us off at the entrance. I squeeze her hand. She looks over at me and my heart does its usual burn for her. I've given up on trying to curb my hunger for Gia.

My craving for her grows daily, but tonight belongs to her. The torrent of flashing bulbs and studio lighting illuminates the night. But all I see is her stunning face as she sits in a gown that makes her look almost too beautiful to be real.

I'd planned for us take the Cadillac SUV, but when she came down our stairs in that dress, I had Ace get the limo.

It's couture, apparently. Her designer friend Alberto made it especially for her and for this night.

Shut Your Muff, our documentary, is premiering tonight. I peer out the window. As with anything concerning Hunter Falcon, it's a huge fucking event. The red carpet runs all the way down Hollywood Boulevard, for fuck's sake.

I reach into my suit jacket and pull out my black sunglasses.

Gia snaps her compact shut after fixing her lipstick. There was no way I wasn't going to fuck her in that dress. As soon as the door shut, the dress was over her head and I fucked her from behind. It's my cock's job to relieve all her stress, and this is a big night for her.

"Rhys, I swear to God, knock it off." She looks at me and I adjust my dick. When I think about her freshly waxed pink pussy, it grows hard again.

"Stop." She laughs, but her eyes narrow while watching me rub my cock.

"They're going to open the door," she warns, licking her lips and looking out at the screaming insanity that is our lives.

If fucking Axel and Antoinette weren't sitting with us tonight, I'd finger fuck her in the dark theater. Just slip my hand up her leg and into her slick, swollen cunt that's stuffed full of my seed. Rub her clit and watch her come undone while everyone else is enthralled in the film. But alas, Gia insisted they come since Axel is in it, and apparently, it's his job to support her.

That, and Antoinette was absolutely losing it. She's a fan. I love it. Drives Axel insane.

"You're stunning."

"Rhys." She starts laughing. "You can wait until we get home."

"I'm not waiting until we get home, Brat—" Ace's knock on the window, giving us a warning that he's opening the door, cuts off my filthy tirade.

The door swings open and he helps my goddess out as I follow. The frenzy is wild tonight, and it's not only from our fans. The elite of Hollywood are walking the carpet too.

"Granger, Gia, over here," they scream. The velvet ropes barely hold them back. They reach out to touch us.

"Keep them away from Gia," I grumble at Ace and my security team. They move us fast toward the red carpet.

"Christ." I look around at all the adoring fans, wondering where Ammo is. I catch sight of Axel. He's wearing black sunglasses, too, and I smirk.

Fucking dick.

In the last year that I've been with Gia, Axel and I have had no less than three fistfights. I guess he finally got it through his thick skull that I'm not going anywhere when Gia and I bought a house in Malibu.

It's a small world, at least in Malibu—our neighbors are Reed and Tess Saddington. Reed is David's best friend, so we've kind of gotten close with them.

Gia decided to start BBQ Sundays when we're in town. Our backyard is filled with the ocean, Disciples, and my band.

I even talked Axel into laying a couple of songs down with me in the studio with the rest of The Stuffed Muffins. Our new album, *Fast and Fierce,* is coming out next month.

Now all we need to do is slow down enough so that I can knock her up. As if she knows what I'm thinking, she turns to me.

"What?" She smiles and waves at the cameras. I lean down and growl into her ear. She starts laughing.

"I'm sorry, what was that growl supposed to mean?"

"I'll show you later."

She waves, then shrieks when Sebastian runs up from behind her. Turning, she throws her arms around him, and I stand back and let her shine. When Alberto brought the dress out tonight, I almost said no. It's silver, which is good, but the top part of the dress is so tight her tits almost fall out. The rest is made up of layers and layers of chiffon with a slit so high it lets you see one of her long, tan legs when she walks.

"You look ravishing." His eyes go straight for her breasts.

"Goddammit." I pull her toward my chest. "Back off, Sebastian."

Throwing his head back, he laughs and pats my shoulder. He waves to the cameras. "Good luck, Granger." He winks as he links his fingers with a beautiful redhead and walks toward the entrance.

"Let's move." I bite her ear while she laughs and talks about the film with a reporter.

"Gia." We both turn as Axel and Antoinette walk up. Of course, he's wearing jeans and a black T-shirt, along with his black cut.

She squeals and hugs Antoinette who's wearing a skintight pink dress, but at least her tits aren't falling out.

"The fuck?" Axel stares at Gia. "Why would you let her wear that?" He looks at me like I've lost my mind.

"I'm trying to be supportive," I say.

"Stop, you pussy-whipped asshole," he retorts, shaking his head and guiding Antoinette toward the entrance.

"Axel," Gia yells. I bite the side of my cheek. She truly does look like she's gonna spill out of that dress.

"One picture, please?"

He rolls his eyes. We all pose, and the cameras go crazy. Rafe thankfully rescues me, saying the rest of the band is already inside. His eyes take in Gia, and he raises a brow at me but wisely stays quiet.

My hand goes to her lower back as I move us toward the venue, smiling and waving at the crowd. The Chinese Theatre is a historical landmark. Outside are the famous handprints of the stars, forever captured on the sidewalk. Inside, the deep red velvet curtain with gold palm trees covers the massive screen. So many legends have walked through those doors.

I spin her toward me like I'm going to kiss her. Instead, I whisper, "Your tits are *mine* and they're falling out."

She smiles and kisses me, whispering back, "That's impossible. I'm taped inside this dress."

"The hell?"

"Granger," Hunter yells and waves as I guide her in, allowing the usher to show us our seats.

The excitement in the room makes me look for my brothers. Nuke sits a couple of rows down with his newest girlfriend, a yoga instructor. He's looked good lately. Apparently, she helped him detox off the smack, so of course, he thought it was wise to move in with her. That'll last until we go on the road.

Ammo sits close to Axel. With his bottle of Jäger in one hand, and his other arm snaked around a large-breasted blonde, he laughs with Cash who brought his kid.

"You ready?" Gia leans her head on my shoulder. Hunter is, once again, being Hunter, rambling on about how this was a true labor of love. I tune him out and take her hand. Her big diamond engagement ring sparkles beneath the chandelier lights.

The audience claps. Our loud music spills out of the surround sound system. The screen stays black as I hear my voice say "Fuck off" along with Axel's loud voice as he screams, "We are the Dicks." Cash laughs.

The screen blinks white, then shifts to footage from a video camera. The person holding it walks toward Axel's garage. It's followed by fast cuts of all of us playing, laughing, sleeping, and hanging out with various girls who always seemed to surround us in Axel's garage.

Then it zeros in on me as I sit smoking in the corner writing something.

My hand squeezes Gia's. She turns and smiles and my heart aches. I turn back and watch her light up the screen. She's maybe nine with that damn camera of hers, taking pictures, clearly bugging me. She twirls in a red dress, her long legs and bare feet covered in dirt. Stopping, she places her hands on her hips, saying something that makes the girl filming laugh.

Then she turns and runs up to the camera saying, "I'm Gia Fontaine and I'm their number one fan." The crowd in the theater claps as I look at her.

"Where did you get that video?"

"I have my ways." She winks.

Axel stands in the middle of the garage drinking and playing. Cash walks over to him as they both look up at the camera and flip it off.

I can't look away. I had no idea this would affect me, but it's wild seeing the past. We all have come so far, yet here we all sit.

I feel a hand on my shoulder and look back at Axel. He leans forward as if he's going to say something but doesn't.

Turning back to the screen, I hear myself say my name while Nuke twirls his drumsticks.

I breathe in and exhale as music fills my head.

"I love you," Gia whispers.

Love. That doesn't even start to describe this feeling that eats me up inside when I think of her.

Hunger, craving, rapture. My heart pounds, and I almost rub it, if only to feel it beat.

My muse.

Everything that I love is in this room. My brothers, my fans, and *her.*

I take a breath and watch us all screaming and performing at our early gigs. My face looks haunted and dark. I was the boy who was destined to never love, the man who was cursed to be alone.

I'm called a Rock God. But I'm not a god. I'm a man who has flaws, but I was given my shot and I took it. I thought that was my music—the fame and money.

I was wrong.

My shot, my greatest opportunity was her, my chance to have something that will last forever. Fame didn't make me happy. In fact, it almost destroyed me.

I glance back at Axel, whose draped his arm around his ballerina's shoulders. He raises a brow at me. I used to be confused as to why he didn't want this life, how could he possibly walk away.

Now I know.

I turn to Gia. She reaches to touch my lips and I smile at her. All my ghosts are gone.

I take a breath.

One. Two. Three.

I'm home, finally at peace.

I hope you enjoyed Rhys and Gia's love story. My rock stars will be back, but first I'm diving back into my Disciples series. Get ready for the dark and delicious world of my enforcer and his secret obsession.

Add Disciples #5 on Goodreads today:
https://bit.ly/TheDisciples5TBR

Speaking of the Disciples, are you missing them?
You can revisit them in
A Very Naughty MC Christmas Anthology
Coming November 30th!

Preorder here...
AMAZON: http://mybook.to/AVNMCChristmasAMZ
EVERYWHERE ELSE:
https://books2read.com/u/49NXXW

Want to see more from Rhys and Axel's glory days?
Rock God Twins

Sign up for my newsletter HERE (https://dl.bookfunnel.com/d4yb30mo3o) and receive my *Rock God Twins* short story!
https://dl.bookfunnel.com/j6dlie17py

Don't forget to follow THE STUFFED MUFFINS
on Instagram for VIP ACCESS!
Stalk the naughty bad boys of Rock 'n' Roll!
bit.ly/TheStuffedMuffinsIG

Would you like to read more by me?

All books are available in Kindle
Unlimited and Audio

ALSO BY CASSANDRA ROBBINS

The Disciples Series

Lethal

Atone

Repent

Ignite

The Entitled Duet

The Entitled

The Enlightened

LETHAL

Blade McCormick is not a nice guy.

He's pure adrenaline and smells like smoke and leather—the kind of guy you look at and know he's going to be a combination of nasty and irresistible. The moment I allowed myself to touch his hot skin and kiss his full lips, I. Was. Done.

Like currency, I've become part of a transaction. Blade took me to *pay off a debt*. I try to tell myself, *Eve, you should hate him. He's a bad guy*. But then again, I'm not a good girl. Blade's the president of the Disciples, the notorious motorcycle club. I should be frightened, yet somehow, he doesn't scare me. If anything, I think I scare him.

It takes a lot of work to become the club's Queen, but I'll stop at nothing to have the King!

ATONE

I don't apologize or regret the destruction I'm about to cause. I'm at peace with what I must do... nothing can or will stand in my way. Not even the raven-haired beauty with golden eyes who haunts my dreams.

No one is innocent in the story of my life. Fairy tales don't exist!

I. Make. No. Excuses.

Everyone needs to *atone*, and I'm the man who is going to see to it.

REPENT

There are two sides to every story.

I fell in love with a redheaded boy, a boy who was kind and good.

Until he wasn't.

He broke my heart once, twice... I've lost count. Like a dark god, he haunts me. He smells like smoke and cinnamon, with danger seeping from every pore. He is my savior, my lover, exciting and addictive.

I should've seen it coming...

Never trust a Disciple. You have to sell your soul to the devil to get one to love you. I would.

I did.

My name is Dolores Dunghart, and I might have done the unforgivable.

I don't care if you judge me... I've judged myself.

But this is how we live.

And this is our love story.

Edge and Dolly forever.

IGNITE

ANTOINETTE

Axel Fontaine has a giant...

At least that's what everyone says. Unfortunately, it's true.

All. Of. It.

He's dangerous, scary, and addictive. Without a doubt, the last person I should fall for is the VP of the Disciples MC.

I'm out of my league.

He's a six-foot-four, blue-eyed biker god.

I'm an ex-ballerina turned stripper who should run away.

But how do you escape the one man who ignites your body and consumes your very soul?

Axel doesn't do relationships. But I'm betting on ME to change his mind.

AXEL

I don't do relationships. I don't do drama, and I definitely don't do love.

I'm not Prince Charming. I'm the VP of the Disciples and the club is my family.

The last thing I need is a violet-eyed enchantress who smells like candy and has some sort of voodoo chemistry that's messing with my mind.

She needs to go.

She's a distraction...a weakness I can't have.

Men like me fall in lust, not love.

So, why is she still here?

**Let's not forget my deliciously HOT Reed Saddington!
Venture into my angsty world of**

The Entitled.

The Entitled

People say you can't find your soulmate at eight years old. I did.I found Reed and loved him more than I loved myself.We were young... beautiful... *entitled.*Money and private schools, our families' lavish parties and posh, New York City apartments—it was all mere window dressing. What was real was our obsessive love, which grew right along with us as we moved toward adulthood. It consumed me, and only in his arms did I feel wanted and safe.

But I have a secret. It's big and to some, unforgivable. And it's why I let Reed destroy me, or maybe I destroyed us. Either way, I'm worse than broke—I'm broken.

Once upon a time, we were happy... Yet privilege has an ugly underside, and in the blink of an eye, my world crashed down around me.

I don't feel *entitled* anymore.*The Entitled* is first in *The Entitled* duet. Reed and Tess's story concludes in *The Enlightened.*

CONNECT

Website: http://www.cassandrafayerobbins.com
Facebook: http://www.facebook.com/cassandrafayerobbins/
Twitter: https://twitter.com/CassFayeRobbins | @
CassFayeRobbins
Instagram: www.instagram.com/cassandrafayerobbins/ | @
CassandraFayeRobbins
Goodreads: http://bit.ly/CassandraRobbins
Newsletter: www.cassandrafayerobbins.com
BookBub: https://bit.ly/2KIOeqB
Book+Main: https://bit.ly/2HZdc7D
Personal Facebook Group: https://www.facebook.com/groups/
cassiessassycrew/
Amazon: https://amzn.to/2Gz8ETe

ACKNOWLEDGEMENTS

First and always, to my husband and my two beautiful children. Their patience when I'm trying to figure out how to do this self-publishing journey is amazing. I love you guys more than you can imagine.

My brother Chris, my baby brother Duke, and my cousin Jake: I'm so lucky to have you. My dad and Susie, my Minnesota family: thank you for all your support.

To my editor Nikki Busch: You are the best at what you do. You truly make all my stories incredible. Not only are you a wonderful friend, I would be lost without you.

Michelle Clay and Annette Brignac: What can I say besides you two complete me! I'm beyond honored to be part of our Tribe but also to call you both my best friends. When I ask for one-hundred percent, you give me one-hundred-and-fifty percent, and I love you both so much.

To Candi Kane PR, my master at calm: You're simply fantastic! To my incredibly talented cover designer Lori Jackson: You amaze me with how you understand my vision and bring it to life. Thank you. Elaine York: you're a genius at making the inside of my books look so incredibly beautiful. Betty at Tease Diaries – Ms Betty's Design Studio, Cat Imb at TRC Designs: you know my vision and make the most beautiful teasers. I adore you all. Thank you to my incredibly talented tattoo artist Mathew Franklin, I'm such a fan of your work. Thank you, Michelle Lancaster and Mitchell Wick for my incredibly hot cover and video!

I have, without a doubt, the best betas: Michelle, Annette, and Rea, thank you from the bottom of my heart.

Robyn, thank you for your extra set of eyes.

A very special thank you to Rea. You're amazing! Not only are you a dear friend, but I have to give a shout-out for sharing your incredibly talented verses, and graciously allowing me to use some of your poetry.

To my daughter, Sophia, you also get a shout-out for helping me write a verse or two.

Monica, do you remember telling me I should write a rock star and name him Rhys? A big thank-you to you.

To my supporters: Without you I could not do this. You're all so special to me. Megan, Kelly, Teresa, Melinda, Cameel, Heather, Cat, Cindy, Erin, Gladys, Rebecca, Stephanie, Tammy, Jennifer, Robyn, Myen, Chayo, Stracey, Violet, Nichole, Mandy, Melissa, Tiffany, Laura, Lucia, Danielle, Clayr, and Sophie: Your friendship and support mean the world to me. Love you all so much.

To my reader group, Robbins Entitled: I adore all of you and am honored to be able to get to know you all. It makes my day to get up and talk to you.

Huge thank you to all the amazing bloggers & IG bookstagrammers who supported this release. I'm beyond grateful for your sharing Rhys and Gia.

Lastly, and most importantly, I thank you, *my readers*. You're what matters most.

XXXX

ABOUT THE AUTHOR

Cassandra Robbins is a *USA Today,* Amazon Top 100, KDP All-Star, and international bestselling author. She threatened to write a romance novel for years, and finally let the voices take over with her debut novel, *The Entitled*. She's a self-proclaimed hopeless romantic, driven to create obsessive, angst-filled characters who have to fight for their happily ever after. Cassandra resides in Los Angeles with her hot husband, two beautiful children, and a fluffy Samoyed, Stanley, and Goldendoodle, Fozzie. Her family and friends are her lifeline, but writing is her passion.